Acclaim for Stephen R. Lawhead's works

"[*Hood*] will leave readers anxious for the next installment."
—*Publishers Weekly*

"[*Hood* is] a highly imaginative, earthy adventure."
—*Booklist*

"*Hood* is rich in the historical and sensory details Lawhead's readers expect."
—*Aspiring Retail*

"[T]he narrative has the excitement of a fantasy novel, a vivid historical setting, and a lengthy, credible, and satisfying plot —just the right elements, in fact, that have made Lawhead a commercial success time and again."
—*Publishers Weekly* review of *Byzantium*

"In a style reminiscent of Tolkien, Lawhead presents a world of vivid imagery. This book is a delight."
—*Bookstore Journal* regarding *The Paradise War*

"*Patrick* is unfailingly sympathetic and believable, and his story of losing and finding his faith will resonate with a wide spectrum of readers."
—*Publishers Weekly*

"Celtic twilight shot with a brighter, fiercer light, and tinged with modern villainy . . . savagely beautiful."
—Michael Scott Rohan, author of the Winter of the World trilogy regarding *The Endless Knot*

KING RAVEN

TRILOGY

England and The March

1080 - 1100 AD

RHI BRAN'S WORLD

to Lundein

King's Road

England

to Lundein

Winton Castle
(East Winton)

HOOD

KING RAVEN: BOOK I

KING RAVEN
TRILOGY

STEPHEN R. LAWHEAD

THOMAS NELSON
Since 1798

NASHVILLE DALLAS MEXICO CITY RIO DE JANEIRO BEIJING

This book is dedicated to
the Schloss Mittersill Community
with heartfelt thanks and gratitude
for their understanding,
encouragement, and support.

Published in Nashville, Tennessee, by Thomas Nelson. Thomas Nelson is a registered trademark of Thomas Nelson, Inc.

Thomas Nelson, Inc., titles may be purchased in bulk for educational, business, fund-raising, or sales promotional use. For information, please e-mail SpecialMarkets@ThomasNelson.com.

Publisher's Note: This novel is a work of fiction. Names, characters, places, and incidents are either products of the author's imagination or used fictitiously. All characters are fictional, and any similarity to people living or dead is purely coincidental.

Map illustration created by Mary Hooper.

Library of Congress Cataloging-in-Publication Data

Lawhead, Steve.
    Hood / by Stephen R. Lawhead.
      p. cm.— (The King Raven trilogy ; bk. 1)
    ISBN 978-1-59554-085-0 (hardcover)
    ISBN 978-1-59554-088-1 (trade paper)
    ISBN 978-1-59554-329-5 (mass market)
    I. Title. II. Series: Lawhead, Steve. King Raven trilogy ; bk. 1.
    PS3562.A865H66 2006
    813'.54—dc22

                           2006014183

Printed in the United States of America

09 10 11 12 QW 8 7 6 5 4 3

The pig was young and wary, a yearling boar timidly testing the wind for strange scents as it ventured out into the honey-coloured light of a fast-fading day. Bran ap Brychan, Prince of Elfael, had spent the entire day stalking the greenwood for a suitable prize, and he meant to have this one.

Eight years old and the king's sole heir, he knew well enough that he would never be allowed to go out into the forest alone. So rather than seek permission, he had simply taken his bow and four arrows early that morning and stolen from the caer unnoticed. This hunt, like the young boar, was dedicated to his mother, the queen.

She loved the hunt and gloried in the wild beauty and visceral excitement of the chase. Even when she did not ride herself, she would ready a welcome for the hunters with a saddle cup and music, leading the women in song. "Don't be afraid," she told Bran when, as a toddling boy, he had been dazzled and a little frightened by the noise and revelry. "We belong to the land. Look, Bran!" She lifted a slender hand toward the hills and the forest rising like a living rampart beyond. "All that you see is the work of our Lord's hand. We rejoice in his provision."

Stricken with a wasting fever, Queen Rhian had been sick most of the summer, and in his childish imaginings, Bran had determined that if he could present her with a stag or a boar that he had brought down all by himself, she would laugh and sing as she always did, and she would feel better. She would be well again.

All it would take was a little more patience and . . .

Still as stone, he waited in the deepening shadow. The young boar stepped nearer, its small pointed ears erect and proud. It took another step and stopped to sample the tender shoots of a mallow plant. Bran, an arrow already nocked to the string, pressed the bow forward, feeling the tension in his shoulder and back just the way Iwan said he should. "Do not aim the arrow," the older youth had instructed him. "Just *think* it to the mark. Send it on your thought, and if your thought is true, so, too, will fly the arrow."

Pressing the bow to the limit of his strength, he took a steadying breath and released the string, feeling the sharp tingle on his fingertips. The arrow blazed across the distance, striking the young pig low in the chest behind the front legs. Startled, it flicked its tail rigid, and turned to bolt into the wood . . . but two steps later its legs tangled; it stumbled and went down. The stricken creature squealed once and tried to rise, then subsided, dead where it fell.

Bran loosed a wild whoop of triumph. The prize was his!

He ran to the pig and put his hand on the animal's sleek, slightly speckled haunch, feeling the warmth there. "I am sorry, my friend, and I thank you," he murmured as Iwan had taught him. "I need your life to live."

It was only when he tried to shoulder his kill that Bran realised his great mistake. The dead weight of the animal was more than he could lift by himself. With a sinking heart, he stood gazing at his glorious prize as tears came to his eyes. It was all for nothing if he could not carry the trophy home in triumph.

Sinking down on the ground beside the warm carcass, Bran put his head in his hands. He could not carry it, and he would not leave it. What was he going to do?

As he sat contemplating his predicament, the sounds of the forest grew loud in his ears: the chatter of a squirrel in a treetop, the busy click and hum of insects, the rustle of leaves, the hushed flutter of wings above him, and then . . .

"Bran!"

Bran started at the voice. He glanced around hopefully.

"Here!" he called. "Here! I need help!"

"Go back!" The voice seemed to come from above. He raised his eyes to see a huge black bird watching him from a branch directly over his head.

It was only an old raven. "Shoo!"

"Go back!" said the bird. "Go back!"

"I won't," shouted Bran. He reached for a stick on the path, picked it up, drew back, and threw it at the bothersome bird. "Shut up!"

The stick struck the raven's perch, and the bird flew off with a cry that sounded to Bran like laughter. "Ha, ha, haw! Ha, ha, haw!"

"Stupid bird," he muttered. Turning again to the young pig beside him, he remembered what he had seen other hunters do with small game. Releasing the string on his bow, he gathered the creature's short legs and tied the hooves together with the cord. Then, passing the stave through the bound hooves and gripping the stout length of oak in either hand, he tried to lift it. The carcass was still too heavy for him, so he began to drag his prize through the forest, using the bow.

It was slow going, even on the well-worn path, with frequent stops to rub the sweat from his eyes and catch his breath. All the while, the day dwindled around him.

No matter. He would not give up. Clutching the bow stave in his hands, he struggled on, step by step, tugging the young boar along the trail, reaching the edge of the forest as the last gleam of twilight faded across the valley to the west.

"Bran!"

The shout made him jump. It was not a raven this time, but a voice he knew. He turned and looked down the slope toward the valley to see Iwan coming toward him, long legs paring the distance with swift strides.

"Here!" Bran called, waving his aching arms overhead. "Here I am!"

"In the name of all the saints and angels," the young man said when he came near enough to speak, "what do you think you are doing out here?"

"Hunting," replied Bran. Indicating his kill with a hunter's pride, he said, "It strayed in front of my arrow, see?"

"I see," replied Iwan. Giving the pig a cursory glance, he turned and started away again. "We have to go. It's late, and everyone is looking for you."

Bran made no move to follow.

Looking back, Iwan said, "Leave it, Bran! They are searching for you. We must hurry."

"No," Bran said. "Not without the boar." He stooped once more to the carcass, seized the bow stave, and started tugging again.

Iwan returned, took him roughly by the arm, and pulled him away. "Leave the stupid thing!"

"It is for my mother!" the boy shouted, the tears starting hot and quick. As the tears began to fall, he bent his head and repeated more softly, "Please, it is for my mother."

"Weeping Judas!" Iwan relented with an exasperated sigh. "Come then. We will carry it together."

Iwan took one end of the bow stave, Bran took the other, and between them they lifted the carcass off the ground. The wood bent but did not break, and they started away again—Bran stumbling ever and again in a forlorn effort to keep pace with his long-legged friend.

Night was upon them, the caer but a brooding black eminence on its mound in the centre of the valley, when a party of mounted searchers appeared. "He was hunting," Iwan informed them. "A hunter does not leave his prize."

The riders accepted this, and the young boar was quickly secured behind the saddle of one of the horses; Bran and Iwan were taken up behind other riders, and the party rode for the caer. The moment they arrived, Bran slid from the horse and ran to his mother's chamber behind the hall. "Hurry," he called. "Bring the boar!"

Queen Rhian's chamber was lit with candles, and two women stood over her bed when Bran burst in. He ran to her bedside and knelt down. "Mam! See what I brought you!"

She opened her eyes, and recognition came to her. "There you are, my dearling. They said they could not find you."

"I went hunting," he announced. "For you."

"For me," she whispered. "A fine thing, that. What did you find?"

"Look!" he said proudly as Iwan strode into the room with the pig slung over his shoulders.

"Oh, Bran," she said, the ghost of a smile touching her dry lips. "Kiss me, my brave hunter."

He bent his face to hers and felt the heat of her dry lips on his. "Go now. I will sleep a little," she told him, "and I will dream of your triumph."

She closed her eyes then, and Bran was led from the room. But she had smiled, and that was worth all the world to him.

Queen Rhian did not waken in the morning. By the next evening she was dead, and Bran never saw his mother smile again. And although he continued to hone his skill with the bow, he lost all interest in the hunt.

PART ONE

DAY OF
THE WOLF

KING RAVEN
TRILOGY

Bran!" The shout rattled through the stone-flagged yard. "Bran! Get your sorry tail out here! We're leaving!"

Red-faced with exasperation, King Brychan ap Tewdwr climbed stiffly into the saddle, narrowed eyes scanning the ranks of mounted men awaiting his command. His feckless son was not amongst them. Turning to the warrior on the horse beside him, he demanded, "Iwan, where is that boy?"

"I have not seen him, lord," replied the king's champion. "Neither this morning nor at the table last night."

"Curse his impudence!" growled the king, snatching the reins from the hand of his groom. "The one time I need him beside me and he flits off to bed that slut of his. I will not suffer this insolence, and I will not wait."

"If it please you, lord, I will send one of the men to fetch him."

"No! It does not bloody please me!" roared Brychan. "He can stay behind, and the devil take him!"

Turning in the saddle, he called for the gate to be opened.

The heavy timber doors of the fortress groaned and swung wide. Raising his hand, he gave the signal.

"Ride out!" Iwan cried, his voice loud in the early morning calm.

King Brychan, Lord of Elfael, departed with the thirty-five Cymry of his mounted warband at his back. The warriors, riding in twos and threes, descended the rounded slope of the hill and fanned out across the shallow, cup-shaped valley, fording the stream that cut across the meadow and following the cattle trail as it rose to meet the dark, bristling rampart of the forest known to the folk of the valley as *Coed Cadw*, the Guarding Wood.

At the edge of the forest, Brychan and his escort joined the road. Ancient, deep-rutted, overgrown, and sunken low between its high earthen banks, the bare dirt track bent its way south and east over the rough hills and through the broad expanse of dense primeval forest until descending into the broad Wye Vale, where it ran along the wide, green waters of the easy-flowing river. Farther on, the road passed through the two principal towns of the region: Hereford, an English market town, and Caer Gloiu, the ancient Roman settlement in the wide, marshy lowland estuary of Mor Hafren. In four days, this same road would bring them to Lundein, where the Lord of Elfael would face the most difficult trial of his long and arduous reign.

"There was a time," Brychan observed bitterly, "when the last warrior to reach the meeting place was put to death by his comrades as punishment for his lack of zeal. It was deemed the first fatality of the battle."

"Allow me to fetch the prince for you," Iwan offered. "He could catch up before the day is out."

"I will not hear it." Brychan dismissed the suggestion with a sharp chop of his hand. "We've wasted too much breath on that worthless whelp. I will deal with him when we return," he said, adding under his breath, "and he will wish to heaven he had never been born."

With an effort, the aging king pushed all thoughts of his profligate son aside and settled into a sullen silence that lasted well into the day. Upon reaching the Vale of Wye, the travellers descended the broad slope into the valley and proceeded along the river. The road was good here, and the water wide, slow flowing, and shallow. Around midday, they stopped on the moss-grown banks to water the horses and take some food for themselves before moving on.

Iwan had given the signal to remount, and they were just pulling the heads of the horses away from the water when a jingling clop was heard on the road. A moment later four riders appeared, coming into view around the base of a high-sided bluff.

One look at the long, pallid faces beneath their burnished warcaps, and the king's stomach tightened. "Ffreinc!" grumbled Brychan, putting his hand to his sword. They were Norman *marchogi*, and the British king and his subjects despised them utterly.

"To arms, men," called Iwan. "Be on your guard."

Upon seeing the British warband, the Norman riders halted in the road. They wore conical helmets and, despite the heat of the day, heavy mail shirts over padded leather jerkins that reached down below their knees. Their shins were covered with polished steel greaves, and leather gauntlets protected their hands, wrists, and forearms. Each carried a sword on his hip and a short spear tucked into a saddle pouch. A narrow shield shaped like an elongated raindrop, painted blue, was slung upon each of their backs.

"Mount up!" Iwan commanded, swinging into the saddle.

Brychan, at the head of his troops, called a greeting in his own tongue, twisting his lips into an unaccustomed smile of welcome. When his greeting was not returned, he tried English—the hated but necessary language used when dealing with the backward folk of the southlands. One of the riders seemed to understand. He made a curt reply in French and then turned and spurred his horse back the way he had come; his three companions remained in place, regarding the British warriors with wary contempt.

Seeing his grudging attempt at welcome rebuffed, Lord Brychan raised his reins and urged his mount forward. "Ride on, men," he ordered, "and keep your eyes on the filthy devils."

At the British approach, the three knights closed ranks, blocking the road. Unwilling to suffer an insult, however slight, Brychan commanded them to move aside. The Norman knights made no reply but remained planted firmly in the centre of the road.

Brychan was on the point of ordering his warband to draw their swords and ride over the arrogant fools when Iwan spoke up, saying, "My lord, our business in Lundein will put an end to this unseemly harassment. Let us endure this last slight with good grace and heap shame on the heads of these cowardly swine."

"You would surrender the road to them?"

"I would, my lord," replied the champion evenly. "We do not want the report of a fight to mar our petition in Lundein."

Brychan stared dark thunder at the Ffreinc soldiers.

"My lord?" said Iwan. "I think it is best."

"Oh, very well," huffed the king at last. Turning to the warriors behind him, he called, "To keep the peace, we will go around."

As the Britons prepared to yield the road, the first Norman rider returned, and with him another man on a pale grey mount with a high leather saddle. This one wore a blue cloak fastened at the throat with a large silver brooch. "You there!" he called in English. "What are you doing?"

Brychan halted and turned in the saddle. "Do you speak to me?"

"I do speak to you," the man insisted. "Who are you, and where are you going?"

"The man you address is Rhi Brychan, Lord and King of Elfael," replied Iwan, speaking up quickly. "We are about business of our own which takes us to Lundein. We seek no quarrel and would pass by in peace."

"Elfael?" wondered the man in the blue cloak. Unlike the others, he carried no weapons, and his gauntlets were white leather. "You are British."

"That we are," replied Iwan.

"What is your business in Lundein?"

"It is our affair alone," replied Brychan irritably. "We ask only to journey on without dispute."

"Stay where you are," replied the blue-cloaked man. "I will summon my lord and seek his disposition in the matter."

The man put spurs to his mount and disappeared around the bend in the road. The Britons waited, growing irritated and uneasy in the hot sun.

The blue-cloaked man reappeared some moments later, and with him was another, also wearing blue, but with a spotless white linen shirt and trousers of fine velvet. Younger than the others, he wore his fair hair long to his shoulders, like a woman's; with his sparse, pale beard curling along the soft line of his jaw, he appeared little more than a youngster preening in his father's clothes. Like the others with him, he carried a shield on his shoulder and a long sword on his hip. His horse was black, and it was larger than any plough horse Brychan had ever seen.

"You claim to be Rhi Brychan, Lord of Elfael?" the new-comer asked in a voice so thickly accented the Britons could barely make out what he said.

"I make no claim, sir," replied Brychan with terse courtesy, the English thick on his tongue. "It is a very fact."

"Why do you ride to Lundein with your warband?" inquired the pasty-faced youth. "Can it be that you intend to make war on King William?"

"On no account, sir," replied Iwan, answering to spare his lord the indignity of this rude interrogation. "We go to swear fealty to the king of the Ffreinc."

At this, the two blue-cloaked figures leaned near and put their heads together in consultation. "It is too late. William will not see you."

"Who are *you* to speak for the king?" demanded Iwan.

"I say again, this affair does not concern you," added Brychan.

"You are wrong. It has become my concern," replied the young man in blue. "I am Count Falkes de Braose, and I have been given the commot of Elfael." He thrust his hand into his shirt and brought out a square of parchment. "This I have received in grant from the hand of King William himself."

"Liar!" roared Brychan, drawing his sword. All thirty-five of his warband likewise unsheathed their blades.

"You have a choice," the Norman lord informed them imperiously. "Give over your weapons and swear fealty to me . . ."

"Or?" sneered Brychan, glaring contempt at the five Ffreinc warriors before him.

"Or die like the very dogs you are," replied the young man simply.

"Hie! Up!" shouted the British king, slapping the rump of his horse with the flat of his sword. The horse bolted forward. "Take them!"

Iwan lofted his sword and circled it twice around his head to signal the warriors, and the entire warband spurred their horses to attack. The Normans held their ground for two or three heartbeats and then turned as one and fled back along the road, disappearing around the bend at the base of the bluff.

King Brychan was first to reach the place. He rounded the bend at a gallop, flying headlong into an armed warhost of more than three hundred Norman marchogi, both footmen and knights, waiting with weapons at the ready.

Throwing the reins to the side, the king wheeled his mount and headed for the riverbank. "Ambush! Ambush!" he cried to those thundering up behind him. "It's a trap!"

The oncoming Cymry, seeing their king flee for the water with a score of marchogi behind him, raced to cut them off. They reached the enemy flank and careered into it at full gallop, spears couched.

Horses reared and plunged as they went over; riders fell and were trampled. The British charge punched a hole in the Norman flank and carried them deep into the ranks. Using spears and swords, they proceeded to cut a swathe through the dense thicket of enemy troops.

Iwan, leading the charge, sliced the air with his spear, thrusting again and again, carving a crimson pathway through horseflesh and manflesh alike. With deadly efficiency, he took the fight to the better-armed and better-protected marchogi and soon outdistanced his own comrades.

Twisting in the saddle, he saw that the attack had bogged down behind him. The Norman knights, having absorbed the initial shock of the charge, were now surrounding the smaller Cymry force. It was time to break off lest the warband become engulfed.

With a flick of the reins, Iwan started back over the bodies of those he had cut down. He had almost reached the main force of struggling Cymry when two massive Norman knights astride huge destriers closed the path before him. Swords raised, they swooped down on him.

Iwan thrust his spear at the one on the right, only to have the shaft splintered by the one on the left. Throwing the ragged end into the Norman's face, he drew his sword and, pulling back hard on the reins, turned his mount and slipped aside as the two closed within striking distance. One of the knights lunged at him, swinging wildly. Iwan felt the blade tip rake his upper back, then he was away.

King Brychan, meanwhile, reached the river and turned to face his attackers—four marchogi coming in hard behind levelled spears. Lashing out with his sword, Brychan struck at the first rider, catching him a rattling blow along the top of the shield. He then swung on the second, slashing at the man's exposed leg. The warrior gave out a yelp and threw his shield into Brychan's face. The king smashed it aside with the pommel of his sword. The shield swung away and down, revealing the point of a spear.

Brychan heaved himself back to avoid the thrust, but the spear caught him in the lower gut, just below his wide belt. The blade burned as it pierced his body. He loosed a savage roar and hacked wildly with his sword. The shaft of the spear sheared away, taking a few of the soldier's fingers with it.

Raising his blade again, the king turned to meet the next attacker . . . but too late. Even as his elbow swung up, an enemy blade thrust in. He felt a cold sting, and pain rippled up his arm. His hand lost its grip. The sword spun from his fingers as he swayed in the saddle, recoiling from the blow.

Iwan, fighting free of the clash, raced to his lord's aid. He saw the king's blade fall to the water as Brychan reeled and then slumped. The champion slashed the arm of one attacker and opened the side of another as he sped by. Then his way was blocked by a sudden swirl of Norman attackers. Hacking with wild and determined energy, he tried to force his way through by dint of strength alone, but the enemy riders closed ranks against him.

His sword became a gleaming flash around him as he struck out again and again. He dropped one knight, whose misjudged thrust went wide, and wounded another, who desperately reined his horse away and out of range of the champion's lethal blade.

As he turned to take the third attacker, Iwan glimpsed his king struggling to keep his saddle. He saw Brychan lurch forward and topple from his horse into the water.

The king struggled to his knees and beheld his champion fighting to reach him a short distance away. "Ride!" he shouted. "Flee! You must warn the people!"

Rhi Brychan made one last attempt to rise, got his feet under him and took an unsteady step, then collapsed. The last thing Iwan saw was the body of his king floating face-down in the turgid, bloodstained waters of the Wye.

CHAPTER 2

A kiss before I go," Bran murmured, taking a handful of thick dark hair and pressing a curled lock to his lips. "Just one."

"No!" replied Mérian, pushing him away. "Away with you."

"A kiss first," he insisted, inhaling the rosewater fragrance of her hair and skin.

"If my father finds you here, he will flay us both," she said, still resisting. "Go now—before someone sees you."

"A kiss only, I swear," Bran whispered, sliding close.

She regarded the young man beside her doubtfully. Certainly, there was not another in all the valleys like him. In looks, grace, and raw seductive appeal, he knew no equal. With his black hair, high handsome brow, and a ready smile that was, as always, a little lopsided and deceptively shy—the mere sight of Bran ap Brychan caused female hearts young and old to flutter when he passed.

Add to this a supple wit and a free-ranging, unfettered charm, and the Prince of Elfael was easily the most ardently discussed bachelor amongst the marriageable young women of the region. The fact that he also stood next in line to the kingship was not lost on any of them. More than one lovesick young lady sighed herself to sleep at night in the fervent hope of winning Bran ap Brychan's heart for her own—causing more than one determined father to vow to nail that wastrel's head to the nearest doorpost if he ever caught him within a Roman mile of his virgin daughter's bed.

Yet and yet, there was a flightiness to his winsome ways, a fickle inconstancy to even his most solemn affirmations, a lack of fidelity in his ardour. He possessed a waggish capriciousness that most often showed itself in a sly refusal to take seriously the genuine concerns of life. Bran flitted from one thing to the next as the whim took him, never remaining long enough to reap the all-too-inevitable consequences of his flings and frolics.

Lithe and long-limbed, habitually clothed in the darkest hues, which gave him an appearance of austerity—an impression completely overthrown by the puckish glint in his clear dark eyes and the sudden, unpredictable, and utterly provocative smile—he nevertheless gorged on an endless glut of indulgence, forever helping himself to the best of everything his noble position could offer. King Brychan's rake of a son was unashamedly pleased with himself.

"A kiss, my love, and I will take wings," Bran whispered, pressing himself closer still.

Feeling both appalled and excited by the danger Bran always brought with him, Mérian closed her eyes and brushed his cheek with her lips. "There!" she said firmly, pushing him away. "Now off with you."

"Ah, Mérian," he said, placing his head on her warm breast, "how can I go, when to leave you is to leave my heart behind?"

"You promised!" she hissed in exasperation, stiff arms forcing him away again.

There came the sound of a shuffling footstep outside the kitchen door.

"Hurry!" Suddenly terrified, she grabbed him by the sleeve and pulled him to his feet. "It might be my father."

"Let him come. I am not afraid. We will have this out once and for all."

"Bran, no!" she pleaded. "If you have any thought for me at all, do not let anyone find you here."

"Very well," Bran replied. "I go."

He leaned close and stole a lingering kiss, then leapt to the window frame, pushed open the shutter, and prepared to jump. "Until tonight, my love," he said over his shoulder, then dropped to the ground in the yard outside.

Mérian rushed to the window and pulled the heavy wooden shutter closed, then turned and began busying herself, stirring up the embers on the hearth as the sleep-numbed cook shambled into the large, dark room.

Bran leaned back against the side of the house and listened to the voices drifting down from the room above—to the cook's mumbled question and Mérian's explanation of what she was doing in the kitchen before break of day. He smiled to himself. True, he had not yet succeeded in winning his way into Mérian's bed; Lord Cadwgan's fetching daughter was proving a match worthy of his wiles. Even so, before summer was gone he would succeed. Of that he was certain.

Oh, but the season of warmth and light was everywhere in full retreat. Already the soft greens and yellows of summer were fading into autumn drab. Soon, all too soon, the fair, bright days would give way to the endless grey of clouds and mist and icy, wind-lashed rain.

That was a concern for another time; now he must be on his way. Drawing the hood of his cloak over his head, Bran darted across the yard, scaled the wall at its lowest span, and ran to his horse, which was tethered behind a hawthorn thicket next to the wall.

With the wind at his back and a little luck, he would reach Caer Cadarn well before his father departed for Lundein.

The day was breaking fair, and the track was dry, so he pushed his mount hard: pelting down the broad hillsides, splashing across the streams, and flying up the steep, wheel-rutted trails. Luck was not with him, however, for he had just glimpsed the pale shimmer of the caer's whitewashed wooden palisade in the distance when his horse pulled up lame. The unfortunate beast jolted to a halt and refused to go farther.

No amount of coaxing could persuade the animal to move. Sliding from the saddle, Bran examined the left fore-leg. The shoe had torn away—probably lost amidst the rocks of the last streambed—and the hoof was split. There was blood on the fetlock. Bran lowered the leg with a sigh and, retrieving the reins, began leading his limping mount along the track.

His father would be waiting now, and he would be angry. But then, he thought, when was Lord Brychan *not* angry?

For the last many years—indeed, ever since Bran could remember—his father had nursed one continual simmering rage. It forever seethed just beneath the surface and was only too likely to boil over at the slightest provocation. And then, God help whoever or whatever was nearby. Objects were hurled against walls; dogs were kicked, and servants too; everyone within shouting distance received the ready lash of their surly lord's tongue.

Bran arrived at the caer far later than he had intended, slinking through the wide-open gate. Like a smith opening the forge furnace door, he braced himself for the heat of his father's angry blast. But the yard was empty of all save Gwrgi, the lord's half-blind staghound, who came snuffling up to put his wet muzzle in Bran's palm. "Everyone gone?" Bran asked, looking around. The old dog licked the back of his hand.

Just then his father's steward stepped from the hall. A dour and disapproving stilt of a man, he loomed over all the comings and goings of the caer like a damp cloud and was never happy unless he could make someone else as miserable as himself. "You are too late," he informed Bran, ripe satisfaction dripping from his thin lips.

"I can see that, Maelgwnt," said Bran. "How long ago did they leave?"

"You won't catch them," replied the steward, "if that's what you're thinking. Sometimes I wonder if you *think* at all."

"Get me a horse," ordered Bran.

"Why?" Maelgwnt asked, eyeing the mount standing inside the gate. "Have you ruined another one?"

"Just get me a horse. I don't have time to argue."

"Of course, sire, right away," sniffed the steward. "As soon as you tell me where to find one."

"What do you mean?" demanded Bran.

"There are none."

With a grunt of impatience, Bran hurried to the stable at the far end of the long, rectangular yard. He found one of the grooms mucking out the stalls. "Quick, Cefn, I need a horse."

"Lord Bran," said the young servant, "I'm sorry. There are none left."

"They've taken them *all*?"

"The whole warband was summoned," the groom explained. "They needed every horse but the mares."

Bran knew which horses he meant. There were four broodmares to which five colts had been born in early spring. The foals were of an age to wean but had not yet been removed from their mothers.

"Bring me the black," Bran commanded. "She will have to do."

"What about Hathr?" inquired the groom.

"Hathr threw a shoe and split a hoof. He'll need looking after for a few days, and I must join my father on the road before the day is out."

"Lord Brychan said we were not to use—"

"I *need* a horse, Cefn," said Bran, cutting off his objection. "Saddle the black—and hurry. I must ride hard if I am to catch them."

While the groom set about preparing the mare, Bran hurried to the kitchen to find something to eat. The cook and her two young helpers were busy shelling peas and protested the intrusion. With smiles and winks and murmured endearments, however, Bran cajoled, and old Mairead succumbed to his charm as she always did. "You'll be king one day," she chided, "and is this how you will fare? Snatching meals from the hearth and running off who-knows-where all day?"

"I'm going to Lundein, Mairead. It is a far journey. Would you have your future king starve on the way, or go a-begging like a leper?"

"Lord have mercy!" clucked the cook, setting aside her chore. "Never let it be said anyone went hungry from my hearth."

She ladled some fresh milk into a bowl, into which she broke chunks of hard brown bread, then sat him down on a stool. While he ate, she cut a few slices of new summer sausage and gave him two green apples, which he stuffed into the pouch at his belt. Bran spooned down the milk and bread and then, throwing the elderly servant a kiss, bounded from the kitchen and back across the yard to the stable, where Cefn was just tightening the saddle cinch on his horse.

"A world of thanks to you, Cefn. You have saved my life."

"Olwen is the best broodmare we have—see you don't push her too hard," called the groom as the prince clattered out into the yard. Bran gave him a breezy wave, and the groom added under his breath, "And may our Lord Brychan have mercy on you."

Out on the trail once more, Bran felt certain he could win his way back into his father's good graces. It might take a day or two, but once the king saw how dutifully the prince was prepared to conduct himself in Lundein, Brychan would not fail to restore his son to favour. First, however, Bran set himself to think up a plausible tale to help excuse his apparent absence.

Thus, he put his mind to spinning a story which, if not entirely believable, would at least be entertaining enough to lighten the king's foul mood. This task occupied him as he rode easily along the path through the forest. He had just started up the long, meandering track leading to the high and thickly forested ridge that formed the western boundary of the broad Wye Vale and was thinking that with any luck at all, he might still catch his father and the warband before dusk. This thought dissolved instantly upon seeing a lone rider lurching toward him on a hobbling horse.

He was still some distance away, but Bran could see that the man was hunched forward in the saddle as if to urge his labouring mount to greater speed. *Probably drunk, rotten sot,* thought Bran, *and doesn't realise his horse is dead on its feet.* Well, he would stop the empty-headed lout and see if he could find out how far ahead his father might be.

Closer, something about the man seemed familiar.

As the rider drew nearer, Bran grew increasingly certain he knew the man, and he was not wrong.

It was Iwan.

CHAPTER 3

Bernard de Neufmarché stormed down the narrow corridor leading from the main hall to his private chambers deep in the protecting stone wall of the fortress. His red velvet cloak was grey with the dust of travel, his back throbbed with the dull, persistent ache of fatigue, and his mind was a spinning maelstrom of dark thoughts as black as his mood. Seven years lost! he fumed. Ruined, wasted, and lost!

He had been patient, prudent, biding his time, watching and waiting for precisely the right moment to strike. And now, in one precipitous act, unprovoked and unforeseen, the red-haired brigand of a king, William, had allied himself with that milksop Baron de Braose and his mewling nephew, Count Falkes. That was bad enough. To make a disastrous business worse, the irresponsible king had also reversed the long-held royal policy of his father and allowed de Braose to launch an invasion into the interior of Wales.

Royal let to plunder Wales was the very development Neufmarché had been waiting for, but now it had been ruined by the greedy, grasping de Braose mob. Their ill-conceived thrashing around the countryside would put the wily Britons on their guard, and any advancement on Bernard's part would now be met with stiff-necked resistance and accomplished only at considerable expense of troops and blood.

So be it!

Waiting had brought him nothing, and he would wait no longer.

At the door to his rooms, he shouted for his chamberlain. "Remey!" he cried. "My writing instruments! At once!"

Flinging open the door, he strode to the hearth, snatched up a reed from the bundle, and thrust it into the small, sputtering fire. He then carried the burning rush to the candletree atop the square oak table that occupied the centre of the room and began lighting the candles. As the shadows shrank beneath the lambent light, the baron dashed wine from a jar into his silver cup, raised it to his lips, and drank a deep, thirsty draught. He then shouted for his chamberlain again and collapsed into his chair.

"Seven years, by the Virgin!" he muttered. He drank again and cried, "Remey!" This time his summons was answered by the quick slap of soft boots on the flagstone threshold.

"Sire," said the servant, bustling into the room with his arms full of writing utensils—rolls of parchment, an inkhorn, a bundle of quills, sealing wax, and a knife. "I did not expect you to return so soon. I trust everything went well?"

"No," growled the baron irritably, "it did not go well. It went very badly. While I was paying court to the king, de Braose and his snivelling nephew were sending an army through my lands to snatch Elfael and who knows what all else from under my nose."

Remey sighed in commiseration. An aging lackey with the face of a ferret and a long, narrow head perpetually covered by a shapeless cap of thick grey felt, he had been in the service of the Neufmarché clan since he was a boy at Le Neuf-March-en-Lions in Beauvais. He knew well his master's moods and appetites and was usually able to anticipate them with ease. But today he had been caught napping, and this annoyed him almost as much as the king had annoyed the baron.

"The de Braose are unscrupulous, as we all know," Remey observed, arranging the items he had brought on the table before the baron.

"Cut me a pen," the baron ordered. Taking up a roll of parchment, he sliced off a suitable square with his dagger and smoothed the prepared skin on the table before him.

Remey, meanwhile, selected a fine long goose quill and expertly pared the tip on an angle and split it with the pen knife. "See if this will suffice," he said, offering the prepared writing instrument to his master.

Bernard pulled the stopper from the inkhorn and dipped the pen. He made a few preliminary swirls on the parchment and said, "It will do. Now bring me my dinner. None of that broth, mind. I've ridden all day, and I'm hungry. I want meat and bread—some of that pie, too. And more wine."

"At once, my lord," replied the servant, leaving his master to his work.

By the time Remey returned, accompanied this time by two kitchen servants bearing trays of food and drink, Neufmarché was leaning back in his chair studying the document he had just composed. "Listen to this," said the baron, and holding the parchment before his eyes, he began to read what he had written.

Remey held his head to one side as his master read. It was a letter to the baron's father in Beauvais requesting a transfer of men and equipment to aid in the conquest of new territories in Britain.

"... the resulting acquisitions will enlarge our holdings at least threefold," Bernard read, "with good land, much of which is valley lowlands possessing tillable soil suitable for a variety of crops, while the rest is mature forest which, besides timber, will provide excellent hunting . . ." Here the baron broke off. "What do you think, Remey? Is it enough?"

"I should think so. Lord Geoffrey was out here two years ago and is well aware of the desirability of the Welsh lands. I have no doubt he will send the required aid."

"I concur," decided Bernard. Bending once more to the parchment, he finished the letter and signed his name. Then, rolling the parchment quickly, he tied the bundle and sealed it, pressing his heavy gold ring into the soft puddle of brown wax dripped from the stick in Remey's hands. "There," he said, setting the bundle aside, "now bring me that tray and fill my cup. When you've done that, go find Ormand."

"Of course, sire," replied the chamberlain, gesturing for the two kitchen servants to place the trays of food before the baron while he refilled the silver cup from a flagon. "I believe I saw young Ormand in the hall only a short while ago."

"Good," said Bernard, spearing one of the hard-crusted pies from the tray with his knife. "Tell him to prepare to ride out at first light. This letter must reach Beauvais before the month is out."

The baron bit into the cold pie and chewed thoughtfully. He ate a little more and then took another long draught of wine, wiped his mouth with the back of his hand, and said, "Now then, go find my wife and tell her I have returned."

"I have already spoken to my lady's maidservant, sire,"

replied Remey, starting for the door. "I will inform Ormand that you wish to see him."

Baron Neufmarché was left alone to eat his meal in peace. As the food and wine soothed his agitated soul, he began to look more favourably on the conquest to come. *Perhaps*, he thought, *I have been overhasty.* Perhaps, in the heat of temper, he had allowed his anger to cloud his perception. He might have lost Elfael, true enough, but Buellt was the real prize, and it would be his; and beyond Buellt lay the ripe, fertile heartland of Dyfed and Ceredigion. It was all good land—wild, for the most part, and undeveloped—just waiting for a man with the boldness of vision, determination, and ambition to make it prosper and produce. Bernard de Neufmarché, Baron of the Shires of Gloucester and Hereford, imagined himself just that man.

Yes, the more he thought about it, the more he was certain he was right; despite the king's outrageous behaviour, things were working out for the best after all. Under the proper circumstances, Elfael, that small and undistinguished commot in the centre of the Welsh hill country, could ensnare the rash invaders in difficulties for years to come. In fact, with the timely application of a few simple principles of subterfuge, the baron could ensure that little Elfael would become the grasping de Braose family's downfall.

The baron was basking in the warmth of this self-congratulatory humour when he heard the latch on his door rattle. The soft cough with which his visitor announced herself indicated that his wife had joined him. His momentary feeling of pleasure dimmed and faded.

"You have returned earlier than expected, my lord," she said, her voice falling soft and low in the quiet of the room.

Bernard took his time answering. Setting aside his cup, he turned his head and looked at her. Pale and wan, she appeared even more wraithlike than when he had last seen her, only a few days ago. Her eyes were large, dark-rimmed circles in the ashen skin of her thin face, and her long lank hair hung straight, making her seem all the more frail and delicate.

"You are looking well, my lady," he lied, smiling. He rose stiffly and offered her his chair.

"Thank you, my lord," she replied. "But sit; you are at meat. I will not disturb you. I only wished to acknowledge your return." She bowed slightly from the waist and turned to leave.

"Agnes, stay," he said and noticed the tremor that coursed through her body.

"I have had my dinner and was just about to go to prayers," she informed her husband. "But very well, I will sit with you awhile. If that is what you wish."

Bernard removed his chair and placed it at the side of the table. "Only if it is no trouble," he said.

"Far from it," she insisted. "It is a very pleasure in itself."

He seated her and then pulled another chair to his place. "Wine?" he asked, lifting the flagon.

"I think not, thank you." Head erect, shoulders level, slender back straight as a lance shaft, she perched lightly on the edge of her chair—as if she feared it might suddenly take wing beneath her negligible weight.

"If you change your mind . . ." The baron refilled his cup and resumed his seat. His wife was suffering, to be sure, and that was real enough. Even so, he could not help feeling that she brought it on herself with her perverse unwilling-ness to adapt in the slightest measure to the demands of her new home and its all-too-often inhospitable climate. She refused to dress more warmly or eat more heartily—as conditions warranted. Thus, she lurched from one vague illness to another, enduring febrile distempers, agues, fluxes, and other mysterious maladies, all with the resigned patience of an expiring saint.

"Remey said you summoned Ormand."

"Yes, I am sending him to Beauvais with a letter for the duke," he replied, swirling the wine in his cup. "The conquest of Wales has begun, and I will not be left out of it. I am requesting troopsmen-at-arms and as many knights as he can spare."

"A letter? For your father?" she asked, the light leaping up in her eyes for the first time since she had entered the room. "Do not bother Ormand with such a task—I will take the letter for you."

"No," replied Bernard. "The journey is too arduous for you. It is out of the question."

"Nonsense," she countered. "The journey would do me a world of good—the sea air and warmer weather would be just the elixir to restore me."

"I need you here," said the baron. "There is going to be a campaign in the spring, and there is much to make ready." He raised the silver cup to his lips, repeating, "It is out of the question. I am sorry."

Lady Agnes sat in silence for a moment, studying her hands in her lap. "This campaign is important to you, I suppose?" she wondered.

"Important? What a question, woman! Of course, it is of the highest importance. A successful outcome will extend our holdings into the very heart of Wales," the baron said, growing excited at the thought. "Our estates will increase threefold

. . . fivefold—and our revenues likewise! I'd call that *important*, wouldn't you?" he sneered.

"Then," Agnes suggested lightly, "I would think it equally important to ensure that success by securing the necessary troops."

"Of course," answered Bernard irritably. "It goes without saying—which is why I wrote the letter."

His wife lifted her thin shoulders in a shrug of studied indifference. "As you say."

He let the matter rest there for a moment, but something in her tone suggested she knew more than she had said.

"Why?" he asked, his suspicion getting the better of him at last.

"Oh," she said, turning her eyes to the fire once more, "no reason."

"Come now, my dear. Let us have it out. You have a thought in this matter, I can tell, and I will hear it."

"You flatter me, I'm sure, husband," she replied. "I am content."

"But I am not!" he said, anger edging into his tone. "What is in your mind?"

"Do not raise your voice to me, sire!" she snapped. "I assure you it is not seemly."

"Very well!" he said, his voice loud in the chamber. He glared at her for a moment and then tried again. "But see here, it is folly to quarrel. Consider that I am overtired from a long journey—it is that making me sharp, nothing more. Therefore, let us be done with this foolishness." He coaxed her with a smile. "Now tell me, my dear, what is in your mind?"

"Since you ask," she said, "it occurs to me that if the

campaign is as gravely important as you contend, then I would not entrust such an undertaking to a mere equerry."

"Why not? Ormand is entirely trustworthy."

"That is as may be," she allowed primly, "but if you really need the troops, then why place so much weight on a mere letter in the hand of an insignificant menial?"

"And what would you do?"

"I'd send a suitable emissary instead."

"An emissary."

"Yes," she agreed, "and what better emissary than the sole and beloved daughter-in-law of the duke himself?" She paused, allowing her words to take effect. "Duke Geoffrey can easily refuse a letter in Ormand's hand," she concluded, "as you and I know only too well. But refuse me? Never."

Bernard considered this for a moment, tapping the silver base of his cup with a finger. What she suggested was not entirely without merit. He could already see certain advantages. If she went, she might obtain not only troops but money as well. And it was true that the old duke could never deny his daughter-in-law anything. He might fume and fret for a few days, but he would succumb to her wishes in the end.

"Very well," decided the baron abruptly, "you shall go. Ormand will accompany you—and your maidservants, of course—but you will bear the letter yourself and read it to the duke when you judge him in a favourable mood to grant our request."

Lady Agnes smiled and inclined her head in acquiescence to his desires. "As always, my husband, your counsel is impeccable."

CHAPTER 4

Bran stirred his mount to speed. "Iwan!" he cried. At the sound of his name, the king's champion raised himself in the saddle, and Bran saw blood oozing down the warrior's padded leather tunic.

"Bran!" the warrior gasped. "Bran, thank God. Listen—"

"Iwan, what has happened? Where are the others?"

"We were attacked at Wye ford," he said. "Ffreinc—three hundred or more . . . sixty, maybe seventy knights, the rest footmen."

Lurching sideways, he seized the young prince by the arm. "Bran, you must ride . . . ," he began, but his eyes rolled up into his head; he slumped and toppled from the saddle.

Bran, holding tight to his arm, tried to lower his longtime friend more gently to the ground. Iwan landed hard nonetheless and sprawled between the horses. Bran slid off the mare and eased the wounded man onto his back. "Iwan! Iwan!" he said, trying to rouse him. "My father, the warband—where are the others?"

"Dead," moaned Iwan. "All . . . all of them dead."

Bran quickly retrieved a waterskin from its place behind his saddle. "Here," he said, holding the skin to the warrior's mouth, "drink a little. It will restore you."

The battlechief sucked down a long, thirsty draught and then shoved the skin away. "You must raise the alarm," he said, some vigour returning to his voice. He clutched at Bran and held him fast. "You must ride and warn the people. Warn everyone. The king is dead, and the Ffreinc are coming."

"How much time do we have?" asked Bran.

"Enough, pray God," said the battlechief. "Less if you stay. Go now."

Bran hesitated, unable to decide what should be done.

"Now!" Iwan said, pushing the prince away. "There is but time to hide the women and children."

"We will go together. I will help you."

"Go!" snarled Iwan. "Leave me!"

"Not like this."

Ignoring the wounded man's curses, Bran helped him to his feet and back into the saddle. Then, taking up the reins of Iwan's horse, he led them both back the way he had come. Owing to the battlechief's wound, they travelled more slowly than Bran would have wished, eventually reaching the western edge of the forest, where he paused to allow the horses and wounded man to rest. "Is there much pain?" he asked.

"Not so much," Iwan said, pressing a hand to his chest. "Ah, a little . . ."

"We'll wait here awhile." Bran dismounted, walked a few paces ahead, and crouched beside the road, scanning the valley for any sign of the enemy invaders.

The broad, undulating lowlands of Elfael spread before him, shimmering gently in the blue haze of an early autumn day. Secluded, green, fertile, a region of gentle, wooded hills seamed through with clear-running streams and brooks, it lay pleasantly between the high, bare stone crags of mountains to the north and east and the high moorland wastes to the south. Not the largest cantref beyond the Marches, in Bran's estimation it tendered in charm what it lacked in size.

In the near distance, the king's fortress on its high mound, whitewashed walls gleaming in the sunlight, stood sentinel at the gateway to Elfael, which seemed to drowse in the heavy, honeyed light. So quiet, so peaceful—the likelihood of anything disturbing such a deep and luxurious serenity seemed impossibly remote, a mere cloud shadow passing over a sun-bright meadow, a little dimming of the light before the sun blazed forth again. Caer Cadarn had been his family's home for eight generations, and he had never imagined anything could ever change that.

Bran satisfied himself that all was calm—at least for the moment—then returned to his mount and swung into the saddle once more.

"See anything?" asked Iwan. Hollow-eyed, his face was pale and dripping with sweat.

"No Ffreinc," Bran replied, "yet."

They started down into the valley at a trot. Bran did not stop at the hill fort but rode straight to Llanelli, the tiny monastery that occupied the heel of the valley and stood halfway between the fortress and Glascwm, the chief town of the neighbouring cantref—and the only settlement of any size in the entire region. Although merely an outpost of the larger abbey of Saint Dyfrig at Glascwm, the Llanelli monastery served the people of Elfael well. The monks, Bran had decided, not only would know best how to raise an alarm to warn the people, but also would be able to help Iwan.

The gates of the monastery were open, so they rode through and halted in the bare-earth yard outside the little timber and mud-daubed church. "Brother Ffreol! Brother Ffreol!" Bran shouted; he leapt from the saddle and ran to the door of the church. A lone priest was kneeling before the altar. An elderly man, he turned as Bran burst in upon his prayers.

"Lord Bran," said the old man, rising shakily to his feet. "God be good to you."

"Where is Brother Ffreol?"

"I am sure I cannot say," replied the aging monk. "He might be anywhere. Why all this shouting?"

Without reply, Bran seized the bell rope. The bell pealed wildly in response to his frantic pulling, and soon monks were hurrying to the church from every direction. First through the door was Brother Cefan, a local lad only slightly older than Bran himself. "Lord Bran, what is wrong?"

"Where is Ffreol?" demanded Bran, still tugging on the bell rope. "I need him."

"He was in the scriptorium a short while ago," replied the youth. "I don't know where he is now."

"Find him!" ordered Bran. "Hurry!"

The young brother darted back through the door, colliding with Bishop Asaph, a dour, humourless drone of advancing age and, as Bran had always considered, middling ability. "You there!" he shouted, striding into the church. "Stop that! You hear? Release that rope at once!"

Bran dropped the rope and spun around.

"Oh, it's you, Bran," said the bishop, his features arranging themselves in a frown of weary disapproval. "I might have guessed. What, pray, is the meaning of this spirited summons?"

"No time to waste, bishop," said Bran. Rushing up, he snatched the churchman by the sleeve of his robe and pulled him out of the church and into the yard, where twenty or so of the monastery's inhabitants were quickly gathering.

"Calm yourself," said Bishop Asaph, shaking himself free of Bran's grasp. "We're all here, so explain this commotion if you can."

"The Ffreinc are coming," said Bran. "Three hundred marchogi—they are on their way here now." Pointing to the battlechief sitting slumped in the saddle, he said, "Iwan fought them, and he's wounded. He needs help at once."

"Marchogi!" gasped the gathered monks, glancing fearfully at one another.

"But why tell *us*?" wondered the bishop. "Your father should be the one to—"

"The king is dead," Bran said. "They murdered him—and the rest of the warband with him. Everyone is dead. We have no protection."

"I do not understand," sputtered the bishop. "What do you mean? Everyone?"

Fear snaked through the gathered monks. "The warband dead! We are lost!"

Brother Ffreol appeared, pushing his way through the crowd. "Bran, I saw you ride in. There is trouble. What has happened?"

"The Ffreinc are coming!" he said, turning to meet the priest and pull him close. "Three hundred marchogi. They're on their way to Elfael now."

"Will Rhi Brychan fight them?"

"He already did," said Bran. "There was a battle on the road. My father and his men have been killed. Iwan alone escaped to warn us. He is injured—here," he said, moving to the wounded champion, "help me get him down."

Together with a few of the other brothers, they eased the warrior down from his horse and laid him on the ground. While Brother Galen, the monastery physician, began examining the wounds, Bran said, "We must raise the alarm. There is still time for everyone to flee."

"Leave that with me. I will see to it," replied Ffreol. "You must ride to Caer Cadarn and gather everything you care to save. Go now—and may God go with you."

"Wait a moment," said the bishop, raising his hand to stop them from hurrying off. Turning to Bran, he said, "Why would the Ffreinc come here? Your father has arranged to swear a treaty of peace with William the Red."

"And he was on his way to do just that!" snapped Bran, growing angry at the perfunctory insinuation that he was lying. "Am I the Red King's counsellor now that I should be privy to a Ffreinc rogue's thoughts?" He glared at the suspicious bishop.

"Calm yourself, my son," said Asaph stiffly. "There is no need to mock. I was only asking."

"They will arrive in force," Bran said, climbing into the saddle once more. "I will save what I can from the caer and return here for Iwan."

"And then?" wondered Asaph.

"We will flee while there is still time!"

The bishop shook his head. "No, Bran. You must ride to Lundein instead. You must finish what your father intended."

"No," replied Bran. "It is impossible. I cannot go to Lundein —and even if I did, the king would never listen to me."

"The king will listen," the bishop insisted. "William is not unreasonable. You must talk to him. You must tell him what has happened and seek redress."

"Red William will not see me!"

"Bran," said Brother Ffreol. He came to stand at the young man's stirrup and placed his hand on his leg as if to restrain him. "Bishop Asaph is right. You will be king now. William will certainly see you. And when he does, you must swear the treaty your father meant to undertake."

Bran opened his mouth to object, but Bishop Asaph stopped him, saying, "A grave mistake has been made, and the king must provide remedy. You must obtain justice for your people."

"Mistake!" cried Bran. "My father has been killed, and his warband slaughtered!"

"Not by William," the bishop pointed out. "When the king hears what has happened, he will punish the man who did this and make reparations."

Bran rejected the advice out of hand. The course they urged was childish and dangerous. Before he could begin to explain the utter folly of their plan, Asaph turned to the brothers who stood looking on and commanded them to take the alarm to the countryside and town. "The people are not to oppose the Ffreinc by force," instructed the bishop sternly. "This is a holy decree, tell them. Enough blood has been shed already—and that needlessly. We must not give the enemy cause to attack. God willing, this occupation will be brief. But until it ends, we will all endure it as best we can."

The bishop sent his messengers away, saying, "Go now, and with all speed. Tell everyone you meet to spread the word— each to his neighbour. No one is to be overlooked."

The monks hurried off, deserting the monastery on the

run. Bran watched them go, grave misgivings mounting by the moment. "Now then," said Bishop Asaph, turning once more to Bran, "you must reach Lundein as quickly as possible. The sooner this error can be remedied, the less damage will result and the better for everyone. You must leave at once."

"This is madness," Bran told him. "We'll all be killed."

"It is the only way," Ffreol asserted. "You must do it for the sake of Elfael and the throne."

Bran stared incredulously at the two churchmen. Every instinct told him to run, to fly.

"I will go with you," offered Ffreol. "Whatever I can do to aid you in this, trust it will be done."

"Good," said the bishop, satisfied with this arrangement. "Now go, both of you, and may God lend you his own wisdom and the swiftness of very angels."

Racing up the ramp, Bran flew through the gates of Caer Cadarn. He leapt from the saddle, shouting before his feet touched the ground. The disagreeable Maelgwnt drifted into the yard. "What now?" he asked. "Foundered another horse? Two in one day—what will your father say, I wonder?"

"My father is dead," Bran said, his tone lashing, "and all who rode with him, save Iwan."

The steward's eyes narrowed as he tried to work out the likelihood of Bran's wild assertion. "If that is a jest, it is a poor one—even for you."

"It is God's own truth!" Bran snarled. Clutching the startled man by the arm, he turned him around and marched swiftly toward the king's hall. "They were attacked by a Ffreinc warhost that is on its way here now," he explained. "They will come here first. Take the strongbox and silver to the monastery —the servants, too. Leave no one behind. The marchogi will take the fortress and everything in it for their own."

"What about the livestock?" asked Maelgwnt.

"To the monastery," replied Bran, dashing for the door.

"Use your head, man! Anything worth saving—take it to Llanelli. The monks will keep it safe for us."

He ran through the hall to the armoury beyond: a square, thick-walled room with long slits for windows. As he expected, the best weapons were gone; the warband had taken all but a few rusty, bent-bladed swords and some well-worn spears. He selected the most serviceable of these and then turned to the rack of longbows hanging on the far wall.

For some reason—probably for decorum's sake in Lundein—his father had left all the warbows behind. He picked one up, tried it, and slung it over his shoulder. He tucked a red-rusted sword into his belt, grabbed up a sheaf of arrows and several of the least blunt spears, and then raced to the stables. Dumping the weapons on the floor, Bran commanded Cefn to saddle another of the mares. "When you're finished, bring it to the yard. Brother Ffreol is on his way here by foot; I want to leave the moment he arrives."

Cefn, wan and distraught, made no move to obey. "Is it true?"

"The massacre?" Bran asked. "Yes, it's true. Ffreol and I ride now to Lundein to see the Red King, swear allegiance, and secure the return of our lands. As soon as I leave, run and find Maelgwnt—do everything he says. We're moving everything to the monastery. Never fear, you will be safe there. Understand?"

Cefn nodded.

"Good. Hurry now. There is not much time."

Bran returned to the kitchen to find the old cook comforting her young helpers. They were huddled beneath her ample arms like chicks beneath the wings of a hen, and she held them, patting their shoulders and stroking their heads. "Mairead, I need provisions," Bran said, striding quickly into the room. "Brother Ffreol and I are riding to Lundein at once."

"Bran! Oh, Bran!" wailed the woman. "Rhi Brychan is dead!"

"He is," Bran replied, pulling the two whimpering girls from her grasp.

"And all who rode with him?"

"Gone," he confirmed. "And we will mourn them properly when we have rid ourselves of these scabby Ffreinc thieves. But you must listen to me now. As soon as I am gone, Maelgwnt will take everyone to Llanelli. Stay there until I return. The Ffreinc will not harm you if you remain at the monastery with the monks. Do you hear me?"

The woman nodded, her eyes filled with unshed tears. Bran turned her and pushed her gently away. "Off with you now! Hurry and bring the food to the yard."

Next, Bran dashed to his father's chamber and to the small wooden casket where the king kept his ready money. The real treasure was kept in the strongbox that Maelgwnt would see hidden at the monastery—two hundred marks in English silver. The smaller casket contained but a few marks used for buying at the market, paying for favours, bestowing largesse on the tenants, and other occasional uses.

There were four bags of coins in all—more than enough to see them safely to Lundein and back. Bran scooped up the little leather bags, stuffed them into his shirt, then ran back out to the yard, where Brother Ffreol was just coming through the gate, leading Iwan on horseback behind him.

"Iwan, what are you doing here?" Bran asked, running to meet them. "You should stay at the monastery where they can tend you."

"Save your breath," advised Ffreol. "I've already tried to dissuade him, but he refuses to heed a word I say."

"I am going with you," the battlechief declared flatly. "That is the end of it."

"You are wounded," Bran pointed out needlessly.

"Not so badly that I cannot sit in a saddle," answered the big man. "I want to see the look in the Red King's eye when we stand before him and demand justice. And," he added, "if a witness to this outrage is required, then you will have one."

Bran opened his mouth to object once more, but Ffreol said, "Let him be. If he feels that way about it, nothing we say will discourage him, and stubborn as he is, he'd only follow us anyway."

Glancing toward the stable, Bran muttered, "What is keeping Cefn?" He shouted for the groom to hurry; when that brought no response, he started for the stable to see what was taking so long.

Brother Ffreol held him back, saying, "Calm yourself, Bran. You've been running all day. Rest when you can. We will be on our way soon enough."

"Not soon enough for me," he cried, racing off to the stable to help Cefn finish saddling the horses. They were leading two mares into the yard when Mairead appeared with her two kitchen helpers, each carrying a cloth sack bulging with provisions. While the priest blessed the women and prayed over them, Bran and Cefn arranged the tuck bags behind the saddles and strapped them down, secreting the money in the folds. "Come, Ffreol," Bran said, taking the reins from the groom and mounting the saddle, "if they catch us here, all is lost."

". . . and may the Lord make his face to shine upon you and give you his peace through all things whatsoever may befall you," intoned the priest, bestowing a kiss on the bowed head of each woman in turn. "Amen. Now off with you! Help Maelgwnt, and then all of you hie to Llanelli as soon as you can."

The sun was already low in the west by the time the three riders crossed the stream and started up the long rising slope toward the edge of the forest; their shadows stretched long on the road, going before them like spindly, misshapen ghosts. They rode in silence until entering the shady margin of the trees.

Coed Cadw, the Guarding Wood, was a dense tangle of ancient trees: oak, elm, lime, plane—all the titans of the wood. Growing amongst and beneath these giants were younger, smaller trees and thickets of hazel and beech. The road itself was lined with blackberry brambles that formed a hedge wall along either side so thick and lush that three paces off the road in any direction and a person could no longer be seen from the path.

"Is it wise, do you think," asked the priest, "to keep to the road? The marchogi are certain to be on it too."

"I do not doubt it," replied Bran, "but going any other way would take far too long. If we keep our wits about us, we will hear them long before they hear us, and we can easily get off the road and out of sight."

Iwan, his face tight with pain, said nothing. Brother Ffreol accepted Bran's assurances, and they rode on.

"Do you think we should have seen the Ffreinc by now?" asked the monk after a while. "If they had been in a hurry to reach Elfael, we would certainly have met them. They probably stopped to make camp for the night. God be praised."

"You praise God for that?"

"I do," admitted the monk. "It means the Cymry have at least one night to hide their valuables and get to safety."

"One night," mocked Bran. "As much as all that!"

"Wars have turned on less," the priest pointed out. "If the Conqueror's arrow had flown but a finger's breadth to the right of Harold's eye, the Ffreinc would not be here now."

"Yes, well, it seems to me that if God really wanted praising, he'd have prevented the filthy Ffreinc and their foul marchogi from coming here in the first place."

"Do you have the mind of God now that you know all things good and ill for each and every one of his creatures?"

"It does not take the mind of God," replied Bran carelessly, "to know that anytime a Norman stands at your gate it is for ill and never good. That is a doctrine more worthy than any Bishop Asaph ever professed."

"Jesu forgive you," sighed the priest. "Such irreverence."

"Irreverent or not, it is true."

They fell silent and rode on. As the sun sank lower, the shadows on the trail gathered, deepening beneath the trees and brushwood; the sounds became hushed and furtive as the forest drew in upon itself for the night.

The road began to rise more steeply toward the spine of the ridge, and Bran slowed the pace. In a little while the gloom had spread so that the gap between trees was as dark as the black boles themselves, and the road shone as a ghost-pale ribbon stretching dimly away into the deepening night.

"I think we should stop," suggested Brother Ffreol. "It will soon be too dark to see. We could rest and eat something. Also, I want to tend Iwan's wound."

Bran was of a mind to ride all night, but one look at the wounded warrior argued otherwise, so he gave in and allowed the monk to have his way. They picketed the horses and made camp at the base of an oak just out of sight of the road, ate a few mouthfuls of bread and a little hard cheese, and then settled down to sleep beneath the tree's protecting limbs. Wrapped in his cloak, Bran slept uneasily, rising again as it became light enough to tell tree from shadow.

He roused Ffreol and then went to Iwan, who came awake at his touch. "How do you feel?" he asked, kneeling beside the champion.

"Never better," Iwan said as he tried to sit up. The pain hit him hard and slammed him back once more. He grimaced and blew air through his mouth, panting like a winded hound. "Perhaps I will try that again," he said through clenched teeth, "more slowly this time."

"Wait a moment," said Ffreol, putting out his hand. "Let me see your binding." He pulled open the big man's shirt and looked at the bandage wrapped around his upper chest. "It is clean still. There is little blood," he announced, greatly reassured.

"Then it is time we made a start."

"When we have prayed," said the monk.

"Oh, very well," sighed Bran. "Just get on with it."

The priest gathered his robe around him, and folding his hands, he closed his eyes and began to pray for the speedy and sure success of their mission. Bran followed the sound of his voice more than the words and imagined that he heard a low, rhythmic drumming marking out the cadence. He listened for a while before realising that he was not imagining the sound. "Quiet!" he hissed. "Someone's coming."

Ffreol helped Iwan to his feet, and the two disappeared into the underbrush; Bran darted to the horses and threw his cloak over their heads to keep them quiet, then stood and held the cloak in place so the animals would not shake it off. Brother Ffreol, flat on the ground, watched the narrow slice of road that he could see from beneath his bush. "Ffreinc!" he whispered a few moments later. "Scores of them." He paused, then added, "Hundreds."

Bran, holding the horses' heads, heard the creak and rattle of wagon wheels, followed by the dull, hollow clop of hundreds of hooves and the tramp of leather-shod feet—a pulsing beat that seemed to go on and on and on.

At long last, the sound gradually faded and the bird-fretted silence of the forest returned. "I believe they have gone," said Ffreol softly. He rose and brushed off his robe. Bran stood listening for a moment longer, and when no one else appeared on the road, he uncovered the horses' heads. Working quickly and quietly, he saddled the horses and then led the animals through the forest, within sight of the road. When, after walking a fair distance, no more marchogi appeared, he allowed them to leave the forest path and return to the road. The three travellers took to the saddle once more and bolted for Lundein.

CHAPTER 6 ⚕

By midmorning Bran, Iwan, and Brother Ffreol had begun the long, sloping ascent of the ridge overlooking the Vale of Wye. Upon reaching the top, they paused and looked down into the broad valley and the glittering sweep of the lazy green river. In the distance they could see the dark flecks of birds circling and swooping in the cloudless sky. Bran saw them, and his stomach tightened with apprehension.

As the men approached the river ford, the strident calls of carrion feeders filled the air—ravens, rooks, and crows for the most part, but there were others. Hawks, buzzards, and even an owl or two wheeled in tight circles above the trees.

Bran stopped at the water's edge. The soft ground of the riverbank was raggedly churned and chewed, as if a herd of giant boar had undertaken to plough the water marge with their tusks. There were no corpses to be seen, but here and there flies buzzed in thick black clouds over congealing puddles where blood had collected in a horse's hoofprint. The air was heavy and rank with the sickly sweet stench of death.

Bran dismounted and walked back toward the road, where

most of the fighting had taken place. He looked down and saw that in the place where he stood the earth took on a deeper, ruddy hue where a warrior's lifeblood had stained the ground on which he died.

"This is where it happened," mused Brother Ffreol with quiet reverence. "This is where the warriors of Elfael were overthrown."

"Aye," confirmed Iwan, his face grim and grey with fatigue and pain. "This is where we were ambushed and massacred." He lifted his hand and pointed to the wide bend of the river. "Rhi Brychan fell there," he said. "By the time I reached him, his body had been washed away."

Bran, mouth pressed into a thin white line, stared at the water and said nothing. Once he might have felt a twinge of regret at his father's passing, but not now. Years of accumulated grievances had long ago removed his father from his affections. Sorrow alone could not surmount the rancour and bitterness, nor span the aching distance between them. He whispered a cold farewell and turned once more to the battleground.

Images of chaos sprang into his mind—a desperate battle between woefully outnumbered and lightly armed Britons and heavy, hulking, mail-clad Ffreinc knights. He saw the blood haze hang like a mist in the air above the slaughter and heard the echoed clash of steel on steel, of blade on wood and bone, the fast-fading shouts and screams of men and horses as they died.

Looking toward the wood to the north, he saw the birds flocking to their feeding frenzy. Squawking, shrieking, they fought and fluttered, battering wings against one another in their greed. Grabbing up stones from the riverbank, he ran to the place, throwing rocks into the midst of the feathered scavengers as he ran.

Reluctant to leave the mound on which they fed, the scolding birds fluttered up and settled again as the angry stones sailed past. Stooping once more, he took up another handful of rocks and, screaming at the top of his lungs, let fly. One of the missiles struck a greedy red-beaked crow and snapped its neck. The wounded bird flopped, beating its wings in a last frantic effort to rise; Bran threw again and the bird lay still.

The hillock was covered with brush and branches cut from the thickets and trees along the riverbank. Pulling a stick from the pile, Bran began beating at the flesh eaters; they hopped and dodged, reluctant to give ground. Bran, screaming like a demon, lashed with the branch, driving the scavengers away. They fled with angry reluctance, crying their outrage to the sky as Bran pulled brushwood from the stack to lay bare a massed heap of corpses.

The stick in his hand fell away, and Bran staggered backward, overwhelmed by the calamity that had taken the lives of his kinsmen and friends. The birds had feasted well. There were gaping hollows where eyes had been; flesh had been stripped from faces; ragged holes had been wrested in rib cages to expose the soft viscera. Human no longer, they were merely so much rotting meat.

No! These were men he knew. They were friends, riding companions, fellow hunters, drinking mates—some of them from times before he could remember. They had taught him trail craft, had given him his first lessons with blunted wooden weapons made for him with their own hands. They had picked him up when he fell from his horse, corrected his aim when he practised with the bow, and along the way, taught him much of what he knew of life. To see them now with their empty eyes and livid, blackening faces, their ruined bodies beginning to bloat, was more than he could bear.

As he gazed in mute horror at the confused tangle of slashed and bloodied limbs and torsos, something deep inside himself gave way—as if a ligament or sinew suddenly snapped under the strain of a load too heavy to bear. His soul spun into a void of bloodred rage. His vision narrowed, and it seemed as if his surroundings had taken on a keener, harder edge but were now viewed from a long way off. It seemed to Bran that he gazed at the world through a red-tinged tunnel.

There was another hill nearby—also crudely covered with brush and lopped-off tree branches. Bran ran to it, uncovered it, and without realising what he was doing, climbed up onto the tangled jumble of bodies. He sank to his knees and grasped the arms of the corpses with his hands, tugging on them as if urging their sleeping owners to wake again and rise. "Get up!" he shouted. "Open your eyes!" He saw a face he recognised; seizing the corpse's arm, he jerked on it, crying, "Evan, wake up!" He saw another: "Geronwy! The Ffreinc are here!" He began calling the names of those he remembered, "Bryn! Ifan! Oryg! Gerallt! Idris! Madog! Get up, all of you!"

"Bran!" Brother Ffreol, shocked and alarmed, ran to pull him away. "Bran! For the love of God, come down from there!"

Stumbling up over the dead, the monk reached out and snagged Bran by the sleeve and hauled him down, dragging the prince back to solid ground and back to himself once more.

Bran heard Ffreol's voice and felt the monk's hands on him, and awareness came flooding back. The blood-tinged veil through which he viewed the world dimmed and faded, and he was himself once more. He felt weak and hollow, like a man who has slaved all night in his sleep and awakened exhausted.

"What were you doing up there?" demanded Brother Ffreol.

Bran shook his head. "I thought . . . I—" Suddenly, his stomach heaved; he pitched forward on hands and knees and retched.

Ffreol stood with him until he finished. When Bran could stand again, the priest turned to the death mound and sank to his knees in the soft earth. Bran knelt beside him, and Iwan painfully dismounted and knelt beside his horse as Brother Ffreol spread his arms, palms upward in abject supplication.

Closing his eyes and turning his face to heaven, the priest said, "Merciful Father, our hearts are pierced with the sharp arrow of grief. Our words fail; our souls quail; our spirits recoil before the injustice of this hateful iniquity. We are undone.

"God and Creator, gather the souls of our kinsmen to your Great Hall, forgive their sins and remember only their virtues, and bind them to yourself with the strong bands of fellowship.

"For ourselves, Mighty Father, I pray you keep us from the sin of hatred, keep us from the sin of vengeance, keep us from the sin of despair, but protect us from the wicked schemes of our enemies. Walk with us now on this uncertain road. Send angels to go before us, angels to go behind, angels on either side, angels above and below—guarding, shielding, encompassing." He paused for a moment and then added, "May the Holy One give us the courage of righteousness and grant us strength for this day and through all things whatsoever shall befall us. Amen."

Bran, kneeling beside him, stared at the ground and tried to add his "Amen," but the word clotted and died in his throat. After a moment, he raised his head and gazed for the last time on the heap of corpses before turning his face away.

Then, while Bran bathed in the river to wash the stink of death and gore from his hands and clothes, Ffreol and Iwan covered the bodies once more with fresh-cut branches of hazel and holly, the better to keep the birds away. Bran finished, and the three grief-sick men remounted and rode on as the cacophony of carrion feeders renewed behind them. Just after midday they crossed the border into England and a short while later approached the English town of Hereford. The town was full of Ffreinc now, so they moved on quickly without stopping. From Hereford, the road was wide and well used, if deeply rutted. They encountered few people and spoke to none, pretending to be deep in conversation with one another whenever they saw anyone approaching, all the while remaining watchful and wary.

Beyond Hereford, the land sloped gently down toward the lowlands and the wide Lundein estuary still some way beyond the distant horizon of rumpled, cultivated hills. As daylight began to fail, they took refuge in a beech grove beside the road near the next ford; while Bran watered the horses, Ffreol prepared a meal from the provisions in their tuck bags. They ate in silence, and Bran listened to the rooks flocking to the woods for the night. The sound of their coarse calls renewed the horror of the day. He saw the broken bodies of his friends once more. With an effort, he concentrated on the fire, holding the hateful images at bay.

"It will take time," Ffreol said, the sound of his voice a distant buzz in Bran's ears, "but the memory will fade, believe me." At the sound of his voice, Bran struggled back from the brink. "The memory of this black day will fade," Ffreol was saying as he broke twigs and fed them to the fire. "It will vanish like a bad taste in your mouth. One day it will be gone, and you will be left with only the sweetness."

"There was little sweetness," sniffed Bran. "My father, the king, was not an easy man."

"I was talking about the others—your friends in the warband."

Bran acknowledged the remark with a grunt.

"But you are right," Ffreol continued; he snapped another twig. "Brychan was not an easy man. God be praised, you have the chance to do something about that. You can be a better king than your father."

"No." Bran picked up the dried husk of a beechnut and tossed it into the fire as if consigning his own fragile future to the flames. He cared little enough for the throne and all its attendant difficulties. What difference did it make who was king anyway? "That's over now. Finished."

"You *will* be king," declared Iwan, stirring himself from his bleak reverie. "The kingdom will be restored. Never doubt it."

But Bran did doubt it. For most of his life he had maintained a keen disinterest in all things having to do with kingship. He had never imagined himself occupying his father's throne at Caer Cadarn or leading a host of men into battle. Those things, like the other chores of nobility, were the sole occupation of his father. Bran always had other pursuits. So far as Bran could tell, to reign was merely to invite a perpetual round of frustration and aggravation that lasted from the moment one took the crown until it was laid aside. Only a power-crazed thug like his father would solicit such travail. Any way he looked at it, sovreignty exacted a heavy price, which Bran had seen firsthand and which, now that it came to it, he found himself unwilling to pay.

"You will be king," Iwan asserted again. "On my life, you will."

Bran, reluctant to disappoint the injured champion with a facile denial, held his tongue. The three were silent again for a time, watching the flames and listening to the sounds of the wood around them as its various denizens prepared for night. Finally, Bran asked, "What if they will not see us in Lundein?"

"Oh, William the Red will see us, make no mistake." Iwan raised his head and regarded Bran over the fluttering fire. "You are a subject lord come to swear fealty. He will see you and be glad of it. He will welcome you as one king welcomes another."

"I am not the king," Bran pointed out.

"You are heir to the throne," replied the champion. "It is the same thing."

Ffreol said, "When we return to Elfael, we will observe the proper rites and ceremonies. But this will be the first duty of your reign—to place Elfael under the protection of the English throne and—"

"And all of us become boot-licking slaves of the stinking Ffreinc," Bran said, his tone bitter and biting. "What is the stupid bloody point?"

"We keep our land!" Iwan retorted. "We keep our lives."

"If God and King William allow!" sneered Bran.

"Nay, Bran," said Ffreol. "We will pay tribute, yes, and count it a price worth paying to live our lives as we choose."

"Pay tribute to the very brutes that would plunder us if we didn't," growled Bran. "That stinks to high heaven."

"Does it stink worse than death?" asked Iwan. Bran, shamed by the taunt, merely glared.

"It is unjust," granted Ffreol, trying to soothe, "but that is ever the way of things."

"Did you think it would be different?" asked Iwan angrily. "Saints and angels, Bran, it was never going to be easy."

"It could at least be fair," muttered Bran.

"Fair or not, you must do all you can to protect our lands and the lives of our people," Ffreol told him. "To protect those least able to protect themselves. That much, at least, has not changed. That was ever the sole purpose and duty of kingship. Since the beginning of time it has not changed."

Bran accepted this observation without further comment. He stared gloomily into the fire, wishing he had followed his first impulse to leave Elfael and all its troubles as far behind as possible.

After a time, Iwan asked about Lundein. Ffreol had been to the city several times on church business in years past, and he described for Bran and Iwan what they might expect to find when they arrived. As he talked, night deepened around them, and they continued to feed the fire until they grew too tired to keep their eyes open. They then wrapped themselves in their cloaks and fell asleep in the quiet grove.

Rising again at dawn, the travellers shook the leaves and dew from their cloaks, watered the horses, and continued on. The day passed much like the one before, except that the settlements became more numerous and the English presence in the land became more marked, until Bran was convinced that they had left Britain far behind and entered an alien country, where the houses were small and dark and crabbed, where grim-faced people dressed in curious garb made up of coarse dun-coloured cloth stood and stared at passing travellers with suspicion in their dull peasant eyes. Despite the sunlight streaming down from a clear blue sky, the land seemed dismal and unhappy. Even the animals, in their woven willow enclosures, appeared bedraggled and morose.

Nor was the aspect to improve. The farther south they went, the more abject the countryside appeared. Settlements of all kinds became more numerous—how the English loved their villages—but these were not wholesome places. Clustered together in what Bran considered suffocating proximity anywhere the earth offered a flat space and a little running water, the close-set hovels sprouted like noxious mushrooms on earth stripped of all trees and greenery—which the mud-dwellers used to make humpbacked houses, barns, and byres for their livestock, which they kept in muck-filled pens beside their low, smoky dwellings.

Thus, a traveller could always smell an English town long before he reached it, and Bran could only shake his head in wonder at the thought of abiding in perpetual fug and stench. In his opinion, the people lived no better than the pigs they slopped, slaughtered, and fed upon.

As the sun began to lower, the three riders crested the top of a broad hill and looked down into the Vale of Hafren and the gleaming arc of the Hafren River. A smudgy brown haze in the valley betrayed their destination for the night: the town of Gleawancaester, which began life in ancient times as a simple outpost of the Roman Legio Augusta XX. Owing to its pride of place by the river and the proximity of iron mines, the town begun by legionary veterans had grown slowly over the centuries until the arrival of the English, who transformed it into a market centre for the region.

The road into the vale widened as it neared the city, which to Bran's eyes was worse than any he had seen so far—if only because it was larger than any other they had yet passed. Squatting hard by the river, with twisting, narrow streets of crowded hovels clustered around a huge central market square of beaten earth, Gleawancaester—Caer Gloiu of the Britons —had long ago outgrown the stout stone walls of the Roman garrison, which could still be seen in the lower courses of the city's recently refurbished fortress.

Like the town's other defences—a wall and gate, still unfinished—a new bridge of timber and stone bore testimony to Ffreinc occupation. Norman bridges were wide and strong, built to withstand heavy traffic and ensure that the steady stream of horses, cattle, and merchant wagons flowed unimpeded into and out of the markets.

Bran noticed the increase in activity as they approached the bridge. Here and there, tall, clean-shaven Ffreinc moved amongst the shorter, swarthier English residents. The sight of these horse-faced foreigners with their long, straight-cut hair and pale, sun-starved flesh walking about with such toplofty arrogance made the gorge rise in his throat. He forcibly turned his face away to keep from being sick.

Before crossing the bridge, they dismounted to stretch their legs and water the horses at a wooden trough set up next to a riverside well. As they were waiting, Bran noticed two barefoot, ragged little girls walking together, carrying a basket of eggs between them—no doubt bound for the market. They fell in with the traffic moving across the bridge. Two men in short cloaks and tunics loitered at the rail, and as the girls passed by, one of the men, grinning at his companion, stuck out his foot, tripping the nearest girl. She fell sprawling onto the bridge planks; the basket overturned, spilling the eggs.

Bran, watching this confrontation develop, immediately started toward the child. When, as the second girl bent to retrieve the basket, the man kicked it from her grasp, scattering eggs every which way, Bran was already on the bridge.

Iwan, glancing up from the trough, took in the girls, Bran, and the two thugs and shouted for Bran to come back.

"Where is he going?" wondered Ffreol, looking around.

"To make trouble," muttered Iwan.

The two little girls, tearful now, tried in vain to gather up the few unbroken eggs, only to have them kicked from their hands or trodden on by passersby—much to the delight of the louts on the bridge. The toughs were so intent on their merriment that they failed to notice the slender Welshman bearing down on them until Bran, lurching forward as if slipping on a broken egg, stumbled up to the man who had tripped the girl. The fellow made to shove Bran away, whereupon Bran seized his arm, spun him around, and pushed him over the rail. His surprised yelp was cut short as the dun-coloured water closed over his head. "Oops!" said Bran. "How clumsy of me."

"Mon Dieu!" objected the other, backing away.

Bran turned on him and drew him close. "What is that you say?" he asked. "You wish to join him?"

"Bran! Leave him alone!" shouted Ffreol as he pulled Bran off the man. "He can't understand you. Let him go!"

The oaf spared a quick glance at his friend, sputtering

and floundering in the river below, then fled down the street. "I think he understood well enough," observed Bran.

"Come away," said Ffreol.

"Not yet," said Bran. Taking the purse at his belt, he untied it and withdrew two silver pennies. Turning to the older of the two girls, he wiped the remains of an eggshell from her cheek. "Give those to your mother," he said, pressing the coins into the girl's grubby fist. Closing her hand upon the coins, he repeated, "For your mother."

Brother Ffreol picked up the empty basket and handed it to the younger girl; he spoke a quick word in English, and the two scampered away. "Now unless you have any other battles you wish to fight in front of God and everybody," he said, taking Bran by the arm, "let us get out of here before you draw a crowd."

"Well done," said Iwan, his grin wide and sunny as Bran and Ffreol returned to the trough.

"We are strangers here," Ffreol remonstrated. "What, in the holy name of Peter, were you thinking?"

"Only that heads can be as easily broken as eggs," Bran replied, "and that justice ought sometimes to protect those least able to protect themselves." He glowered dark defiance at the priest. "Or has that changed?"

Ffreol drew breath to object but thought better of it. Turning away abruptly, he announced, "We have ridden far enough for one day. We will spend the night here."

"We will not!" objected Iwan, curling his lip in a sneer. "I'd rather sleep in a sty than stay in this stinking place. It is crawling with vermin."

"There is an abbey here, and we will be welcome," the priest pointed out.

"An abbey filled with Ffreinc, no doubt," Bran grumbled. "You can stay there if you want. I'll not set foot in the place."

"I agree," said Iwan, his voice dulled with pain. He sat on the edge of the trough, hunched over his wound as if protecting it.

The monk fell silent, and they mounted their horses and continued on. They crossed the bridge and passed through the untidy sprawl of muddy streets and low-roofed hovels. Smoke from cooking fires filled the streets, and all the people Bran saw were either hurrying home with a bundle of firewood on their backs or carrying food to be prepared—a freshly killed chicken to be roasted, a scrap of bacon, a few leeks, a turnip or two. Seeing the food reminded Bran that he had eaten very little in the last few days, and his hunger came upon him with the force of a kick. He scented the aroma of roasting meat on the evening air, and his mouth began to water. He was on the point of suggesting to Brother Ffreol that they should return to the centre of town and see if there might be an inn near the market square, when the monk suddenly announced, "I know just the place!" He urged his horse to a trot and proceeded toward the old south gate. "This way!"

The priest led his reluctant companions out through the gate and up the curving road as it ascended the steep riverbank. Shortly, they came to a stand of trees growing atop the bluff above the river, overlooking the town. "Here it is—just as I remembered!"

Bran took one look at an odd eight-sided timber structure with a high, steeply pitched roof and a low door with a curiously curved lintel and said, "A barn? You've brought us to a barn?"

"Not a barn," the monk assured him, sliding from the saddle. "It is an old cell."

"A priest's cell," Bran said, regarding the edifice doubtfully. There was no cross atop the structure, no window, no outward markings of any kind to indicate its function. "Are you sure?"

"The blessed Saint Ennion once lived here," Ffreol explained, moving toward the door. "A long time ago."

Bran shrugged. "Who lives here now?"

"A friend." Taking hold of a braided cord that passed through one doorpost, the monk gave the cord a strong tug. A bell sounded from somewhere inside. Ffreol, smiling in anticipation of a glad welcome, pulled the cord again and said, "You'll see."

CHAPTER 7

Ffreol waited a moment, and when no one answered, he gave the braided cord a more determined pull. The bell sounded once more—a clean, clear peal in the soft evening air. Bran looked around, taking in the old oratory and its surroundings.

The cell stood at the head of a small grove of beech trees. The ground was covered with thick grass through which an earthen pathway led down the hillside into the town. In an earlier time, it occupied the grove as a woodland shrine overlooking the river. Now it surveyed the squalid prospect of a busy market town with its herds and carts and the slow-moving boats bearing iron ore to be loaded onto ships waiting at the larger docks downriver.

When a third pull on the bell rope brought no response, Ffreol turned and scratched his head. "He must be away."

"Can we not just let ourselves in?" asked Bran.

"Perhaps," allowed Ffreol. Putting his hand to the leather strap that served for a latch, he pulled, and the door opened inward. He pushed it farther and stuck in his head. "Pax vobiscum!" he shouted and waited for an answer. "There is no one here. We will wait inside."

Iwan, wincing with pain, was helped to dismount and taken inside to rest. Bran gathered up the reins of the horses and led them into the grove behind the cell; the animals were quickly unsaddled and tethered beneath the trees so they could graze. He found a leather bucket and hauled water from a stoup beside the cell. When he had finished watering the horses and settled them for the night, he joined the others in the oratory; by this time, Ffreol had a small fire going in the hearth that occupied one corner of the single large room.

It was, Bran thought, an odd dwelling—half house, half church. There was a sleeping place and a stone-lined hearth, but also an altar with a large wooden cross and a single wax candle. A solitary narrow window opened in the wall high above the altar, and a chain of sausages hung from an iron hook beside the hearth directly above a low three-legged stool. Next to the stool was a pair of leather shoes with thick wooden soles—the kind worn by those who work the mines. Crumbs of bread freckled both the altar and the hearthstones, and the smell of boiled onions mingled with incense.

Ffreol approached the altar, knelt, and said a prayer of blessing for the keeper of the cell. "I hope nothing has happened to old Faganus," he said when he finished.

"Saints and sinners are we all," said a gruff voice from the open doorway. "Old Faganus is long dead and buried."

Startled, Bran turned quickly, his hand reaching for his knife. A quick lash of a stout oak staff caught him on the arm. "Easy, son," advised the owner of the staff. "I will behave if you will."

Into the cell stepped a very short, very fat man. The crown of his head came only to Bran's armpit, and his bulk filled the doorway in which he stood. Dressed in the threadbare brown robes of a mendicant priest, he balanced his generous girth on two absurdly thin, bandy legs; his shoulders sloped and his back was slightly bent, giving him a stooped, almost dwarfish appearance; however, his thick-muscled arms and chest looked as if he could crush ale casks in his brawny embrace.

He carried a slender staff of unworked oak in one hand and held a brace of hares by a leather strap with the other. His tonsure was outgrown and in need of reshaving; his bare feet were filthy and caked with river mud, some of which had found its way to his full, fleshy jowls. He regarded his three intruders with bold and unflinching dark eyes, as ready to wallop them as welcome them.

"God be good to you," said Ffreol from the altar. "Are you priest here now?"

"Who might you be?" demanded the rotund cleric. He was one of the order of begging brothers which the Ffreinc called *frères* and the English called friars. They were all but unknown amongst the Cymry.

"We might be the King of England and his barons," replied Iwan, rising painfully. "My friend asked you a question."

Quick as a flick of a whip, the oak staff swung out, catching Iwan on the meaty part of the shoulder. He started forward, but the priest thumped him with the knob end of the staff in the centre of the chest. The champion crumpled as if struck by lightning. He fell to his knees, gasping for breath.

"It was only a wee tap, was it not?" the priest said in

amazement, turning wide eyes to Bran and Ffreol. "I swear on Sweet Mary's wedding veil, it was only a tap."

"He was wounded in a battle several days ago," Bran said. Kneeling beside the injured warrior, he helped raise him to his feet.

"Oh my soul, I didn't mean to hurt the big 'un," he sighed. To Ffreol, he said, "Aye, I am priest here now. Who are you?"

"I am Brother Ffreol of Llanelli in Elfael."

"Never heard of it," declared the brown-robed priest.

"It is in Cymru," Bran offered in a snide tone, "which you sons of Saecsens call Wales."

"Careful, boy," snipped the priest. "Come over high-handed with me, and I'll give you a thump to remind you of your manners. Don't think I won't."

"Go on, then," Bran taunted, thrusting forward. "I'll have that stick of yours so far up your—"

"Peace!" cried Ffreol, rushing forward to place himself between Bran and the brown priest. "We mean no harm. Pray, forgive my quick-tempered friends. We have suffered a grave calamity in the last days, and I fear it has clouded our better judgement." This last was said with a glare of disapproval at Bran and Iwan. "Please forgive us."

"Very well, since you ask," the priest granted with a sudden smile. "I forgive you." Laying his staff aside, he said, "So now! We know whence you came, but we still lack names for you all. Do they have proper names in Elfael? Or are they in such short supply that you must hoard them and keep them to yourselves?"

"Allow me to present Bran ap Brychan, prince and heir of Elfael," said Ffreol, drawing himself upright. "And this is Iwan ap Iestyn, champion and battlechief."

"Hail and welcome, friends," replied the little friar, raising his hands in declamation. "The blessings of a warm hearth beneath a dry roof are yours tonight. May it be so always."

Now it was Bran's turn to be amazed. "How is it that you speak Cymry?"

The brown priest gave him a wink. "And here was I, thinking you hotheaded sons of the valleys were as stupid as stumps." He chuckled and shook his head. "It took you long enough. Indeed, sire, I speak the tongue of the blessed."

"But you're English," Bran pointed out.

"Aye, English as the sky is blue," said the friar, "but I was carried off as a boy to Powys, was I not? I was put to work in a copper mine up there and slaved away until I was old enough and bold enough to escape. Almost froze to death, I did, for it was a full harsh winter, but the brothers at Llandewi took me in, did they not? And that is where I found my vocation and took my vows." He smiled a winsome, toothy grin and bowed, his round belly almost touching his knees. "I am Brother Aethelfrith," he declared proudly. "Thirty years in God's service." To Iwan, he said, "I'm sorry if I smacked you too hard."

"No harm done, Brother Eathel . . . Aelith . . . ," Iwan stuttered, trying to get his British tongue around the Saxon name.

"Aethelfrith," the priest repeated. "It means 'nobility and peace,' or some such nonsense." He grinned at his guests. "Here now, what have you brought me?"

"Brought you?" asked Bran. "We haven't brought you anything."

"Everyone who seeks shelter here brings me something," explained the priest.

"We didn't know we were coming," said Bran.

"Yet here you are." The fat priest stuck out his hand.

"Perhaps a coin might suffice?" said Ffreol. "We would be grateful for a meal and a bed."

"Aye, a coin is acceptable," allowed Aethelfrith doubtfully. "Two is better, of course. Three, now! For three pennies I sing a psalm and say a prayer for all of you—*and* we will have wine with our dinner."

"Three it is!" agreed Ffreol.

The brown priest turned to Bran expectantly and held out his hand.

Bran, irked by the friar's brash insistence, frowned. "You want the money now?"

"Oh, aye."

With a pained sigh, Bran turned his back on the priest and drew the purse from his belt. Opening the drawstring, he shook out a handful of coins, looking for any clipped coins amongst the whole. He found two half pennies and was looking for a third when Aethelfrith appeared beside him and said, "Splendid! I'll take those."

Before Bran could stop him, the priest had snatched up three bright new pennies. "Here, boyo!" he said, handing Bran the two fat hares on the strap. "You get these coneys skinned and cleaned and ready to roast when I get back."

"Wait!" said Bran, trying to snatch back the coins. "Give those back!"

"Hurry now," said Aethelfrith, darting away with surprising speed on his ludicrous bowed legs. "It will be dark soon, and I mean to have a feast tonight."

Bran followed him to the door. "Are you certain you're a priest?" Bran called after him, but the only reply he heard was a bark of cheerful laughter.

Resigned to his task, Bran went out and found a nearby

stone and set to work skinning and gutting the hares. Ffreol soon joined him and sat down to watch. "Strange fellow," he observed after a time.

"Most thieves are more honest."

Brother Ffreol chuckled. "He is a good hand with that staff."

"When his victim is unarmed, perhaps," allowed Bran dully. He stripped the fur from one plump animal. "If I'd had a sword in my hand . . ."

"Be of good cheer," said Ffreol. "This is a fortuitous meeting. I feel it. We now have a friend in this place, and that is well worth a coin or two."

"Three," corrected Bran. "And all of them new."

Ffreol nodded and then said, "He will repay that debt a thousand times over—ten thousand."

Something in his friend's tone made Bran glance up sharply. "Why do you say that?"

Ffreol offered a small, reticent smile and shrugged. "It is nothing—a feeling only."

Bran resumed his chore, and Ffreol watched him work. The two sat in companionable silence as evening enfolded them in a gentle twilight. The hares were gutted and washed by the time Friar Aethelfrith returned with a bag on his back and a small cask under each arm. "I did not know if you preferred wine or ale," he announced, "so I bought both."

Handing one of the casks to Bran, he gave the other to Ffreol and then, opening the bag, drew out a fine loaf of fresh-baked bread and a great hunk of pale yellow cheese. "Three moons if a day since I had fresh bread," he confided. "Three threes of moons since I had a drink of wine." Offering Bran another of his preposterous bows, he said, "A blessing on the

Lord of the Feast. May his days never cease and his tribe increase!"

Bran smiled in spite of himself and declared, "Bring the jars and let the banquet begin!"

They returned to the oratory, where Iwan, reclining beside the hearth, had built up the fire to a bright, crackling blaze. While Aethelfrith scurried around readying their supper, Ffreol found wooden cups and poured out the ale. Their host paused long enough to suck down a cup and then returned to his preparations, spitting the fat hares and placing them at the fireside for Iwan to tend. He then brought a wooden trencher with broken bread and bite-sized chunks of cheese, and four long fire-forks, which he passed to his guests.

They sat around the hearth and toasted bread and cheese and drank to each other's health while waiting for the meat to cook. Slowly, the cares of the last days began to release their hold on Bran and his companions.

"A toast!" said Iwan at one point, raising his cup. "I drink to our good host, Aethleth—" He stumbled at the hurdle of the name once more. He tried again, but the effort proved beyond him. Casting an eye over the plump priest, he said, "Fat little bag of vittles that he is, I will call him Tuck."

"*Friar* Tuck to you, boyo!" retorted the priest with a laugh. Cocking his head to one side, he said, "And it is Iwan, is it not? What is that in couth speech?" He tapped his chin with a stubby finger. "It's *John*, I think. Yes, John. So, overgrown infant that he is, I will call him Little John." He raised his cup, sloshing ale over the rim, "So, now! I lift my cup to Little John and to his friends. May you always have ale enough to wet your tongues, wit enough to know friend from foe, and strength enough for every fight."

Ffreol, moved as much by the camaraderie around the hearth as by the contents of his cup, raised his voice in solemn, priestly declamation, saying, "I am not lying when I say that I have feasted in the halls of kings, but rarely have I supped with a nobler company than sits beneath this humble roof tonight." Lofting his cup, he said, "God's blessing on us. Brothers all!"

CHAPTER 8

The sun was high and warm by the time the men were ready to depart Aethelfrith's oratory. Bran and Iwan bade the priest farewell, and Brother Ffreol bestowed a blessing, saying, "May the grace and peace of Christ be upon you, and the shielding of all the saints be around you, and nine holy angels aid and uphold you through all things." He then raised himself to the saddle, saying, "Do not drink all the wine, brother. Save some for our return. God willing, we will join you again on our way home."

"Then you had better hurry about your business," Aethelfrith called. "That wine will not last long."

Bran, eager to be away, slapped the reins and trotted out onto the road. Ffreol and Iwan followed close behind, and the three resumed their journey to Lundein. The horses were just finding their stride when they heard a familiar voice piping, "Wait! Wait!"

Turning around in the saddle, Bran saw the bandy-legged friar running after them. Thinking they had forgotten something, he pulled up.

"I'm coming with you," Aethelfrith declared.

Bran regarded the man's disgraceful robe, bare feet, ragged tonsure, and untidy beard. He glanced at Ffreol and shook his head.

"Your offer is thoughtful, to be sure," replied Brother Ffreol, "but we would not burden you with our affairs."

"Maybe not," he allowed, "but God wants me to go."

"God wants you to go," Iwan scoffed lightly. "You speak for God now, do you?"

"No," the priest allowed, "but I know he wants me to go."

"And how, pray, do you know this?"

Aethelfrith offered a diffident smile. "He told me."

"Well," replied the battlechief lightly, "until he tells *me*, I say you stay here and guard the wine cask."

Ffreol lifted a hand in farewell, and the three started off again, but after only a few dozen paces, Bran looked around again to see the plump priest hurrying after them, robes lifted high, his bowed legs churning. "Go back!" he called, not bothering to stop.

"I cannot," replied Aethelfrith. "It is not your voice I heed, but God's. I am compelled to come with you."

"I think we should take him," Brother Ffreol said.

"He is too slow afoot," Bran pointed out. "He could never keep pace."

"True," agreed Ffreol as the priest came puffing up. Reaching down his hand, he said, "You can ride with me, Tuck." Aethelfrith took the offered hand and began wriggling labouriously up onto the back of the horse.

"What?" said Iwan. Indicating Bran and himself, he said, "Are we not to have a say in this?"

"Say whatever you like," Aethelfrith replied. "I am certain God is willing to listen."

Iwan grumbled, but Bran laughed. "Stung you," he chuckled, "eh, Little John?"

For five days they journeyed on, following the road as it bent its way south and east over the broad lowland hills from whose tops could be seen a land of green and golden fields strewn with the smudgy brown blots of innumerable settlements. They travelled more slowly with four; owing to the extra weight, they had to stop and rest the horses more frequently. But what he cost them in time, Tuck made up in songs and rhymes and stories about the saints—and this made the journey more enjoyable.

The countryside became ever more densely populated—roads, lanes, and trackways seamed the valleys, and the cross-topped steeples of churches adorned every hilltop. Over all hung the odour of the dung heap, pungent and heavy in the sultry air. By the time the sprawl of Lundein appeared beyond the wide gleaming sweep of the Thames, Bran was heartily sick of England and already longing to return to Elfael. Ordinarily, he would not have endured such a misery in silence, but the sight of the city brought the reason for their sojourn fresh to mind, and his soul sank beneath the weight of an infinitely greater grief. He merely bit his lip and passed through the wretched realm, his gaze level, his face hard.

On its way into the city, the road widened to resemble a broad, bare, wheel-rutted expanse hemmed in on each side by row upon row of houses, many flanked by narrow yards out of which merchants and craftsmen pursued their various trades. Carters, carpenters, and wheelwrights bartered with customers ankle deep in wood shavings; blacksmiths hammered glowing rods on anvils to produce andirons, fire grates, ploughshares, door bands and hinges, chains, and horseshoes; corders sat in their doorways, winding jute into hanks that rose in mounded coils at their feet; potters ferried planks lined with sun-dried pitchers, jars, and bowls to their nearby kilns. Everywhere Bran looked, people seemed to be intensely busy, but he saw no place that looked at all friendly to strangers.

They rode on and soon came to a low house fronting the river. Several dozen barrels were lined up outside the entrance beside the road. Some of the barrels were topped with boards, behind which a young woman with hair the colour of spun gold and a bright red kerchief across her bare shoulders dispensed jars of ale to a small gathering of thirsty travellers. Without a second thought, Bran turned aside, dismounted, and walked to the board.

"Pax vobiscum," he said, dusting off his Latin.

She gave him a nod and patted the board with her hand—a sign he took to mean she wanted to see his money first. As Bran dug out his purse and searched for a suitable coin, the others joined him.

"Allow me," said Aethelfrith, pushing up beside him. He brought out an English penny. "Coin of the realm," he said, holding the small silver disc between thumb and forefinger. "And for this we should eat like kings as well, should we not?" He handed the money to the alewife. "Four jars, good woman," he said in English. "And fill them full to overflowing."

"There is food, too?" asked Bran as the woman poured out three large jars from a nearby pitcher.

"Inside the house," replied the cleric. Following Bran's gaze, he added, "but we'll not be going in there."

"Why not? It seems a good enough place." He could smell the aroma of roast pork and onions on the light evening breeze.

"Oh, aye, a good enough place to practise iniquity, per-haps, or lose your purse—if not your life." He shook his head at the implied depravity. "But we have a bed waiting for us where we will not be set upon by anything more onerous than a psalm."

"You know of such a place?" asked Ffreol.

"There is a monastery just across the river," Friar Aethelfrith informed them. "The Abbey of Saint Mary the Virgin. I have stayed there before. They will give us a bowl and bed for the night."

Aethelfrith's silver penny held good for four more jars and half a loaf of bread, sliced and smeared with pork drippings, which only served to rouse their appetites. Halfway through the second jar, Bran had begun to feel as if Lundein might not be as bad as his first impression had led him to believe. He became more certain when he caught the young alewife watch-ing him; she offered him a saucy smile and gave a little toss of her head, indicating that he should follow. With a nod and a wink, she disappeared around the back of the house, with Bran a few steps behind her. As Bran came near, she lifted her skirt a little and extended her leg to reveal a shapely ankle.

"It is a lovely river, is it not?" observed Aethelfrith, falling into step beside him.

"It is not the river I am looking at," said Bran. "Go back and finish your ale, and I will join you when I've finished here."

"Oh," replied the friar, "I think you've had enough already." Waving to the young woman, he took Bran by the arm and steered him back the way they had come. "Evening is upon us," he observed. "We'll be going on."

"I'm hungry," said Bran. Glancing back at the alewife, he saw that she had gone inside. "We should eat something."

"Aye, we will," agreed Tuck, "but not here." They rejoined the others, and Bran returned to his jar, avoiding the stern glance of Brother Ffreol. "Drink up, my friends," ordered Tuck. "It is time we were moving along."

With a last look toward the inn, Bran drained his cup and reluctantly followed the others back to their mounts and climbed back into the saddle. "How many times have you been to Lundein?" he asked as they continued their slow plod into the city.

"Oh, a fair few," Aethelfrith replied. "Four or five times, I think, though the last time was when old King William was on the throne." He paused to consider. "Seven years ago, perhaps."

At King's Bridge they stopped in the road. Bran had never seen a bridge so wide and long, and despite the crowds now hurrying to their homes on the other side of the river, he was not certain he wanted to venture out too far. He was on the point of dismounting to lead his horse across when Aethelfrith saw his hesitation. "Five hundred men on horseback cross this bridge every day," he called, "and oxcarts by the score. It will yet bear a few more."

"I was merely admiring the handiwork," Bran told him. He gave his mount a slap and started across. Indeed, it was ingeniously constructed with beams of good solid oak and iron spikes; it neither swayed nor creaked as they crossed. All the same, he was happy to reach the far side, where Aethelfrith, now afoot, began leading them up one narrow, shadowed street and down another until the three Welshmen had lost all sense of direction.

"I know it is here somewhere," said Aethelfrith. They paused at a small crossroads to consider where to look next.

The twisting streets were filling up with smoke from the hearth fires of the houses round about.

"Night is upon us," Ffreol pointed out. "If we cannot find it in the daylight, we will fare no better in the dark."

"We are near," insisted the fat little priest. "I remember this place, do I not?"

Just then a bell rang out—a clear, distinct tone in the still evening air.

"Ah!" cried Aethelfrith. "That will be the call to vespers. This way!" Following the sound of the bell, they soon arrived at a gate in a stone wall. "Here!" he said, hurrying to the gate. "This is the place—I told you I would remember."

"So you did," replied Bran. "How could we have doubted?"

The mendicant priest pulled a small rope that passed through a hole in the wooden door. Another bell tinkled softly, and presently the door swung open. A thin, round-shouldered priest dressed in a long robe of undyed wool stepped out to greet them. One glance at the two priests in their robes, and he said, "Welcome, brothers! Peace and welcome."

A quick word with the porter, and their lodgings for the night were arranged. They ate soup with the brothers in the refectory, and while Ffreol and Aethelfrith attended the night vigil with the resident monks, Bran and Iwan went to the cell provided for them and fell asleep on fleece-covered straw mats. Upon arising with the bell the next morning, Bran saw that Ffreol and Aethelfrith were already at prayer; he pulled on his boots, brushed the straw from his cloak, and went out into the abbey yard to wait until the holy office was finished.

While he waited, he rehearsed in his mind what they should say to William the Red. Now that the fateful day had dawned, Bran found himself lost for words and dwarfed by the awful knowledge of how much depended upon his ability to persuade the English king of the injustice being perpetrated on his people. His heart sank lower and lower as he contemplated the dreary future before him: an impoverished lackey to a Ffreinc bounder whose reputation for profligate spending was exceeded only by his whoring and drinking.

When at last Ffreol and Aethelfrith emerged from the chapel, Bran had decided he would swear an oath to the devil himself if it would keep the vile invaders from Elfael.

The travellers took their leave and, passing beyond the monastery gates, entered the streets of the city to make their way to the White Tower, as the king's stronghold was known.

Bran could see the pale stone structure rising above the rooftops of the low, mean houses sheltering in the shadows of the fortress walls. At the gates, Brother Ffreol declared Bran's nobility and announced their intent to the porter, who directed them into the yard and showed them where to tie their horses. They were then met by a liveried servant, who conducted them into the fortress itself and to a large anteroom lined with benches on which a score or more men—mostly Ffreinc, but some English—were already waiting; others were standing in clumps and knots the length of the room. The thought of having to wait his turn until all had been seen cast Bran into a dismal mood.

They settled in a far corner of the room. Every now and then a courtier would appear, summon one or more petitioners, and take them away. For good or ill, those summoned never returned to the anteroom, so the mood remained one of hopeful, if somewhat desperate, optimism. "I have heard of people waiting twenty days or more to speak to the king," Friar Aethelfrith confided as he cast his glance around the room at the men lining the benches.

"We will not bide that long," Bran declared, but he sank a little further into gloom at the thought. Some of those in the room did indeed look as if they might have taken up more or less permanent residence there; they brought out food from well-stocked tuck bags, some slept, and others whiled away the time playing at dice. Morning passed, and the day slowly crept away.

It was after midday, and Bran's stomach had begun reminding him that he had eaten nothing but soup and hard bread since the day before, when the door at the end of the great vestibule opened and a courtier in yellow leggings and a short tunic and mantle of bright green entered, passing slowly along the benches and eyeing the petitioners who looked up hopefully. At his approach, Bran stood. "We want to see the king," he said in his best Latin.

"Yes," replied the man, "and what is the nature of your business here?"

"We want to see the king."

"To be sure." The court official glanced at those attending Bran and said, "You four are together?"

"We are," replied Bran.

"The question is *why* would you see the king?"

"We have come to seek redress for a crime committed in the king's name," Bran explained.

The official's glance sharpened. "What sort of crime?"

"The slaughter of our lord and his warband and the seizure of our lands," volunteered Brother Ffreol, taking his place beside Bran.

"Indeed!" The courtier became grave. "When did this happen?"

"Not more than ten days ago," replied Bran.

The courtier regarded the men before him and made up his mind. "Come."

"We will see the king now?"

"You will follow me."

The official led them through the wooden door and into the next room, which, although smaller than the anteroom they had just left, was whitewashed and strewn with fresh straw; at one end was a fireplace, and opposite the hearth was an enormous tapestry hung from an iron rod. The hand-worked cloth depicted the risen Christ on his heavenly throne, holding an orb and sceptre. The centre of the room was altogether taken up by a stout table at which sat three men in high-backed chairs. The two men at each end of the table wore robes of deep brown and skullcaps of white linen. The man in the centre was dressed in a robe of black satin trimmed with fox fur; his skullcap was red silk and almost the same colour as his long, flowing locks. He also wore a thick gold chain around his neck, attached to which were a cross and a polished crystal lens. Before the men were piles of parchments and pots containing goose quills and ink, and all three were writing on squares of parchment before them; the scratch of their pens was the only sound in the room.

"Yes?" said one of the men as the four approached the table. He did not raise his eyes from his writing. "What is it?"

"Murder and the unlawful seizure of lands," intoned the courtier.

"This is not a matter for the royal court," replied the man

dismissively, dipping his pen. "You must take it up with the Court of the Assizor."

"I thought perhaps this particular case might interest you, my lord bishop," the courtier said.

"Interesting or not, we do not adjudicate criminal cases," sighed the man. "You must place the matter before the assizes."

Before the courtier could make a reply, Bran said, "We appeal to the king's justice because the crime was committed in the king's name."

At this the man in the red skullcap glanced up; interest quickened eyes keen and rapacious as a hawk's. "In the king's name, did you say?"

"Yes," replied Bran. "Truly."

The man's eyes narrowed. "You are Welsh."

"British, yes."

"What is your name?"

"Here stands before you Bran ap Brychan, prince and heir to the throne of Elfael," said Iwan, speaking up to save his future king the embarrassment of having to affirm his own nobility.

"I see." The man in the red silk cap leaned back in his chair. The gold cross on his chest had rubies to mark the places where nails had been driven into the saviour's hands and feet. He raised the crystal lens and held it before a sharp blue eye. "Tell me what happened."

"Forgive me, sir, are you the king?" asked Bran.

"My lord, we have no time for such as this. They are—," began the man in the white skullcap. His objection was silenced by a flick of his superior's hand.

"King William has been called away to Normandie,"

explained the man in the red skullcap. "I am Cardinal Ranulf of Bayeux, Chief Justiciar of England. I am authorised to deal with all domestic matters in the king's absence. You may speak to me as you would speak to His Majesty." Offering a mirthless smile, the cardinal said, "Pray, continue. I would hear more of this alleged crime."

Bran nodded and licked his lips. "Nine days ago, my father, Lord Brychan of Elfael, set off for Lundein to swear allegiance to King William. He was ambushed on the road by Ffreinc marchogi, who killed him and all who were with him, save one. My father and the warband of Elfael were massacred and their bodies left to rot beside the road."

"My sympathies," said Ranulf. "May I ask how you know the men who committed this crime were, as you call them, Ffreinc marchogi?"

Bran put out a hand to Iwan. "This man survived and witnessed all that took place. He is the only one to escape with his life."

"Is this true?" wondered the cardinal.

"It is, my lord, every word," affirmed Iwan. "The leader of this force is a man named Falkes de Braose. He claims to have received Elfael by a grant from King William."

Ranulf of Bayeux raised the long white quill and held it lengthwise between his hands as if studying it for imperfections. "It is true that His Majesty has recently issued a number of such grants," the cardinal told them. Turning to his assistant on the left, he said, "Bring me the de Braose grant."

Without a word the man in the chair beside him rose and crossed the room, disappearing through a door behind the tapestry.

"There would seem to be some confusion here," allowed

the cardinal when his man had gone, "but we will soon find the cause." Regarding the three before him, he added, "We keep good records. It is the Norman way."

Friar Aethelfrith stifled a hoot of contempt for the man's insinuation. Instead, he beamed beatifically and loosed a soft fart.

A moment later the cardinal's assistant returned bearing a square of parchment bound by a red satin riband. This he untied and placed before his superior, who took it up and began to read aloud very quickly, skipping over unimportant parts. "Be it known . . . this day . . . by the power and enfranchisement . . . Ah!" he said. "Here it is."

He then read out the pertinent passage for the petitioners. "Granted to William de Braose, Baron, Lord of the Rape of Bramber, in recognition for his support and enduring loyalty, the lands comprising the Welsh commot Elfael so called, entitled free and clear for himself and his heirs in perpetuity, in exchange for the sum of two hundred marks."

"We were sold for two hundred marks?" wondered Iwan.

"A token sum," replied the cardinal dryly. "It is customary."

"The Norman way, no doubt," put in Aethelfrith.

"But it is Count Falkes de Braose who has taken the land," Bran pointed out, "not the baron."

"Baron William de Braose is his uncle, I believe," said the cardinal. "But, yes, that is undoubtedly where the confusion has arisen. There is no provision for Falkes to assume control of the land, as he is not a direct heir. The baron himself must occupy the land or forfeit his claim. Therefore, as Chief Justiciar, I will allow this grant to be rescinded."

"I do thank you, my lord," said Bran, sweet relief surging through him. "I am much obliged."

The cardinal raised his hand. "Please, hear me out. I will allow the grant to be revoked for a payment to the crown of six hundred marks."

"Six hundred!" gasped Bran. "It was given to de Braose for two hundred."

"In recognition of his loyalty and support during the rebellion of the Barons," intoned the cardinal. "Yes. For you it will be six hundred *and* fealty sworn to King William."

"That is robbery!" snapped Bran.

The cardinal's eyes snapped quick fire. "It is a bargain, boy." He stared at Bran for a moment and then pulled the parchment to himself, adding, "In any case, that is my decision. The matter will be held in abeyance until such time as the money is paid." He gestured to his assistant, who began writing an addendum to the grant.

Bran stared at the churchman and felt the despair melt away in a sudden surge of white-hot rage. His vision became blood-tinged and hard. He saw the bland face and shrewd eyes, the man's flaming red hair, and it was all he could do to keep from seizing the imperious cleric, pulling him bodily across the table, and beating the superior smirk off that smug face with his fists.

Rigid as a stump, hands clenched in rage, he stared at the courtiers as his grip on reality slipped away. In a blood-tinted vision, he saw a tub of oil at his feet, and before anyone could stop him, he snatched up the tub and emptied it over the table, drenching the cardinal, his clerks, and their stacks of parchment. As the irate courtiers spluttered, Bran calmly withdrew an oil-soaked parchment from the pile; he held it to a torch in a wall sconce and set it ablaze. He blew on it to strengthen the flame, then tossed it back onto the table. The oil flared, igniting the table, parchments, and men in a single conflagration. The clerks pawed at the flames with their hands and succeeded only in spreading them. The cardinal, gripped with terror, cried out like a child as tongues of fire leapt to his hair and turned the rich fox fur trim into a collar of living flame. Bran glimpsed himself standing gaunt and grim as the howling clerics fled the room, each oil-soaked footprint alighting behind them as they ran. He saw Ranulf of Bayeux's face bubble and crack like the skin of a pig on a spit, and as the cardinal fought for his last breath—

"Abeyance, my lord," said Ffreol. "Forgive me, but does that mean Baron de Braose keeps the land?"

At the sound of Ffreol's voice, Bran came to himself once more. He felt drained and somewhat light-headed. Without awaiting the cardinal's reply, he turned on his heel and strode from the chamber.

"Until the money is paid, yes," Cardinal Ranulf replied to Ffreol. He reached for a small bronze bell to summon the porter. "Do not bother to return here until you have the silver in hand." He rang the bell to end the audience, saying, "God grant you a good day and pleasant journey home."

CHAPTER 9

And a pleasant journey home," minced Aethelfrith in rude parody of Cardinal Ranulf. "Bring me my staff, and I will give that bloated toad a pleasant journey hence!"

Bran, scowling darkly, said nothing and walked on through the gates, leaving the White Tower without a backward glance. The unfairness, the monstrous injustice of the cardinal's demand sent waves of anger surging through him. Into his mind flashed the memory of a time years ago when a similar injustice had driven him down and defeated him: Bran had been out with some of the men; as they rode along the top of a ridgeway, they spied in the valley below a band of Irish raiders herding stolen cattle across the cantref. Outnumbered and lightly armed, Bran had let the raiders pass unchallenged and then hurried back to the caer to tell his father. They met the king in the yard, along with the rest of the warriors of the warband. "You let them go—and yet dare to show your face to me?" growled the king when Bran told him what had happened.

"We would have been slaughtered outright," Bran explained, backing away. "There were too many of them."

"You worthless little coward!" the king shouted. The warriors gathered in the yard looked on as the king drew back his hand and let fly, catching Bran on the side of the head. The blow sent the boy spinning to the ground. "Better to die in battle than live as a coward!" the king roared. "Get up!"

"Lose ten good men for the sake of a few cows?" countered Bran, climbing to his feet. "Only a fool would think that was better."

"You snivelling brat!" roared Brychan, lashing out again. Bran stood to the blow this time, which only enraged his father the more. The king struck him again and yet again— until Bran, unable to bear the abuse any longer, turned and fled the yard, sobbing with pain and frustration.

The bruises from that encounter lasted a long time, the humiliation longer still. Any ambition Bran might have held for the crown died that day; the throne of Elfael could crumble to dust for all he cared.

They did not stay in Lundein again that night but fled the city sprawl as if pursued by demons. The moon rose nearly full and the sky remained clear, so they rode on through the night, stopping only a little before dawn to rest the horses and sleep. Bran had little to say the next day or the day after. They reached the oratory, and Brother Aethelfrith prevailed upon them to spend the night under his roof, and for the sake of wounded Iwan, Bran agreed. While the friar scurried about to prepare a meal for his guests, Bran and Ffreol took care of the horses and settled them for the night.

"It isn't fair," muttered Bran, securing the tether line to the slender trunk of a beech tree. He turned to Ffreol and exclaimed, "I still don't see how the king could sell us like that. Who gave him the right?"

"Red William?" replied the monk, raising his eyebrows at the sudden outburst from the all-but-silent Bran.

"Aye, Red William. He has no authority over Cymru."

"The Ffreinc claim that kingship descends from God," Ffreol pointed out. "William avows divine right for his actions."

"What has England to do with us?" Bran demanded. "Why can't they leave us alone?"

"Answer that," replied the monk sagely, "and you answer the riddle of the ages. Throughout the long history of our race, no tribe or nation has ever been able to simply leave us alone."

That night Bran sat in the corner by the hearth, sipping wine in sombre silence, brooding over the unfairness of the Ffreinc king, the inequity of a world where the whims of one fickle man could doom so many, and the seemingly limitless injustices—large and small—of life in general. And why was everyone looking to him to put it right? *"For the sake of Elfael and the throne,"* Ffreol had said. Well, the throne of Elfael had done nothing for him—save provide him with a distant and disapproving father. Remove the throne of Elfael—take away Elfael itself and all her people. Would the world be so different? Would the world even notice the loss? Besides, if God in his wisdom had bestowed his blessing on King William, favouring the Ffreinc ascendancy with divine approval, who were any of them to disagree?

When heaven joined battle against you, who could stand?

Early the next morning, the three thanked Friar Aethelfrith for his help, bade him farewell, and resumed the homeward journey. They rode through that day and the next, and it was not until late on the third day that they came in sight of the great, rumpled swath of forest that formed the border between England and Cymru. The dark mood that had dogged them since Lundein began to lift at last. Once amongst the sheltering trees of Coed Cadw, the oppression of England and its rapacious king dwindled to mere annoyance. The forest had weathered the ravages of men and their petty concerns from the beginning of time and would prevail. What was one red-haired Ffreinc tyrant against that?

"It is only money, after all," observed Ffreol, optimism making him expansive. "We have only to pay them and Elfael is safe once more."

"If silver is what the Red King wants," said Iwan, joining in, "silver is what he will get. We will buy back our land from the greedy Ffreinc bastards."

Bran said, "There are two hundred marks in my father's strongbox. That is a start."

"And a good one," declared Iwan. All three fell silent for a moment. "How will we get the rest?" Iwan asked at last, voicing the thought all three shared.

"We will go to the people and tell them what is required," said Bran. "We will raise it."

"That may not be so easy," cautioned Brother Ffreol. "If you could somehow empty every silver coin from every pocket, purse, and crock in Elfael, you might get another hundred marks at most."

To his dismay, Bran realised that was only too true. Lord Brychan was the wealthiest man in three cantrefs, and he had never possessed more than three hundred marks all at once in the best of times.

Six hundred marks. Cardinal Ranulf might as well have

asked for the moon or a hatful of stars. He was just as likely
to get one as the other.

Unwilling to succumb to despair again so soon, Bran gave
the mare a slap and picked up the pace. Soon he was racing
through the darkening wood, speeding along the road, feeling
the cool evening air on his face. After a time, his mount began
to tire, so at the next fording place, Bran reined up. He slid
from the saddle and led the horse a little way along the stream,
where the animal could drink. He cupped a few handfuls of
water to his mouth and drew his wet hands over the back of
his neck. The water cooled his temper somewhat. It would be
dark soon, he noticed; already the shadows were thickening,
and the forest was growing hushed with the coming of night.

Bran was still kneeling at the stream, gazing at the darkening forest, when Ffreol and Iwan arrived. They dismounted and
led their horses to the water. "A fine chase," said Ffreol. "I
have not ridden like that since I was a boy." Squatting down
beside Bran, he put a hand to the young man's shoulder and
said, "We'll find a way to raise the money, Bran, never fear."

Bran nodded.

"It will be dark soon," Iwan pointed out. "We will not
reach Caer Cadarn tonight."

"We'll lay up at the next good place we find," said Bran.

He started to climb into the saddle, but Ffreol said, "It is
vespers. Come, both of you, join me, and we will continue
after prayers."

They knelt beside the ford then, and Ffreol raised his
hands, saying:

> I am bending my knee
> In the eye of the Father who created me,

In the eye of the Son who befriended me,
In the eye of the Spirit who walks with me,
In companionship and affection.
Through thine own Anointed One, O God,
Bestow upon us fullness in our need . . .

Brother Ffreol's voice flowed out over the stream and along the water. Bran listened, and his mind began to wander. Iwan's hissed warning brought him back with a start. "Listen!" The champion held up his hand for silence. "Did you hear that?"

"I heard nothing but the sound of my own voice," replied the priest. He closed his eyes and resumed his prayer. "Grant us this night your peace—"

There came a shout behind them. *"Arrêt!"*

The three rose and turned as one to see four Ffreinc marchogi on the road behind them. Weapons drawn, the soldiers advanced, walking warily, their expressions grave in the dim light.

"Ride!" shouted Iwan, darting to his horse. "Hie!"

The cry died in his throat, for even as the three prepared to flee, five more marchogi stepped from the surrounding wood. Their blades glimmered dimly in the dusky light. Even so, Iwan, wounded as he was, would have challenged them and taken his chances, but Ffreol prevented him. "Iwan! No! They'll kill you."

"They mean to kill us anyway," replied the warrior carelessly. "We must fight."

"No!" Ffreol put out a restraining hand and pulled him back. "Let me talk to them."

Before Iwan could protest, the monk stepped forward. Stretching out empty hands, he walked a few paces to meet the advancing knights. "Pax vobiscum!" he called. Continuing in Latin, he said, "Peace to you this night. Please, put up your swords. You have nothing to fear from us."

One of the Ffreinc made a reply that neither Bran nor Iwan understood. The priest repeated himself, speaking more slowly; he stepped closer, holding out his hands to show that he had no weapons. The knight who had spoken moved to intercept him. The point of his sword flicked the air. Ffreol took another step, then stopped and looked down.

"Ffreol?" called Bran.

The monk made no answer but half turned as he glanced back toward Bran and Iwan. Even in the failing light, Bran could see that blood covered the front of the monk's robe.

Ffreol himself appeared confused by this. He looked down again, and then his hands found the gaping rent in his throat. He clutched at the wound, and blood spilled over his fingers. "Pax vobiscum," he spluttered, then crashed to his knees in the road.

"You filthy scum!" screamed Bran. Leaping to the saddle, he drew his sword and spurred his horse forward to put himself between the wounded priest and the Ffreinc attackers. He was instantly surrounded. Bran made but one sweeping slash with his blade before he was hauled kicking from the saddle.

Fighting free of the hands that gripped him, he struggled to where Brother Ffreol lay on his side. The monk reached out a hand and brought Bran's face close to his lips. "God keep you," he whispered, his voice a fading whisper.

"Ffreol!" cried Bran. "No!"

The priest gave out a little sigh and laid his head upon the road. Bran fell upon the body. Clutching the priest's face between his hands, he shouted, "Ffreol! Ffreol!" But his friend

and confessor was dead. Then Bran felt the hands of his captors on him; they hauled him to his feet and dragged him away.

Jerking his head around, he saw Iwan thrashing wildly
with his sword as the marchogi swarmed around him. "Here!"
Bran shouted. "To me! To me!"

That was all he could get out before he was flung to the
ground and pinned there with a boot on his neck, his face
shoved into the dirt. He tried to wrestle free but received a
sharp kick in the ribs, and then the air was driven from his
lungs by a knee in his back.

With a last desperate effort, he twisted on the ground,
seized the leg of the marchogi, and pulled him down.
Grasping the soldier's helmet, Bran yanked it off and began
pummelling the startled soldier with it. In his mind, it was not
a nameless Ffreinc soldier he bludgeoned senseless, but ruthless King William himself.

In the frenzy of the fight, Bran felt the handle of the soldier's knife, drew it, and raised his arm to plunge the point
into the knight's throat. As the blade slashed down, however,
the marchogi fell on him, pulling him away, cheating him of
the kill. Screaming and writhing in their grasp, kicking and
clawing like an animal caught in a net, Bran tried to fight free.
Then one of the knights raised the butt of a spear, and the
night exploded in a shower of stars and pain as blow after
blow rained down upon him.

CHAPTER 10

Y ou are Welsh, yes? A Briton?"

Bruised, bloodied, and bound at the wrists by a rope that looped around his neck, Bran was dragged roughly forward and forced to his knees before a man standing in the wavering pool of light from a handheld torch. Dressed in a long tunic of yellow linen with a short blue cloak and boots of soft brown leather, he carried neither sword nor spear, and the others deferred to him. Bran took him to be their lord.

"Are you a Briton?" He spoke English with the curious flattened nasal tone of the Ffreinc. "Answer me!" He nodded to one of the soldiers, who gave Bran a quick kick in the ribs.

The pain of the blow roused Bran. He lifted his head to gaze with loathing at his inquisitor.

"I think you are Welsh, yes?" the Ffreinc noble said.

Unwilling to dignify the word, Bran merely nodded.

"What were you doing on the road?" asked the man.

"Travelling," mumbled Bran. His voice sounded strange and loud in his ears; his head throbbed from the knocks he had taken.

"At night?"

"My friends and I—we had business in Lundein. We were on our way home." He raised accusing eyes to his Ffreinc interrogator. "The man your soldiers killed was a priest, you bloody—" Bran lunged forward, but the soldier holding the rope yanked him back. He was forced down on his knees once more. "You will all rot in hell."

"Perhaps," admitted the man. "We think he was a spy."

"He was a man of God, you murdering bastard!"

"And the other one?"

"What about the other one?" asked Bran. "Did you kill him, too?"

"He has eluded capture."

That was something at least. "Let me go," Bran said. "You have no right to hold me. I've done nothing."

"It is for my lord to hold or release you as he sees fit," said the Ffreinc nobleman. "I am his seneschal."

"Who is your lord? I demand to speak to him."

"Speak to him you shall, Welshman," replied the seneschal. "You are coming with us." Turning to the marchogi holding the torches, he said, *"Liez-le."*

Bran spent the rest of the night tied to a tree, nursing a battered skull and a consuming hatred of the Ffreinc. His friend, Brother Ffreol, cut down like a dog in the road and himself taken captive . . . This, added to the gross injustice of Cardinal Ranulf's demands, overthrew the balance of Bran's mind—a balance already made precarious by the loss of his father and the warband.

He passed in and out of consciousness, his dreams merging with reality until he could no longer tell one from the other. In his mind he walked a dark forest pathway, longbow in hand and a quiver of arrows on his hip. Over and over again, he heard the sound of hoofbeats, and a Ffreinc knight would thunder out of the darkness, brandishing a sword. As the knight closed on him, blade held high, Bran would slowly raise the bow and send an arrow into his attacker's heart. The shock of the impact lifted the rider from the saddle and pinned him to a tree. The horse would gallop past, and Bran would walk on. This same event repeated itself throughout the long night as Bran moved through his dream, leaving an endless string of corpses dangling in the forest.

Sometime before morning, the moon set, and Bran heard an owl cry in the treetop above him. He came awake then and found himself bound fast to a stout elm tree, but uncertain how he had come to be there. Groggily, like a man emerging from a drunken stupor, he looked around. There were Ffreinc soldiers sleeping on the ground nearby. He saw their inert bodies, and his first thought was that he had killed them.

But no, they breathed still. They were alive, and he was a captive. His head beat with a steady throb; his ribs burned where he had been kicked. There was a nasty metallic taste in his mouth, as if he had been sucking on rusty iron. His shirt was wet where he had sweat through it, and the night air was cold where the cloth clung to his skin. He ached from head to heel.

When the owl called again, memory came flooding back in a confused rush of images: an enemy soldier writhing and moaning, his face a battered, bloody pulp; mailed soldiers swarming out of the shadows; the body of his friend Ffreol crumpled in the road, grasping at words as life fled through a slit in his throat; a blade glinting swift and sharp in the moonlight; Iwan, horse rearing, sword sweeping a wide, lethal arc as he galloped away; a Ffreinc helmet, greasy with blood, lifted high against a pale summer moon . . .

So it was true. Not *all* of it was a dream. He could still tell the difference. That was some small comfort at least. He told himself he had to keep his wits about him if he was to survive, and on that thought, he closed his eyes and called upon Saint Michael to help him in his time of need.

The Ffreinc marchogi broke camp abruptly. Bran was tied to his own horse as the troops made directly for Caer Cadarn. The invaders moved slowly, burdened as they were with ox-drawn wagons full of weapons, tools, and provisions. Alongside the men-at-arms were others—smiths and builders. A few of the invaders had women and children with them. They were not raiders, Bran concluded, but armed settlers. They were coming to Elfael, and they meant to stay.

Once free of the forest, the long, slow cavalcade passed through an apparently empty land. No one worked the fields; no one was seen on the road or even around the few farms and settlements scattered amongst the distant hillsides. Bran took this to mean that the monks had been able to raise the alarm and spread the word; the people had fled to the monastery at Llanelli.

At their approach to the caer, the Ffreinc seneschal rode ahead to inform his lord of their arrival. By the time they started up the ramp, the gates were open. Everything in the caer appeared to be in good order—nothing out of place, no signs of destruction or pillage. It appeared as though the new residents had simply replaced the old, continuing the steady march of life in the caer without missing a step.

The marchogi threw Bran, still bound, into the tiny root cellar beneath the kitchen, and there he languished through the rest of the day. The cool, damp dark complemented his misery, and he embraced it, mourning his losses and cursing the infinite cruelty of fate. He cursed the Ffreinc, and cursed his father, too.

Why, oh why, had Rhi Brychan held out so long? If he had sworn fealty to Red William when peace was first offered—as Cadwgan, in the neighbouring cantref of Eiwas, and other British kings had long since done—then at least the throne of Elfael would still be free, and his father, the warband, and Brother Ffreol would still be alive. True, Elfael would be subject to the Ffreinc and much the poorer for it, but they would still have their land and their lives.

Why had Rhi Brychan refused the Conqueror's repeated offers of peace?

Stubbornness, Bran decided. Pure, mean, pigheaded stubbornness and spite.

Bran's mother had always been able to moderate her husband's harsher views, even as she lightened his darker moods. Queen Rhian had provided the levity and love that Bran remembered in his early years. With her death, that necessary balance and influence ceased, never to be replaced by another. At first, young Bran had done what he could to imitate his mother's engaging ways—to be the one to brighten the king's dour disposition. He learned riddles and songs and made up amusing stories to tell, but of course it was not the same. Without his queen, the king had grown increasingly severe. Always a demanding man, Brychan had become a bitter, exacting, dissatisfied tyrant, finding fault with everyone and everything. Nothing was ever good enough. Certainly, nothing Bran ever did was good enough. Young Bran, striving to please and yearning for the approving touch of a father's hand, only ever saw that hand raised in anger.

Thus, he learned at an early age that since he could never please his father, he might as well please himself. That is the course he had pursued ever since—much to his father's annoyance and eventual despair.

So now the king was dead. From the day the Conqueror seized the throne of the English overlords, Brychan had resisted. Having to suffer the English was bad enough; their centuries-long presence in Britain was, to him, still a fresh wound into which salt was rubbed almost daily. Brychan, like his Celtic fathers, reckoned time not in years or decades but in whole generations. If he looked back to a time when Britain and the Britons were the sole masters of their island realm, he also looked forward to a day when the Cymry would be free again. Thus, when William, Duke of Normandie, settled his bulk on Harold's throne that fateful Christmas Day, Rhi Brychan vowed he would die before swearing allegiance to any Ffreinc usurper.

At long last, thought Bran, that oft-repeated boast had been challenged—and the challenge made good. Brychan was dead, his warriors with him, and the pale high-handed foreigners ran rampant through the land.

How now, Father? Bran reflected bitterly. *Is this what you hoped to achieve? The vile enemy sits on your throne, and your heir squats in the pit. Are you proud of your legacy?*

It was not until the following morning that Bran was finally released and marched to his father's great hall. He was brought to stand before a slender young man, not much older than himself, who, despite the mild summer day, sat hunched by the hearth, warming his white hands at the flames as if it were the dead of winter.

Dressed in a spotless blue tunic and yellow mantle, the thin-faced fellow observed Bran's scuffed and battered appearance with a grimace of disgust. "You will answer me— if you can, Briton," said the young man. His Latin, though heavily accented, could at least be understood. "What is your name?"

The sight of the fair-haired interloper sitting in the chair Rhi Brychan used for a throne offended Bran in a way he would not have thought possible. When he failed to reply quickly enough, the young man who, apparently, was lord and leader of the invaders rose from his seat, drew back his arm, and gave Bran a sharp, backhanded slap across the mouth.

Hatred leapt up hot and quick. Bran swallowed it down with an effort. "I am called Gwrgi," he answered, taking the first name that came to mind.

"Where is your home?"

"Ty Gwyn," Bran lied. "In Brycheiniog."

"You are a nobleman, I think," decided the Norman lord. His downy beard and soft dark eyes gave him a look of mild innocence—like a lamb or a yearling calf.

"No," replied Bran, his denial firm. "I am not a nobleman."

"Yes," asserted his inquisitor, "I think you are." He reached out and took hold of Bran's sleeve, rubbing the cloth between his fingers as if to appraise its worth. "A prince, per-haps, or at least a knight."

"I am a merchant," Bran replied with dull insistence.

"I think," the Ffreinc lord concluded, "you are not." He gave his narrow head a decisive shake, making his curls bounce. "All noblemen claim to be commoners when captured. You would be foolish to do otherwise."

When Bran said nothing, the Norman drew back his hand and let fly again, catching Bran on the cheek, just below the eye. The heavy gold ring on the young man's finger tore the flesh; blood welled up and trickled down the side of his face. "I am not a nobleman," muttered Bran through clenched teeth. "I am a merchant."

"A pity," sniffed the young lord, turning away. "Noblemen we ransom—beggars, thieves, and spies we kill." He nodded to his attending soldiers. "Take him away."

"No! Wait!" shouted Bran. "Ransom! You want money? Silver? I can get it."

The Ffreinc lord spoke a word to his men. They halted, still holding Bran tightly between them. "How much?" inquired the young lord.

"A little," replied Bran. "Enough."

The Norman gathered his blue cloak around his shoulders and studied his captive for a moment. "I think you are lying, Welshman." The word was a slur in his mouth. "But no matter. We can always kill you later."

He turned away and resumed his place by the fire. "I am Count Falkes de Braose," he announced, settling himself in the chair once more. "I am lord of this place now, so mind your tongue, and we shall yet come to a satisfactory agreement."

Bran, determined to appear pliant and dutiful, answered respectfully. "That is my fervent hope, Count de Braose."

"Good. Then let us arrange your ransom," replied the count. "The amount you must pay will depend on your answers to my questions."

"I understand," Bran said, trying to sound agreeable. "I will answer as well as I can."

"Where were you and that priest going when my men found you on the road?"

"We were returning from Lundein," replied Bran. "Brother Ffreol had business with the monastery there, and I was hoping to buy some cloth to sell in the markets hereabouts."

"This business of yours compelled you to ride at night. Why?"

"We had been away a long time," answered Bran, "and Brother Ffreol was anxious to get home. He had an important message for his bishop, or so he said."

"I think you were spies," de Braose announced.

Bran shook his head. "No."

"What about the other one? Was he a merchant, too?"

"Iwan?" said Bran. "Iwan is a friend. He rode with us to provide protection."

"A task at which he failed miserably," observed the count. "He escaped, but we will find him—and when we do, he will be made to pay for his crimes."

Bran took this to mean he had injured or killed at least one of the marchogi in the skirmish on the road.

"Only a coward would kill a priest," observed Bran. "Since you require men to pay for their crimes, why not begin with your own?"

The count leaned forward dangerously. "If you wish to keep your tongue, you will speak with more respect." He sat back and smoothed his tunic with his long fingers. "Now then, you knew my men were attacked by your people on that same road some days ago?"

"I was in Lundein, as I said," Bran replied. "I heard nothing of it."

"No?" wondered the count, holding his head to one side. "I can tell you the attack was crushed utterly. The lord of this place and his pitifully few warriors were wiped out."

"Three hundred against thirty," Bran replied, bitterness sharpening his tone. "It would not have been difficult."

"Careful," chided the count. "Are you certain you knew nothing of this battle?"

"Not a word," Bran told him, trying to sound both sincere and disinterested. "But I know how many men the King of Elfael had at his command."

"And you say you know nothing of the priest's business?"

"No. He did not tell me—why would he? I am no priest," Bran remarked. "Churchmen can be very secretive when it suits them."

"Could it have something to do with the money the priest was carrying?" inquired the count. He gestured to a nearby table and the four bags of coins lying there. Bran glanced at the table; the thieving Ffreinc had, of course, searched the horses and found the money Bran had hidden amongst the provisions.

"It is possible," allowed Bran. "I did not think priests carry so much money otherwise."

"No," agreed de Braose, "they do not." He frowned, apparently deciding there was nothing more to be learned. "Very well," he said at last, "about the ransom. It will be fifty marks."

Bran felt bitter laughter rising in his throat. Cardinal Ranulf wanted six hundred; what was fifty more?

"Fifty marks," he repeated. Determined not to allow the enemy the pleasure of seeing him squirm, Bran shrugged and adopted a thoughtful air. "A heavy price for one who is neither lord nor landholder."

De Braose regarded him with an appraising look. "You think it too high. What value would you place on your life?"

"I could get ten marks," Bran told him, trying to make himself sound reasonable. "Maybe twelve."

"Twenty-five."

"Fifteen, maybe," Bran offered reluctantly. "But it would take time."

"How much time?"

"Four days," said Bran, pursing his lips in close calculation. "Five would be better."

"You have one," the Norman lord decided. "And the ransom will be twenty marks."

"Twenty, then," agreed Bran reluctantly. "But I will need a horse."

De Braose shook his head slowly. "You will go afoot."

"If I am not to have a horse, I will certainly need more time," said Bran. He would have the money before the morning was out but did not want the Ffreinc to know that.

"Either you can find the ransom or you cannot," concluded de Braose, making up his mind. "You have one day—no more. And you must swear on the cross that you will return here with the money."

"Then I am free to go?" asked Bran, surprised that it should be so easy.

"Swear it," said de Braose.

Bran looked his enemy in the eye and said, "I do swear on the cross of Christ that I will return with money enough to purchase my ransom." He glanced at the two knights standing by the door. "I can go now?"

110 STEPHEN R. LAWHEAD

De Braose inclined his long head. "Yes, and I urge you to make haste. Bring the money to me before sunset. If you fail, you will be caught and your life will be forfeit, do you understand me?"

"Of course." Bran turned on his heel and strode away. It was all he could do to refrain from breaking into a run the moment he left the hall. To maintain the pretence, he calmly crossed the yard under the gaze of the marchogi and strode from the caer. He suspected that his new overlords watched him from the fortress, so he continued his purposeful, unbroken stride until the trees along the river at the valley bottom took him from sight—then he ran all the way to Llanelli to tell Bishop Asaph the grievous news about Brother Ffreol.

CHAPTER 11

"Where is everyone?" shouted Bran, dashing through the gate and into the tidy spare yard of the Llanelli monastery. He had expected the yard to be full to overflowing with familiar faces of cowering, frightened Cymry seeking refuge from the invaders.

"Lord Bran! Thank God you are safe," replied Brother Eilbeg, the porter, hurrying after him.

Bran turned on him. "What happened to those I sent here?" he demanded.

"They've been taken to Saint Dyfrig's. Bishop Asaph thought they would be better cared for at the abbey until it is safe to return."

"Where is the bishop?"

"At prayer, sire," replied the monk. He looked through the door behind Bran, as if hoping to see someone else, then asked, "Where is Brother Ffreol?"

Bran made no answer but sped to the chapel, where he found Bishop Asaph on his knees before the altar, hands outstretched. "My lord," said Bran abruptly, "I have news."

The bishop concluded his prayer and turned to see who it

was that interrupted his communion. One quick glance at Bran's bruised face told him there had been more trouble. "How bad is it?" asked the bishop, grasping the edge of the altar to pull himself to his feet.

"As bad as can be," Bran replied. "Brother Ffreol is dead. Iwan escaped, but they are searching for him to kill him."

The bishop's shoulders dropped, and he sagged against the near wall. He put a hand out to steady himself and paused a long moment, eyes closed, his lips moving in a silent prayer. Bran waited, and when the bishop had composed himself, he quickly explained how they had been caught on the road by marchogi who had killed the good brother without provocation.

"And you?" asked Asaph. "You fought free?"

Bran shook his head. "They took me captive and brought me to the caer. I was released to raise ransom for myself."

The bishop shook his head sadly. He gazed at Bran as if trying to fathom the depths of such outrageous events. "Cut down in the road, you say? For no reason?"

"No reason at all," confirmed Bran. "They are murderous Ffreinc bastards—that is all the reason they need."

"Did he suffer at all?"

"No," replied Bran with a quick shake of his head. "His death was quick. There was little pain."

Asaph gazed back at him with damp, doleful eyes and fingered the knotted ends of his cincture. "And yet they let you simply walk away?"

"The count thinks I am a nobleman."

Asaph's wizened face creased in a frown of incomprehension. "But you *are* a nobleman."

"I told him otherwise—although he refused to believe me."

"What will you do now?"

"I agreed to give him twenty marks in exchange for my freedom. I am honour-bound to bring him the money; otherwise he would never have let me go."

"We must go to Ffreol," murmured the bishop, starting for the chapel door. "We must go find his body and—"

"Did you hear me?" demanded Bran. Gripping the bishop's shoulder tightly, he spun the old man around. "I said I need the money."

"The ransom, yes—how much do you need?"

"Twenty marks in silver," repeated Bran quickly. "The strongbox—my father's treasure box—where is it? There should be more than enough to pay—" The sudden expression of anxiety on the bishop's face stopped him. The bishop looked away.

"The strongbox, Asaph," Bran said, his voice low and tense. "Where is it?"

"Count de Braose has taken it," the bishop replied.

"What!" cried Bran. "You were supposed to hide it from them!"

"They came here, the count and some of his men—they asked if we had any treasure," replied the churchman. "They wanted it. I had to give it to them."

"Fool!" shouted Bran. "In the name of all that is holy, why?"

"Bran, I could not lie," answered Asaph, growing indignant. "Lying is a venal sin. Love in the heart, truth on the lips—that is our rule."

"You just *gave* it to them?" Bran glared at the sanctimonious cleric, anger flicking like a whip from his gaze. "You've just killed me; do you know that?"

"I hardly think—"

"Listen to me, you old goat," spat Bran. "I must pay de Braose the ransom by sunset today, or I will be hunted down and executed. Where am I going to find that money now?"

The bishop, unrepentant, raised a finger heavenward. "God will provide."

"He already did!" snarled Bran. "The money was here, and you let them take it!" He growled with frustration and stalked to the open doorway of the chapel, then turned back suddenly. "I need a horse."

"That will be difficult."

"I do not care how difficult it is. Unless you want to see me dead this time tomorrow, you will find a horse at once. Do you understand me?"

"Where will you go?"

"North," answered Bran decisively. "Ffreol would still be alive and I would be safe there now if we had not listened to you."

The bishop bent his head, accepting the reproach.

Bran said, "My mother's kinsmen are in Gwynedd. When I tell them what has happened here, they will take me in. But I need a horse and supplies to travel."

"Saint Ernin's abbey serves the northern cantrefs," observed the bishop. "If you need help, you can call on them."

"Just get me that horse," commanded Bran, taking the cleric roughly by the arm and steering him toward the door.

"I will see what I can find." The bishop left, shaking his head and murmuring, "Poor Ffreol. We must go and claim his body so that he can be buried here amongst his brothers."

Bran walked alongside him, urging the elderly churchman to a quicker pace. "Yes, yes," he agreed. "You must claim the body, by all means. But first the horse—otherwise you will be digging *two* graves this time tomorrow."

The bishop nodded and hurried away. Bran watched him for a moment and then walked to the small guest lodge beside the gate; he looked around the near-empty cell. In one corner was a bed made of rushes overspread with a sheepskin. He crossed to the bed, lay down, and, overcome by the accumulated exertions of the last days, closed his eyes and sank into a blessedly dreamless sleep.

It was late when he woke again; the sun was well down, and the shadows stretched long across the empty yard. The bishop, he soon learned, had sent three monks in search of a horse; none of the three had yet returned. The bishop himself had taken a party with an oxcart to retrieve the body of Brother Ffreol. There was nothing to do, so he returned to the guest lodge to stew over the stupidity of churchmen and rue his rotten luck. He sprawled on the bench outside the chapter house, listening to the intermittent bell as it tolled the offices. Little by little, the once-bright day faded to a dull yellow haze.

He dozed and awoke to yet another bell. Presently the monks began appearing; in twos and threes they entered the yard, hurrying from their various chores. "That bell—what was it?" Bran asked one of the brothers as he passed.

"It is only vespers, sire," replied the priest respectfully.

Bran's heart sank at the word: *vespers*. Eventide prayer—the day gone, and he was still within shouting distance of the caer. He slumped back against the mud-daubed wall and stuck his feet out in front of him. Asaph was worse than useless, and he felt a ripe fool for trusting him. If he had known the silly old man had given his father's treasure to de Braose—simply handed it over, by Job's bones—he could have lit out for the northern border the moment the count set him free.

He was on the point of fleeing Llanelli when an errant breeze brought a savoury aroma from the cookhouse, and he suddenly remembered how hungry he was. An instant later he was on his feet and moving toward the refectory. He would eat and then go.

Nothing was easier than cadging a meal from Brother Bedo, the kitchener. A cheerful, red-faced lump with watery eyes and a permanent stoop from bending over his pots and steaming cauldrons, no creature that begged a crust was ever turned away from his door.

"Lord Bran, bless me, it's you," he said, pulling Bran into the room and sitting him down on a three-legged stool at the table. "I heard what happened to you on the road—a sorry business, a full sorry business indeed, God's truth. Brother Ffreol was one of our best, you know. He would have been bishop one day, he would—if not abbot also."

"He was my confessor," volunteered Bran. "He was a friend and a good man."

"I don't suppose it could have been helped?" asked the kitchener, placing a wooden trencher of roast meat and bread on the table before Bran.

"There was nothing to be done," Bran said. "Even if he'd had a hundred warriors at his back, it would not have made the slightest difference."

"Ah, so, well . . ." Bedo poured out a jar of thin ale into a small leather cup. "Bless him—and bless you, too, that you were there to comfort him at his dying breath."

Bran accepted the monk's words without comment. There had been precious little comforting in Ffreol's last moments.

The chaos of that terrible night rose before him once more, and Bran's eyesight dimmed with tears. He finished his meal without further talk, then thanked the brother and went out, already planning the route he would take through the valley, away from the caer and Count de Braose's ransom demand.

The moon had risen above the far hills when Bran slipped through the gate. He had walked only a few dozen paces when he heard someone calling after him. "Lord Bran! Wait!" He looked around to see three dusty, footsore monks leading a swaybacked plough horse.

"What is that?" asked Bran, regarding the animal doubtfully.

"My lord," the monk said, "it is the best we could find. Anyone with a seemly mount has sent it away, and the Ffreinc have already taken the rest." The monk regarded the horse wearily. "It may not be much, but trust me, it is this or nothing."

"Worse than nothing," Bran grumbled. Snatching the halter rope from the monk's hands, he clambered up onto the beast's bony back. "Tell the bishop I have gone. I will send word from Gwynedd." With that, he departed on his pathetic mount.

Bran had never ridden a beast as slow and stumble-footed as the one he now sat atop. The creature plodded along in the dying moonlight, head down, nose almost touching the ground. Despite Bran's most ardent insistence, piteous begging, and harrowing threats, the animal refused to assume a pace swifter than a hoof-dragging amble.

Thus, night was all but spent by the time Bran came in

sight of Caer Rhodl, the fortress of Mérian's father, King Cadwgan, rising up out of the mists of the morning that would be. Tethering the plough horse to a rowan bush in a gully beside the track, Bran ran the rest of the way on foot. He scaled the low wall at his customary place and dropped into the empty yard. The caer was silent. The watchmen, as usual, were asleep.

Quick and silent as a shadow, Bran darted across the dark expanse of yard to the far corner of the house. Mérian's room was at the back, its single small window opening onto the kitchen herb garden. He crept along the side of the house until he came to her window and then, pressing his ear to the rough wooden shutter, paused to listen. Hearing nothing, he pulled on the shutter; it swung open easily, and he paused again. When nothing stirred inside, he whispered, "Mérian, . . . ," and waited, then whispered again, slightly louder, "Mérian! Be quick!"

This time his call was answered by the sound of a hushed footfall and the rustle of clothing. In a moment, Mérian's face appeared in the window, pale in the dim light. "You should not have come," she said. "I won't let you in—not tonight."

"There was a battle," he told her. "My father has been killed—the entire warband with him. The Ffreinc have taken Elfael."

"Oh, Bran!" she gasped. "How did it happen?"

"They have a grant from King William. They are taking everything."

"But this is terrible," she said. "Are you hurt?"

"I was not in the battle," he said. "But they are searching for me."

"What are you going to do?"

"I'm leaving for Gwynedd—now, at once. I have kinsmen there. But I need a horse."

"You want me to give you a horse?" Mérian shook her head. "I cannot. I dare not. My father would scream the roof down."

"I will pay him," said Bran. "Or find a way to return it. Please, Mérian."

"Is there not some other way?"

He raised a hand and squeezed her arm. "Please, Mérian, you're the only one who can help me now." He gazed at her in the glowing light of a rising sun and, in spite of himself, felt his desire quicken. On a sudden inspiration, he said, "I love you, Mérian. Come with me. We will go together, you and I—far away from all of this."

"Bran, think what you're saying!" She pulled free. "I cannot just run away, nor can you." Leaning forward as far as the small window would allow, she clutched at him. "Listen to me, Bran. You must go back. It is the people of Elfael who will need you now and in the days to come. You will be king. You must think of your people."

"The Ffreinc will kill me!" protested Bran.

"Shh!" she said, placing her fingertips to his lips. "Someone will hear you."

"I failed to pay the ransom," Bran explained, speaking more softly. "If I go back to Elfael empty-handed, they'll kill me—they mean to kill me anyway, I think. The only reason I'm still alive is because they want the money first."

"Come," she said, making up her mind. "We must go to my father. You must tell him what you have told me. He will know what to do."

"Your father hates me." Bran rejected the idea outright. "No. I am not going back. Elfael is lost. I have to get away now while I still have a chance." He raised a hand to stroke her cheek. "Come with me, Mérian. We can be together."

"Bran, listen. Be reasonable. Let my father help you."

"Will he give twenty marks to free me?" Mérian bit her lip doubtfully. "No?" sneered Bran. "I thought not. He'd sooner see my head on a pike."

"He will go with you and talk to them. He stands in good stead with Baron Neufmarché. The Ffreinc will listen to him. He will help you."

"I'm leaving, Mérian." Bran backed away from the window. "It was a mistake to come here . . ."

"Just wait there," she said and disappeared suddenly. She was back an instant later. "Here, take this," she said. Reaching out, she dropped a small leather bag into his hand. It chinked as he caught it. "It is not much," she said, "but it is all I have."

"I need a weapon," he said, tucking the bag away. "Can you get me a sword? Or a spear? Both would be best."

"Let me see." She darted away again and was gone longer this time. Bran waited. The sky brightened. The rising sun bathed his back with its warming rays. It would be daylight before he could start out, and that would mean finding a way north that avoided as much of Elfael as possible. He was pondering this when Mérian returned to the window.

"I couldn't get a sword," she said, "but I found this. It belongs to my brother." She pushed the polished ash-wood shaft of a longbow out to him, followed by a sheaf of arrows.

Bran took the weapons, thanked her coolly, and stepped away from the window. "Farewell, Mérian," he said, raising a hand in parting.

"Please don't go." Reaching out, she strained after him, brushing his fingertips with her own. "Think of your people,

Bran," she said, her voice pleading. "They need you. How can you help them in Gwynedd?"

"I love you, Mérian," he said, still backing away. "Remember me."

"Bran, no!" she called. "Wait!"

But he was already running for his life.

CHAPTER 12

By the time Bran reached the stream separating the two cantrefs, the sun was burning through the mist that swathed the forest to the east and collected in the hollows of the lowlands. Astride his slow horse, he cursed his luck. He had considered simply taking a horse from Cadwgan's stable but could not think how to do so without waking one of the stable hands. And even if he had been able to achieve that, adding the wrath of Lord Cadwgan to his woes was not a prospect to be warmly embraced. The last thing he needed just now was an irate king's search party hot on his heels.

Despite his slow pace, he rode easily along the valley bottom through fields glistening with early morning dew. The crops were ripe, and soon the harvest season would be upon them. Long before the first scythe touched a barley stalk, however, Bran would be far away beyond the forest and mountain fastness to the north, enjoying the warmth and safety of a kinsman's hearth.

There were, Bran considered as he clopped along, two ways to Gwynedd through the Cymraic heartland. Elfael straddled both, and neither was very good.

The first and most direct way was straight across Elfael to Coed Cadw and then through dense woodland all the way to the mountains. They were not high mountains, but they were rough, broken crags of shattered stone, and difficult to cross—all the more so for a man alone and without adequate supplies. The second route was less direct; it meant skirting the southern border of Elfael and working patiently through the intricate interlacing of low hills and hidden valleys to the west before turning north along the coast.

This second route was slower and passed uncomfortably close to Caer Cadarn before bending away to the west. There was a risk that he might be seen. Still, it kept him out of the treacherous mountain pathways and made best use of his mount's limited value as a steady plodder.

Bran did not relish the idea of passing so close to the unfriendly Ffreinc, but it could not be helped. He considered laying up somewhere and waiting until nightfall; however, the idea of trying to remain hidden under de Braose's nose and then thrashing around the countryside in the dark lacked the allure of ready flight. The day was new, he reckoned, and he would pass Caer Cadarn at the nearest point while it was still early morning and the invaders would most likely be otherwise occupied. Perhaps they were not even looking for him yet.

He reached the boundary stream but did not cross. Instead, he turned his slow steed west and, in the interest of keeping well out of sight of Caer Cadarn, followed the narrow waterway as it snaked through the gorsy lowlands that formed the border between Elfael and Brycheiniog to the south. In time, the stream would swing around to the northwest, entering Maelienydd, a region of rough hills and cramped valleys that he hoped to cross as quickly as possible. Then he would head for Arwstli, angling north all the while toward Powys—and so work his way cantref by cantref to Gwynedd and a glad welcome amongst his mother's people.

Bran was thinking about how distraught and outraged his kinsmen would be upon learning the news of his father's cruel murder and the loss of Elfael when the distant echo of a scream brought him up short. He tried telling himself he had imagined it only and was halfway down the path toward believing that when the terrified shriek came again: a woman's voice, carried on the breeze and, though faint, clearly signifying terrible distress. Bran halted, listened again, and then turned his mount in the direction of the cry.

He crossed the stream into the far southwestern toe of Elfael. Over the nearest hill, he saw the first threads of black smoke rising in the clear morning air. He crested the hill and looked over into the valley on the other side, where he saw the settlement called Nant Cwm, a fair-sized holding comprised of a large house and a yard with several barns and a few out-buildings. Even from a distance, he could see that it was under attack; smoke was spewing from the door of the barn and from the roof of the house. There were five saddled horses in the yard between the house and barn, but no riders. Then, as Bran watched, a man burst from the front door of the house, almost flying. He ran a few steps, his feet tangled, then fell sprawling on his side. Right behind him came his attackers—two Ffreinc men-at-arms with drawn swords. Two more marchogi emerged from the house, dragging a woman between them.

Bran saw the hated Ffreinc, and his anger flared white hot in an instant. Snatching up the bow Mérian had given him, he grabbed the sheaf of arrows, and before he knew his feet had touched ground, he was racing down the hill toward the settlement.

In the yard, the farmer cried out, throwing his hands before him—clearly pleading for his life. The two Ffreinc standing over him raised their swords. The woman screamed again, struggling in the grasp of her captors. The farmer shouted again and tried to rise. Bran saw the swords glint hard and bright in the sun as they slashed and fell. The farmer writhed in a vain attempt to avoid the blows. The fierce blades slashed again, and the man lay still.

At the farmer's death, Bran's vision hardened to a single, piercing beam, and the world flashed crimson. He bit his lip to keep from crying out his rage as he flew toward the fight. As soon as he judged he was within the longbow's range, he squatted down and opened the cloth bundle.

There were but six arrows. Every arrow would have to count. Bran nocked the first onto the string, pulled the feathered shaft close to his cheek, and took aim—his target the nearer of the two soldiers struggling with the farmer's wife.

Just as he was about to let fly, the farmhouse door opened and out of the burning building ran a young boy of, perhaps, six or seven summers.

One of the marchogi shouted, and from around the far side of the house another Ffreinc soldier appeared with a sword in one hand and the leash of an enormous hunting dog in the other. This was the commander—a knight with a round steel helmet and a long hauberk of ringed mail. The knight saw the boy escaping across the yard and gave a shout. When the child failed to stop, he loosed the hound.

With staggering speed, the snarling, slavvering beast ran down the boy. The mother screamed as the hound, fully as big as her son, closed on the fleeing child.

The hound leapt, and the terrified boy stumbled. Bran let fly in the same instant.

The arrow whirred as it streaked home, burying itself in the hound's slender neck, even as the beast's jaws snatched at the child's unprotected throat. The dog crumpled and rolled to the side, teeth still gnashing, forelegs raking the air.

As the whimpering boy climbed to his feet, the Ffreinc men-at-arms searched the surrounding hills for the source of the unexpected arrow. The knight who had released the dog was the first to spot Bran crouching on the hill above the settlement. He shouted a command to his marchogi, pointing toward the hillside with his sword.

He was still pointing when an arrow—like a weird, feathered flower—sprouted in the middle of his mail-clad stomach.

The sword spun from his hand, and the knight crashed to his knees, clutching the shaft of the arrow. He gave out a roar of pain and outrage, and the two soldiers standing over the dead farmer leapt to life. They charged at a run, blades high, across the yard and up the hill.

Bran, working with uncanny calm, placed another arrow on the string, took his time to pull, hold, and aim. When he let fly, the missile sang to its mark. The first warrior was struck and spun completely around by the force of the arrow. The second ran on a few more steps, then halted abruptly, jerked to his full height by the slender oak shaft that slammed into his chest.

Next, Bran turned his attention to the two marchogi holding the woman. No one was struggling now; all three were staring in flatfooted disbelief at the lone archer crouching on the hillside.

By the time Bran had another arrow on the string and was taking aim, the two had released the woman and were running for the horses. One of the marchogi had the presence of mind to try to cut off any possible pursuit; he gathered the reins of the riderless horses, leapt into the saddle, and fled the slaughter ground.

Bran raced down to the farmyard, pausing at the foot of the hill to release another arrow. He drew and loosed at the nearest of the two fleeing riders. The arrow flew straight and true, sizzling through the air to sink its sharp metal head deep between the shoulders of the Ffreinc warrior, who arched his back and flung his arms wide as if to embrace the sky. The galloping horse ran on a few more steps, and the warrior slumped sideways and plunged heavily to the ground.

Bran's last arrow streaked toward the sole remaining soldier as he gained the low rise at the far end of the yard. Lashing his mount hard, the rider swerved at the last instant as the missile ripped by, slashing through the tall grass. The fleeing warrior sped on and did not look back.

Bran hurried to the farmwife, who was on her knees, clutching her wailing son. "You must get away from here!" he told her, urgency making him sharp. "They might come back in force." The woman just stared at him. "You must go!" he insisted. "Do you understand?"

She nodded and, still holding tight to her child, turned her tearful gaze back to the yard where her husband lay. Bran saw the look and relented. He allowed her a moment and then took her gently by the shoulder and turned her to face him.

"They will come back," he said, softening his tone. "You must get away while you can."

"I have no place to go," cried the woman, turning again to the twisted, bloody body of her dead husband. "Oh, Gyredd!" Her face crumpled, and she began to weep.

"Lady, you will mourn him in good time," Bran said, "but later, when you are safe. You must think of your child now and do what is best for him."

Taking the crying boy into his arms, he walked quickly to the horse on the hill, urging the woman to hurry. Its rider slain, the animal had stopped running and was now grazing contentedly. If he considered taking the good horse for himself and giving the plough horse to the farmwife, one look at the woman struggling valiantly to bear up under the calamity that had befallen her abolished any such thought. Here was a woman with a boy so much like himself at that age they could have been brothers.

"Here is what you will do," Bran said, speaking slowly. "You will take the lad and ride to the abbey. The monks at Saint Dyfrig's will take care of you until it is safe to return, or until you find somewhere else to go."

He helped her onto the horse, holding the boy as she climbed into the saddle. "Go now," he commanded, lifting the child and placing him in the saddle in front of his mother. "Tell them what happened here, and they will take care of you."

Putting his hand to the bridle, Bran ran the horse to the top of the rise where he could get a clear view of the countryside around. There were no marchogi to be seen, so he pointed the woman in the direction of the monastery. "Take good care of your mother, lad," he told the boy, then gave the horse a slap on the rump to send them off. "Do not stop until you reach the abbey," he called. "I will see to things here."

"God bless you," said the woman, turning in the saddle as the horse jolted into motion.

Bran watched until they were well away and then hurried back to the farm. He dragged the dead farmer to the grassy hillside, then fetched a wooden shovel from the barn; the fire had been hastily set, and the flames had already burned down to smouldering ash, leaving the barn intact. Working quickly, he dug a shallow grave in the green grass at the foot of the hill, then rolled the body into the long depression and began piling the soft earth over the corpse.

He left the shovel at the head of the grave to mark the place and then ran to retrieve his arrows. Pulling them from the bodies was a grim task, but they were too valuable to waste, and he had no way to replace them. Despite his care, one of them broke when he tried to worry it free from the rib cage of the dead soldier, and the one that had missed its target could not be found. In the end, he had to settle for recovering but four of the six.

He wiped the iron heads on the grass, bundled them up again, and then hurried to retrieve his shamble-footed mount. Grabbing a handful of mane, he swung up onto the sway-backed creature once more and, with much kicking and cursing, clopped away.

He did not get far.

Upon reaching the top of the hill, he glanced back toward the settlement. At that moment, five marchogi on horseback crested the rise beyond Nant Cwm. The riders paused, as if searching out a direction to follow. Bran halted and sat very still, hoping they would not see him. This hope, like all the others he had conceived since the Ffreinc arrived, died as it was born.

Even as he watched, one of the riders raised an arm and pointed in his direction. Bran did not wait to see more. He slapped the reins hard across the withers of his plough horse mount and kicked back hard with his heels. The startled animal responded with a gratifying burst of speed that carried him over the crest of the hill and out of sight of the riders.

Once over the hilltop, the nag slowed and stopped, and Bran swiftly scanned the descent for his best chance of escape. The slope fell away steeply to the stream he had been following. On the other side the land opened onto a meadow grazing land—flat and bereft of any rock or tree big enough to hide behind. Away to the northeast rose the thick dark line of Coed Cadw.

He turned his face to the north, kicked his mount to life once more, and rode for the strong, protecting wall of the forest.

CHAPTER 13

The ancient woodland rampart rose before him in vast dark folds, like a great bristling pelt covering the deep, rocky roots of Yr Wyddfa, the Region of Snows in the north. His rickety mount trotted along at a pace resembling a canter, and still some distance away from the nearest trees, Bran despaired of reaching them before his galloping pursuers overtook him.

Midway between himself and the forest, a course of rock jutted up out of the mounded earth, forming a narrow spine of stone that ran all the way to the forest. Tiring quickly now, his slow-footed animal resumed its customary amble. Bran slung the bow across his chest and, gripping his clutch of arrows, slid off the beast's back and sent it on. As it sauntered away without him, he bounded to the rocky outcrop and ducked behind it.

He knew the marchogi would not follow a riderless horse, and the lazy animal would not wander far, but he hoped the slight misdirection would distract them at least long enough to allow him to reach the shelter of the forest. Once amongst the trees, he had no doubt at all that he could elude pursuit without difficulty. The forest was a place he knew well.

Crouching low to keep his head below the jagged line of rock, Bran worked his way quickly up the rising slope toward the tree line, pausing now and again to scan the open ground behind him. He saw no sign of the marchogi and took heart. Perhaps they had given up the chase and returned to pillage the farm instead.

The last few hundred paces rose up a steep embankment, at the top of which lay the forest edge. Bran paused and gathered himself for the last mad scramble. Gulping air, he tried to calm his racing heart as, with a final glance behind him, he ran to the escarpment. It took longer than he thought to reach it, but clambering over the grey lichen-covered rocks on hands and knees, he eventually gained the top, pulling himself up the last rise with his hands and gripping the arrow bundle with his teeth.

The trees lay just ahead. He put his head down and staggered on. He had taken but a half-dozen steps when a Ffreinc rider appeared from the edge of the forest and stepped directly into his path. Bran did not have time even to raise his bow before the warrior was on him. Sword drawn, the soldier spoke a command that Bran could not understand and indicated that Bran was to turn around and start back the way he had come.

Instead, Bran ran toward him, dove under the belly of the horse, and, legs churning, continued running. The rider gave a shout and put spurs to his mount. Bran flew to the forest.

This first rider cried after him, and his shout was answered by another. A second rider appeared, racing along the margin of the forest to cut off Bran's flight before he could reach the wood.

Desperation lent him speed. He gained the entrance to the dark refuge of Coed Cadw as two more riders joined the chase. The rippling thud of the horses' hooves thrummed on the turf, punctuated by gusting blasts of air through the galloping animals' nostrils. On the riders came, whooping and shouting as they converged on his trail, readying their spears as if he were a deer for the kill.

They were loud, and they were overconfident. And they had not enough wit to know to quit the saddle before entering the wood. Realising this, Bran stopped dead on the trail and turned to face his attacker. The oncoming rider gave out a wild shriek of triumph and heaved his lance. Bran saw the spearhead spin as the lance left the rider's hand. He gave a simple feint to the side, and the spear sliced the air where his head had been. The rider cursed and came on, drawing his sword.

Whirling around, Bran retrieved the spear and, turning back, knelt and planted the butt of the shaft in the ground as the charger sped forward—too fast to elude the trap. Unable to stop, the hapless animal ran onto the blade. With a scream of agony, the horse plunged on a few more strides before it became tangled in the undergrowth and went down in a heap of flailing hooves and thrashing legs. The rider was thrown over the neck of his mount and landed on hands and knees. Bran rushed to the stunned knight, ripped the knife from his belt, and with a shriek like the cry of a banshee, plunged the blade into the exposed flesh of the man's neck, between his helmet and mail shirt. The knight struggled to his knees, clawing at the blade, as Bran ran for the shelter of the trees.

A few strides into the wood, the main trail split into several smaller paths, fanning out into the tangle of trees and undergrowth. Bran chose one that passed between two close-grown trees—wide enough to admit him, but narrow enough to hinder a rider. His feet were already on the path, and he was through the gap when the second rider reached the place.

He heard a frustrated shout behind him and the tormented whinny of a horse. Bran glanced back to see that the rider had halted because his mount was tangled in the branches of a low-lying bramble thicket, and the warrior was having difficulty extricating himself.

Unslinging his bow, Bran shook the arrows from the bundle and snatched one from the ground. He pressed the bow forward, took aim, and let fly. The missile sped through the trees and took the rider in the chest just below the collarbone. The force of the impact slammed the warrior backward in the saddle, but he kept his seat. Bran sent a second arrow after the first. It flew wide of the mark by a mere hairsbreadth.

He had two arrows left. He bent down to snatch them up, and as he straightened, he glimpsed a blur of movement out of the corner of his eye.

The spear sped through the air. Bran tried to leap aside, but the steel-tipped length of ash was expertly thrown, and the blade caught him midstride, striking high on the right shoulder. The force of the throw knocked him off his feet and sent him sprawling forward.

Bran fell hard and heard something snap beneath him. He had landed on the arrows, breaking one of the slender shafts in the fall. One arrow left. Gasping for breath, he rolled onto his side, and the spear came free.

The rider drove in fast behind his throw, sword drawn and raised high, ready to part Bran's head from his shoulders.

Bran, crouching in the path, picked up the bow and the last arrow; he nocked the shaft to the string, pressing the longbow forward in the same swift motion.

The wound in his shoulder erupted with a ferocious agony. Bran gasped aloud, his body convulsed, and his fingers released their grip on the string. The arrow scudded off along the trail, to no effect. He threw down the bow, picked up the Ffreinc lance that had wounded him, and stumbled from the path, pushing deeper into the wood.

The coarse shouts of his attackers grew louder and more urgent as they ordered their pursuit. The branches were now too close grown and tangled, the trail too narrow for men on horseback. Bran sensed the marchogi were dismounting; they would continue the chase on foot.

Using their momentary inattention, he turned off the trail and dove into the undergrowth. Moving as quickly and quietly as possible, he slipped through the crowded ranks of slender young hazel and beech trees, scrambling over the fallen trunks of far older elms until he came to another, wider path.

He paused to listen.

The voices of his pursuers reached him from the trail he had left behind. Soon they would realise their quarry was no longer on the path they pursued; when that happened, they would spread out and begin a slower, more careful search.

He put his hand to his injured shoulder and probed the wound with his fingers. The ache was fierce and fiery, and blood was trickling down his back in a sticky rivulet. It would be best to find some way to bind the wound lest one of the pursuers see the blood and pick up his trail that way. Luckily, he thought with grim satisfaction, the marchogi no longer had a dog with them.

As if in answer to this thought, there came a sound that turned his bowels to water: the hoarse baying of a hound on scent. It was still some way off, but once the animal reached the trailhead, the hunt would be all but finished.

Turning away, Bran lurched on, following the path as it twisted and turned, pressing ever deeper into the wood. He ran, listening to the cry of the hound grow louder by degrees, keenly alert for something, anything, that might throw the beast off his scent.

Then, all at once the sound ended. The forest went quiet. Bran stopped.

His shoulder was aflame, and cold sweat beaded on his brow. He waited, drawing air deep into his lungs, trying to steady his racing heart.

Suddenly, the hound gave out a long, rising howl that was followed instantly by a shout from one of the soldiers. The dog had found his trail again.

Bran staggered forward once more. He knew he could not long elude his pursuers now—a few moments, more or less, and the chase would end.

And then, just ahead, he spied a low opening in the brush and, beneath it, dark, well-churned earth: the telltale sign of a run used by wild pigs. He dove for it and scrambled forward on hands and knees, dragging the spear with him. His pursuers were still on the trail he had just quit.

He drove himself on, wriggling through the undergrowth, around rocks and over roots. Low-hanging branches tore at him, snagging his clothing and skin.

The hound reached the end of the pig run and hesitated. At first the marchogi assumed the dog had been distracted by the scent of the pigs. There was a shout and a yelp as they dragged the dog away from the entrance to the run and moved on down the trail.

Bran gathered himself for another push. Pulling himself up by the shaft of the spear, he lurched ahead——four heart-beats later, the hound loosed another rising howl, and the chase resumed behind him.

Gritting his teeth against the pain, Bran ran on.

Above the crashing and thrashing in the wood behind him, he heard something else: the liquid murmur of falling water. Bran followed the sound and in a moment came to a small, boulder-strewn clearing. A swift-flowing stream cut through its centre, coursing around the base of the huge, round moss-covered stones.

Bran picked his way amongst the rocks, only to find that the path ended in a sheer drop. The stream plunged into a pool beneath the stony ledge on which Bran was standing. The waters gathered in the pool and then flowed away into the hidden heart of Coed Cadw.

Bran gazed at the pool and realised that, like the path, his flight had ended, too.

With his back to the waterfall, he turned to make his last stand. His breath came in shaky gasps. Sweat flowed down his face and neck. The shaft of the spear was slick with his blood. He wiped his hands on his clothes and tightened his grip on the spear as the marchogi approached, their voices loud in the silence of the forest.

They reached the clearing all at once——the hound and three men——bursting into the glade in a blind rush. Two sol-diers held spears, and the third grasped the leash of the hound. The dog saw Bran and began straining at its lead, snarling with slavering fury and clawing the air to reach him.

The soldiers hesitated, uncertain where they were. Bran saw the cast of their eyes as they took in the rocks, the waterfall, and then . . . himself, standing perfectly still on a stone above the fall.

The dog handler shouted to the others; the knight on his left raised his spear and drew back his arm. Bran readied himself to dodge the throw.

There came a shout, and a fourth man entered the rock-filled hollow behind the others; he wielded a sword, and the front of his hauberk was stained with blood from the arrow wound beneath his collarbone. He made a motion with his hand, and the marchogi under his command spread out.

Bran tightened his grip on the spear and braced himself for the attack.

The man with the sword raised his hand, but before he could give the signal, there was a sharp snap, like that of a slap in the face. The hound, suddenly and unexpectedly free of its broken leash, bounded toward Bran, its jaws agape.

Bran turned to meet the hound. One of the soldiers, seeing Bran move, launched his spear.

Both dog and spear reached Bran at the same time. Bran jerked his body to the side. The spear sailed harmlessly by, but the jaws of the hound closed on his arm. Bran dropped his spear and threw his free arm around the neck of the dog, trying to strangle the animal as its teeth ripped into the skin and tendons of his arm.

Two more spears were already in the air. The first found its mark, passing through the dog and striking Bran. The hound gave out a yelp, and Bran felt a wicked sting in the centre of his chest.

Wounded, his vision suddenly blurred with the pain, Bran

fought to keep his balance on the rock ledge. Too late he saw the glint in the air of a spear streaking toward him. Thrown high, it missed his throat but sliced through the soft part of his cheek as it grazed along his jaw.

The jolt rocked him backward.

He teetered on the ledge for an instant, and then, still clasping the dying dog like a shield before his body, he plunged over the waterfall and into the pool below.

The last thing he saw was the face of one of his attackers peering cautiously over the edge of the fall. Then Bran closed his eyes and let the stream bear him away.

PART TWO

IN COED
CADW

Mérian took the news of Bran's death hard —much harder than she herself might have predicted had she ever dreamed such a possibility could occur. True, she heartily resented Bran ap Brychan for running away and deserting his people in their time of need; she might have forgiven him all else, if not for that. On the other hand, she knew him to be a selfish, reckless, manipulating rascal. Thus, though utterly irritated and angry with him, she had not been at all surprised by his decision to flee. She told herself that she would never see him again.

Even so, never in her most resentful disposition did she conceive—much less *wish*—that any harm would come to him. That he had been caught and killed trying to escape filled her with morbid anguish. The news—reported by her father's steward and overheard by her as he related the latest marketplace gossip to the cook and scullery girls—hit her like a blow to the stomach. Unable to breathe, she sagged against the doorpost and stifled a cry with her fist.

Sometime later, when summoned to her father's chamber, where she was informed, she was able to bear up without betraying the true depth of her feelings. Shocked, horrified, mournful, and leaden with sorrow, Mérian moved through the first awful day feeling as if the ground she trod was no longer solid beneath her feet—as if the very earth was fragile, delicate, and thin as the shell of a robin's egg, and as if any moment the crust on which she stood might shatter and she would instantly plunge from the world of light and air into the utter, perpetual, suffocating darkness of the tomb.

Soon, everyone in King Cadwgan's court was talking of nothing else but Bran's sad, but really only-too-predictable, demise. That was harder still for Mérian. She put on a brave face. She tried to appear as if the news of Bran and the misfortune that had befallen Elfael meant little to her, or rather that it meant merely as much as bad news from other places ever meant to anyone not directly concerned—as if, lamentable though it surely was, the fate of the wayward son of a neighbouring king ultimately was nothing to do with her.

"Yes," she would agree, "isn't it awful? Those poor people—what will they do?"

She told herself time and again that Bran had been an unreliable friend at best; that his apparent interest in her was nothing more than carnal, which was entirely true; and that his sad death had, at the very least, delivered her from a life of profound and perpetual unhappiness. These things and more she told herself—spoke them aloud, even. But no matter how often she rehearsed the reasons she should be relieved to be free of Bran ap Brychan, she could not make herself believe them. Nor, for all the truth of her assertions, could she make herself feel less wretched.

She kept a tight rein on herself when others were nearby. She neither wept nor sobbed; not one sorrowing sigh escaped her lips. Her features remained composed, thoughtful perhaps, but not distraught, less yet grief-stricken. Anyone observing Mérian might have thought her distracted or concerned. Knowing that nothing good could come of any overt display of emotion where Bran was concerned, she swallowed her grief and behaved as if the news of Bran's death was a thing of negligible significance amidst the more troubling news of the murder of Brychan ap Tewdwr and all his warband and the unwarranted Ffreinc advance into neighbouring Elfael. Here, if only here, she and her stern father agreed: the Ffreinc had no right to kill a sitting king and seize his cantref.

"It is a bad business," King Cadwgan told her, shaking his grey head. "Very bad. It should not have happened, and William Rufus should answer. But Brychan had been warned more than once to make his peace. I urged him to go to Lundein long ago—*years* ago! We all did! Would he listen? He was a hell-bent, bloody-minded fool—"

"Father!" Mérian objected. "It is beneath you to speak ill of the dead, and bad luck besides."

"Beneath me?" wondered Cadwgan. "Daughter, it is kindness itself! I knew the man, and of times would have called him my friend. You know that. On Saint Becuma's knees, I swear that man could be so maddeningly pigheaded—and mean with it! If there was ever a man with a colder heart, I don't want to know him." He raised an admonishing finger to his daughter. "Mark my words, girl, now that Brychan and his reprobate son are gone, we will soon count it a blessing in disguise."

"Father!" she protested once more, her voice quivering slightly. "You should not say such things."

"If I speak my mind, it is not out of malice. You know me better than that, I hope. Though we may not like it, that is God's own truth. Brychan's son was a rogue, and his death saved a hangman's fee."

"I will not stay and listen to this," declared Mérian as she turned quickly and hurried away.

"What did I say?" called her father after her. "If anyone has cause to mourn Bran ap Brychan's death, it is the hangman who was cheated out of his pay!"

Mérian's mother was more sympathetic but no more comforting. "I know it is hard to accept," said Queen Anora, threading her embroidery needle, "when someone you know has died. He was such a handsome boy—if only he had been better brought up, he might have made a good king. Alas, his mother died so young. Rhian was a beauty, and kindness itself—if a little flighty, so they say. Still, it's a pity she was not there to raise him." She sighed, then went back to her needle. "You can thank God you were not allowed to receive him in company."

"I know, Mother," said Mérian glumly, turning her face away. "How well I know."

"Soon you will forget all about him." She offered her daughter a hopeful smile. "Time will heal, and the hurt will pass. Mark my words, the pain will pass."

Mérian knew her parents were right, though she would not have expressed her opinions quite so harshly. Even so, she could not make her heart believe the things they said: it went on aching, and nothing anyone said soothed the pain. In the end, Mérian determined to keep her thoughts, like her grief, to herself.

Each day, she went about her chores as if the raw wound of sorrow was already skinning over. She attended her weaving with care and patience. She helped the women prepare the animal skins that would become furs to adorn winter cloaks and tunics. She stood barefoot in the warm sun and raked the newly harvested beans over the drying floor. She twirled the spindle between her deft fingers to spin new-carded wool into thread, watching the skein grow as she wound it round and round. Though she laboured with diligence, she did not feel the thread pass through her fingertips, nor the rake in her hands; she did not smell the strong curing salts she rubbed into the skins; her fingers gathered the wool of their own accord without her guidance.

Each day, she completed her duties with her usual care—as if the thought of Bran hunted down and speared to death like some poor, fear-crazed animal was not the sole occupation of her thoughts, as if the anguish at his passing was not continually churning in her gentle heart.

And if, each night, she cried silently in her bed, each morning she rose fresh faced and resolved not to allow any of these secret feelings to manifest themselves in word or deed. In this she made good.

As the weeks passed, she thought less about Bran and his miserable death and more about the fate of his leaderless people. Of course, they were not—as Garran, her elder brother, so helpfully pointed out—leaderless. "They have a new king now—William Rufus," he told her. "And his subject lord, Count de Braose, is their ruler."

"De Braose is a vile murderer," Mérian snapped.

"That may be," Garran granted with irritating magnanimity, "but he has been given the commot by the king. And," he delighted in pointing out, "the crown is divinely appointed by God. The king is justice, and his word is law."

"The king is himself a usurper," she countered.

"As were most of those before him," replied her brother, smug in his argument. "Facts are facts, dear sister. The Saxon stole the land from us, and now the Ffreinc have stolen it from them. We possess what we hold by King William's sufferance. He is our sovereign lord now, and it is no good wishing otherwise, so you had best make peace with how things are."

"*You* make peace with how things are," she answered haughtily. "I will remain true to our own kind."

"Then you will continue to live in the past," Garran scoffed. "The old ways are over for us. Times are changing, Mérian. The Ffreinc are showing us the way to peace and prosperity."

"They are showing us the way to *hell!*" she shouted, storming from his presence.

That young Prince Bran had died needlessly was bad enough. That he had been killed trying to flee was shameful, yes, but anyone might have done the same in his place. What she found impossible to comprehend or accept was her brother's implied assertion that their Norman overlords were somehow justified in their crime by the innate superiority of their customs or character, or whatever it was her brother found so enamouring.

The Ffreinc are brutes and they are wrong, she insisted to herself. *And that King William of theirs is the biggest brute of all!*

After that last exchange, she refused to talk to anyone further regarding the tragedy that had befallen Bran and Elfael. She kept her thoughts to herself and buried her feelings deep in the fastness of her heart.

CHAPTER 15

Baron de Neufmarché, along with twenty men-at-arms, accompanied his wife to the ship waiting at Hamtun docks. Although he had used the ship Le Cygne in the past and knew both the captain and pilot by name, he nevertheless inspected the vessel bow to stern before allowing his wife to board. He supervised the loading of men, horses, provisions, and weapons—his wife would travel with Ormand, his seneschal, and a guard of seven men. Inside a small casket made of elm wood, Lady Agnes carried the letter he had written to his father and the gift of a gold buckle received from the Conqueror himself in recognition of the baron's loyalty during the season of northern discontent in the years following the invasion.

Once Agnes was established in her quarters beneath the ship's main deck, the baron bade his wife farewell. "The tide is on the rise. Godspeed, lady wife," he said. Raising her hand to his lips, he kissed her cold fingers and added, "I wish you a mild and pleasant winter, and a glad Christmas."

"It may be that I can return before the snow," she ventured, hope lending a lightness to her voice. "We could observe Christmas together."

"No"—Bernard shook his head firmly—"it is far too dangerous. Winter gales make the sea treacherous. If anything should happen to you, I could not forgive myself." He smiled. "Enjoy your sojourn at home—it is brief enough. Time will pass swiftly, and we will celebrate the success of your undertaking with the addition of a new estate."

"*Très bien,*" replied Lady Agnes. "Have a care for yourself, my husband." She leaned close and put her lips against his cheek. "Until we meet again, *adieu, mon chéri.*"

The pilot called down from the deck above that the tide was beginning to run. The baron kissed his wife once more and returned to the wharf. A short time later, the tide had risen sufficiently to put out to sea. The captain called for a crewman to cast off; the ropes were loosed, and the ship pushed on poles away from the dock. Once in the centre of the river, the vessel was caught by the current, turned, and headed out into the estuary and the unprotected sea beyond.

Bernard watched all this from the wooden dock. Only when the ship raised sail and cleared the headland at the wide river mouth did he return to his waiting horse and give the order to start for home. The journey took two days, and by the time he reached his westernmost castle at Hereford, he had decided to make a sortie into Welsh territory, into the cantref of Brycheiniog, to see what he could learn of the land he meant to possess.

Bran no longer knew how long he had been dragging his wounded body through the underbrush. Whole days passed in blinding flashes of pain and shuddering sickness. He could feel his strength departing, his lucid times growing fewer and further apart. He could no longer count on his senses to steer him aright; he heard the voices of people who were not there, and often what he saw before him was, on nearer examination, mere phantasm.

Following his plunge into the pool, he had been swept downstream a fair distance. The current carried him along high-sided banks overhung with leafless branches and great moss-covered limbs, deeper and ever deeper into the forest until finally washing him into the shallows of a green pool surrounded by the wrecks of enormous trees, the boles of which had toppled and fallen over one another like the colossal pillars of a desolated temple.

The warm, shallow water revived him, and he opened his eyes to find himself surrounded by half-sunk, waterlogged trunks and broken boughs. Green slime formed a thick sludge on the surface of the pool, and the air was rank with the stench of fetid stagnant water and decay, and black with shifting clouds of mayflies. Bran struggled upright and, on hands and knees, hauled himself over a sunken log and into the soft, soggy embrace of a peat bog, where he collapsed, a quivering, pain-wracked lump.

Evening was fast upon him when he had finally roused himself that first day and, aching in every joint and muscle, gathered his feet beneath him and climbed up on unsteady legs. Following a deer trail, he lurched like a half-drowned creature from the swamp and staggered into the haven of the greenwood. His chief concern that first night was finding shelter where he could rest and bind his wounds.

He did not know how badly he was injured—only that he was alive and grateful to be so. Once he found shelter, he would remove his tunic and see what he could do to bandage himself. After he had rested and regained his strength, he would make his way to the nearest habitation and secure the aid of his fellow Cymry to continue his flight to safe haven in the north.

As twilight cast a purple gloom over the forest at the end of that first day, Bran found a great oak with a hollowed-out cavity down in the earth beneath the roots. The place had been used by a bear or badger; the earthy musk of the creature still lingered in the cavity. But the hole was dry and warm, and Bran fell asleep the moment he lay down his head.

He woke with a burning thirst, and light-headed from hunger. His wounds throbbed, and his muscles were stiff. There was nothing for his hunger, but he could hear the soft burble of a brook nearby, and easing himself upright, he made his unsteady way to the moss-carpeted bank. He knelt and, with some difficulty because of the cut that ran along the side of his face, stretching from cheekbone to ear, cupped water to his mouth. The inside of his cheek was as raw as sliced meat, and his tongue traced an undulating line like a thick, blood-soaked string.

The cold water made the inside of his mouth sting and brought tears to his eyes, but he quenched his thirst as best he could and then carefully removed his tunic and mantle to better assess his injuries. He could not see the cut in his upper back, but by reaching around cautiously, he was able to feel that it had stopped bleeding. The deep rent in his chest was easier to examine. Caked with dried blood that he gently washed away, the cut was ragged and ratty, the skin puckered along the edges. The wound ached with a persistent throb; the bones had been nicked when the blade forced his ribs apart, but he did not think any had been broken.

Lastly, he examined the bite on his arm. The limb was tender—the hound's teeth had broken the skin, nothing worse—the flesh swollen and sore, but the ragged half circle of raised, red puncture wounds did not seem to be festering. He bathed his arm in the brook and washed the dried blood from his chest and stomach. He tried to bathe the spear cut on his upper back but succeeded only in dribbling water over his shoulders and making himself cold. He drew on his clothes and contemplated the choices before him.

So far as he could see, he had but two courses: return to Elfael and try to find someone to take him in, or continue on to Gwynedd and hope to find help somewhere along the way before he reached the mountains.

The land to the north was rough and inhospitable to a man alone. Even if he had the great good fortune of making it through the forest unaided, the chances of finding help were remote. Elfael, on the other hand, was very nearly deserted; most of his countrymen had fled, and the Ffreinc were seeking his blood. It came to him that he could do no better than try to take his own advice and go to Saint Dyfrig's to seek sanctuary with the monks.

The decision was easily made, and he gathered what strength he could muster and set out. With any luck, he allowed himself to think, day's end would find him behind friendly walls, resting in the guest lodge.

Bran's luck had so far proved as irksomely elusive as the trail. It served him no better now. The forest pathways crossed one another in bewildering profusion, each one leading on to others—over and under fallen trunks, down steep grades into rills and narrow defiles, up sharp-angled ridges and scrub-covered hillsides. Hunger had long since become a constant, gnawing pain in his stomach. He could drink from the streams and brooks he encountered, but nourishing food was scarce. There were mushrooms in extravagant overabundance, but most, he knew, were poisonous, and he did not trust himself to recognise the good ones. Finding nothing else, he chewed hazel twigs just to have something in his mouth.

Hungry, pain-riddled, he allowed his mind to wander.

He imagined himself received into the safety of the abbey and welcomed to a dinner of roast lamb, braised leeks, and oat bread and ale. This comforting dream awakened a ferocious appetite that refused to subside—even when he tried to appease it with sour blackberries gobbled by the purple handful from a bramble bush. In his haste, he bit the inside of his cheek, breaking open the wound afresh and driving him to his knees in agony. He lay for a long time on the ground, rocking back and forth in misery until he became aware that he was being watched.

"What?" asked a voice somewhere above him. "What?"

Raising his eyes, Bran saw a big black rook on a branch directly over his head. The bird regarded him with a shiny bead of an eye. "What?"

He dimly remembered a story about a starving prophet fed by crows. "Bring me bread."

"What?" asked the bird, stretching its wings.

"Bread," Bran said, his voice a breathless groan. "Bring me some bread."

The rook cocked its head to one side. "What?"

"Stupid bird." Angered by the rook's refusal to aid in his revival, Bran dragged himself to his feet once more. The bird started at the movement; it flew off shrieking, its cry of "Die! Die!" echoing through the wood.

Bran looked around and realised with a sinking heart that he had dreamed most of the day away. He moved on then, dejected and afraid to trust his increasingly unreliable judgement. The wounds to his chest and back throbbed with every step and were hot to the touch. As daylight deteriorated around him, his steps slowed to an exhausted shuffle; hunger burned like a flame in his gut, and it hurt his chest to breathe. The long day ended, leaving him worse off than when it had begun, and night closed over him like a fist. He closed his eyes beneath the limbs of a sheltering elm and spent an uncomfortable night on the ground.

When he rose again the next morning, he was just as weary as when he lay down. Climbing to his feet on that second day, he felt fear circling him like a preying beast. He remembered thinking that if he did not find a trail out of the wood, this day might be his last. That was when he had decided to follow the next stream he found, thinking that it would eventually lead to the river that ran through the middle of Elfael.

This he did, and at first it seemed his determination would be rewarded, for the forest thinned and he glimpsed open sky ahead. Closer, he saw sunlight on green grass and imagined the valley spreading beyond. He limped toward the place and, as he passed the last trees, stepped out into a wide meadow—at the centre of which was a shimmering pool. Dragonflies flitted around the water's edge, and larks soared high above. The stream he had been following emptied itself into the pool and, so far as he could tell, did not emerge again.

It had taken him the better part of two days to reach another dead end, and now, as he gazed around him, he knew his strength was gone. Hope crushed to a cold cinder, Bran staggered stiff legged through the long grass to stand gazing down into the water, too tired to do anything but stand.

After a time, he lowered himself painfully down to kneel at the water's edge, drank a few mouthfuls, then sat down beside the pool. He would rest a little before moving on. He fell back in the grass and closed his eyes, giving way to the fatigue that paralysed him. When he woke again, it was dark. The moon was high above a line of clouds moving in from the northwest. Exhausted still, he closed his eyes and went back to sleep.

It rained before morning, but Bran did not rise. And that was how the old woman found him the next day.

She hobbled from the forest on her stout legs and stood for a long time contemplating the wreck of him. "Dost thou ever seek half measures?" she asked, glancing skyward. "Whether 'tis meet or ill, I know not. But heavy was the hand that broke this reed."

She paused, as if listening. "Oh, aye," she muttered. "Aye and ever aye. Your servant obeys."

With that she removed the moth-eaten rag that was her cloak and placed it over the wounded man. Then she retreated to the forest the way she had come. It was midday before she returned, leading two ragged men pulling a handcart. She directed them to the place where she had found the unconscious young man; he was where she left him, still covered by her cloak.

"We could dig a grave," suggested one of the men upon observing the wounded stranger's pale, bloodless flesh. "I do believe 'twould be a mercy."

"Nay, nay," she said. "Take him to my hearth."

"He needs more than hearth care," observed the man, scratching a bristly jaw. "This 'un needs holy unction."

"Go to, Cynvar," the old woman replied. "If thou wouldst but stir thyself to action—and yon stump with thee"—she indicated the second man still standing beside the cart—"methinks we mayest yet hold death's angel at bay."

"You know best, *hudolion*," replied the man. He motioned to his fellow, and the two lifted the stranger into the cart. The movement caused the wounded man to moan softly, but he did not waken.

"Gently, gently," chided the old woman. "I have work enough without thee breaking his bones."

She laid a wrinkled hand against the pale young stranger's wounded cheek and then touched two fingers to his cold brow. "Peace, beloved," she crooned. "In my grasp I hold thee, and I will not let thee go."

Turning to the men once more, she said, "Grows the grass beneath thy feet? About thy business, lads! Be quick."

CHAPTER 16

Count Falkes de Braose anticipated the arrival
of his cousin with all the fret and ferment of a maid awaiting a suitor. He could not remain seated for more than a few
moments at a time before he leapt to his feet and ran to
inspect some detail he had already seen and approved twice
over. Ill at ease in his own skin, he started at every stray
sound, and each new apprehension caused his heart to sink:
What if Earl Philip arrived late? What if he met trouble on
the way? What if he did not arrive at all?

He fussed over the furnishings of his new stronghold:
Were they adequate? Were they too spare? Would he be considered niggardly—or worse yet, a spendthrift? He worried
about the preparation of the feast: Was the fare sumptuous
enough? Was the wine palatable? Was the meat well seasoned?
Was the bread too hard, the soup too thin, the ale too sweet
or too sour? How many men would come with Philip? How
long would they stay?

When these and all the other worries overwhelmed him, he
grew resentful of the torment. What cause did Philip have to
be angry with him? After all, he had taken Elfael with but a

bare handful of casualties. Most of the footmen had not even used their weapons. His first campaign, and it was an absolute triumph! What more could anyone ask?

By the time Philip, Earl of Gloucester, arrived with his retinue late in the day, Falkes was limp with nervous exhaustion. "Cousin!" boomed Philip, striding across the pennon-festooned yard of Caer Cadarn. He was a tall, long-legged man, with dark hair and an expanding bald spot that he kept hidden beneath a cap trimmed in marten fur. His riding gauntlets were trimmed in the same fur, as were the tops of his boots. "It is good to see you, I do declare it! How long has it been? Three years? Four?"

"Welcome!" uttered Falkes in a strangled cry. He loped across the yard with unsteady strides. "I pray you had an uneventful journey—peaceful, that is."

"It was. God's grace, it was," answered Philip, pulling his kinsman into a rough embrace. "But you now—are you well?" He cast a quizzical eye over his younger cousin. "You seem pale and fevered."

"It is nothing—an ague born of anticipation—it will pass." Falkes turned and flapped a hand in the vague direction of the hall. "Valroix Palace it is not," he apologised, "but consider it yours for as long as you desire to stay."

Philip cast a dubious glance at the crude timber structure. "Well, so long as it keeps the rain off, I am satisfied."

"Then come, let us share the welcome cup, and you can tell me how things stand at court." Falkes started across the yard, then remembered himself and stopped. "How is Uncle? Is he well? It is a shame he could not accompany you. I should like to properly thank him for entrusting the settlement of his newest commot to me."

"Father is well, and he is pleased, never fear," replied Philip de Braose. Removing his gauntlets, he tucked them in his belt. "He would have liked nothing better than to accompany me, but the king has come to rely on him so that he will not abide the baron to remain out of sight for more than a day or two before calling him to attendance. Nevertheless, the baron has instructed me to bring him a full account of your deeds and acquisitions."

"*Bien sûr!* You shall have it," said Falkes, nervousness making his voice a little too loud. Turning to the knights and men-at-arms in Philip's company, he called, "Messires, you are most welcome here. Quarters have been arranged, and a feast has been prepared for your arrival. But first, it would please me if you would join me in raising a cup of wine."

He then led his guests into the great hall, the walls of which had been newly washed until they gleamed as white as the Seven Maidens. Fresh green rushes had been strewn over the sand-scoured wooden floor, permeating the enormous room with a clean scent of mown hay. A great heap of logs was blazing on the hearth at one end of the room, where, on an iron spit, half an ox was slowly roasting, the juices sizzling in a pan snugged in the glowing coals.

Several board-and-trestle tables had been erected, draped in cloths, and decked with fir branches. As the men settled on the long benches, the steward and his serving boys filled an assortment of vessels with wine drawn from a tun brought from Aquitaine. When each of the guests was in possession of a cup, their host raised his chalice and called, "My friends, let us drink to King William and his continued good health! Long may he reign!"

"King William!" they all cried and downed the first of

many such cups that night. With the men thus fortified, the celebration soon turned into a revel, and Count Falkes's anxiety slowly gave way to a pleasant, wine-induced contentment. Cousin Philip seemed happy with his efforts and would certainly return to his uncle with a good report. As the evening wore on, Falkes became more and more the jovial host, urging his guests to eat and drink their fill; and when they had done so, he invited his own men, and some of their wives, to join the festivities. Those who knew how to play music brought their instruments, and there was singing and dancing, which filled the hall and lasted far into the night.

Accordingly, it was not until late the next day that Falkes and Philip found opportunity to sit down together. "You have done well, Cousin," Philip asserted. "Father always said that Elfael was a plum ripe for the plucking."

"How right he was," agreed Falkes readily. "I hope you will tell him how grateful I am for his confidence. I look forward to an early demonstration of my loyalty and thanks."

"Rest assured I will tell him. Know you, he has charged me to convey a secret—all being well."

"I hope you think it so," said Falkes.

"It could not be better," replied Philip. "Therefore, I am eager to inform you that the baron intends to make Elfael his staging ground for the conquest of the territories."

"Which territories?" wondered Falkes.

"Selyf, Maelienydd, and Buellt."

"Three commots!" Falkes exclaimed. "That is . . . ambitious."

Falkes had no idea his uncle entertained such far-reaching plans. But then, with the endorsement of the king, what was to prevent Baron de Braose from laying claim to the whole of Wales?

"Ambitious, to be sure," avowed Philip pleasantly. "My father is intent, and he is determined. Moreover, he has the fortune to make it possible."

"I would never doubt it."

"Good," replied Philip, as if a knotty issue had been decided. "To this end, the baron requires you to undertake a survey of the land to be completed before spring."

"Before spring——," repeated Falkes, struggling to keep up. "But we have only just begun to establish——"

"*Zut!*" said Philip, brushing aside his objection before it could be spoken aloud. "The baron will send his own men to perform the survey. You need only aid them with an appropriate guard to ensure their safety while they work."

"I see." The pale count nodded thoughtfully. "And what is this survey to determine?"

"The baron requires three castles to be built—one on the border to the north, one south, and one west—on sites best suited for controlling the territories beyond each of those borders. This the surveyors will determine."

"Three castles," mused Falkes, stroking his thin, silky beard. The cost of such an undertaking would be staggering. He hoped he would not be expected to help pay for the project.

Philip, seeing the shadow of apprehension flit across his cousin's face, quickly explained. "You will appreciate," he continued, "that the building will be funded out of the baron's own treasury."

Falkes breathed easier for the reassurance. "What about the people of Elfael?" he wondered.

"What about them?"

"I assume they will be required to supply ready labour."

"Of course—we must have workers in sufficient number."

"They may resist."

"I don't see how they can," declared Philip. "You said the king and his son have already been removed, along with their men-at-arms. If you were to encounter any meaningful resistance, you would certainly have done so by now. Whatever opposition we meet from here on will be easily overcome."

Despite his cousin's effortless assurance, Falkes remained sceptical. He had no clear idea how many of the original inhabitants remained in Elfael. Most seemed to have fled, but it was difficult to determine their numbers, for even in the best of times they rarely stayed in one place, preferring to wander here and there as the whim took them, much like the cattle they raised and which formed their chief livelihood. Be that as it may, those few who remained in the scattered farms and steadings were certain to have something to say about invaders taking their property, even if it was mostly grazing land.

"You can tell your father, my uncle, that he will find everything in good order by next spring, God willing. In the meantime, I will await the arrival of the surveyors—and what is more, I will accompany them personally to see that all is carried out according to the baron's wishes."

They talked of the work to be done, the materials to be obtained, the number of men who would be needed, and so on. In all that followed, Count Falkes paid most stringent attention—especially when it came to the labourers who would be required.

It was common practise amongst the Ffreinc to entice the local population of conquered lands to help with construction work; for a little pay, parcels of land, or promises of preferential dealings, an ample workforce could often be gathered from the immediate area. The custom had been applied to rousing effect amongst the Saxons. This is how the Conqueror and his barons had accomplished so much so quickly in the subjugation and domination of England. There was no reason why the same practise should not also work in Wales.

The prospect of ready silver went a long way toward slaking any lingering thirst for rebellion. Often those who shouted the loudest about rising up against the invaders were the same ones who profited most handily from the invasion. God knows, Baron de Braose's renowned treasury had won more battles than his soldiers and could be relied upon to do so again. And as everyone knew, the Welsh, for all their prideful bluster, were just as greedy for gain as the most grasping, lackland Saxon.

It was with this in mind that the two kinsmen rode out the following day to view the commot. Philip wanted to get a better idea of the region and see firsthand the land that had so quickly fallen under their control.

The day began well, with a high, bright sky and a fresh breeze pushing low clouds out of the west. Autumn was advancing; everywhere the land was slumping down toward its winter rest. The leaves on the trees had turned and were flying from the branches like golden birds across a pale blue sky. Away in the distance, always in the distance, defining the boundary of the commot, towered the green-black wall of the forest, looming like a line of clouds, dark and turbulent, heralding the advance of a coming storm.

The two noblemen, each accompanied by a knight and three men-at-arms, rode easily together through the valley and across the rolling hills. They passed by the little monastery at Llanelli and paused to examine the setting of the place and the construction of the various buildings before riding on. They also visited one of Elfael's few far-flung settlements, cradled amongst the branching valleys. This one, huddled in the wind shadow of the area's highest hill, consisted of a house and barn, a granary, and a coop for chickens. It, like so many others, was abandoned. The people had gone—where, Falkes had no idea.

After visiting a few of the dwellings, they returned to their horses. "A piss-poor place," observed Earl Philip, climbing back into the saddle. "I would not allow one of my dogs to live here." He shook his head. "Are they all like this?"

"More or less," replied Falkes. "They are mostly herdsmen, from what I can tell. They follow their cattle, and these holdings are often abandoned for months at a time."

"What about the farms, the crops?" wondered Philip, taking up the reins.

"There are few enough of those," answered Falkes, turning his horse back onto the trackway. "Most of the open land is used for grazing."

"That will change," decided Philip. "This soil is rich—look at the grass, lush and thick as it is! You could grow an abundance of grain here—enough to feed an army."

"Which is precisely what will be needed," replied Falkes, urging his mount forward. He thought about the baron's plans to subdue the next commots. "Two or three armies."

They rode to the top of the hill above the settlement and looked out over the empty valley with its narrow stream snaking through the deep green grass, rippling in the wind. In his mind's eye, Earl Philip could see farms and villages springing up throughout the territory. There would be mills—for wood and wool and grain—and storehouses, barns, and granaries. There would be dwellings for the farmers, the workers, the craftsmen: tanners, chandlers, wainwrights, ironsmiths, weavers, bakers, dyers, carpenters, butchers, fullers, leatherers, and all the rest.

There would be churches, too, one for each village and town, and perhaps a monastery or two as well. Maybe, in time, an abbey.

"A good place," mused Falkes.

"Yes." His cousin smiled and nodded. "And it is a good thing we have come." He let his gaze sweep over the hilltops and up to the blue vault of heaven and felt the warm sun on his face. "Elfael is a rough gem, but with work it will polish well."

"To be sure," agreed Falkes. "God willing."

"Oh, God has already willed it," Philip assured him. "As sure as William is king, there is no doubt about that." He paused, then added, "None whatsoever."

CHAPTER 17

The day following the feast of Saint Edmund
—three weeks after Earl Philip's visit—and the weather had
turned raw. The wind was rising out of the north, gusting
sharply, pushing low, dirty clouds over the hills. Count Falkes's
thin frame was aching with the chill, and he longed to turn
around and ride back to the scorching, great fire he kept blazing in the hearth, but the baron's men were still disputing over
the map they were making, and he did not want to appear
irresolute or less than fully supportive of his uncle's grand
enterprise.

There were four of them—an architect, a surveyor, and
two apprentices—and although Falkes could not be sure, he
suspected that in addition to their charting activities, they
were also spies. The questions they asked and the interest they
took in his affairs put the count on his guard; he knew only
too well that he enjoyed his present position through the sufferance of Baron de Braose. Not a day went by that he did
not ponder how to further advance his uncle's good opinion
of him and his abilities, for as Elfael had been given, so Elfael
could be taken away. Without it, he would become again what

he had been: one more impoverished nobleman desperate to win the favour of his betters.

Fate had reached down and plucked him from the heaving ranks of desperate nobility. Against every expectation, he had been singled out for advancement and granted this chance to make good. Spoil this, and Falkes knew another opportunity would never come his way. For him, it was Elfael . . . or nothing.

Thus, he must ever and always remain vigilant and ruthless in his dealings with the Welsh under his rule, nor could he afford to show any weakness to his countrymen, however insignificant, that might give the baron cause to send him back to Normandie in disgrace.

Although his cousin Philip heartily assured him that his uncle, the baron, applauded his accomplishments, Falkes reckoned he would not be secure in his position as Lord of Elfael until the de Braose banner flew unopposed over the surrounding commots. So despite the bone-cracking cold, a most miserable Falkes remained with his visitors, sitting on his horse and shivering in the damp wind.

The surveying party had arrived the day before when the first wains rolled down into the shallow bowl of the valley. Bumping across the stream that was now a swift-running torrent, the high-sided, wooden-wheeled vehicles toiled up the slope and came to a stop at the foot of the mound on which the fortress stood. The wagons, five in all, were full of tools and supplies for the men who would oversee the construction of the three castles Baron de Braose had commissioned. Building work would not begin until the spring, but the baron was anxious to waste not a single day; he wanted everything to be ready when the masons and their teams of apprentices arrived with the thaw.

By the time the wildflowers brushed the hilltops with gold, the foundations of each defensive tower would be established. When the stars of the equinox shone over the sites, the ditches would be man deep and the walls shoulder high. By midsummer, the central mound would belly to the sky, and stone curtains twice the height of the workmen would crown the hillcrests. And when the time came for the master mason to call his men to pack their tools and load the wains to return to their families in Wintancaester, Oxenforde, and Gleawancaester, the walls and keep, bailey, donjon, and ditch would be half-finished.

For now, however, the wagons and animals would remain in sight of Caer Cadarn, where their drivers would camp in the lee of the fortress to shelter from the perpetual wind and icy rain that roared down out of the northwest. All winter long, Count Falkes's men-at-arms would be kept busy hunting for the table, while the footmen and servants foraged for wood to keep the fires ablaze in hearth and fire ring of caer and camp.

It was not at all a convivial country, Falkes decided, for although winter had yet to arrive in force, the count had never been so cold in all his life. Curse the baron's impatience! If only the invasion of Elfael could have waited until the spring. As it was, Falkes and his men had come so late to Wales that they had not had time to adequately prepare for the season of snow and ice. Falkes found he had seriously underestimated the severity of the British weather; his clothes—he wore two or three tunics and mantles at a time, along with his heaviest cloak—were too thin and made of the wrong stuff. His fingers and toes suffered perpetual chilblains. He stamped his way around the fortress, clapping his hands and flapping his arms across his chest to keep warm. By night, he took to his bed after supper and burrowed deep under the fleeces and skins and cloaks that served him for bedclothes in his dank, wind-fretted chamber.

Just this morning he had awakened in his bed, aghast to find that frost had formed on the bedclothes overnight; he swore an oath that he would not sleep another night in that room. If it meant he had to bed down with the servants and dogs beside the hearth in the great hall, so be it. The only time his hands and feet were ever warm was when he sat in his chair before the hearth, with arms and legs outstretched toward the fire—a position he could maintain only for a few moments altogether; but those were moments of pure bliss in what looked to be a long, grinding, bitter winter—more ordeal than season.

It was not until the light was beginning to fail and the surveyor could no longer read the chart he was making that the builders decided to stop for the day and return to Caer Cadarn. The count was the first to turn his horse and head for home. As the work party came in sight of the fortress, the skies opened and rain began hammering down in driving sheets. Falkes lashed his mount to speed and covered the remaining distance at a gallop. He raced up the long ramp, through the gates, and into the yard to find a half dozen unfamiliar horses tethered to the rail outside the stable.

"Who has come?" he asked, throwing the reins of his mount to the head stabler.

"It is Baron Neufmarché of Hereford," replied the groom. "He arrived only a short while ago."

Neufmarché here? Mon Dieu! This is a worry, thought the count. *What could he possibly want with me?*

Dashing back across the rain-scoured yard, a very wet Falkes de Braose entered the great hall. There, standing before a gloriously radiant hearth, was his uncle's compatriot and chief rival, accompanied by five of his men: knights every one. "Baron Neufmarché!" called Falkes. He shrugged off his sodden cloak and tossed it to a waiting servant. "This is an unexpected pleasure," he brayed, trying to sound far more gracious than he felt at the moment. Striding quickly forward, he rubbed the warmth back into his long hands. "Welcome! Welcome, messires, to you all!"

"My dear Count de Braose," replied the baron with a polite bow of courtesy. "Pray forgive our intrusion—we were on our way north, but this vile weather has driven us to shelter. I hope we do not trespass on your hospitality."

"Please," replied Falkes, oozing cordiality, "I am honoured." He glanced around to see the cups in the hands of his guests. "I see my servants have seen to your refreshment. *Bon.*"

"Yes, your seneschal is most obliging," the baron assured him. Taking up a spare cup, already poured, he handed it to the count. "Here, drink and warm yourself by the fire. You have had an inclement ride."

Feeling uncomfortably like a guest in his own house, Falkes nevertheless thanked the baron and accepted the cup. Withdrawing a poker from the fire, he plunged it into the wine; the hot iron sizzled and sputtered. The count then raised his steaming cup and said, "To King William!" Several cups later, when a meal had been prepared and they all sat down together, the count at last discovered the errand that brought the baron to his door, and it had nothing to do with seeking shelter from the rain.

"I have long wished to visit the Earl of Rhuddland," the baron informed him, spearing a piece of roast beef with his knife. "I confess I may have waited too far into the autumn, but affairs at court kept me in Lundein longer than I anticipated." He lifted a shoulder. *"C'est la vie."*

Count Falkes allowed himself a sly, secret smile; he knew Baron Neufmarché had been summoned by King William to attend him in Lundein and kept waiting several days before finally being sent away. William the Red had still not completely forgiven the contrary noblemen who had upheld his brother Robert's claim to the throne, legitimate though it undoubtedly was. When the dust of revolt had settled, William had tacitly pardoned those he considered rebels, returning them to rank and favour—although he could not resist harassing them in small ways just to prove the point.

The delay Neufmarché complained of had allowed the count's uncle to make good the de Braose clan's first foray into Wales without interference from the lords of neighbouring territories. While Neufmarché was idling in Lundein, Count Falkes had, with uncommon swiftness and ease, conquered Elfael. The whole campaign had been closely planned to avoid extraneous entanglements from the likes of rival lords such as Neufmarché, for if Baron de Braose had had to beg Neufmarché for permission to cross his lands that lay between Norman England and the Welsh provinces, Falkes was fairly certain they would all be waiting still.

"You have done well," the baron said, gazing around the hall approvingly, "and in a very short time. I take it the Welsh gave you no trouble?"

"Very little," affirmed Falkes. "There is a monastery nearby, with a few monks and some women and children in hiding. The rest seem to have scattered to the hills. I expect we won't see them until the spring." He cut into a plump roast fowl on the wooden trencher before him. "By then we will be well fortified hereabouts, and opposition will be futile." He sliced into the succulent breast of the bird, raised a bite on his knife, and nibbled daintily.

Neufmarché caught the veiled reference to increased fortification. *No one builds fortresses to hold down a few monks and some women and children,* he thought and guessed the rest. "They are a strange people," he observed, and several of his knights grunted their agreement. "Sly and secretive."

"*Bien sûr,*" Falkes replied. He chewed thoughtfully and asked, trying to sound casual, "Do you plan to make a foray yourself?"

The bluntness of the question caught the baron off guard. "Me? I have no plans," he lied. "But now that you mention it, the thought has crossed my mind." He raised his cup to give himself time to think and then continued, "I confess, your example gives me heart. If I imagined that acquiring land would be so easy, I might give it some serious consideration." He paused as if entertaining the possibility of an attack in Wales for the very first time. "Busy as I am ruling the estates under my command, I'm not at all certain a campaign just now would be wise."

"You would know better than I," Falkes conceded. "This is my first experience ruling an estate of any size. No doubt I have much to learn."

"You are too modest," Neufmarché replied with a wide, expansive smile. "From what I have seen, you learn very quickly." He drained his cup and held it aloft. A servant appeared and refilled it at once. "I drink to your every success!"

"And I to yours, *mon ami,*" said Count Falkes de Braose. "And I to yours."

The next morning, the baron departed with an invitation

for Falkes to visit him whenever he passed through his lands in Herefordshire. "I will look forward to it with keenest pleasure," said the count as he waved his visitors away. He then hurried to his chamber, where he drafted a hasty letter to his uncle, informing him of the progress with the ongoing survey of the building sites—as well as his adversary's unannounced visit. Falkes sealed the letter and dispatched a messenger the moment his guests were out of sight.

CHAPTER 18

Angharad stirred the simmering contents of the cauldron with a long wooden spoon and listened to the slow *plip, plip, plip* of the rain falling from the rim of stone onto the wet leaves at the entrance to the cave. She took up the bound sprig of a plant she had gathered during the summer and with a deft motion rolled the dry leaves back and forth between her palms, crumbling the herb into the broth. The aroma of her potion was growing ever more pungent in the close air of the cave.

Every now and then she would cast a glance toward the fleece-wrapped bundle lying on a bed of pine boughs and covered with moss and deer pelts. Sometimes the man inside the bundle would moan softly, but for the most part his sleep was as silent as the dead. Her skill with healing unguents and potions extended to that small mercy if nothing more.

When the infusion was ready, she lifted the cauldron from the fire and carried it to a nearby rock, where it was left to cool. Then, taking up an armful of twigs from the heap just inside the cave entrance, she returned to her place by the fire.

"One for the Great King on his throne so white," she said,

tossing a twig onto the embers. She waited until the small branch flared into flame, then reached for another, saying, "Two for the Son the King begat."

This curious ritual continued for some time—taking up a twig and consigning it to the flames with a little verse spoken in a child's rhythmic singsong—and the simple chant reached the young man in his pain-fretted sleep.

> Three for the Errant Goose both swift and wild.
> Four for Pangur Ban the cat.
> Five for the Martyrs undefiled—
> Aye, five for the Martyrs undefiled.

She paused and cupped a hand above the fire for a moment, allowing the smoke to gather, then turned her palm, releasing a little white cloud. As the smoke floated up and dispersed, she continued her verse.

> Six for the Virgins who watch and wait.
> Seven for the Bards in halls of oak.
> Eight for the patches on Padraig's cloak.
> Nine for the lepers at the gate.
> Ten for the rays of Love's pure light—
> Aye, ten for the rays of Love's pure light.

Though the young man did not wake, the softly droning words and the simple rhythm seemed to soothe him. His breathing slowed and deepened, and his stiff muscles eased.

Angharad heard the change in his breathing and smiled to herself. She went to test the heat of the potion in the cauldron; it was still hot but no longer bubbling. Picking up the big copper kettle, she carried it to where Bran lay, drew her three-legged stool near, and began gently pulling away the fleeces that covered him.

His flesh was dull and waxen, his wounds livid and angry. The right side of his face was roundly swollen, the skin discoloured. The teeth marks on his arm where the hound had fastened its jaws were puncture wounds, deep but clean—as was the slash between his shoulder blades. Painful as any of these wounds might have been, none were life-threatening. Rather, it was the ragged gash in the centre of his chest that worried her most. The iron blade had not pricked a lung, nor pierced the watery sac of the heart; but the lance head had driven cloth from his tunic and hair from the hound deep into the cut. These things, in her experience, could make even insignificant injuries fester and turn sour, bringing on fever, delirium, and finally death.

She sighed as she placed her fingertips on the bulbous swelling. The flesh was hot beneath her gentle fingertips, oozing watery blood and yellow pus. He had been wandering a few days before she had found him, and the wounds had already begun to go rancid. Therefore, she had taken great pains to prepare the proper infusion with which to wash the wound and had gathered the instruments to enlarge it so she could carefully dig out any scraps of foreign matter.

Angharad had expected him to come to her injured. She had foreseen the fight and knew the outcome, but the wounds he had suffered would tax her skill sorely. He was a strong one, his strength green and potent; even so, he would need all of it, and more besides, if he was to survive.

Bending to the cauldron, she took up a bit of clean cloth from a neat stack she had prepared; she folded the cloth and soaked it in the hot liquid and then gently, gently applied it to the gash in his chest. The heat caused him to moan in his sleep, but he did not wake. She let the cloth remain and, taking up another, soaked it and placed it on the side of his face.

When the second cloth had been carefully arranged, she returned to the first, removed it, placed it back in the cauldron, and began again.

So it went.

All through the night, the old woman remained hunched on her little stool, moving with slow purpose from one wound to the next, removing the cloth, dipping it, and replacing it. When the potion in the cauldron cooled, she returned it to the embers of her fire and brought it back to the boil. Heat was needed to draw out the poison of the wounds.

While she worked, she sang—an old song in the Elder Tongue, something she had learned from her own banfáith many, many years ago—the tale of Bran the Blesséd and his journey to Tir na' Nog. It was a song about a champion who, after a long sojourn in the Otherworld, had returned to perform the Hero Feat for his people: a tale full of hope, longing, and triumph—fitting, she thought, for the man beneath her care.

As dawn seeped into the rainy sky to the east, Angharad finished. She set aside the cauldron and rose slowly, arching her back to ease the ache there. Then she knelt once more and, taking up a handful of dried moss, placed it gently over the young man's wounds before covering him with the sheepskins. Later that day, she would begin the purification procedure all over again, and the next day, too, and perhaps the next. But for now, it was enough.

She rose and returned the cauldron to the edge of the fire

ring, and settling herself once more on the three-legged stool, she pulled her cloak around her shoulders and closed her eyes on the day.

Bran did not know how long he had been lying in the dark, listening to the rain: a day, perhaps many days. Try as he might, he could not remember ever hearing such a sound before. He could vaguely remember what rain was and what it looked like, but so far as he could recall, this was the first time he had ever heard it patter down on earth and rocks and drip from the canopy of leaves to the sodden forest pathways below.

Unable to move, he was content to lie with his eyes closed, listening to the oddly musical sound. He did not want to open his eyes for fear of what he might see. Flitting through his shattered memory were weird and worrisome images: a snarling dog that snapped at his throat; a body floating in a pool; a black-shadowed hole in the ground that was both stronghold and tomb; and a hideous, decrepit old woman bearing a steaming cauldron. It was a nightmare, he told himself: the dreams of a pain-haunted man and nothing more.

He knew he was badly injured. He did not know how this had come to be nor even how he knew it to be true. Nevertheless, he accepted this fact without question. Then again, perhaps it was part of the same nightmare as the old crone—who could say?

However it was, the woman seemed to be intimately connected with another curious image that kept spinning through his mind: that of himself, wrapped in soft white fleece and lying full-length on a bed of pine boughs and moss covered by deerskins. Now and then, the image changed, taking on the quality of a dream—a peculiar reverie made familiar through repetition. In this dream he hovered in the air like a hawk, gazing down upon his own body from some place high above. At first he did not know who this hapless fellow in the rude bed might be. The young man's face was round and oddly misshapen, one side purple black and bloated beyond all recognition. His skin was dull and lustreless and of an awful waxy colour; no breath stirred the unfortunate's lungs. The poor wretch was dead, Bran concluded.

And that is when the old woman had first appeared. A hag with a bent back and a face like a dried apple, she limped to the dead man's bed, carrying the gurgling pot fresh from the fire. She leaned low and peered into the fellow's face, shaking her head slowly as she carefully positioned the cauldron and settled herself cross-legged on the ground beside him. Then, rocking back and forth, she began to sing. Bran thought he had heard the song before but could not say where. And then, abruptly, the dream ended—always at the same place. The injured man and the old woman simply vanished in a blinding white haze, and most upsetting, Bran found himself waking in the dark and occupying the injured man's place.

This distressing transformation did not upset him as much as it might have because of the overwhelming sympathy Bran felt for the unfortunate fellow. Not only did he feel sorry for the young man, but he felt as if they might have been friends in the past. At the same time, he resented the repulsive old woman's intrusions. If not for her, Bran imagined he and the wounded man would have been free to leave that dark place and roam at will in the fields of light.

He knew about these far-off fields because he had seen

them, caught fleeting glimpses of them in his other dreams. In these dreams he was often flying, soaring above an endless landscape of softly rounded hills over which the most wonderful, delicate, crystalline rays of sunlight played in ever-shifting colours—as if the soft summer breeze had become somehow visible as it drifted over the tall grass in richly variegated hues to delight the eye. Nor was this all, for accompanying the blithe colours was a soft flutelike music, buoyant as goose down on the breeze, far-off as the remembered echo of a whisper. Soft and sweet and low, it gradually modulated from one note to the next in fine harmony.

The first time he saw the fields of light, the sight made his heart ache with yearning; he wanted nothing more than to go there, to explore that wondrous place, but something prevented him. Once, in his dream, he had made a determined rush toward the glorious fields, and it appeared he would at last succeed in reaching them. But the old woman suddenly arose before him—it was Angharad; he knew her by the quick glance of her dark eye—except that she was no longer the hideous hag who dwelt in the darksome hole. Gone were her bent back and filthy tangles of stringy hair; gone her withered limbs, gone her coarse-woven, shapeless dress.

The woman before him was beauty made flesh. Her tresses were long and golden hued, her skin flawless, soft, and supple; her gown was woven of glistening white samite and trimmed in ermine; the slippers on her feet were scarlet silk, beaded with tiny pearls. She gazed upon him with large, dark eyes that held a look of mild disapproval. He moved to step past her, but she simply raised her hand.

"Where do you go, *mo croi*?" she asked, her voice falling like gentle laughter on his ear.

He opened his mouth to frame a reply but could make no sound.

"Come," she said, smiling, "return with me now. It is not yet time for you to leave."

Reaching out, she touched him lightly on the arm, turning him to lead him away. He resisted, still staring at the wonderful fields beyond.

"Dearest heart," she said, pressing luscious lips to his ear, "yon meadow will remain, but you cannot. Come, return you must. We have work to do."

So she led him back from the edge of the field, back to the warm darkness and the slow *plip, plip, plip* of the falling rain. Sometime later—he could not say how long—Bran heard singing. It was the voice from his dream, and this time he opened his eyes to dim shadows moving gently on the rock walls of his primitive chamber.

Slowly, he turned his head toward the sound, and there she was. Although it was dark as a dovecote inside the cave, he could see her lumpen, ungainly form as she stood silhouetted by the fitful, flickering flames. She was as hideous as the hag of his recent nightmares, but as he knew now, she was no dream. She, like the hole in the ground where he lay, was only too real.

"Who are you?" asked Bran. His head throbbed with the effort of forming the words, and his voice cracked, barely a whisper. The old woman did not turn or look around but continued stirring the foul-smelling brew.

It was some time before Bran could work up the strength to ask again, with slightly more breath, "Woman, who are you?"

At this, the crone dropped her stirring stick and turned her wrinkled face to peer at him over a hunched shoulder, regarding him with a sharp, black, birdlike eye. Her manner put Bran in mind of a crow examining a possible meal or a bright bauble to steal away to a treetop nest.

"Can you speak?" asked Bran. Each word sent a peal of agony crashing through his head, and he winced. The side of his face felt as stiff and unyielding as a plank of oak.

"Aye, speak and sing," she replied, and her voice was far less unpleasant than her appearance suggested. "The question is, methinks, can thee?"

Bran opened his mouth, but a reply seemed too much effort. He simply shook his head—and instantly wished he had not moved at all, for even this slight motion sent towering waves of pain and nausea surging through his gut. He closed his eyes and waited for the unpleasantness to pass and the world to right itself once more.

"I thought not," the old woman told him. "Thou best not speak until I bid thee."

She turned from him then, and he watched her as she rose slowly and, bending from her wide hips, removed the pot from the flames and set it on a nearby rock to cool. She then came to his bed, where she sat for some time, gazing at him with that direct, unsettling glance. At length, she said, "Thou art hungry. Some broth have I made thee."

Bran, unable to make a coherent reply, merely blinked his eyes in silent assent. She busied herself by the fire, returning a short time later with a wooden bowl. Taking up a spoon made from a stag's horn, she dipped it into the bowl and brought it to Bran's mouth, parting his lips with a gentle yet insistent pressure.

Barely able to open his mouth, he allowed some of the lukewarm liquid to slide over his teeth and down his throat.

It had a dusky, herb-rich flavour that reminded him of a greenwood glen in deep autumn.

She lifted the spoon once more, and he sucked down the broth. "There, and may it well become you," she said soothingly. "Thou mayest yet make good your return to Tir na' Nog."

An inexplicable sense of pride and accomplishment flushed his cheeks, and he suddenly found himself eager to please her with this trifling display of infant skill. The broth, although thin and clear, was strangely filling, and Bran found that after only a few more sips from the spoon, he could hold no more. The food settled his stomach, and exhausted with the small effort expended, he closed his eyes and slept.

When he woke again, it was brighter in the cave, and he was hungry again. As before, the old woman was there to serve him some of the herbal broth. He ate gratefully, but without trying to speak, and then slept after his meal.

Life proceeded like this for many days: he would wake to find his guardian beside him, ready to feed him his broth, whereupon, after only a few sips from the stag horn spoon, he would be overcome by the urge to sleep. Upon waking, he would find himself better refreshed than before, and what is more, Bran not only found that he was eating more each time, but also suspected that the intervals between sleeping and eating were shorter.

The comforting routine was interrupted one day when Bran awoke to find himself alone in the cave. He moved his head to look around, but the hag was nowhere to be seen. The *pit-pat* drip of water that had accompanied his waking moments for the last many days was gone. Alone and unobserved, he decided to stand up.

Slowly, cautiously, he levered himself onto the elbow of his good arm. His shoulders were stiff, and his chest ached; even the tiniest movement set off a crippling surge of agony that left him panting. At each attack he would pause, eyes squeezed shut, clutching his chest, until the waves of pain receded and he could see straight again.

On the ground near his bed was a shallow iron basin full of water; guarding against any sudden moves, he stretched out his hand and was able to hook two fingers over the rim and pull the heavy vessel closer. When the water stopped sloshing around the basin, he leaned over it and looked in. The face staring back at him was woefully misshapen; the right side was puffy and discoloured, and a jagged black line ran from the lower lip to the earlobe. The flesh along this lightning-strike line was pinched and puckered beneath a rough beard, which had been unevenly shaved to keep the hair away from the wound.

Angry at what he saw reflected in the water, he gave the basin a shove and instantly regretted it. The violent movement caused another upwelling of pain, greater than any before. He could not bear it and fell back, tears streaming down the sides of his face. He moaned, and that started him coughing, which opened the wound in his chest. The next thing he knew, he was coughing up blood.

The stuff came bubbling up his throat, thick and sweet, and spilled over his chin. He gagged and hacked, spitting blood in a fine red mist over himself. Each cough brought forth another, and he could not catch his breath. Just when he thought he would choke to death on his own blood, the old woman appeared beside him.

"What hast thou done?" she asked, kneeling beside him.

Unable to reply, he wheezed and spluttered, blood welling up over his teeth. With a quick motion, Angharad tore aside the sheepskin covering and placed a gentle hand on his chest. "Peace!" she whispered, like a mother to a distraught and unquiet child.

> Power of moon have I over thee,
> Power of sun have I over thee,
> Power of stars have I over thee,
> Power of rain have I over thee,
> Power of wind have I over thee,
> Power of heaven have I over thee,
> Power of heaven have I over thee in the power
>   of God to heal thee.

She moved her hand over his chest, her fingertips softly brushing the injured flesh. "Closed for thee thy wound, and stanched thy blood. As Christ bled upon the cross, so closeth he thy wound for thee," she intoned, her voice a caress.

> A part of this hurt on the high mountains,
> A part of this hurt on the grass-deep meadow,
> A part of this hurt on the heathered moors,
> A part of this hurt on the great surging sea
>   that has best means to bear it.
> This hurt on the great surging sea, she herself
>   has the best means to bear it for
>   thee . . . away . . . away . . . away.

Under Angharad's warm touch, the pain subsided. His lungs eased their laboured pumping, and his breathing calmed. Bran lay back, his chin and chest glistening with gore, and mouthed the words, *Thank you.*

Taking a bit of rag, she soaked it in the basin and began washing him clean, working patiently and slowly. She hummed as she worked, and Bran felt himself relaxing under her gentle ministrations. "Now wilt thou sleep," the old woman told him when she finished.

Eyelids heavy, he closed his eyes and sank into the soft, dark, timeless place where his dreams kindled and flared with strange visions of impossible feats, of people he knew but had never met, of things past—or perhaps yet to come—when the king and queen gave life and love to the people, when bards lauded the deeds of heroes, when the land bestowed its gifts in abundance, when God looked with favour upon his children and hearts were glad. Over all he dreamed that night, there loomed the shape of a strange bird with a long beak and a face as smooth and hard and black as charred bone.

CHAPTER 19

Spring could not come soon enough for Falkes de Braose. The count ached for an end to the roof-rattling, teeth-chattering cold of the most inhospitable winter he had ever known—and it had only just begun! As he shivered in his chair, wrapped in cloaks and robes—a very hillock of dun-coloured wool—he consoled himself with the thought that when winter came next year, he would be firmly ensconced in his own private chamber in a newly built stone keep. In blissful dreams he conjured snug, wood-panelled rooms hung with heavy tapestries to keep out the searching fingers of the frigid wind, and a down-filled bed set before a blazing hearth all his own. He would never again suffer the dank drear of the great hall, with its drafts and smoke and freezing damp.

He would not abide another winter swaddled like a grotesquely oversized worm waiting for spring so it could shrug off its cocoon. Next winter, a ready supply of fuel would be laid in; he would determine how much was required and then treble the amount. This daily struggle to squeeze inadequate warmth from wet timber was slow insanity, and the count vowed never to endure it again. This time next year, he would laugh at the rain and cheerfully thumb his nose at each snowflake as it floated to the ground.

Meanwhile, he waited in perpetual dudgeon for the spring thaw, studying the plans drawn by the master architect for the baron's new borderland castles: one facing the yet-to-be-conquered northwestern territories, one to anchor the centre and the lands to the south, and one to defend the backs of the other two from any attacks arising from the east. The castles were, with only slight variations, all the same, but Falkes studied each sheaf of drawings with painstaking care, trying to think of improvements to the designs that he could suggest and that might win his uncle's approval. So far, he had come up with only one: increasing the size of the cistern that captured rainwater for use in times of emergency. As this detail was not likely to impress his uncle, he kept at his scrutiny and dreamed of warmer climes.

Five days after the feast of Saint Benedict, a messenger arrived with a letter from the baron. "Good news, I hope," said Falkes to the courier, taking receipt of the wrapped parchment. "Will you stay?"

"My lord baron requires an answer without delay," replied the man, shaking rainwater from his cloak and boots.

"Does he indeed?" Falkes, his interest sufficiently piqued, waved the courier away to the cookhouse. Alone again, he broke the seal, unrolled the small scrap of parchment, and settled back in his chair, holding the crabbed script before his eyes. He read the letter through to the end and then scanned it again to make sure he had not missed anything.

The message was simple enough: his uncle, eager to strengthen his grasp on Elfael so that he could begin his long-anticipated invasion into fresh territories, desired the construction of his new castles to begin without further delay. The baron was sending masons and skilled workers at once. Further, many of these would be bringing their families, eliminating the need to return home when the building season ended, thus allowing them to work longer before winter brought a halt to their labours. Therefore, Baron de Braose wanted his nephew to put every available resource of time and energy into building a town and establishing a market so that the workers and their families would have a place to live while the construction continued.

"A town!" spluttered Falkes. "He wants an entire town raised before next winter!"

The baron concluded his letter saying that he knew he could rely on his nephew to carry out his command with utmost zeal and purpose, and that when the baron arrived on Saint Michael's Day to inspect the work, he trusted he would find all ready and in good order.

Falkes was still sitting in his chair with a stunned expression on his long face when the messenger returned. "My lord?" asked the man, approaching uncertainly.

Falkes stirred and glanced up. "Yes? Oh, it is you. Did you find something to eat?"

"Thank you, sire, I have had a good meal."

"Well," replied Falkes absently, "I am glad to hear it. I suppose you want to get back, so I . . ." His voice trailed off as he sat gazing into the flames on the hearth.

"Ahem," coughed the messenger after a moment. "If you please, sire, what reply am I to make to the baron?"

Raising the letter to his eyes once more, Falkes took a deep breath and said, "You may tell the baron that his nephew is eager to carry out his wishes and will press ahead with all speed. Tell him . . ." His voice grew small at the thought of the enormity of the task before him.

"Pardon?" asked the messenger. "You were saying?"

"Yes, yes," resumed the count irritably. "Tell the baron his nephew wishes him success in all his undertakings. No, tell him . . . Tell the baron nothing. Wait but a little, and I will compose a proper reply." He flicked his long fingers at the messenger. "You may go see to your mount."

Bowing quickly, the messenger departed. Falkes went to his table, took up his pen, and wrote a coolly compliant answer to his uncle's demand on the same parchment, then rolled and resealed it and called for a servant to take the letter to the waiting messenger. He heard the clatter of iron-shod hooves in the courtyard a short time later and, closing his eyes, leaned his head against the back of his chair.

An entire town to raise in one summer. Impossible! It could not be done. Was his uncle insane? The baron himself, with all his men and money, could surely not accomplish such a thing.

He slumped farther into his chair and pulled the woollen cloaks more tightly under his chin as hopelessness wrapped its dark tendrils around him. Three castles to erect, and now a complete town as well. His own dream of a warm chamber in a newly enlarged fortress receded at an alarming pace.

By the Blessèd Virgin, a town!

So lost in his despair was he that it was not until the next day that Falkes found a way out of the dilemma: it did not have to be a *whole* town. That would come, in time and in good order. For now, the undertaking could be something much more modest—a market square, a meeting hall, a few houses, and, of course, a church. Constructing even that much would be difficult enough—where was he to find the labourers? Why, a church alone would require as many men as he had ready to hand; where would he find the rest?

The church alone . . . , he thought, and the thought brought him upright in his chair. *Yes! Of course!* Why, the answer was staring him full in the face.

He rose and, leaving the warmth of his hall behind, rushed out into the snow-covered yard, calling for his seneschal. "Orval! Orval!" he cried. "Bring me Bishop Asaph!"

The summons came while the bishop was conducting an audit of food supplies with the kitchener. It was turning into a hard winter, and this year's harvest had been poor; the monastery was still sheltering a dozen or so people who, for one reason or another, could not escape to Saint Dyfrig's. Thus, the bishop was concerned about the stock of food on hand and wanted to know how long it would last.

Together with Brother Brocmal, he was examining the monastery's modest storerooms, making an exact accounting, when the riders arrived to fetch him. "Bishop Asaph!" called the porter, running across the yard. "The Ffreinc—the Ffreinc have come for you!"

"Calm yourself, brother," Asaph said. "Deliver your charge with some measure of decorum, if you please."

The porter gulped down a mouthful of air. "Three riders in de Braose livery have come," he said. "They have a horse for you and say you are to accompany them to Caer Cadarn."

"I see. Well, go back and tell them I am busy just now but will attend them as soon as I have finished."

"They said I was to bring you at once," countered the porter. "If you refused, they said they would come and drag you away by your ears!"

"Did they indeed!" exclaimed the bishop. "Well, I will save them the trouble." Handing the tally scroll to the kitchener, he said, "Continue with the accounting, Brother Brocmal, while I deal with our impatient guests."

"Of course, bishop," replied Brother Brocmal.

Asaph returned with the porter and found three marchogi on horseback waiting with a saddled fourth horse. "Pax vobiscum," said the bishop, "I am Father Asaph. How may I be of assistance?" He spoke his best Latin, slowly, so they would understand.

"Count de Braose wants you," said the foremost rider.

"So I have been given to understand," replied the bishop, who explained that he was in the midst of a necessary undertaking and would come as soon as he was finished.

"No," said the horseman. "He wants you now."

"Now," explained the bishop, still smiling, "is not convenient. I will come when my duties allow."

"He doesn't care if it is convenient," replied the soldier. "We have orders to bring you without delay."

He nodded to his two companions, who began dismounting. "Oh, very well," said Asaph, moving quickly to the waiting horse. "The sooner gone, the sooner finished."

With the help of the porter, the bishop mounted the saddle and took up the reins. "Well? Are you coming?" he asked in a voice thick with sarcasm. "Apparently, it does not do to keep the count waiting."

Without another word, the marchogi turned their mounts and rode from the yard out into a dazzling, sun-bright day.

The soldiers led the way across the snow-covered valley, and the bishop followed at an unhurried pace, letting his mind wander as it would. He was still trying to get the measure of these new overlords, and each encounter taught him a new lesson in how to deal with the Ffreinc invaders.

Strictly speaking, they were not Ffreinc, or Franks, at all; they were Normans. There was a difference—not that any of the Britons he knew cared for such fine distinctions. To the people of the valleys beyond the March, the tall strangers were invaders from France—that was all they knew, or needed to know. To the Britons, be they Ffreinc, Angevin, or Norman, they were merely the latest in a long line of would-be conquerors.

Before the Normans, there were the English, and before the English, the Danes, and the Saxons before them. And each invader had carved out dominions for themselves and had gradually been gathered in and woven into the many-coloured mantle that was the Island of the Mighty.

These Normans were, from what he knew of them, ambitious and industrious, capable of great acts of piety and even greater brutality. They built churches wherever they went and filled them on holy days with devout worshippers, who nevertheless lived like hellions the rest of the time. It was said of the Ffreinc that they would blithely burn a village, slaughter all the men, and hang all the women and children, and then hurry off to church lest they miss a Mass.

Be that as it may, the Normans were Christian at least—which was more than could be said for the Danes or English when they had first arrived on Britain's fair shores. That being the case, the Church had decided that the Normans were to be treated as brothers in Christ—albeit as one would treat a domineering, wildly violent, and unpredictable older brother.

There was, so far as Bishop Asaph could see, no other alternative. Had he not urged King Brychan—if once, then a thousand times over the years—to acknowledge the Conqueror, swear fealty, pay his taxes, and do what he could to allow his people to live in peace? *"What?"* Asaph could hear the king cry in outrage. *"Am I to kneel and kiss the rosy rump of that usurping knave? And me a king in my own country? Let me be roasted alive before I stoop to pucker!"*

Well, he had sown his patch and reaped his reward, God save him—and his feckless son, too. Now that was a very shame. Profligate, recklessly licentious, and dissolute the prince may have been—no mistake about it, he was all that and more—yet he had qualities his father lacked, hidden though they might have been. Were they hidden so deeply as to never be recovered? That was the question he had often asked himself.

Alas, the question was moot, and would so forever remain. With Bran's death, the old era passed and a new had begun. Like it or not, the Ffreinc were a fact of life, and they were here to stay. The path was as clear as the choice before him: his only hope of guiding his scattered flock through the storms ahead was to curry favour with the ruling powers. Bishop Asaph intended to get along with them however he could and hope—and pray—for the best.

It was in this frame of mind that Llanelli's deferential senior cleric entered the fortress where Count Falkes de Braose sat blowing on numb fingers in his damp, smoke-filled hall, beside a sputtering fire of green wood.

"Ah, Bishop Asaph," said the count, glancing around as the

churchman was led into the hall. "It is good to see you again. I trust you are well?" Falkes sniffed and drew a sleeve under his runny nose.

"Yes," answered the bishop stiffly, "well enough."

"I, on the other hand, seem destined to endure no end of suffering," opined the count, "what with one thing and another—and this vile weather on top of it all."

"And yet despite your sufferings, you remain alive to complain," observed the bishop, his voice taking on the chill of the room. In Falkes's presence he felt anew the loss of Brother Ffreol and the death of Bran—not to mention the massacre at Wye Ford. Ffreol's death had been an accident— that was what he had been told. The slaughter of the king and warband was, regrettably, a consequence of war he would have to accept. Bran's death was, in his mind, without justification. That the prince had been killed trying to escape without paying the ransom was, he considered, beside the point. Whatever anyone thought of the young man, he was Elfael's rightful king and should have been accorded due respect and courtesy.

"Mind your tongue, priest, if you value it at all," threatened de Braose, who promptly sneezed. "I am in no mood for your insolence."

Duly chastised, Asaph folded his hands and said, "I was told you required my assistance. How may I be of service?"

Waving a long hand toward the empty chair on the other side of the fireplace, de Boase said, "Sit down and I will tell you." When the churchman had taken his seat, the count declared, "It has been determined that Elfael needs a town."

"A town," the bishop repeated. "As it happens, I have long advocated a similar plan."

"Have you indeed?" sniffed Falkes. "Well then. We agree. It is to be a market town." He went on to explain what would be required and when.

The cleric listened, misgiving mounting with every breath. When the count paused to sneeze once more, the bishop spoke up. "Pray, excuse me, my lord, but who do you expect to build this town?"

"Your people, of course," confirmed the count, stretching his hands toward the fire. "Who else?"

"But this is impossible!" declared Asaph. "We cannot build you an entire town in a single summer."

The count's eyes narrowed dangerously. "It will profit both of us."

"Be that as it may, it cannot be done," objected the churchman. "Even if we possessed a ready supply of tools and material, who would do the building?"

"Be at ease," said the count. "You are growing distraught over nothing. Have I not already said that we will use as much existing building work as possible? We will begin with that and add only what is necessary. It does not have to be a city, mind— a small market village will do."

"What *existing* buildings do you mean?"

"I mean," replied the count with exaggerated patience, "those buildings already established—the church and outbuildings and whatnot."

"But . . . but . . . ," cried the bishop in a strangled voice. "That is my monastery you are talking about!"

"*Oui*," agreed the count placidly. "We will begin there. Those structures can easily be converted to other uses. We need only raise a few houses, a grange hall, smithery, and such like. Your monastery serves . . . what? A paltry handful of monks? My town will become a centre of commerce and prosperity for the whole valley. Where is the difficulty?"

"The difficulty, Count de Braose," replied the bishop, fighting to keep his voice level, "is that I will no longer have a monastery."

"Your monastery is no longer required," stated the count. "We need a market town, not a monkery."

"There has been a monastery in this valley for eleven generations," Asaph pointed out. He raised his hands and shook his head vehemently. "No. I will not preside over its destruction. It is out of the question."

The churchman's outright and obstinate refusal irritated de Braose; he felt the warmth of anger rising in him, and his voice grew hushed. "*Au contraire*, bishop," he said, "it *is* the question. See here, we must have a town, and quickly. People are coming to settle in the valley; we need a town."

He paused, gathered his nerves, and then continued in a more conciliatory tone, "The labourers will be drawn from the residents of the valley, and the materials will be supplied from the woods and stone fields of Elfael. I have already undertaken the requisition of the necessary tools and equipment, as well as oxen and wagons for transport. Anything else that you require will be likewise supplied. All that remains," he said in conclusion, "is for you to supply the men. They will be ready to work as soon as the last snow has melted. Is that clear?"

"Which *men* do you imagine I command?" demanded the bishop in his anger at being thrown out of his beloved monastery. "There are no men," he snapped, "only a paltry handful of monks."

"The Welsh," said Falkes. "The people of Elfael, your countrymen—that is who I mean."

"The men of Elfael are gone," scoffed the bishop. "The best were slaughtered on their way to Lundein," he said pointedly, "and the rest fled. The only ones left are those who had nowhere else to go, and if they have any sense at all, they will stay far away from this valley."

The count glared from beneath his brows. "Courtesy, priest," warned de Braose. "Sarcasm ill becomes you."

"Count de Braose," appealed the bishop, "every able-bodied man gathered his family and his flocks and fled the valley the moment you and your soldiers arrived. There *are* no men."

"Then you must find some," said Falkes, growing weary of the bishop's unwillingness to see things from his point of view. "I do not care where you find them, but find them you will."

"And if I decline to aid you in this?"

"Then," replied Falkes, his voice falling to a whisper, "you will quickly learn how I repay disloyalty. I assure you it can be extremely unpleasant."

Bishop Asaph stared in disbelief. "You would threaten a priest of Christ?"

The young count shrugged.

"And this . . . after I delivered the king's treasury to you? This is how I am to be repaid? We agreed that the church would not be harmed. You gave me your word."

"Your church will be in a town," said the count. "Where is the harm?"

"We are under the authority of Rome," Asaph pointed out. "You hold no power over us."

"I hold a royal grant for this commot. Any interference in the establishment of my rule will be reckoned treason, which is punishable by death." He spread his hands as if to indicate that the matter was beyond his immediate control. "But we need not dwell on such unhappy things. You have plenty of time to make the right decision."

"You cannot do this," blurted the bishop. "In the name of God, you cannot."

"Oh, I think you will find that I can," replied Falkes. "One way or another there will be a town in this valley. You can help me, or you and your precious monks will perish. The choice, my dear bishop, is yours."

CHAPTER 20

Winter laid siege to the forest and set up encampment on the hilltops and valleys throughout Elfael. The tiny, branch-framed patch of sky that could be seen from the mouth of the cave was often obscured, cast over with heavy, snow-laden clouds. Bran, warm beneath layered furs and skins, would sometimes wake in the night and listen to the gale as it shrieked through the naked trees outside, beating the bare branches together and sending the snow drifting high and deep over the forest trails and trackways.

The cave, however fierce the storm outside, remained dry and surprisingly comfortable. Bran spent his days dozing and planning his eventual departure; when he grew strong enough to leave this place, he would resume his flight to the north. Having no other plan, that was as good as any. For now, however, he remained content to sleep and eat and recover his strength. Sometimes he would wake to find himself alone, but Angharad always returned by day's end—often with a fat hare or two slung over her shoulder, and once with half a small deer, which she hung from an iron hook set in the rock at the entrance to the cave. In the evenings, she cooked their simple meals and tended his wounds while the pot bubbled on the fire.

And at night, each night of that long winter, the cave was transformed. No longer a rock-bound hole in a cliff face, it became a shining gateway into another world. For each night after they had eaten, Angharad sang.

The first time it took Bran by surprise. Without any hint or warning of what was to come, the old woman disappeared into the dark interior of the cave and returned bearing a harp. Finely made of walnut and elm wood, with pegs of oak, the curve of its shapely prow was polished smooth by years of handling.

Bran watched as she carefully brushed away the dust with the hem of her mantle, tightened the strings, and tuned the instrument. Then, settled on her stool, her head bent near as if in close communion with an old friend, a frown of concentration on her puckered face, Angharad had begun to play—and Bran's bemusement turned to astonished delight.

The music those gnarled old fingers coaxed from the harp strings that night was pure enchantment, woven tapestries of melody, wonder made audible. And when she opened her mouth to sing, Bran felt himself lifted out of himself and transported to places he never knew existed. Like the ancient harp cradled in her lap, Angharad's voice took on a beauty and quality far surpassing the rude instrument. At once agile and sure and gentle, the old woman's singing voice possessed a fluid, supple strength—now soaring like the wind over the far-off mountains, now a bird in flight, now a cresting wave rolling upon the shore.

And was it not strange that when Angharad sang, she herself was subtly changed? No longer the gray hag in a tattered robe, she assumed a more noble, almost regal aspect, a dignity her shabby surroundings ordinarily denied, or at least obscured from view. Well accustomed to her presence now, Bran was no longer repulsed by her appearance; in the same way, he no longer noticed her odd, archaic way of speaking with her thee and thou and wouldst and goest, and all the rest. Neither her aspect nor her speech seemed remarkable; he accepted both the same way he recognized her healing skill: they seemed natural to her, and most naturally her.

In fact, as Bran soon came to appreciate, with a harp in her weathered hands, Angharad became more herself.

Extraordinary as it was to Bran, that first night's performance was merely the seeding of a disused well, or the clearing of a brush-filled spring to let fresh new waters flow. Thereafter, as night after night she took her place on the stool and cradled the harp to her bosom, Angharad's voice, like fine gold, began to take on added luster through use. A voice so rare, Bran mused, must come from somewhere else, from some other time or place, from some other world—perhaps from the very world Angharad's songs described.

The world Angharad sang into being was the Elder World, the realm of princely warriors and their noble lovers. She sang of long-forgotten heroes, kings, and conquerors; of warrior queens and ladies of such beauty that nations rose and fell at the fleeting glance of a limpid eye; of dangerous deeds and queer enchantments; of men and women of ancient renown at whose names the heart rose and the blood raced faster.

She sang of Arianrhod, Pryderi, Llew, Danu, and Carridwen, and all their glorious adventures; of Pwyll and Rhiannon, and their impossible love; of Taliesin, Arthur Pendragon, and wise Myrddin Embries, whose fame made Britain the Island of the Mighty. She sang of the Cauldron of

Rebirth, the Isle of the Everliving, and the making of many-splendoured Albion.

One night, Bran realised that he had not heard such tales since he was a child. This, he thought, was why the songs touched him so deeply. Not since the death of his mother had anyone sung to him. This is why he listened to them all with the same awed attention. Caught up in the stories, he lived them as they took life within him; he became Bladudd, the blighted prince who sojourned seven years in unjust servitude; he became the lowly swineherd Tucmal, who challenged the giant champion Ogygia to mortal combat; he flew with doomed Yspilladan on his beautiful wings of swan feathers and wax; he spent a lonely lifetime in hopeless pining for the love of beautiful, inconstant Blodeuwedd; he was a warrior standing shoulder to shoulder with brave Meldryn Mawr to fight against dread Lord Nudd and his demon horde in a land of ice and snow . . . All these and many more did Bran become.

After each night's song, Angharad laid aside the harp and sat for a time, gazing into the fire as if into a window through which she could see the very things she sang about. After a time, her body would give a little shake, and she would come to herself again, like one emerging from a spell. Sometimes the sense of what he had heard eluded him—she could tell by the frown that knitted his brow and tugged at the corner of his mouth that he had not understood. So, wrapping her arms around her knees as she sat on her three-legged stool, she would gaze into the fire and talk about the story and its inner meaning—the spirit of the song, Angharad called it.

As Bran's knowledge grew, so did his appreciation of the stories themselves. He began to behold possibilities and portents, glimmerings of distant hope, flashes of miracle. The things he heard in Angharad's songs were more than mere fancy—the stuff itinerant minstrels plied—they were tokens of knowledge in another, deeper, rarer form. Perhaps they were even a form of power, but one long dormant. At the very least, these songs were markers along a sacred and ancient pathway that led deep into the heart of the land and its people—his land, his people—a spirit and life that would be crushed out of existence beneath the heavy, unfeeling rule of the coldhearted Ffreinc.

It snowed the day Bran finally regained his feet. Leaning heavily on the old woman, he shuffled with agonizing slowness to the mouth of the cave to stand and watch silent white flakes drift down from the close grey sky to cover the forest in a fine seamless garment of glistening white. He felt the cold air on his face and hands and drew it deep into his lungs, shivering with the icy tingle. The sensation made him cough; it still hurt, but the coughing no longer made him gasp with pain. He braved it for the chance to simply stand and watch the swirling flakes spin and dance as they floated to earth.

After being so long abed, with nothing to look at but the dull grey rock walls of the cave, Bran considered that he had rarely seen anything so beautiful. The dizzying sweep and curl and gyre of the falling flakes made him smile as he turned his light-dazzled eyes to the sky. The old woman seemed to approve of the pleasure he took in the sight; she bore him up with her sturdy peasant strength, watching the enjoyment flit across Bran's thin, haggard features.

When he grew tired, Angharad fetched him a staff. She

returned with a sturdy length of hawthorn; placing it in his hands, she indicated that Bran should go and relieve himself. He hobbled gingerly out into the little clearing; the snow fell on him, the fat, wet flakes stinging sweetly as they alighted on his exposed skin, stuck, and instantly melted.

Although it felt odd standing in the snow within sight of the old woman at the mouth the cave, Bran was glad to be able to stand like a man on his own two feet once more and not have to squat on a pot like a child. He returned to the cave, shaking and sweating and tottering like an invalid no longer able to lift his feet, but beaming as if he had journeyed to the very edge of the earth and lived to tell the tale.

The old woman did not rush out to help him but waited at the cave mouth for each stumbling step to bring him back. When he entered the cave, she took his face between her rough hands and blew her warm breath upon him. "You can speak," she told him, "if you will."

Up until that moment, Bran did not feel he had anything to say, but now all the pent-up words came bubbling up in a confused and tangled rush, only to stick in his throat. He stood swaying on the staff, his tongue tingling with half-formed thoughts and questions, struggling to frame the words until she laid a sooty finger on his lips and said, "Time enough for all your questions anon, but sit down now and rest."

She did not lead him back to his bed as he expected, but sat him on her three-legged stool beside the fire ring. While he warmed himself, she made a meal for them—a stew with meat this time, a nice fat hare, along with some leeks and wild turnips and dried mushrooms gathered through the autumn and dried in the sun. When she had cut up everything and tossed it into the cauldron, she took a few handfuls of ground wheat, some salt, water, honey, dried berries, and dried herbs and began making up little cakes with dough left over from the last batches.

Bran sat and watched her deft fingers prepare the food, and his thoughts slowed and clarified. "What is your name?" he asked at last, and was surprised to hear a voice that sounded much like the one he knew as his own.

She smiled without glancing up and continued kneading the dough for a moment before answering. She shaped a small loaf and set it to warm and rise on a stone near the fire. Then, looking him full in the face, she replied, "I am Angharad."

"Are you a *gwrach*," he asked, "a sorceress?"

She bent to her work once more, and Bran thought she would not answer. "Please, I mean no disrespect," he said. "Only it seems to me that no one can do what you do without the aid of powerful magic." He paused, watching her mix the flour, and then asked again, "Truly, are you a sorceress?"

"I am as you see me," she replied. She shaped another small loaf and put it beside the first. "Different people see different things. What do you see?"

Embarrassed now to tell her what he really thought—that he saw a repulsive crone with bits of leaf and seeds in her hair; that he saw a grotesque hag with smoke-darkened skin in a filthy, grease-stained rag of a dress; that he saw a hunch-backed, shambling wreck of a human being—Bran swallowed his blunt observations and instead replied, "I see the woman who with great skill and wisdom has saved my life."

"I ask you now," she replied, rolling the dough between her calloused palms, "was it a life worth the saving?"

"I do hope you think so," he replied.

Angharad stopped her work. Her face grew still as she

regarded him with an intensity like the lick of a naked flame over his skin. "It is my most fervent hope," she said, her voice solemn as a pledge. "What is more, all of Elfael joins me in that hope."

Bran, feeling suddenly very unworthy of such esteem, lowered his gaze to the fire and said no more that night.

Many more days passed, and Bran's strength slowly increased. Restless and frustrated by his inability to move about as he would like, he sat and moped by the fire, idly feeding twigs and bark and branches to the flames. He knew he was not well enough to leave yet, and even if he could have limped more than a few paces without exhausting himself, winter, with its blizzards and blasts, still raged. That did not hinder him from wishing he could go and making plans to leave.

Angharad, he knew, would not prevent him. She had said as much, and he had no reason to believe otherwise. Indeed, she seemed more than sympathetic to his plight, for she, too, nursed a low-smouldering hatred for the Ffreinc who had seized Elfael, killed the king, and wiped out the warband. Outlanders, she called them, whose presence was an offence under heaven, a stink in the nostrils of God.

While Bran shared this view, he could not see himself effecting any significant change in the situation. Even if he had been so inclined, as the matter stood, he was a man marked for death. If he was caught in Elfael again, Bran knew Count de Braose would not hesitate to finish what he had almost succeeded in accomplishing at the forest's edge.

The fear of that attack would come swarming out of the night to kindle in him an intense passion to escape, to flee to a safe haven in the north, to leave Elfael and never look back. Other times, he saw himself standing over the body of Count de Braose, his lance blade deep in his effete enemy's guts. Occasionally, Bran imagined there might be a way to unite those two conflicting ambitions. Perhaps he could fly away to safety, persuade his kinsmen in the north to join with him, and return to Elfael with a conquering warhost to drive the Ffreinc invaders from the land.

This last idea was late in coming. His impulse from the beginning had been escape, and it still claimed first place in his thoughts. The notion of staying to fight for his land and people had occurred to him in due course—seeded, no doubt, by the stories Angharad told, stories that filled his head with all kinds of new and unfamiliar thoughts.

One morning, Bran rose early to find his wizened guardian gone and himself alone. Feeling rested and able, he set himself the task of walking from the cave to the edge of the clearing. The day was clear and bright, the sun newly risen, the air crisp. He drew a deep breath and felt the tightness in his chest and side—as if inner cords still bound him. His shoulder ached with the cold, but he was used to it now, and it no longer bothered him. His legs felt strong enough, so he began to walk— slowly, with exaggerated care.

The ground sloped down from the mouth of the cave, and he saw the path trodden by Angharad on her errands and, judging by the other tracks in the well-trampled snow, a multitude of forest creatures as well. He hobbled across the open expanse and arrived in good order at the edge of the clearing.

Flushed with the exhilaration of this small achievement, he decided to press himself a little further. He entered the forest, walking with greater confidence along the well-packed snow track. It felt good to move and stretch. The downhill path was gentle, and soon he reached a small rill. The stream was covered by a thin layer of translucent ice; he could hear water running underneath.

The track turned and ran alongside the stream; without thinking, he followed. In a little while he came to a place where the ground dropped away steeply. The water entered a deep cutting carved into the slope and disappeared in a series of stony cascades. The path followed this ravine, but it was far too steep for Bran, so he turned and started back the way he had come. When he reached the place where the path joined the stream, he continued on, soon reaching another impasse. On his left hand, a rocky shelf jutted up, twice his height; on his right the stream flowed at the bottom of a rough defile, and dead ahead, the trunk of a fallen elm blocked the path like a gnarled, black, bark-covered wall.

He did not trust his ability to clamber over the fallen log —in his present condition, he did not dare risk it. He had no choice but to retrace his steps, so he turned around and started back to the cave. It was then he learned that he had walked farther than he intended, and also that he had seriously mis-judged the slight uphill climb.

The rise was steep, and the snow slick underfoot. Twice he slipped and fell; he caught himself both times, but each fall was accompanied by a sharp tearing sensation—as if his wounds were being ripped open once more. The second time, he paused on his hands and knees in the snow and waited until the waves of pain subsided.

After that, he proceeded much more carefully, but the exer-tion soon taxed his rapidly tiring muscles; he was forced to stop to rest and catch his breath every few dozen paces. Despite the cold, he began to sweat. His tunic and mantle were soon soaked through, and his damp clothes grew clammy and froze, chilling him to the bone. By the time the cave came into sight, he was shaking with cold and gasping with pain.

Head down, wheezing like a wounded bear, Bran shuffled the last hundred paces to the cave, staggered in, and collapsed on his bed. He lay a long time, shivering, too weak to pull the fleeces over himself.

This was how Angharad found him sometime later when she returned with a double brace of woodcocks.

Bran sensed a movement and opened his eyes to see her bending over him, the birds dangling in her hand and her brow creased with concern. "You went out," she said simply.

"I did," he said, his voice husky with fatigue. He clenched his jaw tightly to keep his teeth from chattering.

"You should not have done so." Laying aside the birds, she straightened his limbs in his bed, then arranged the fleeces over him.

"I am sorry," he murmured, sinking gratefully beneath the coverings. He closed his eyes and shivered.

Angharad built up the fire again and set about preparing the woodcocks for their supper. Bran dozed on and off through the rest of the day; when he finally roused himself once more, it was dark outside. The cave was warm and filled with the aroma of roasting meat. He sat up stiffly and rubbed his chest; the wound was sore, and he felt a burning deep inside.

The old woman saw him struggle to rise and came to him. "You will stay abed," she told him.

"No," he said, far more forcefully than he felt. "I want to get up."

"You have overtired yourself and must rest now. Tonight you will stay abed."

"I won't argue," he said, accepting her judgement. "But will you still sing to me?"

Angharad smiled. "One would almost think you liked my singing," she replied.

That night after supper, Bran lay in his bed, aching and sore, skin flushed with fever, barely able to keep his eyes open. But he listened to that incomparable voice, and as before, the cave disappeared and he travelled to that Elder Realm, where Angharad's tales took life. That night he listened as, for the first time, she sang him a tale of King Raven.

CHAPTER 21

Angharad settled herself beside Bran on her three-legged stool. She plucked a harp string and silenced it with the flat of her hand. Closing her eyes, she held her head to one side, as if listening to a voice he could not hear. He watched her shadow on the cave wall, gently wavering in the firelight as she cradled the harp to her breast and began to stroke the lowest string—softly, gently releasing a rich, sonorous note into the silence of the cave.

Angharad began to sing—a low whisper of exhaled breath that gathered force to become an inarticulate moan deep in her throat. The harp note pulsed quicker, and the moan became a cry. The cry became a word, and the word a name: *Rhi Bran*.

Bran heard it, and the small hairs on his arms stood up.

Again and again, Angharad invoked the name, and Bran felt his heart quicken. Rhi Bran. King Raven—his own name and his rightful title—but cast in a newer, fiercer, almost frightening light.

Angharad's fingers stroked a melody from the harp, her voice rose to meet it, and the tale of King Raven began. This is what she sang:

In the Elder Time, when the dew of Creation was still fresh on the ground, Bran Bendigedig awakened in this worlds-realm. A beautiful boy, he grew to be a handsome man, renowned amongst his people for his courage and valour. And his valour was such that it was exceeded only by his virtue, which was exceeded only by his wisdom, which was itself exceeded only by his honesty. Bran the Blesséd he was called, and no one who saw him doubted that if ever there was a man touched by the All Wise and granted every boon in abundance, it was he. Thus, he possessed all that was needful for a life of utter joy and delight, save one thing only. A single blessing eluded him, and that was contentment.

Bran Bendigedig's heart was restless, always seeking, never finding—for if it was known what would satisfy his unquiet heart, that knowledge was more completely hidden than a single drop of water in all the oceans of the world. And the knowledge of his lack grew to become a fire deep inside him that burned his bones and filled his mouth with the taste of ashes.

One day, when he could endure his discontent no longer, he put on his best boots, kissed his mother and father farewell, and began to walk. "I will not stop walking until I have found the thing which will quell my restless heart and fill this hunger in my soul."

Thus, he began a journey through many lands, through kingdoms and dominions of every kind. At the end of seven years, he reached a distant shore and gazed across a narrow sea, where he beheld the fairest island that he or anyone else had ever seen. Its white cliffs glowed in the dying sunlight like a wall of fine pale gold, and larks soared high above the green-topped hills, singing in the gentle evening air. He wanted nothing more than to go to the island without delay, but night was coming, and he knew he could not reach the far shore in time, so he settled down to spend the night on the strand, intending to cross over the narrow sea with the next morning's new light.

Unable to sleep, he lay on the beach all night long, listening to the fitful wash of the waves over the pebbles, feeling as if his heart would burst for restlessness. When the sun rose again, he rose with it and looked out at the many-splendoured island as it lay before him in the midst of the silver sea. Then, as the rising sun struck the white cliffs, setting them aglow with a light that dazzled the eyes, Bran struck out. Drawing himself up to full height, he grew until his head brushed the clouds, whereupon he waded out into the narrow sea, which reached only to the knot of his belt. He reached the opposite shore in nine great strides, emerging from the water at his normal height.

He spread his arms to the sun, and while he stood waiting for the bright rays to dry his clothes, he heard the most delightful music, and he turned to see a lady on a milk-white horse approaching a little way off. The music arose from a flute that she played as she cantered along the water's edge in the sweet, honeyed light of the rising sun. Her hair shone with the brightness of a flame, and her skin was firm and soft. Her limbs were fine and straight, her gown was yellow satin, edged in blue, and her eyes were green as new grass or apples in summer.

As she came near, she caught sight of Bran, standing alone on the strand, and she stopped playing. "I give you good greeting, sir," she said; her voice, so light and melodious, melted Bran in his innermost parts. "What is your name?"

"I am Bran Bendigedig," said he. "I am a stranger here."

"Yet you are welcome," said the lady. "I see that you are beguiled by the sight of this fair island."

"That I am," Bran confessed. "But no less than by the sight of you, my lady. If ever I boast of seeing a fairer face in all this wide world, may I die a liar's death. What is your name?"

"Would that you had asked me anything else," she told him sadly, "for I am under a strong *geas* never to reveal my name to anyone until the day of Albion's release."

"If that is all that prevents you, then take heart," Bran replied boldly, for the moment she spoke those first words in his ear, he knew beyond all doubt that the thing required to bring contentment to his restless heart was the name of the lady before him—just to know her name and, knowing it, to possess it and, possessing it, to hold her beside him forever. With her as his wife, his heart would find peace at last. "Only tell me who or what Albion might be," Bran said, "and I will achieve its release before the sun has run its course."

"Would that you had promised anything else," the lady told him. "Albion is the name of this place, and it is the fairest island known. Ten years ago a plague came to these shores, and it is this which now devastates the island. Every morning I come to the sea-strand in the time-between-times in the hope of finding someone who can break the wicked spell that holds Albion in thrall."

"Today your search has ended," replied Bran, his confidence undimmed. "Only tell me what to do, and it will be done."

"Though your spirit may be bold and your hand strong, Albion's release will take more than that. Many great men have tried, but none have succeeded, for the plague is no ordinary illness or disease. It is an evil enchantment, and it takes the form of a race of giants who by their mighty strength cause such havoc and devastation that my heart quails at the mere mention of them."

"Fear for nothing, noble lady," Bran said. "The All Wise in his boundless wisdom has granted me every good gift, and I can do wonderfully well whatever I put my hand to."

At this the lady smiled, and, oh, her smile was even more radiant than the sunlight on the shining cliffs. "The day you deliver Albion, I will give you my name—and more than that, if you only ask."

"Then rest assured," replied Bran, "that on that very day, I will return to ask for your hand and more— I will ask for your heart also." The lady bent her shapely neck in assent and then told him what he had to do to release Albion from the evil spell and break the geas that bound her.

Bran the Blesséd listened well to all she said; then,

bidding her farewell, he started off. He came to a river that the lady had told him to expect, then followed it to the centre of the isle. For three days and nights he walked, stopping only now and then to drink from the pure waters of the river, for his heart burned within him at the thought of marrying the most beautiful woman in the world.

As the sun rose on the fourth day, he came to a great dark wood—the forest from which all other forests in the world had their beginning. He entered the forest, and just as the lady had told him, after walking three more days, he came to a glade where two roads crossed. He strode to the centre of the cross-roads and sat down to wait. After a time, he heard the sound of someone approaching and looked up to see an old man with a white beard hobbling toward him. The man was bent low to the ground beneath heavy bundles of sticks he was carrying, so low that his beard swept the ground before him.

Seeing this man whom the lady had told him to expect, Bran jumped up and hailed him. "You there! You see before you a man of purpose who would speak to you."

"And *you* see before *you* a man who was once a king in his own country," the man replied. "A little respect would become you."

"My lord, forgive me," replied Bran. "May I come near and speak to you?"

"You may approach—not that I could prevent you," answered the old man. Nevertheless, he motioned Bran to come near. "What is your name?" asked the old man.

"I am Bran Bendigedig," he answered. "I have come to seek the release of Albion from the plague that assails it."

"Too bad for you," said the bent-backed man, straining beneath his load of sticks. "Many good men have tried to break the spell; as many as have tried, that many have failed."

"It may be as you say," offered Bran, "but I doubt there are two men like me in all the world. If there is another, I have never heard of him." He explained how he had met the noble lady on the strand and had pledged himself to win her hand.

"I ween that you are a bold man, perhaps even a lucky one," said the aged noble. "But though you were an army of like-minded, hardy men, you would still fail. The enchantment that besets Albion cannot be broken except by one thing, and one thing alone."

"What is that thing?" asked Bran. "Tell me, and then stand back and watch what I will do."

"It is not for me to say," replied the former lord.

Pointing to the road that led deeper into the forest, the old man said, "Go down that road until you come to a great forest, and continue on until you come to a glade in the centre of the wood. You will know it by a mound that is in the centre of the glade. In the centre of the mound is a standing stone, and at the foot of the standing stone, you will find a fountain. Beside the fountain is a slab of white marble, and on the slab you will find a silver bowl attached by a chain so that it may not be stolen away. Dip a bowl of water from the fountain and dash it upon the marble slab. Then stand aside and wait. Be patient, and it will be revealed to you what to do."

Bran thanked the man and journeyed on along the forest road. In a little while, he began seeing signs of devastation of which the noble lady had warned him: houses burned; fields trampled flat; hills gouged out; streams diverted from their natural courses; whole trees uprooted, overturned, and thrust back into the hole with roots above and branches below. The mutilated bodies of dead animals lay everywhere on the ground, their limbs rent, their bodies torn asunder. Away to the east, a great fire burned a swathe through the high wooded hills, blotting out the sun and turning the sky black with smoke.

Bran looked upon this appalling destruction. *Who could do such a thing?* he wondered, and his heart moved within him with anger and sorrow for the ruined land.

He moved on, walking through desolation so bleak it made tears well up in his eyes to think what had been so cruelly destroyed. After two days, he came to the glade in the centre of the forest. There, as the old man had said, he saw an enormous mound, and from the centre of this mound rose a tall, slender standing stone. Bran ascended the mound and stood before the narrow stone; there at his feet he saw a clear-running fountain and, beside it, the marble slab with the silver bowl attached by a thick chain. Kneeling down, he dipped the silver bowl into the fountain, filled it, and then dashed the water over the pale stone.

Instantly, there came a peal of thunder loud enough to shake the ground, the wind blew with uncommon fury, and hail fell from the sky. So fiercely did it fall that Bran feared it would beat through his skin and flesh to crack his very bones. Clinging to the standing stone, he pressed himself hard against it for shelter, covered his head with his arms, and bore the assault as best he could.

In a short while the hail and wind abated, and the thunder echoed away. He heard then a grinding noise—like that of a millstone as it crushes the hard seeds of grain. He looked and saw a crevice open in the ground and a yellow vapour issuing from the gap like a foul breath. In the midst of the yellow fumes there appeared a woman—so old and withered that she looked as if she might be made of sticks wrapped in a dried leather sack.

Her hair—what little remained—was a tangled, ratty mass of leaves and twigs, moss and feathers, and bird droppings; her mouth was a slack gash in the lower part of her face, through which Bran could see but a single rotten tooth; her clothing was a filthy rag so threadbare it resembled cobwebs, and so small her withered dugs showed above one end and her spindly thighs below the other. Her face was more skull than visage, her eyes sunken deep in their sockets, where they gleamed like two shiny stones.

Bran took but a single brief look before turning away, swallowing his disgust as she advanced toward him.

"You there!" she called, her voice cracking like a dry husk. "Do you know what you have done? Do you have any idea?"

Half-shielding his eyes with his hand, Bran offered a sickly smile and answered, "I have done that which was required of me, nothing more."

"Oh, have you now?" queried the hag. "By heaven's lights, you will soon wish you had not done that."

"Woman," said Bran, "I am wishing that already!"

"Tell me your name and what it is that you want," said the woman, "and I will see if there is any help for you."

"I am Bran Bendigedig, and I have come to break the vile enchantment that ravages Albion."

"I did not ask *why* you have come," the old crone laughed. "I asked what it is that you want."

"I was born with an unquiet heart that has never been satisfied—not that it is any of your affair," Bran told her.

"Silence!" screeched the woman in a voice so loud that Bran clapped his hands over his ears lest he lose his hearing. "Respect is a valuable treasure that costs nothing. If you would keep your tongue, see that it learns some courtesy."

"Forgive me," Bran spluttered. "It was not my wish to offend you. If I spoke harshly just then, it was merely from impatience. You see, I have met a noble lady who is all my heart's desire, and I have set myself to win her if I can. To do that, I have vowed to rid Albion of the plague that even now wreaks such havoc on this fairest of islands."

The wretched hag put her face close to Bran's—so close that Bran could smell the stink she gave off and had to pinch his nostrils shut. She squinted her eyes with the intensity of her scrutiny. "Is that what you are about?" she asked at last.

"I am," replied Bran. "If you can help me, I will be in your debt. If not, only tell me someone who can, and I will trouble you no more."

"You ask my help," said the ancient woman, "and though you may not know it, you could not have asked a better creature under heaven, for help you shall receive—though it comes at a cost."

"It is ever the way of things," sighed Bran. "What is the price?"

"I will tell you how to break the wicked enchantment that binds Albion—and I hope you succeed, for unless you do, Albion is lost and will soon be a wasteland."

"And the price?" asked Bran, feeling the restlessness beginning to mount like a sneeze inside him.

"The price is this: that on the day Albion is released, you will take the place of the man the giants have killed."

"That is no burden to me," remarked Bran with relief. "I thought it would be more."

"There are some who think the cost too great." She shrugged her skinny shoulders, and Bran could almost hear them creak. "Nevertheless, that is the price. Do you agree?"

"I do," said Bran the Blesséd. "In truth, I would pay whatever you asked to break the curse and win my heart's desire."

"Done! Done!" crowed the old woman in triumph. "Then listen well, and do exactly as I say."

Laying her bony fingers on Bran's strong arm, the

hag led him from the mound and into the ruined forest. They passed through death and devastation that would have made the very stones weep, and walked on until they came to a high hill that was topped by a magnificent white fortress. At the base of the hill flowed a river; once sparkling and clear, it now ran ruddy brown with the blood of the slaughtered.

Pointing to the fortress, the hag said, "Up there you will find the tribe of giants who have enthralled this fair island and whose presence is a very plague. Kill them all and the spell will be broken, and your triumph will be assured."

"If that is all," replied Bran grandly, "why did you not tell me sooner? It is as good as done." He made to start off at once.

The ancient crone prevented him, saying, "Wait! There is more. You should know also that the giants have slain the Lord of the Forest and taken possession of his cauldron, called the Cauldron of Rebirth on account of its miraculous virtue: that whatever living creature, man or animal it matters not, though he were dead and dismembered, mutilated, torn into a thousand pieces, and those pieces eaten, if any part of the corpse is put into the cauldron when it is on the boil, life will return, and the creature will emerge hale and whole once more."

Amazed, Bran exclaimed, "Truly, that is a wonder! Rest assured that I will stop at nothing to reclaim this remarkable vessel."

"Do so," promised the hag, "and your deepest desire will be granted."

Off he went, crossing the river of blood and ascending the high hill. As Bran drew closer, he saw that the white fortress was not, as he had assumed, built of choice marble, but of the skulls and bones of murdered beasts and humans, used like so much rubble to erect the high white walls, turrets, and towers. A sickening smell rose from the bones, which, though it made him gag, also raised Bran's fury against the giants.

Boldly he approached the gate, and boldly entered. There was neither guard nor porter to prevent him, so he strode across the courtyard and entered the hall. However much the courtyard stank, the odour inside the hall was that much worse.

From the hall, he could hear the sound of a great roister. He crept to the massive door, peered inside, and instantly wished he had not. He saw seven giants, the least of which was three times the height of any human man, and the greatest amongst them was three times the height of the smallest. Each giant was a gruesomely ugly brute with pale, blotchy skin; shaggy, long hair that hung down his broad back in nasty, tangled hanks; and a single large eyebrow across his thick, overhanging forehead. Each giant was more hideous than the last, with fat, fleshy lips and an enormous, long nose shaped like the beak of a malformed bird. Their necks were short and squat, their arms ridiculously long, and their legs thin through the shank and fat at the thigh. They all carried clubs of iron, which any two human men would have found a burden to lift.

Three long tables filled the hall, and on those tables was a feast of roast meat of every kind of creature under heaven, which the giants ate with ravenous abandon. While they ate—rending the carcasses with their hands, stuffing the meat down their stubby necks, spitting out the bones, and then washing it all down with great, greedy draughts of rendered lard and fat drawn from a score of vats around the hall—they laughed and sang in disagreeable voices and raised such a revel that Bran's head throbbed like a beaten drum with the noise.

The Blesséd Bran stood for a moment, gazing upon the carnage of the feast, and felt an implacable rage rise inside him. Then, across the hall, he spied an enormous kettle of burnished bronze and copper, silver and gold—so large it could easily hold sixteen human men at once; or three teams of oxen; or nine horses; or seven stags, three deer, and a fawn. A fire of oak logs blazed away beneath the prodigious vessel.

Seeing this, Bran thought, *The prize is within my grasp,* and taking a deep breath, he stepped boldly through the door. "Giants!" he called, "The feast is over! You have eaten your last corpse. I give you fair warning— doom is upon you!"

The giants were startled to hear this loud voice, and they were even more surprised when they saw the tiny man who made such a bold and foolish claim. They laughed in their beards and blew their noses at him. Two of them bared their horrible backsides, and the others mocked him with rude gestures. Up rose the chief of the monstrous clan, and he was the most repulsive brute of them all; taller than seven normal men, he was greasy with the blood of the meat he had been gorging.

Sneering, he opened his gate of a mouth and

bellowed, "What you lack in size, you make up for in stupidity. I've eaten five of your race already today and will gladly count you amongst them. What is your name, little man?"

"Call me *Silidons*, for such I am," said Bran, hiding his true name behind a word that means "nobody." "You will have to kill me first, and I have never lost a fight I entered."

"Then you cannot have entered many. Today we will put you to the test." So saying, the giant lifted his massive hand and commanded two of his nearest fellows forward. "Seize him! Show this imbecile how we deal with anyone foolish enough to oppose us!"

The two giants rose and lumbered forth, their fleshy lips wide in distorted grins. Bran stepped forward, and as he did so, he grew in size to half again his height; another step doubled his size. Now the crown of his head came up to the giants' chests.

The giants saw this and were astonished but undaunted. "Is that the best you can do?" they laughed. Taking up their iron clubs, they swung at Bran, first one way and then the other. Bran leapt over the first and ducked under the second; then, leaping straight up into the air, he lashed out with his foot and caught one of the giants in the middle of the forehead. The great brute dropped his club and grabbed his head. Snatching up the enormous weapon, Bran swung with all his might and crushed the skull of the giant, who gave out a throaty groan and lay still.

Seeing his comrade bested so easily infuriated the second attacker. Roaring with rage, he whirled his heavy club around his head and smashed it down, cracking the flagstones. Bran stepped neatly aside as the club struck the floor, then quickly climbed the broad shaft as if it were an iron mounting block. When the giant lifted the club, Bran leapt into the brute's face and drove both fists into the giant's eyes. The ghastly creature screamed and fell to his knees, clutching his eyes with both hands. Calmly, Bran picked up the club and swung hard. The brute pitched forward onto his face and rose no more.

Looking around, he called, "Who will be next?"

Crazed with fear and spitting with rage, the remaining giants rose as one and charged Bran, who ran to meet them, growing bigger with every step until he was a head taller than the tallest. Four blows were thrown, one after another, and four giants fell, leaving only the enormous chieftain still on his feet. Not only bigger, he was also quicker than the others, and before Bran could turn, he reached out and seized Bran by the throat. Drawing a deep breath, Bran willed his neck to become a column of white granite; with all his strength the giant chieftain could not break that thick column.

Meanwhile, Bran took hold of the giant's protruding ears. Grabbing one in each hand, he yanked hard, pulling the giant chieftain forward and driving the point of his granite chin right between the odious monster's bulging eyes. The giant's knees buckled, and he tumbled backward like a toppled pine tree, striking his head on the stone floor and expiring before he could draw his next breath.

Triumphant, Bran strode to the hearth and plucked the still-bubbling cauldron from the flames. Grasping the miraculous pot in his strong arms of stone, Bran walked from the castle of bone, back to the world outside, where he once again met the ancient hag who was waiting for him.

The hag jumped up and scurried to meet him. "Truly, you are a mighty champion!" she cried. "From this day you are my husband."

Bran glanced at her askance. "Lady, if lady you be, I am no such thing," he declared. "You said I would achieve my greatest desire, and marriage to you is far from that. And even if I were so minded, I could not, for I am promised to another."

The wild-haired hag opened her gaping, toothless mouth and laughed in Bran's face. "O man of little understanding! Do you not know that whoever possesses the Cauldron of Rebirth is the Lord of the Forest? He is my husband, and I am his wife." Reaching out, she seized him with her scaly, clawlike hands and pressed her drooling lips close to his face.

Repulsed, Bran reared back and shook off her grip. He started to run away, but she pursued him with uncanny swiftness. Bran changed himself into a stag and bolted away at speed, but the hag became a wolf and raced after him. When Bran saw that he could not elude her that way, he changed into a rabbit; the hag changed into a fox and matched him stride for stride. When he saw that she was gaining on him, Bran changed into an otter, slid into the clear-running stream, and swam away. The hag, however, changed into a great salmon and caught him by the tail.

Bran felt the hag's teeth biting into him and leapt

from the stream, dragging the salmon with him. Once out of the water, the salmon loosed its hold, and instantly Bran turned into a raven and flew away.

But the hag, now become an eagle, flew up, seized him in her strong talons, and pulled him from the sky. "You led me on a fine chase, but I have caught you, my proud raven!" she cackled with glee, resuming her former repulsive shape. "And now you must marry me."

Squirming and pecking at the bony fingers clasped tightly around him, Bran, still in the form of a raven, cried, "I never will! I have promised myself to another. Even now she is waiting for me on the shining shore."

"Bran, Bran," said the hag, "do you not know that I am that selfsame woman?" Smiling grotesquely, she told him all that had happened to him since meeting him that very morning on the strand where she went every day in the guise of a beautiful lady to search for a champion to become her mate. "It was myself you promised to take to wife," she concluded. "Now lie with me and do your duty as a husband."

Horrified, Bran cried out, "I never will!"

"Since you refuse," said the old woman, still clutching him between her hands, "you leave me no choice!" With that, she spat into her right hand and rubbed her spittle on Bran's sleek head, saying, "A raven you are, and a raven you shall remain—until the day you fulfil your vow to take me to wife."

The hag released Bran then, and he found that though he could still change his shape at will—now one creature, now another—he always assumed the form of a raven in the end. Thus, he took up his duties as Rhi

Bran the Hud, Lord of the Forest, whom some call the Dark Enchanter of the Wood. And from that day to this, he abides as a great black raven still.

The last note faded into silence. Laying aside the harp, Angharad gazed at the rapt young man before her and said, "That is the song of King Raven. Dream on it, my son, and let it be a healing dream to you."

PART THREE

THE MAY
DANCE

arm winds from the sea brought an early spring, and a wet one. From Saint David's Day to the Feast of Saint John, the sky remained a low, slate-grey expanse of dribbling rain that swelled the streams and rivers throughout the Marches. Then the skies finally cleared, and the land dried beneath a sun so bright and warm that the miserable Outlanders in their rusting mail almost forgot the hardships of the winter past.

The first wildflowers appeared, and with them wagons full of tools and building materials, rolling into the valley from Baron de Braose's extensive holdings in the south. The old dirt trackways were not yet firm enough, but Baron de Braose was eager to begin, so the first wagons to reach the valley churned the soft earth into deep, muddy trenches to swamp all those who would come after. From morning to night the balmy air was filled with the calls of the drivers, the crack of whips, and the bawling of the oxen as they struggled to haul the heavy-laden vehicles through the muck.

The Cymry also returned to the lower valleys from their winter sanctuaries in the high hills. Although most had fled the cantref, a few remained—farmers for the most part, who could not, like the sheep and cattle herders, simply take their property elsewhere—and a few of the more stubborn herdsmen who had contemplated their choices over the winter and concluded that they were unwilling to give up good grazing land to the Ffreinc. The farmers began readying their fields for sowing, and the herdsmen returned to the pastures. Following the age-old pattern of the clans from time past remembering—working through the season of sun and warmth, storing up for the season of rain and ice, when they took their ease in communal dwellings around a shared hearth—the people of the region silently reasserted their claim to the land of their ancestors. For the first time since the arrival of the Ffreinc, Elfael began to assume something of its former aspect.

Count Falkes de Braose considered the reappearance of the British a good sign. It meant, he thought, that the people had decided to accept life under his rule and would recognise him as their new overlord. He still intended to press them into helping build the town the baron required—and the castles, too, if needed—but beyond that he had no other plans for them. So long as they did what they were told, and with swift obedience, he and the local population would achieve a peaceable association. Of course, any opposition to his rule would be met with fierce retaliation—still, that was the way of the world, and only to be expected, no?

Anticipating a solid season of industry—a town to raise and border fortifications to be established—the count sent a messenger to the monastery to remind Bishop Asaph of his duty to supply British labourers to supplement the ranks of builders the baron would provide. He then busied himself with supervising the allotment of tools and materials for the various sites. Together with the architect and master mason, he inspected each of the sites to make sure that nothing had been overlooked and all was in readiness. He personally marked out the boundaries for the various towers and castle ditch enclosures, spending long days beneath the blue, cloud-crowded sky, and counted it work well done. He wanted to be ready when the baron's promised builders arrived. Time was short, and there was much to be done before the autumn storms brought an end to the year's labour.

Nothing would be allowed to impede the progress he meant to make. Only too aware that his future hung by the slender thread of his uncle, the baron's, good pleasure, Falkes agonised over his arrangements; he ate little and slept less, worrying himself into a state of near exhaustion over the details large and small.

On a sunny, windblown morning, the master mason approached Falkes on one of his visits to the building sites. "If it please you, sire, I would like to begin tomorrow," he said. Having supervised the raising of no fewer than seven castles in Normandie, Master Gernaud—with his red face beneath his battered straw hat and faded yellow sweat rag around his neck—was a solid veteran of the building trade. These were to be the first castles he had raised outside France.

"Nothing would please me more," the count replied. "Pray begin, Master Gernaud, and may God speed your work."

"We will soon have need of the rough labourers," the mason pointed out.

"It has been arranged," replied the count with confidence. "You shall have them."

Two days passed, however, and none of the required British volunteers appeared.

When, after a few more days, not a single British worker had come to any of the building sites, Falkes de Braose sent for Bishop Asaph and demanded to know why.

"Have you spoken to them?" asked Falkes, leaning on the back of his oversized chair. The hall was empty save for the count and his guest; every available hand—excepting his personal servants and a few soldiers required to keep the fortress in order—had been sent to help with the construction.

"I have done as you required," replied the churchman in a tone suggesting he could do no more than that.

"Did you tell them we must have the town established? Each day delayed is another day we must work in the winter cold."

"I told them," said Asaph.

"Then where are they?" queried Falkes, growing irate at the inconvenience perpetrated by the absent locals. "Why don't they come?"

"They are farmers, not quarrymen or masons. It is ploughing season, and the fields must be prepared for sowing. They dare not delay; otherwise there will be no harvest." He paused, plucked up his courage, and added, "Last year's harvest was very poor, as you know. And unless they are allowed to put in their crops, the people will starve. They are hungry enough already."

"What?" cried Falkes. "Do you suggest this is in any way my fault? They fled their holdings. The ignorant louts were in no danger, but they fled anyway. The blame lies with them."

"I merely state the fact that the farmers of Elfael were prevented from gathering in the harvest last year, and now there is precious little ready food in the valleys."

"They should have thought of that before they ran off and abandoned their fields!" Falkes cried, slapping the back of the chair with his long hands. "What of their cattle? Let them slaughter a few of those if they're hungry."

"The cattle are the only wealth they possess, lord count. They cannot slaughter them. Anyway, the herds must be built up through the summer if there is to be food enough to see them through the winter."

"This is not my concern!" Falkes insisted. "This problem is of their own making and will not be laid at *my* door."

"Count de Braose," said the bishop in a conciliatory tone, "they are simple folk, and they were afraid of your troops. Their king and warband had just been slain. They feared for their lives. What did you expect—that they would rush with glad hosannas to welcome you?"

"That tongue of yours will get you hanged yet, priest," warned de Braose, wagging a long finger in warning. "I would guard it if I were you."

"Will that help raise your castles?" asked Asaph. "I merely point out that if they ran away, it was for good reason. They are afraid, and nothing they have seen from you has changed that."

"I meant them no harm," insisted the count, growing petulant. "Nor do I mean them harm now. But the town *will* be raised, and the fortresses *will* be built. This commot *will* be settled and civilised, and that is the end of it." Crossing his arms over his narrow chest, Falkes thrust out his chin as if daring the churchman to disagree.

Bishop Asaph, squeezed between the rock of the count's demands and the hard place of his people's obstinate resistance to any such scheme, decided there was no harm in trying to mitigate the damage and ingratiate himself with the count. "I see you are determined," he said. "Might I offer a suggestion?"

"If you must," granted Falkes.

"It is only this. Why not wait until the fields have been sown and planted?" suggested the churchman. "Once the crops are in, the people will be more amenable to helping with the building. Grant them a reprieve until the sowing is finished. They will thank you for it, and it will demonstrate your fairness and good faith."

"*Dieu défend!* Delay the building? That I will *not* do!" cried Falkes. He took three quick strides and then turned on the bishop once more. "Here now! I give you one more day to inform the people and assemble the required labourers—the two strongest men from each family or settlement. They will come to your monastery, where they will be met and assigned to one of the building sites." Glaring at the frowning cleric, he said, "Is that understood?"

"Of course," the bishop replied diffidently. "But what if they refuse to come? I can only relay your demands. I am not their lord—"

"But I am!" snapped Falkes. "And yours as well." When the bishop made no reply, he added, "If they fail to comply, they will be punished."

"I will tell them."

"See that you do." Falkes dismissed the churchman then. As Asaph reached the door, the count added, "I will come to the monastery yard at dawn tomorrow. The workers will be ready."

The bishop nodded, departing without another word. Upon arriving at the monastery, he commanded the porter to sound the bell and convene the monks, who were quickly dispatched to the four corners of the cantref to carry the count's summons to the people.

When Count de Braose and his men arrived at the

monastery the next morning, they found fifteen surly men and four quarrelsome boys standing in the mostly empty yard with their bishop. The count rode through the gate, took one look at the desultory crew, and cried, "What? Is this all? Where are the others?"

"There are no others," replied Bishop Asaph.

"I distinctly said *two* from every holding," complained the count. "I thought I made that clear."

"Some of the holdings are so small that there is only one man," explained the bishop. Indicating the sullen gathering, he said, "These represent every holding in Elfael." Looking at the unhappy faces around him, he asked the count, "Did you think there would be more?"

"There *must* be more!" roared Falkes de Braose. "Work is already falling behind for lack of labourers. We must have more."

"That is as it may be, but I have done as you commanded."

"It is not enough."

"Then perhaps you should have invaded a more populous cantref," snipped the cleric.

"Do not mock me," growled the count, turning away. He strode to his horse. "Find more workers. Bring them in. Bring everybody in—women too. Bring them all. I want them here tomorrow morning."

"My lord count," said the bishop, "I beg you to reconsider. The ploughing will soon be finished. That is of utmost concern, and it cannot wait."

"My *town* cannot wait!" shouted Falkes. Raising himself to the saddle, he said, "I will not be commanded by the likes of you. Have fifty workers here tomorrow morning, or one holding will burn."

"Count de Braose!" cried the bishop. "You cannot mean that, surely."

"I do most certainly mean exactly what I say. I have been too lenient with you people, but that leniency is about to end."

"But you must reconsider—"

"Must? Must?" the count sneered, stepping his horse close to the cleric, who shrank away. "Who are you to tell me what I *must* or *must not* do? Have the fifty, or lose a farm."

With that, the count wheeled his horse and rode from the yard. As the Ffreinc reached the gate, one of the boys picked up a stone and let fly, striking the count in the middle of the back. Falkes whirled around angrily but could not tell who had thrown the rock; all were standing with hands at their sides, staring with dour contempt, men as well as boys.

Unwilling to allow the insult to stand, Falkes rode back to confront them. "Who threw the stone?" he demanded. When no one answered, he called to the bishop. "Make them tell me!"

"They do not speak Latin," replied the churchman coolly. "They only speak Cymry and a little Saxon."

"Then you ask for me, priest!" said the count. "And be quick about it. I want an answer."

The bishop addressed the group, and there was a brief discussion. "It seems that no one saw anything, count," the cleric reported. "But they all vow to keep a close watch for such disgraceful behaviour in the future."

"Do they indeed? Well, for one, at least, there will be no future." Indicating a smirking lad standing off to one side, the count spoke a command in Ffreinc to his soldiers, and instantly two of the marchogi dismounted and rounded on the panic-stricken youth.

The elder Britons leapt forward to intervene but were

prevented by the swiftly drawn swords of the remaining soldiers. After a momentary scuffle and much shouting, the offending youngster was marched to the centre of the yard, where he was made to stand while the count, drawing his sword, approached his quivering, bawling prisoner.

"Wait! Stop!" cried the bishop. "No, please! Don't kill him!" Asaph rushed forward to place himself between the count and his victim, but two of the soldiers caught him and dragged him back. "Please, spare the child. He will work for you all summer if you spare him. Do not kill him, I beg you."

Count de Braose tested the blade and then raised his arm and, with a fury born of frustration, yanked down the boy's trousers and struck the boy's exposed backside with the flat of his sword—once, twice, and again. Thin red welts appeared on the pale white skin, and the boy began to wail with impotent fury.

Satisfied with the punishment, the count sheathed his sword, then raised his foot and placed his boot against the crying lad's wounded rump and gave him a hard shove. The boy, his legs tangled in his trousers, stumbled and fell on his chin in the dirt, where he lay, weeping hot tears of pain and humiliation.

The count turned from his victim, strode to his horse, and mounted the saddle once more. "Tomorrow I want fifty men here, ready to work," he announced. "Fifty, do you hear?" He paused as the bishop translated his words. "Fifty workmen or, by heaven, a farm will burn." His words were still ringing in the yard as he and his soldiers rode out.

The next morning there were twenty-eight workers waiting when the count's men arrived, and most of those were monks, as the entire monastery—save aged Brother Clyro, who was too old to be of much use at heavy labour—rallied to the cause. Bishop Asaph hastened to explain the deficit and promised more workers the next day, but the count was not of a mood to listen. Since the tally was short the required number, the count ordered his soldiers to ride to the nearest farm and put it to the torch. Later, the smoke from the burning darkened the sky to the west, and the following day, eighteen more Cymry—ten men, six women, and two more boys—joined the labour force, bringing the total to forty-six, only four shy of the number decreed by the count.

Falkes de Braose and his men entered the yard to find the bishop on his knees before a sulky and fearful gathering of native Cymry and monks. The bishop pleaded with the count to rescind his order and accept those who had come as sufficient fulfilment of his demand. When that failed to sway the implacable overlord, Asaph stretched himself out on the ground before the count and begged for one more day to find workers to make up the number.

The count ignored his entreaties and ordered another holding to be burned. That night the monks offered prayers of deliverance all night long. The next morning four more workers appeared—two of them women with babes in arms—bringing up the total to the required fifty, and no more farms were destroyed.

CHAPTER 23

With the onset of warmer weather, Bran felt more and more restless confined to the cave. Angharad observed his discontent and, on fine days, allowed him to sit outside on a rock in the sun; but she never let him venture too far, and he was rarely out of her sight for more than a moment or two at a time. Bran was still weaker than he knew, and his eagerness to resume his flight to the north made him prone to overtax himself. He mistook convalescence for indolence and resented it, seldom missing an opportunity to let Angharad know he felt himself a prisoner under her care. This was natural enough, she knew, but there was more.

Lately, Bran's sleep had grown fitful and erratic; several times as dawn light broke in the east, he had called out; when she rose and went to him, he was asleep still but sweating and breathing hard. The reason, Angharad suspected, was that the story was working on him. His acceptance of the tale that night had been complete. Weak from his wandering in the snow, his fatigue had left him in an unusually receptive condition—unusual, that is, for one so strong-willed and naturally contrary; he had been in that state of alert serenity the bards called the *trwyddo ennyd*, the seeding time, and which they recognised as a singular moment for learning. This condition of attentive repose allowed the song to sink deep into Bran's being, passing beneath his all-too-ready defences. Now it was under his skin, burrowing deep into his bones, seeping into his soul, changing him from the inside out, though he did not know it.

There would come a day when the meaning would break upon him; maybe sooner, maybe later, but it would come. And for this, as much as for the progress of his healing, Angharad watched him so that she would be there when it happened.

She also made plans.

One day, as Bran sat outside in a pool of warm sunlight, Angharad appeared with an ash-wood stave in her hand. She came to where he sat and said, "Stand up, Bran."

Yawning, he did so, and she placed the length of wood against his shoulder. "What is this?" he asked. "Measuring me for a druid staff?" In his restlessness, he had begun mocking her quaintly antiquated ways. The wise woman knew the source of his impatience and astutely ignored it.

"Nay, nay," she said, "you would have to spend seventeen years at least before you could hold one of those—and you would have had to begin before your seventh summer. This," she said, placing the stave in his hands, "is your next occupation."

"Herding sheep?"

"If that is your desire. I had something else in mind, but the choice is yours."

He looked at the slender length of wood. Almost as long as he was tall, it had a good heft and balance. "A bow?" he guessed. "You want me to make a bow?"

She smiled. "And here I was thinking you slow-witted. Yes, I want you to make a bow."

Bran examined the length of ash once more. He held it up and looked down its length. Here and there it bent slightly out of true—not so badly that it could not be worked—but that was not the problem. "No," he said at last, "it cannot be done."

The old woman looked at the stave and then at Bran. "Why not, Master Bran?"

"Do not call me that!" he said roughly. "I am a nobleman, remember, a prince—not a common tradesman."

"You ceased being a prince when you abandoned your people," she said. Though her voice was quiet, her manner was unforgiving, and Bran felt the now-familiar rush of shame. It was not the first time she had berated him for his plan to flee Elfael. Laying a hand on the stave, she said, "Tell me why the wood cannot be worked."

"It is too green," replied Bran, petulance making his voice low.

"Explain, please."

"If you knew anything about making a longbow, you would know that you cannot simply cut a branch and begin shaping. You must first season the wood, cure it—a year at least. Otherwise it will warp as it dries and will never bend properly." He made to hand the length of ash back to her. "You can make a druid staff out of it, perhaps, but not a bow."

"And what leads you to think I have not already seasoned this wood?"

"Have you?" Bran asked. "A year?"

"Not a year, no," she said.

"Well then—" He shrugged and again tried to give the stave back to her.

"Two years," she told him. "I kept it wrapped in leather so it would not dry too quickly."

"Two years," he repeated suspiciously. "I don't believe you." In truth, he *did* believe her; he simply did not care to consider the more far-reaching implications of her remark.

Angharad had turned away and was moving toward the cave. "Sit," she said. "I will bring you the tools."

Bran settled himself on the rock once more. He had made a bow only twice as a lad, but he had seen them made countless times. His father's warriors regularly filled their winter days, as well as the hall itself, with sawdust and wood shavings as they sat around the fire, regaling each other with their impossible boasts and lies. For battle, the longbow was the prime weapon of choice for all True Sons of Prydein—and a fair few of her fearless daughters, too. In skilled hands, a stout warbow was a formidable weapon—light, durable, easily made with materials ready to hand, and above all, devastatingly deadly.

Bran, like most every child who had grown up in the secluded valleys and rough hills of the west, had been taught the bowman's art from the time he could stand on his own two unsteady legs. As a boy he had often gone to sleep with raw, throbbing fingers and aching arms. At seven years, he had earned a permanent scar on his left wrist from the lash of the bowstring all summer. At eight, he had brought down a young boar all by himself—a gift for his dying mother. Although hunting had ceased to interest him after that, he had continued to practise with the warband, and by his thirteenth year, he could pull a man's bow and put a fowler's arrow through the eye of a crow perched on a standing stone three hundred paces away.

This was not a skill unique to himself; every warrior he

knew could do the same—as well as any farmer worth his salt. The ability to direct an arrow with accuracy over implausible lengths was a common, but no less highly prized, facility, and one which made best use of another of the weapon's considerable qualities: it allowed a combatant to strike from a distance, silently if need be—a virtue unequalled by any other weapon Bran knew.

When Angharad shortly reappeared with an adz, a pumice stone, and several well-honed chisels and knives from her trove of unknown treasures somewhere deep in the cave, Bran set to work, tentatively at first, but with growing confidence as his hands remembered their craft. Soon he was toiling away happily, sitting on his rock in the warm sun, stripping the bark from the admittedly well-seasoned length of ash. As he worked, he listened to the birds in the greening trees round about and attuned his ears to the forest sounds. This became, as she had intended, his principal occupation. As the days passed, Angharad noticed that when he was working on the bow, Bran fretted less and was more content. On days when it rained, he sat in the cave entrance beneath the overhanging ledge and laboured there.

Slowly, the slender length of ash took form beneath his hands. He worked with deliberate care; there was no hurry, after all. He knew he was not yet fit enough for the journey across the mountains. It would be high summer when that day came, and by then the bow would be finished and ready to use.

Bran still planned on leaving. As soon as his wrinkled physician pronounced him hale and whole once more, he would wish her farewell and leave the forest and Elfael without looking back.

But one day, as he thought about his plan, something

awakened inside him—a vague uneasiness, almost like a grinding in the pit of his stomach. It was a mildly disagreeable feeling, and he quickly turned his attention to something else. From that moment, however, the discomfort returned whenever his thoughts happened to touch on the point of his leaving. At first, he considered it a form of discontent—a daylight manifestation of the same restlessness he often experienced at night. Even so, the subtle anxiety was growing, and all too soon Bran began experiencing a bitter, unpleasant taste in his mouth whenever he thought about any aspect of his future whatsoever.

Unwilling to confront the pain fermenting inside him, Bran pushed down the disagreeable feeling and ignored it. But there, deep in the inner core of his hidden heart, it festered and grew as he worked the wood—shaping it, smoothing it, slowly creating just the right curve along the belly and back so that it would bend uniformly along its length—and he forgot the blight that was spreading in his soul.

When at last he had the stave shaped just right, he brought it to Angharad, passing it to her with an absurdly inordinate sense of achievement. He could not stop grinning as she held the smooth ash-wood bow in her rough, square hands and tested the bend with her weight. "Well?" he asked, unable to contain himself any longer. "What do you think?"

"I think I was right to call you Master Bran," she replied. "You have a craftsman's aptitude for the tools."

"It *is* good, is it not?" he said, reaching out to stroke the smooth, tight-grained wood. "The stave was excellent."

"You worked it well," she told him, handing it back. "I cannot say when I've seen a finer bow."

"Ash is good," he allowed, "although yew is better."

Glancing up, he caught Angharad's eye and added, "I don't blame you, mind. It is difficult to find a serviceable limb."

"Ah, well, just you finish this," she told him. "I want to see if you can hunt with it."

He caught the challenge in her words. "You think I could not bring down a stag? Or a boar even?"

"Maybe a small one," she allowed, teasing, "if it was also slow of foot and weakhearted."

"I do not hunt anymore," he told her. "But if I did, I'd bring back the biggest, swiftest, strongest stag you've ever seen—a genuine Lord of the Forest."

She regarded him with a curious, bird-bright eye. His use of the term tantalised. Could it be that her pupil was ready for the next step on his journey? "Finish the bow first, Master Bran," she said, "and then we'll see what we shall see."

Completing his work on the bow took longer than he expected. Obtaining the rawhide for the grip, slicing it thin, and braiding it so that it could be wound tightly around the centre of the stave was the work of several days. Making the bowstring proved an even more imposing task. Bran had never made a bowstring; those were always provided by one of the women of the caer.

Faced with this chore, he was not entirely certain which material was best, or where it might be found. He consulted Angharad. "They used hemp," he told her. "Also flax—I think. But I don't know where they got it."

"Hemp is easy enough to find. Given a little time, I could get flax, too. Which would you prefer?"

"Either," he said. "Whichever can be got soonest."

"You shall have it."

Two days later, Angharad presented him with a bound

bundle of dried hemp stalks. "You will have to strip it and beat it to get the threads," she told him. "I can show you."

The next sunny day found them outside the cave, cutting off the leaves and small stems and then beating the long, fibrous stalks on a flat stone. Once the stalks began to break down, it was easy work to pull the loosened threads away. The long outer fibres were tough and hairy, but the inner ones were finer, and these Bran carefully collected into a tidy, coiled heap.

"Now they must be twisted," Bran told her. Selecting a few of the better strands, he tied them to a willow branch; while Angharad slowly, steadily turned the branch, Bran patiently wound the long threadlike fibres over one another, carefully adding in new ones as he went along to increase the length. The process was repeated until he had six long strings of twisted strands, which were then tightly and painstakingly braided together to make two bowstrings of three braided strands each.

Determining the length of the bowstring took some time, too. Bran had to string and unstring the bow a dozen times before he was happy with the bend and suppleness of the draw. When he finished, he proclaimed himself satisfied with the result and declared, "Now for the arrows."

Making arrows was not a chore he had ever undertaken either; but, like the other tasks, he had watched it done often enough to know the process. "Willow is easiest to work, but difficult to find in suitable lengths," he mused aloud before the fire while Angharad cooked their supper. "Beech and birch, also. Ash, alder, and hornbeam are sturdier. Oak is the most difficult to shape, but it is strongest of all. It is also heavier, so the arrows do not fly as far—good for hunting bigger animals, though," he added, "and for battle, of course."

"Each of those trees abounds in the forest," Angharad offered. "Tomorrow, we can go out together and find some branches."

"Very well," agreed Bran. It would be the first time he had been allowed to walk into the forest since the winter ramble that had sent him back to his sickbed. Even so, he did not want to appear too excited lest Angharad change her mind. "If you think I'm ready."

"Bran," she said gently, "you are not a prisoner here."

He nodded, adopting a diffident air, but inwardly he was very much a prisoner yearning for release.

The next day they walked a short distance into the wood to select suitable branches from various trees. "The arrow tips will be difficult to make," Bran offered, swinging the axe as they walked along. "If I could get back into the caer, I'd soon have all the arrowheads I needed—arrows, too."

"What about flint?"

The idea of a stone-tipped arrow was so old-fashioned, it made Bran chuckle. "I doubt if anyone alive in all of Britain still knows how to make an arrowhead of flint."

Now it was Angharad's turn to laugh. "There is one in the Island of the Mighty who remembers."

Bran stopped walking and stared after her. "Who *are* you, Angharad?"

When she did not answer, he hurried to catch her. "I mean it—who are you that you know all these things?"

"And I have already told you."

"Tell me again."

Angharad stopped, turned, and faced him. "Will you listen this time? And listening, will you believe?"

"I will try."

She shook her head. "No. You are not ready." She resumed her pace.

"Angharad!" bawled Bran in frustration. "Please! Anyway, what difference does it make whether I believe or not? Just tell me."

Angharad stopped again. "It makes a world of difference," she declared solemnly. "It matters so much that sometimes it takes my breath away. Greater than life or death; greater than this world and the world to come. There is no end to the amount of difference it can make."

She moved on, but Bran did not follow. "You speak in riddles! How am I to understand you when you talk like that?"

Angharad turned on him with a sudden fury that forced him back a step. "What did you do with your life, Master Bran?" she demanded accusingly. "More to the point, what will you do with your life now that you have it back?"

Bran started to protest but shut his mouth even as he drew breath to speak. It was futile to challenge her—better to keep quiet.

"Answer me that," she told him, "and then I will answer you."

Bran glared back at her. What reply could he make that she would not revile?

"Nothing to say?" inquired Angharad with sweet insincerity. "I thought not. Think long before you speak again."

Her words stung him like a slap, and they did more. They ripped open the hole into which he had pushed all the festering blackness in his soul—soon to come welling up with a vengeance.

CHAPTER 24

Although spies had long ago confirmed his suspicions—three castles were being erected on the borders of Elfael—Baron Neufmarché wished to see the de Braose bastion-building venture for himself.

Now that warmer weather had come to the valleys, he thought it time to pay another visit to the count. Along the way, he could visit his British minions and see how the spring planting progressed. As overlord of a subject people, it never hurt to make an unannounced appearance now and then to better judge the mood and temper of those beneath his rule. Lord Cadwgan had given him little trouble during his reign, and for that the baron was shrewd enough to be grateful. But with the long-awaited expansion into Welsh territory begun, Neufmarché thought it would be best to see how things stood on the ground, reward loyalty and industry, and snuff out any sparks of discontent before they could catch fire.

With this in mind, the baron struck out one bright morning with a small entourage for Caer Rhodl, the stronghold of King Cadwgan. Upon his arrival two days later, the Welsh king received him with polite, if subdued, courtesy. "My

Lord Neufmarché," said Cadwgan, emerging from his hall. "I wonder that you did not send your steward ahead so I would know to expect you. Then you would have received a proper welcome."

"My thanks all the same, but I did not know I was coming here myself," lied the baron with a genial smile. "I was already on the road when I decided to make this stop. I expect no ceremony. Here, ride with me—I have it in mind to inspect the fields."

The king called for horses to be saddled so that he and his steward and a few warriors of his retinue could accompany the baron. Together, they rode out from the stronghold into the countryside. "Winter was hard hereabouts?" asked the baron amiably.

"Hard enough," replied the king. "Harder for those in the next cantref." He indicated Elfael to the north with a slight lift of his chin. "Aye," he continued, as if just considering it for the first time. "They lost the harvest, and that was bad enough, but now they have been prevented from planting."

"Truly?" wondered Baron Neufmarché with genuine curiosity. Any word of others' difficulties interested him. "Why is that, do you know?"

"It's that new count—that kinsman of de Braose! First, he runs them all off, and now that he has them back, he's herded them together and he's making them work on his accursed fortresses."

"He is building fortresses?" wondered the baron. He gazed at the king with an innocent expression.

"Aye, three of them," replied the king grimly. "That's what I hear," he concluded, "and I have no reason to believe otherwise."

"Very ambitious," granted Baron Neufmarché. "I would not think he needed such fortification to govern little Elfael."

"Nay, it's his uncle, the baron, who has eyes on the cantrefs to the north and west. He means to take as much as he can grab."

"So it would seem."

"Aye, and I know it. Greedy bastards," swore Cadwgan, "they cannot even rule the commot they've been given! What do they want with more land?" The king spat again and shook his head slowly—as if contemplating a ruin that could easily be avoided. "Mark my words, nothing good will come of this."

The baron sighed. "I fear you could be right."

Upon reaching the holding, the baron made a thorough inspection, asked many questions of the farmers—about the last harvest, the new planting, the adequacy of the spring rains—and walked out into one of the fields, where he bent down and rubbed dirt between his hands, as if testing the worth of the soil. At the end of his survey, he professed himself well pleased with the farmers' efforts and called to his seneschal to send the head of the settlement two casks of good dark ale as a token of his thanks and good wishes.

The baron and the king rode on to the next holding, where the herdsmen were grazing cattle. The baron asked how the cattle had fared during the winter and how it was going with the spring calving and whether they would see a good increase this year. He received a favourable reply in each case, and after concluding his enquiry, ordered two more casks of ale to be sent to the settlement.

Then, turning their horses, the party rode back to the caer, where King Cadwgan commanded his cooks to prepare a festive supper in honour of his overlord's unexpected, though not altogether unwelcome, visit. The baron had made Cadwgan feel like a knowledgeable confidant, a trusted advisor, and for that he ordered the best of what he had to offer: beeswax candles for the board, fine woven cloths to dress the table, silver plates on which to eat and silver cups for the wine he had been saving for such an occasion, and choice slices from the haunch of venison aging in the larder. Fresh straw was to be spread on the floor and a fragrant fire of apple wood and heather lit in the hearth.

"You will put your feet beneath my board tonight," Cadwgan told him, "and allow me to show you true Cymry hospitality."

"I would like nothing better," replied the baron, pleased with how well his scheme was coming together.

The king ordered his steward to conduct the baron to a chamber for his use and to prepare water for washing. "When you are ready, come join me in the hall. I will have a jar waiting."

The baron dutifully obeyed his host and, after refreshing himself in his room, returned a little while later to the hall, where he was delighted to see that two beautiful young women had joined them. They were standing on each side of the hearth, where a fire brightly burned.

"Baron Neufmarché," announced the king, "I present my daughter, Mérian, and her cousin Essylt."

Mérian, slightly older of the two, tall and willowy with long, dark hair, was wearing a simple gown of pale green linen; her cousin Essylt, fair with a pleasant, plump face and a delicate mouth, was dressed in a gown the colour of fresh butter. Both possessed an air of demure yet guileless confidence.

Mérian regarded him with frank appraisal as she extended

a small wooden trencher with pieces of bread torn from a loaf. "Be welcome here, Baron Neufmarché," she said in a voice so soft and low that it sent a pang of longing through the baron's tough heart.

"May you want for nothing while you are here," said Essylt, stepping forward with a small dish of salt in her cupped hands.

"I am charmed, my ladies," professed the baron, speaking the complete truth for the first time that day. Taking a piece of bread from the offered board, he dipped it in the salt and ate it. "Peace to this house tonight," he said, offering his hand.

"Your servant, Baron Neufmarché," replied the king's daughter. She accepted the baron's hand, performed a graceful curtsy, and bowed her head; her long, dark curls parted, slightly exposing the nape of a slender neck and the curve of a shapely shoulder.

"As I am yours," said the baron, delighted by the splendid young woman. Although he also accepted the courtesy of the young woman called Essylt, his eyes never left the dark-haired beauty before him.

"Father tells me you approve of the fieldwork," said Mérian, not waiting to be addressed.

"Indeed," replied the baron. "It is good work and well done."

"And the herds—they were also to your liking?"

"I have rarely seen better," answered the baron politely. "Your people know their cattle—as I have always said. I am pleased."

"Well then, I expect we shall see an increase in our taxes again this year," she said with a crisp smile.

"Here now!" objected her father quickly; he gave the forthright young woman a glance of fierce disapproval. To the baron, he said, "Please forgive my daughter. She is of a contrary mind and sometimes forgets her place."

"That is true," acknowledged Mérian lightly. "I do humbly beg your pardon." So saying, she offered another little bow, which, although performed with simple grace, was in no way deferential.

"Pardon granted," replied the baron lightly. Despite the glancing sting of her remark—which would certainly have earned a less winsome subject stiff punishment—the baron found it easy to forgive her and was glad for the opportunity to do so. Her direct, uncomplicated manner was refreshing; it put him in mind of a spirited young horse that has yet to be trained to the halter. He would, he considered, give much to be the man to bring her to saddle.

The two young women were sent to fetch the jars the king had ordered. They returned with overflowing cups, which they offered the king and his noble guest. The two made to retreat then, but the baron said, "Please, stay. Join us." To the king he said, "I find the company of ladies often a pleasant thing when taking my evening meal."

Queer as the request might be, Cadwgan was not about to offend his guest—there were matters he wished to negotiate before the night was finished—so he lauded the idea. "Of course! Of course, I was just about to suggest the same thing myself. Mérian, Essylt, you will stay. Mérian, fetch your mother and tell her we will all dine together tonight."

Mérian dipped her head in acquiescence to this odd suggestion, so neither her father nor his guest saw her large, dark eyes roll in derision.

The king then offered a health to the baron, ". . . and to King William, may God bless his soul!"

"Hear! Hear!" seconded the baron with far more zeal than he felt. In truth, he still nursed a grudge against the king for the humiliation suffered at Red William's hands when the baron had last been summoned to court.

Still, he drank heartily and asked after his subject lord's interest in hunting. The conversation grew warm and lively then. Queen Anora joined them after a while to say that dinner was ready and they all could be seated. The dining party moved to the board then, and Baron Bernard contrived to have Mérian sit beside him.

The party dined well, if not extravagantly, and the baron enjoyed himself far more than at any time in recent memory. The nearness of the enchanting creature next to him proved as stimulating as any cup of wine, and he availed himself of every opportunity to engage the young lady's attention by passing along news of royal affairs in Lundein, which, he imagined, would be of interest to her, as they were to every young lady he had ever known.

The meal ended all too soon. The baron, unable to think how to prolong it, bade his host a good night and retired to his chamber, where he lay awake a long time thinking about King Cadwgan's lovely dark-haired daughter.

CHAPTER 25

Bran and Angharad spent the next days collecting branches suitable for arrows. The best of these were bundled and carried back to the clearing outside the cave, where Bran set to work, trimming off leaves and twigs, stripping bark, arranging the raw lengths in the sun, and turning them as they dried. He worked alone, with calm, purposeful intent. Outwardly placid, his heart was nevertheless in turmoil— unquiet, gnawing inwardly on itself with ravenous discontent —as if, starving, he hungered for something he could not name.

Meanwhile, Angharad dug chunks of flint from a nearby riverbank to make points for Bran's arrows. With a tidy heap of rocks before her, she settled herself cross-legged on the ground, a folded square of sheepskin on one knee. Then, taking up a piece of flint, she placed it on the pad of sheepskin and, using a small copper hammer, began tapping. From time to time, she would use an egg-shaped piece of sandstone to smooth the piece she was working on. Occasionally, she chose the front tooth of a cow to apply pressure along the worked edge to flake off a tiny bit of flint. With practised precision, Angharad shaped each small point.

Working in companionable silence, she and Bran bent to their respective tasks with only the sound of her slow, rhythmic *tap, tap, tap* between them. When Bran had fifteen shafts finished, and Angharad an equal number of flint tips, they began gathering feathers for the flights—goose and red kite and swan. The goose and swan they picked up at disused nests beside the river, which lay a half day's walk to the northwest of the cave; the red kite feathers they got from another nest, this one in a stately elm at the edge of a forest meadow.

Together they cut the feathers, stripped one side, trimmed them to length, and then bound the prepared flight to the end of the shaft with narrow strips of leather. Bran carefully notched the other end and slotted in one of Angharad's flint tips, which was securely bound with wet rawhide. The resulting arrow looked to Bran like something from an era beyond recall, but it was perfectly balanced and, he expected, would fly well enough.

With a few serviceable arrows to tuck into his belt, the next thing was to try the longbow. His first attempt to draw the bowstring sent crippling pain through his chest and shoulder. It was such a surprise that he let out a yelp and almost dropped the weapon. The arrow spun from the string and slid through the grass before striking the root of a tree.

He tried two more times before giving up, dejected and sore. "Why downcast, Master Bran?" Angharad chided when she found him slumped against the rock outside the cave a little later. "Did you expect to attain your former strength in one day?"

On his next attempt, he lengthened the string to make the bow easier to draw and tried again. This improved the outcome somewhat, but not by much—the arrow flew in an absurdly rounded arc to fall a few dozen paces away. A child might produce a similar effect, but it was progress. After a few more equally dismal attempts, his shoulder began to ache, so he put the bow away and went in search of more branches to make arrows.

This was to become his habit by day: working with the bow, slowly increasing his strength, struggling to reclaim his shattered skills until the ache in his shoulder or chest became too great to ignore, and then putting aside the bow to go off in search of arrow wood or dig in the cliff side for good flints. If he appeared to toil away happily enough by day, each evening he felt the change come over him with the drawing in of the night. Always, he sat at the fireside, staring at the flames: moody, peevish, petulant.

Angharad still sang to him, but Bran could no longer concentrate on the songs. Ever and again, he drifted in his mind to a dark and lonely place, invariably becoming lost in it and overwhelmed by sudden, palpable feelings of hopelessness and despair.

Finally, one night, as Angharad sang the tale of Rhonabwy's Dream, he raised his head and shouted, "Do you have to play that stupid harp all the time? And the singing! Why can't you just shut up for once?"

The old woman paused, the melody still ringing from the harp strings. She held her head to one side and regarded him intently, as if she had just heard the echo of a word long expected.

"And stop staring at me!" Bran snapped. "Just leave me to myself!"

"So," she said quietly, laying aside the harp, "we come to it at last."

Bran turned his face away. Her habit of simply accepting his outbursts was maddening.

Angharad gathered her ragged skirts and stood. She shuffled around the fire ring to stand before him. "The time has come, Master Bran. Follow me."

"No," he said stubbornly. "And stop calling me that!"

"I will call you by a better name when you have earned one."

"You ugly old crone!" he growled savagely. "You are nothing. I cannot stand another moment of your insane mumbling. I am leaving." He glared at her, fists clenched on his knees. "Tomorrow, I will go, and nothing you say can stop me."

"If that is your choice, I will not prevent you," she told him. Moving to the mouth of the cave, she paused and beckoned him. "Tonight, however, you will come with me. I have something to show you."

With that, she turned on her heel and went out into the night. She waited for a moment, and when he did not come, she called him again.

Reluctantly, and with much bitter complaining, Bran emerged from the cave. It was dark, and the pathways she walked could not be seen; yet somehow her feet unerringly found the way. Bran soon stopped grumbling and concentrated instead on keeping up with the old woman and avoiding the branches that reached out and slapped at him.

They walked for some time, and as Bran began to tire, much of the anger dissipated. "Where are we going?" he asked at last, sweating now, slightly winded. "Is it much farther? If it is, I need to rest."

"No," she told him, "just over the top of the next rise."

Sighing heavily, he moved on—trudging along, head down,

hands loose, feet dragging. They mounted the long, rising incline of a ridge, at the crest of which the trees thinned around them. Once over the ridgetop, the ground sloped away sharply, and Bran found himself standing at the edge of the forest, looking down into a shallow, bowl-shaped valley barely discernible in the light of a pale half-moon just clearing the treetops to the southeast.

"So this is what you dragged me out here to see?" he asked. His eyes caught a gleam of light below, and then another.

As he looked down into the valley, he began seeing more lights—tiny flecks, glints and shards of light, moving slowly over the surface of the ground in a weird, slow dance.

"What—," he began, stopped, and gaped again. "In the name of Saint Dafyd, what is that?"

"It is happening all over Elfael," Angharad said, indicating the night-dark land with a wide sweep of her arm. "It is the May Dance."

"The May Dance," repeated Bran without understanding.

"Your people are ploughing their fields."

"Ploughing! By night?" he said, turning toward her. "Why? And why so late in the season?"

"They are made to labour for Count de Braose all day," the old woman explained. "Night is the only time they have to put in the crops. So they toil by lantern light, planting the fields."

"But it is too late," Bran pointed out. "The crops will never mature to harvest before winter."

"That is likely," Angharad agreed, "but starvation is assured if they do nothing." She turned once more to the slowly swinging lights glimmering across the valley. "They dance with death," she said. "What else can they do?"

Bran stiffened at the words. He gazed at the moving lights and felt his anger rising.

"Why did you show me this?" he shouted suddenly.

"So that you will know."

"And what am I supposed to do about it?" he said. "Tell me that. What am I supposed to do?"

"Help them," Angharad said softly.

"No! Not me! I can do nothing!" he insisted. Turning away abruptly, he strode off, retreating back into the forest. "I am leaving tomorrow," he shouted over his shoulder, "and nothing you say can stop me!"

Angharad watched him for a moment; then, turning her face to the sky, she murmured, "You see? You see how it is with him? Everything is a fight. A wild boar would be less headstrong—*and* more charming." She paused, as if listening to an unheard voice, then sighed. "Your servant obeys."

Retracing her steps, she made her way back to the cave.

Determined to make good his vow, Bran rose at dawn to bid Angharad farewell. A night's sleep had softened his mood, if not his resolve. He regretted shouting at her and sought to make amends. He said kindly, "I will be forever grateful to you for saving my life. I will never forget you."

"Nor I you, Master Bran."

He smiled at her use of the disdained name. Unable to put words to the volatile mix of emotions churning in his heart, he stood silent for a moment lest he say something he would regret, then turned to collect his bow and arrows. "Well, I will go now."

"If that is your choice."

Glancing around quickly, he said, "You know that I do not wish to leave this way."

"Oh, I believe you do," the old woman replied. "This *is* your way, and you are ever used to having your way in all things. Why should this leaving be different from any other?"

Her reproach annoyed him afresh, but he had promised himself that nothing she could say would change his mind or alter his course. "Why do you torment me this way?" he said in a tone heavy with resignation. "What do you want from me?"

"What do *I* want?" she threw back at him. "Only this—I want you to be the man you were born to be."

"How do you know what I was born to be?"

"You were born to be a king," Angharad replied simply. "You were born to lead your people. Beyond that, God only knows."

"King!" raged Bran, lashing out with a fury that surprised even himself. "My father was the king. He was a heavy-handed tyrant who thought only of himself and how the world had wronged him. You want me to be like him?"

"Not like him," Angharad countered. "Better." She held the young man with her uncompromising gaze. "Hear me now, Bran ap Brychan. You are not your father. You could be twice the king he was—and ten times the man—if you so desired."

"And you hear *me*, Angharad!" said Bran, his voice rising with his temper. "I do not want to be king!"

The old woman's eyes searched his face. "What did he do to you, Master Bran, that you fear it so?"

"I am not afraid," he insisted. "It is just . . ." His voice faltered. How could he express a lifetime of hurt and humiliation, of need and neglect, in mere words?

"I don't want it. I never wanted it," he said, turning away from the old woman at last. "Find someone else."

"There is no one else, Master Bran," she said. "Without a king, the people will die. Elfael will die."

Bran uttered an inarticulate growl of frustration and, turning away again, strode quickly to the cave entrance. "Farewell, Angharad. I will remember you."

"Go your way, Master Bran. But if you think about me at all, remember only this: a raven you are, and a raven you will remain—until you fulfil your vow."

Bran stopped in the cave entrance and gave a bitter laugh. "I made no vow, Angharad," he said, her name a slur in his mouth. "Just you remember *that*."

With swift strides, his long legs carried him from the cave. Angry and determined to put as much distance as possible between himself and Angharad's unreasonable expectations, he walked far into the forest before it occurred to him that he had not the slightest idea where he was going. As many times as he had been out gathering materials to make arrows, he had paid little heed to directions and pathways; and last night when Angharad led him to the valley overlook—from which he would certainly be able to find his way—it had been dark and the pathway unseen.

Already tired, he stopped walking and sat down on a fallen log to rest and think the matter through. The simplest solution, of course, would be to return to the cave and demand that Angharad lead him to the valley. That smacked too much of humiliation, and he rejected the idea outright. He would exhaust all other possibilities before confronting that disagreeable old hag again.

After trying to work out a direction from the sun, he rose from his perch and set off once more. This time, he walked more slowly and tried to spy out any familiar features that might guide him. Although he found no end of pathways—runs used by deer and wild pigs, and even an old charcoal burners' trackway—the trails were so intertwined and tangled, crossing over one another, circling back, and crossing again, that he only succeeded in disorienting himself further.

He moved with more deliberate care now, reading direction from the moss on the trees. Certainly, he thought, if he kept moving north, he would eventually reach the high, open heathlands, and beyond them the mountains. All he had to do was get clear of the trees.

Morning lengthened, and the day warmed beneath a fulsome sun, and Bran began to grow hungry. How had he forgotten to bring provisions? Despite months of thinking of nothing but escape, now that the day had come, he was appalled to discover how little he had actually prepared. He had no food, no water, no money, nor even any idea which way to go. He looked at the bow in his hand and marvelled that he had remembered to bring that.

Well, he could get something to eat at the first settlement—just as soon as he found a way out of this accursed forest. Shouldering his bow, he trudged on with a growing hunger in his belly to match his unquiet heart.

CHAPTER 26

It was bad enough having to stand by and watch as his beloved monastery was destroyed piecemeal, but the tacit enslavement of his people was more than he could bear. Elfael's men and women toiled like beasts of burden— digging the defensive ditches; building the earthen ramparts; carrying stone and timber to raise the baron's strongholds; and pulling down buildings, clearing rubble, and salvaging materials for the town. From dawn's first light to evening's last gleam, they drudged for the baron. Then, often as not, they went home to work their own fields by the light of the moon, when it shone, and by torchlight and bonfires when it did not.

The bishop pitied them. What choice did they have? To refuse to work meant the loss of another holding—a prospect no one could abide. So they worked and muttered strong curses under their breath for the Ffreinc outlanders.

This was not the way it was supposed to be. He and the count had an understanding, an agreement. The bishop had lived up to his part of the bargain: he had delivered the treasure of Elfael's king to Count de Braose in good faith, had offered no resistance and counselled the same amongst his flock; he had accepted Count de Braose as the new authority in Elfael and had trusted him to do right by the Cymry under his rule. But the Ffreinc did not deal fairly. They took what they wanted and behaved as they pleased, never giving a thought to the Cymry now languishing under their reign.

It could not continue. The scant rations left from the previous winter were dwindling rapidly, and in some places in the valley the Cymry were beginning to run out of food. Something must be done, and with both lord and heir dead, it fell to Bishop Asaph to do it.

Joining Brother Clyro in the chapel, he announced, "I have decided to speak to Count de Braose. I want you to remain in the chapel and uphold me before the Throne of Mercy."

"How would you have me pray, father?" asked old Brother Clyro. "That God would remove this oppression, or that God would turn the hearts of the oppressors toward peace?" A pedantic, unimaginative man, a scribe and a scholar, he could be counted on to carry out the bishop's instructions to the letter but, as ever, insisted on knowing the precise nature of those instructions.

"Pray for a softening of Count de Braose's heart," the bishop sighed, humouring him, "a turning from his ways, and for food to sustain the people through this ordeal."

"It will be done," replied Clyro with a nod.

Leaving the elderly cleric in the chapel, Bishop Asaph walked through the building site that had once been the monastery yard and struck off along the dirt road to the caer. The day had grown warm, and he was thirsty by the time he reached the fortress. The place was all but deserted, save for a crippled stable hand who, in the absence of the others who were aiding construction of the town, had been pressed into duty as a porter.

"Bishop Asaph to see Count de Braose," the cleric declared, presenting himself before the servant, who smelled of the stable. "It is a matter of highest importance. I demand audience with the count at once."

The porter's laugh as he limped across the yard was all the reply he received, and in the end, the bishop was made to wait in the yard until the count consented to receive him.

While he was waiting, however, another visitor arrived: a Norman lord, by the look of him. Astride a fine big horse and splendidly arrayed, with an escort of two retainers and three soldiers, he was, Asaph decided, most likely a count, or perhaps even a baron. Clearly a man of some importance.

Thus, it was with some surprise that the bishop heard himself hailed by the noble visitor. "You there!" the stranger called in a tone well suited to command. "Come here. I would speak to you."

The bishop dutifully obeyed. "Your servant, my lord."

"You are Welsh, yes?" asked the stranger in good, if slightly accented, Latin.

"I am of the Cymry, my lord," answered the bishop. "That is correct."

"And a priest?"

"I am Father Asaph, bishop of what is left of the monastery of Llanelli," replied the churchman. "Whom do I have the pleasure of addressing?"

"I am Bernard de Neufmarché, Baron of Gloucester and Hereford." Indicating that the bishop was to follow, the baron led the churchman aside, out of the hearing of his own men and the count's overcurious porter. "Tell me, how do the people hereabouts fare?"

The question was so unexpected that the bishop could only ask, "Which people?"

"*Your* people—the Welsh. How do they fare under the count's rule?"

"Poorly," answered the bishop without hesitation. "They fare poorly indeed, sire. They are forced to work for the count, building his strongholds, yet he does not feed them— nor do they have any food of their own." Asaph went on to explain about the meagre harvest of the previous year and how the count's ambitious building scheme had interfered with this year's planting. He concluded, saying, "That is why I have come—to make entreaty with the count to release grain from his stores to feed the people."

Baron Neufmarché listened to all the churchman had to say, nodding solemnly to himself. "Word of this has reached me," he confided. "With your permission, bishop, I will see what I can do."

"Truly?" wondered Asaph, greatly impressed. "But why should you do anything for us?"

Neufmarché merely leaned close and, in a lowered voice, said, "Because it pleases me. But see that it remains a secret between ourselves, understood?"

The bishop considered the baron's words for a moment, then agreed. "As you say," he replied. "I praise God for your kind intervention."

The baron rejoined his men, and they were conducted directly to the hall, leaving a bewildered bishop to stand in the yard. "Father of Light," he prayed, "something has just happened which passes all understanding—at least, *I* cannot make any sense of it. Yet, Strong Redeemer, I pray that the meaning will be for good, and not ill, for all of us who wait on the Lord's deliverance in this time of testing."

The bishop remained in a corner of the yard, lifting his voice in prayer. He was still praying when, a little later, Count Falkes's seneschal came looking for him. "My lord will deal with you now," Orval told him and started away again. "At once."

The bishop followed the seneschal to the door of the hall and was conducted inside, where the count was seated in his customary chair beside the hearth. Baron Neufmarché was also in attendance, standing a little to one side; the visiting baron appeared to pay no heed to the bishop as he continued talking quietly to his own men. "Pax vobiscum," said the bishop, raising his hand palm outward and making the sign of the cross.

"Yes? Yes?" said the count, as if irritated by his visitor's display of piety. "Get on with it. As you can see, I am busy. I have important guests."

"I will be brief," replied the bishop. "Simply put, the people are hungry. You cannot make them work all day without food, and if they have none of their own, then you must feed them."

Count de Braose stared at the cleric for a moment, his lip curling with displeasure. "My dear confused bishop," began the count after a moment, "your complaint is unfounded."

"I think not," objected the bishop. "It is the very truth."

The count lifted a long, languid hand and raised a finger. "In the first place," he said, "if your people have no food, it is their own fault—merely the natural consequence of abandoning their land and leaving good crops in the field. This was entirely without cause, as we have already established." Another finger joined the first. "Secondly, it is not—"

"I do beg your pardon," interrupted Neufmarché, stepping forward. Turning away from his knights, he addressed the count directly. "I could not help overhearing—but am I to understand that you make your subjects work for you, yet refuse to feed them?"

"It is a fact," declared the bishop. "He has enslaved the entire valley and provides nothing for the people."

"Enslaved," snorted the count. "You dare use that word? It is an unfortunate circumstance," corrected the count. Turning his attention to the baron, he said, "Do *you* undertake to feed all your subjects, baron?"

"No," replied the baron, "not all of them—only those who render me good service. The ox or horse that pulls plough or wagon is fed—it is the same for any man who labours on my behalf."

The count twitched with growing discomfort. "Well and good," he allowed, "but this is a predicament of their own making. A hard lesson it may be, but they will learn it all the same. I rule here now," the count said, facing the bishop once more, "and the sooner they accept this, the better."

"And who will you rule," asked the baron, "when your subjects have starved to death?" Advancing a few paces toward the bishop, the baron made a small bow of deference and said, "I am Baron Neufmarché, and I stand ready to supply grain, meat, and other provisions if it would aid you in this present difficulty."

"I thank you, and my people thank you, sire," said the bishop, careful not to let on that they had already spoken of the matter in private. "Our prayers for deliverance are answered."

"What?" objected the count. "Am I to have nothing to say about this?"

"Of course," allowed Neufmarché, "I would never intrude in the affairs of another lord in his realm. I merely make the offer as a gesture of goodwill. If you prefer to give them the grain out of your own stores, that is entirely your decision."

The bishop, hands folded as if in prayer, turned hopeful eyes to the count, awaiting his answer.

Falkes hesitated, tapping the arms of his chair with his long fingers. "It is true that the storehouses are nearly empty and that we shall have to bring in supplies very soon. Therefore," he said, making up his mind, "I accept your offer of goodwill, Neufmarché."

"Splendid!" cried the baron. "Let us consider this the first step along the road toward a peaceful and harmonious alliance. We are neighbours, after all, and we should look toward the satisfaction of our mutual interests. I will dispatch the supplies immediately upon my return to Hereford."

Seeing in Baron Neufmarché a resourceful new ally, and emboldened by his presence, the bishop plucked up his courage and announced, "There is yet one more matter I would bring before you, lord count."

Knowing himself the subject of the baron's scrutiny, Falkes sighed. "Go on, then."

"The two farms you burned—special provision must be made for the farmers and their families. They have lost everything. I want tools and supplies to be replaced at once so they can rebuild."

Hearing this, the baron swung toward the count. "You burned their farms?"

The count, aghast to find himself trapped between two

accusers, rose abruptly from his chair as if it had suddenly become too hot. "I burned some barns, nothing more," blustered the count nervously. "The threat was merely an enticement to obedience. It would not have happened if they had complied with my request."

"Those families had little enough already, and that little has been taken from them. I demand redress," said Asaph, far more forcefully than he would have dared had it not been for the baron looking on.

"Oh, very well," said Count Falkes, a sickly smile spreading on his lips. He turned to the baron, who returned his gaze with stern disapproval. "They will be given tools and other supplies so they can rebuild."

Regarding the bishop, the baron said, "Are you satisfied?"

"When the tools and supplies have been delivered to the church," said the bishop, "I will consider the matter concluded."

"Well then," said Baron Neufmarché. He turned to an extremely agitated Count Falkes and offered a sop. "I think we can put this unfortunate incident behind us and welcome a more salutary future." He spoke as a parent coaxing a wayward child back into the warm bosom of family fellowship.

The count was not slow to snatch a chance to regain a measure of dignity. "Nothing would please me more, baron." To the bishop, he said, "If there is nothing else, you are dismissed. Neufmarché and I have business to discuss."

Asaph made a stiff bow and withdrew quietly, leaving the noblemen to their talk. Once outside, he departed Caer Cadarn in a rush to bring the good news of the baron's kindness to the people.

CHAPTER 27

By the end of his second day in the forest, Bran was footsore, weary, and voraciously hungry. Twice he had sighted deer, twice loosed an arrow and missed; his shoulder still pained him, and it would take many more days of practise before he recovered his easy mastery of the weapon. He had retrieved one arrow, but the other had been lost—along with any hope of a meal. And though the berries on the brambles and raspberry canes were still green and bitter, he was proud enough to refuse the growing impulse to return to the cave and beg Angharad's help. The notion smelled of weakness and surrender, and he rejected it outright.

So as the twilight shadows deepened in the leaf-bound glades, he drank his fill from a clear-running stream and prepared to spend another night in the forest. He found the disused den of a roe deer in a hollow beneath the roots of an ancient oak and crawled in. He lay back in the dry leaves and observed a spider enshroud a trapped cricket in a cocoon of silk and leave it dangling, suspended by a single strand above his head.

As Bran watched, he listened to the sounds of the woodland transforming itself for night as the birds flocked to roost and night's children began to awaken: mice and voles, badgers, foxes, bats—all with their particular voices—and it seemed to him then, as never before, that a forest was more than a place to hunt and gather timber, or else better avoided. More than a stand of moss-heavy trees; more than a sweet-water spring bubbling up from the roots of a distant mountain; more than a smooth-pebbled pool, gleaming, radiant as a jewel in a green hidden dell, or a flower-strewn meadow surrounded by a slender host of white swaying birches, or a badger delving in the dark earth beneath a rough-barked elm, or a fox kit eluding a diving hawk; more than a proud stag standing watch over his clan . . . More than these, the forest was itself a living thing, its life made up of all the smaller lives contained within its borders.

This realization proved so strong that it startled him, and he marvelled at its potency. It was, perhaps, the first time a thought like this had ever taken hold in Bran, and after the initial jolt passed, he found himself enjoying the unique freshness of the raw idea—divining the spirit of the Greene Wood, he called it. He turned it over and over in his mind, exploring its dimensions, delighting in its imaginative potential. It occurred to him that Angharad was largely responsible for this new way of thinking: that with her songs and stories and her old-fashioned, earthy ways, she had awakened in him a new kind of sight or understanding. Surely, Angharad had bewitched him, charmed him with some strange arboreal enchantment that made the forest seem a realm over which he might gain some small dominion. Angharad the Hudolion, the Enchantress of the Wood, had worked her wiles on him, and he was in her thrall. Rather than fear or dread, the conviction produced a sudden exultation. He felt, inexplicably, that he had passed some trial, gained some mastery, achieved some virtue. And although he could not yet put a name to the thing he had accomplished, he gloried in it all the same.

He lay back in the hollow of the great oak's roots as if embraced by strong encircling arms. It seemed to him that he was no longer a stranger in the forest, an intruder in a foreign realm . . . He *belonged* here. He could be at home here. In this place, he could move as freely as a king in his caer, a lord of a leaf and branch and living things—like the hero of the story: Rhi Bran.

He fell asleep with that thought still turning in his mind.

Deep in the night, he dreamed that he stood on the high crest of a craggy hill rising in the centre of the forest, the wind swirling around him. Suddenly, he felt the urge to fly, and stretching out his arms, he lifted them high. To his amazement, his arms sprouted long black feathers; the wind gusted, and he was lifted up and borne aloft, rising up and up into the clear blue Cymraic sky. Out over the forest he sailed; looking down, he saw the massed treetops far below—a thick, green, rough and rumpled skin, with the threads of streams seamed through it like veins. He saw the silvery glint of a lake and the bare domes of rock peaks. Away in the misty distance he saw the wide green sweep of the Vale of Elfael with its handful of farms and settlements scattered over a rolling, rumpled land that glowed like a gemstone beneath the light of an untroubled sun. Higher and still higher he soared, revelling in his flight, sailing over the vast extent of the greenwood.

From somewhere far below, there arose a cry—a wild,

ragged wail, like that of a terrorised child who will not be comforted or consoled. The sound grew until it assaulted heaven with its insistence. Unable to ignore it, he sailed out over the valley to see what could cause such anguish. Scanning the ground far below, a movement on the margin of the forest caught his eye. He circled lower for a closer look: hunters. They had dogs with them and were armed with lances and swords. That they should violate the sanctity of his realm angered Bran, and he determined to drive them away. He swooped down, ready to defend his woodland kingdom, only to realise, too late, that it was himself they were hunting.

He plummeted instantly to earth, landing on the path some little way ahead of the invading men. The sharp-sighted dogs saw him and howled to be released. As Bran gathered himself to flee, the hunters loosed the hounds.

Bran ran into the forest, found a dark nook beneath a rock, and crawled in to hide. But the dogs had got his scent, and they came running, baying for his blood . . .

Bran awakened with the sound of barking still echoing through the trees. A soft mist curled amongst the roots of the trees, and dew glistened on the lower leaves and on the grassy path.

The long rising note came again and, close behind, the very beast itself: a lean, long-legged grey hunting hound with clipped ears and a shaggy pelt, bounding with great, galloping strides through the morning fog.

Seizing his bow, Bran nocked an arrow and drew back the string. He was on the point of loosing the missile when a small boy appeared, racing after the dog. Barefoot, dirty-faced, with long, tangled dark hair, the lad appeared to be no more than six or seven years old. He saw Bran the same instant Bran saw him; the boy glimpsed the weapon in Bran's hands and halted just as Bran's fingers released the string.

In the same instant a voice cried, "Pull up!"

Distracted by the shout, Bran's aim faltered, and the arrow went wide; the hound leapt, colliding with Bran and carrying him to the ground. Bran crossed his arms over his neck to protect his throat . . . as the dog licked his face. It took a moment for Bran to understand that he was not being attacked. Taking hold of the dog's iron-studded collar, he tried to free himself from the beast's eager attentions, but it stood on his chest, holding him to the ground. "Off!" cried Bran. "Get off!"

"Look at you now," said Angharad as she came to stand over him. "And is this not how I first found you?"

"I surrender," Bran told her. "Get him off."

The old woman gestured to the boy, who came running and pulled the dog away.

Bran rolled to his feet and brushed at the dog's muddy footprints. Angharad smiled and reached down to help him. "I thought you were away to the north country and the safety of a rich kinsman's hearth," she said, her smile brimming with merry mischief. "How is it that you are still forest bound?"

"You would know that better than I," replied Bran. Embarrassed to be so easily found, he nevertheless welcomed the sight of the old woman.

"Aye," she agreed, "I would. But we have had this discussion before, I think." She extended her hand, and Bran saw that she held a cloth bundle. "Your fast is over, Master Bran. Come, let us eat together one last time."

Bran, chastened by his luckless wandering through the forest, dutifully fell into step behind the old woman as she led her little party a short distance to a glade and there spread out a meal of cold meat, nuts, dried fruit, mushrooms, honey cakes, and eggs. The three of them ate quietly; Angharad divided the meat and shared it out between them. When the edge of his hunger had been blunted, Bran turned to the boy, who seemed curiously familiar to him, and asked, "What's your name?"

The boy raised big dark eyes to him but made no reply.

Thinking the boy had not understood him, Bran asked again, and this time the lad raised a dirty finger to his lips and shook his head.

"He is telling you he cannot speak," explained Angharad. "I call him Gwion Bach."

"He is a kinsman of yours?"

"Not mine," she replied lightly. "He belongs to the forest—one of many who live here. When I told him I was going to find you, he insisted on coming, too. I think he knows you."

Bran examined the boy more closely . . . the attack in the farmyard—could it be the same boy? "One of many," he repeated after a moment. "And *are* there many?"

"More now that the Ffreinc have come," she answered, handing the boy a small boiled egg, which he peeled and popped into his mouth with a smack of his lips.

Bran considered this for a moment and then said, "You knew I would be here. You knew I would not be able to find my way out of the wood alone." He did not accuse her of laying a spell on him, but it was in his mind. "You knew, and still you let me go."

"It was your decision. I said I would not prevent you."

He smiled and shook his head. "I am a fool, Angharad, as we both know. But you could have told me the way out."

"Oh, aye," she agreed cheerfully, "but you did not ask." Growing suddenly serious, she regarded him with a look of unsettling directness. "What is your desire, Bran?" Their meal finished, it was time, once more, for them to part. "What will you do?"

Bran regarded the old woman before him; wrinkled and stooped she might be, but shrewd as a den of weasels. In her mouth the question was more than it seemed. He hesitated, feeling that much depended on the answer.

What answer could he give? Despite his newfound appreciation of the forest, he knew the Ffreinc would kill him on sight. Seeking refuge amongst his mother's kinsmen was still a good plan. In the months he had been living with Angharad, no better scheme had come to him, nor did anything more useful occur to him now. "I will go to my people," he replied, and the words thudded to the ground like an admission of defeat.

"If that is what you wish," the old woman allowed as graciously as Bran could have hoped, "then follow me, and I will lead you to the place where you can find them."

Gathering up the remains of the meal, Angharad set off with Bran following and little Gwion Bach and the dog running along behind. They walked at an unhurried pace along barely discernible trails that Angharad read with ease. After a time, Bran noticed that the trees grew taller, the spaces between them narrower and more shadowed; the sun became a mere glimmer of shattered gold in the dense leaf canopy overhead; the trail became soft underfoot, thick with moss and damp leaves; the very air grew heavier and more redolent of earth and water and softly decaying wood. Here and there, he heard the tiny rustlings of creatures that lived in shady nooks. Everywhere—around this rock, on the other side of that holly bush, beyond the purple beech wall—he heard the sound of water: dripping off branches, trickling along unseen courses.

The morning passed, and they paused to rest and drink from a brook no wider than a man's foot. Angharad passed out handfuls of hazelnuts from the bag she carried. "A good day," observed Bran. He owed his life to the old woman who had saved him, and as much as he wanted to part on good terms, he also wanted her to understand why he had to leave. "A good day to begin a journey," he added.

"Aye," she replied, "it is that." Her answer, though agreeable, did not provide him the opening he sought, and he could think of no way to broach the subject. He fell silent, and they continued on a short while later, pressing ever deeper into the forest. The farther they went, the darker, wilder, and more ancient the woodland became. The smaller trees—beeches, birch, and hawthorn—gave way to the larger woodland lords: hornbeam, plane, and elm. The immense boles rose like pillars from the earth to uphold tremendous limbs, which formed a timber ceiling of intertwined branches. It would be possible, Bran imagined, to move through this part of the forest without ever setting foot on the ground.

Deeper they went, and deeper grew the shadows, and more silent the surrounding wood with a hush that was at once peaceful and slightly ominous—as if the woodland solitude was wary of trespass and imposed a guarded watch on strangers.

Bran's senses quickened. He imagined eyes on him, observing him, marking him as he passed. The impression grew with every step until he began darting glances right and left; the dense wood defied sight; the tangles of branch and vine were impenetrable.

Finally, the old woman stopped, and Bran caught the scent of smoke on the air. "Where are we?" he asked.

Extending a hand, she pointed to an enormous oak that had been struck by lightning during a storm long ago. Half-hollow now, the trunk had split and splayed outward to form a natural arch. The path on which they stood led through the centre of the blast-riven oak. "I am to go through there?"

A quick nod was the only answer he received.

Drawing himself up, he stepped to the fire-blackened arch, passing through the strange portal and into the unknown.

CHAPTER 28 ⚹

Stepping through the dark arch, Bran found himself holding his breath as if he were plunging into the sea, or leaping from a wall from which he could not see the ground below. On the other side of the oak arch was a hedge wall through which passed a narrow path. Two quick strides brought him through the hedge and into an enormous glade—a great wide greensward of a valley in the heart of the wood, bounded by a ring of towering trees that formed a stout palisade of solid oak around the mossy-banked clearing.

And there, spread out across the floor of the dell, was a camp with dwellings unlike any Bran had ever seen, made of brushwood and branches, the antlers of stags and hinds, woven grass, bark, bone, and hide. Some were little more than branches bent over a hollow in the ground. Others were more substantial shelters of such weird and fanciful construction that Bran was at once entranced and a little unsettled by the sight. He did not see the people who inhabited these queer dwellings, but having heard him coming a long way off, they saw him.

Moments before Bran emerged from the arch of the hedge

wall beyond the shattered oak, women whisked children out of sight, men disappeared behind trees and huts, and the settlement that only moments before had been astir with activity now appeared deserted.

"Is anybody here?" called Bran.

As if awaiting his signal, the menfolk emerged from hiding, some carrying sticks and tools for weapons. Seeing that he was alone, they approached. There were, Bran estimated quickly, perhaps thirty men and older boys, ragged, their clothes patched and worn—like those the farmers gave the stick-men in the fields to frighten the birds.

"Pax vobiscum," Bran called. When that brought no response, he repeated it in Cymry, *"Hedd a dy!"* The men continued advancing. Silent, wary as deer, they closed ranks, dark eyes watching the stranger who had appeared without warning in their midst.

"Sefyll!" called Angharad, taking her place beside Bran. Her appearance halted the advance.

One of the menfolk returned the greeting. "Hudolion!" He was joined by others, and suddenly everyone was calling, "Hudoles!" and "Hudolion!"

Ignoring Bran, they hurried to greet the old woman as she scrambled gingerly down the mossy bank into the shallow basin of the glade. The respect and adulation provoked by her appearance impressed Bran. Clearly, she had some place of honour in this rough outcast clan.

"Welcome, hudolion," called one of the men, advancing through the knot of people gathered around her. Tall and lean, there was something of the wolf about him; he wore a short red cloak folded over his shoulder in the manner of a Roman soldier of old. The others parted to let him through, and as he took his place before the old woman, he touched the back of a grimy hand to his forehead in the ancient sign of submission and salutation.

"Greetings, Siarles," she said. "Greetings, everyone." Lifting a hand to Bran, she said, "Do you not recognise Prince Bran ap Brychan when you see him?"

The man called Siarles stepped nearer for a closer look. He peered into Bran's face uncertainly, cool grey eyes moving over the young man's features. He then turned to those behind him. "Call the big 'un," he commanded, and a slender youth with a downy moustache raced away. "I do not," Siarles said, turning once more to Bran and Angharad, "but if it is as you say, then *he* will."

The youth ran to one of the larger huts and called to someone inside. A moment later, a large, well-muscled man stepped from the low entrance of the hut. As he straightened, Bran saw his face for the first time.

"Iwan?" cried Bran, rushing to meet him.

"Bran? Mary and Joseph in a manger, Bran!" A grin spread across his broad face; his thick moustache twitched with pleasure. Seizing Bran, he gathered him in a crushing embrace. "Bran ap Brychan," he said, "I never thought to see you again."

"If it had not been for Angharad, no one ever would," Bran confessed, gazing up into the face of his father's champion. "By heaven, it is good to see you."

Iwan raised his hand high and called out in a voice that resounded through the glade. "Hear me, everyone! Before you stands Bran ap Brychan, heir to the throne of Elfael! Make him welcome!"

Then, turning once more to Bran, the warrior clapped his hand to the young man's shoulder. "Humble it may be,"

Iwan said, "but my hearth will be all the merrier with you for company."

"I would be honoured," Bran told him.

"Come, we will share a cup," announced Iwan. "I am that anxious to hear how you fared all this time without me."

The former champion turned on his heel and started back to his hut. Bran caught Angharad by the arm and whispered, "You did not tell them I was coming?"

"The choice, my son, was always yours alone," she replied.

"You knew this would happen," he insisted. "You must have known all along."

"You said you wanted to go to your people." Extending a gnarled hand to the bedraggled gathering before him, she said, "Here are your people, Bran."

How strange she was, this old woman standing before him—at once aged and ageless. The dark eyes gazing out at him from that wrinkled visage were as keen as blades, her mind sharper still. Bran was, he knew, at her mercy and always had been. "Who are you, Angharad?" he asked.

"You asked me once," she replied, "but you were not ready to receive the answer. Are you ready now?"

"I am—I mean, I think so."

"Then come," Angharad said. "It will not take long. Iwan will wait." She led him to a round moss- and bracken-covered hut in the centre of the settlement. The hide of a red ox served for a door, and here she paused, saying, "If you enter, Master Bran, you must leave your unbelief outside."

"I will," he told her. "So far as I am able, I will."

She regarded him without expression and then smiled. "I suppose that will have to do." To the others who had followed them, she said, "Go about your business. Siarles, tell

Iwan we will join him soon. I would speak to Bran alone a moment." The people moved off reluctantly; Angharad gave Bran a little bow and, drawing aside the red oxhide, said, "Be welcome here, Prince of Elfael."

Bran stepped into the dim interior of the odd dwelling. Although dark, it was surprisingly ample and comfortable. Light filtered in through a single hole in the roof directly over the stone-lined fire pit in the centre of the room. The furnishings were spare. A single three-legged stool, a row of woven grass baskets along the curving wall, and a bed of reeds and fleeces were the only belongings in the room. These Bran took in with a single glance as he entered.

A second look revealed another item he did not see until his eyes had better adjusted to the dusky interior: a robe made entirely of feathers, all of them black. Drawn to the peculiar garment, he ran his hand over the glossy plumage. "What is this?"

"It is the Bird Spirit Cloak," replied the old woman. "Come, sit down." She indicated a place opposite her at the fire ring.

"They called you hudolion," Bran said, settling himself cross-legged on a grass mat. "Are you?" he asked. "Are you an enchantress?"

"I have been called many things," she replied simply. "Hag . . . Whore . . . Leper . . . Witch . . . I am each of these and none. Banfáith of Elfael . . . True Bard of Britain, these titles are also mine. Call me what you will, I am myself alone, the last of my kind."

In her words Bran heard the echo of a long-forgotten time, a time when Britain belonged to Britons alone, and when its sons and daughters walked beneath free skies.

The old woman exhaled gently and closed her eyes. She was silent for a long moment and then drew a deep breath. When she spoke again, her voice had changed, taking on the timbre and cadence of one of her songs. "Not for Angharad the friendly hearth, the silver-strung harp, or torc of gold," she said, almost singing the words. "In the forest she resides, living like the wild things——the nimble fox, elusive bear, or phantom wolf. Like these, her four-footed sisters, the forest is her shelter and her stronghold."

She exhaled again, and another long pause ensued. Bran, accustomed to the old woman's queer moods and eccentric ways, knew better than to interrupt her. He waited in silence for her to continue.

"Oh, beloved, yes, the greenwood is her caer, but it is not her home," she said after a moment. "Angharad was born to a more exalted position. She was born to bless the hall of a king with her song, to adorn and complete a noble sovereign with her strengthening presence. But the world has turned, the kings grown small, and the bards sing no more.

"Listen! Do not turn away. There was a time once, long ago, when the bards were lauded in the halls of kings, when rulers of the Cymry dispensed gold rings and jewelled armbands to the Chieftains of Song, when all men listened to the old tales, gloried in them, and so magnified their understanding; a time when lord and lady alike heeded the Head of Wisdom and sought the counsel of the Learned in all things.

"Alas! That time is gone. Everywhere kings quarrel amongst themselves, wasting their substance on trivialities and the meaningless pursuit of power, each one striving to rise at the expense of the other. They are maggots in manure, fighting for supremacy of the dung heap. Meanwhile, the enemy goes from strength to strength. The invader waxes mighty while the *Gwr Gwyr*, the True Men, melt away like mist on a sun-bright morning.

"The Day of the Wolf has dawned. The dire shape of its coming was seen and foretold, its arrival awaited with fear and dread. At long last it is here, and there are none who can turn it aside. Hear me, O Rhi Bran, the Red King stretches out his hand across the land, grasping, seizing, rending. He will not be satisfied until all lies under his dominion, or until he awakens from his sleep of death and acknowledges the law of love and justice laid down before the foundations of the world."

She spoke with eyes shut, her head weaving from side to side, as if listening to a melody Bran could not hear.

"I am Angharad, and here in the forest I watch and wait. For, as I live and breathe, the promise of my birth will yet be proved. By the grace of the Christ, my druid, I will yet compose a song to be sung before a king worthy of his praise." Then, slowly opening her eyes, she gazed at Bran directly. "Do you believe me when I say this?"

"I do believe," replied Bran without hesitation. More than anything else he had ever wanted, he ached for those words, somehow, to be true.

Bishop Asaph stood in the door of his old wooden chapel, watching the labourers break a hole in the wall of his former chapter house, which was to become the residence of Count de Braose's chief magistrate and tax collector—an ominous development, to be sure, but of a piece with the multitude of changes taking place throughout Elfael almost daily.

The monastery yard had slowly become the market square of the new town, and the various monastic buildings either converted to accommodate new uses or pulled down to make way for bigger, more serviceable buildings. One row of monks' cells was being removed to make way for a blacksmith forge and granary. The long, low wattle-and-daub refectory was to be a guildhall, and the modest scriptorium a town treasury. That there were no guilds in Elfael seemed not to matter; that no one paid taxes was, apparently, beside the point. The guilds would come in due course; the taxman, too.

Lamentable though the thought surely was, the bishop could not give it more than fleeting consideration. His mind was occupied with the far more urgent matter of feeding his hungry people. The grain promised by Baron Neufmarché had not yet arrived, and Asaph had determined to go to Count de Braose and see what might be done. He had hoped his next audience with the count would be on more amiable terms, but the prospect of better dealings seemed always to remain just beyond his grasp.

He tightened the laces of his shoes, then made his way through the building site that had been his home—God's home—and walked out across the valley to Caer Cadarn. Upon presenting himself at the fortress gate, he was, as he had come to expect, made to tarry in the yard until the count deigned to see him. Here, the Bishop of Llanelli loitered in the sun like a friendless farmhand with muck on his feet, while the count sat at meat. He resented this treatment but tried not to take offence; he decided to recite a psalm instead.

Twenty psalms later, the count's seneschal finally came for him. At the door to the audience chamber, Asaph thanked Orval and composed himself, smoothing his robe and adjusting his belt. Stepping through the opened door, Bishop Asaph found the count hunched over a table laden with the half-empty plates of the meal just finished and squares of parchment on which were drawn plans for defensive fortifications.

"Forgive me, bishop, if I do not offer you refreshment," said the count distractedly. "I am otherwise occupied, as you see."

"I would not presume upon your attentions," said the bishop tartly. "You can be sure that I would not come here at all if need did not demand it."

Falkes glanced up sharply. "Pray, what are you prattling about now?"

"We were promised provisions," said the bishop.

"When?"

"Why, when Baron Neufmarché was here. It has been almost a month now, and the need grows ever—"

"Neufmarché promised grain, yes, I remember." Count de Braose returned to the drawings before him. "What of it?"

"My lord count," said the bishop, his palms growing wet with apprehension, "it has not arrived."

"Has it not?" sniffed the count. "Well, perhaps he has forgotten."

"The baron promised to send the supplies immediately upon his return to Hereford. It has been, as I say, almost a month now, and the need is greater than ever. The people are at the end of their resources—they faint with hunger; the children cry. In some settlements, they are already starving. If relief is not forthcoming, they will die."

"In that case," replied the count, picking up a scrap of parchment and holding it at arm's length before his face, "I suggest you take up the matter with the baron himself. It is his affair, not mine."

"But—"

"We are finished here," interrupted Count Falkes. "You may go."

Aghast and confounded, Bishop Asaph stood in silence for a moment. "My lord, do you mean to say that nothing has been sent?"

"Have you taken root?" inquired the count. "The matter is concluded. You are dismissed. Go."

The churchman turned and walked stiffly from the room. By the time he reached the monastery, some semblance of reason had returned, and he had determined that the count was right. The baron had made the promise and must be held to account. Therefore, he would go to the baron and demand a reckoning. If he left at once, he could be in Hereford in four or five days. He would obtain an audience; he would implore; he would plead; he would beg the baron to make good his vow and release the promised food and supplies without delay.

CHAPTER 29

It took the two aging priests of Llanelli more than a week to reach the Neufmarché stronghold in Hereford. Though Bishop Asaph fervently hoped to travel more swiftly, he could not go faster than doddering Brother Clyro could walk, nor could he bring himself to deny the needy who, upon seeing the passing monks, ran to beg them for prayers and blessings.

Weary and footsore, they reached Hereford toward evening of the eighth day and found their way to the Abbey of Saints James and John, where they took beds for the night. They were led by the porter to the guest lodge and provided with basins of water to wash and later joined the priests for prayers and a simple supper before going to sleep. After prime the next morning, the bishop left his companion at prayer and made his way to the baron's fortress. Set on a bluff overlooking the river Wye, the castle could be seen for miles in every direction: an impressive structure built of stone and enclosed by a deep, steep-sided ditch filled with water diverted from the river.

It was not the first fortress on this site; the previous one had been burned to the ground long ago during a battle with the English. The Ffreinc had rebuilt it, but in stone this time; larger, stronger, bristling with battlements, walls, and towers, it was built to last. Its latest inhabitant had extended the grounds around the stronghold to include common grazing lands, cattle pens, granaries, and barns.

The bishop paused before entering the castle gate. "Great of Might," he murmured, lifting a hand toward heaven, "you know our need. Let relief be swiftly granted. Amen." He then proceeded through the gate, where he was met by a gatekeeper in a short red tunic. "Pax vobiscum," said the bishop.

"God with you," answered the gateman, taking in the bishop's robe and tonsure. "What is your business here, father?"

"I seek audience with Baron Neufmarché, if you please. You may tell him that Bishop Asaph of Elfael is here on a matter of highest importance."

The servant nodded and led the cleric across a wooden bridge over the water ditch, through another gate, and into an inner yard, where he waited while the gatekeeper announced his presence to a page, who conveyed the request for an audience to the baron. While he awaited the baron's summons, Bishop Asaph watched the people around him as they went about their daily affairs. He found himself thinking about what a strange race they were, these Ffreinc, made up of many contradictions. Industrious and resourceful, they typically pursued their interests with firmness of purpose and an admirable ardour. Yet from what he had seen of the marchogi in Elfael, they could just as quickly abandon themselves to dejection and despondency when events betrayed them. Devout, stalwart, and reverent in the best of times, they also seemed inordinately subject to weird caprices and silly superstitions. A handsome people, hale and strong bodied, with

long, straight limbs and clear eyes set in broad, open faces—
they nevertheless seemed to suffer from a rare abundance of
infirmities, maladies, and ailments.

All these things and arrogant, too. They were, the bishop
concluded, fiercely ambitious. In appetite for acquisition: insatiable. In intensity for mastery: rapacious. In aspiration for
achievement: merciless. In desire for domination: inexorable.

However, and he had always to remember this, they could
be fair-minded and loyal, and when it suited them, they displayed a laudable sense of justice—at least with their own.
The English and Cymry were treated poorly for the most part,
it was true; but the capacity for evenhanded tolerance was not
entirely lacking. The bishop hoped he would encounter some
of this fairness in his dealings with the baron today.

Presently, the page returned to announce that the baron
would be pleased to see him at once, and Asaph was brought
into a large, stone-flagged anteroom, where he was offered a
cup of wine and some bread before making his way into the
baron's audience chamber—an enormous oak-panelled room
with a narrow arched window of leaded glass that kept out
the wind but allowed the light to come streaming through.

"Bishop Asaph!" boomed the baron as the priest was
announced. "Pax vobiscum!" He crossed the chamber in
long, quick strides and held out his hand in the peculiar
greeting of Ffreinc noblemen. "It is good to see you again."
The bishop grasped the offered hand somewhat awkwardly.
"You should have told me you were coming! I would have
had a dinner prepared in your honour. But come! Come, sit
with me. I will have some refreshment brought, and we will
eat together."

The effusive greeting banished Bishop Asaph's worst fears.

"Thank you, Baron Neufmarché, but your servant was kind enough to offer me bread and wine just now. I would not presume to keep you from your affairs a moment longer than necessary."

"So earnest," observed the baron lightly. "It is a most welcome interruption, bishop. You have an advocate in me. I hope you know that."

"You cannot imagine how it gratifies me to hear those words, Baron Neufmarché. You are very kind."

Neufmarché brushed aside the compliment. "It is nothing. However, I can see that you are troubled—and I think it must be something serious indeed to bring you from your beautiful valley." He gestured his guest to a chair beside his own. "Here, my friend; sit down and tell me what is distressing you."

"To be blunt, it is about the food supplies you promised to send."

"Yes? I trust they were put to good use. I assure you, the grain and meat were the finest I could lay hands to at short notice."

"I am certain they were," Bishop Asaph conceded. "But we never received them."

"Nothing? Nothing at all?" wondered the baron. Asaph shook his head slowly. "How is that possible?"

"That is what I have come to discover," replied the bishop, who then told of his conversation with Count Falkes. "In short," concluded the bishop, "the count gave me to know in no uncertain terms that the supplies had never been sent—or, if they had, they never arrived. He suggested I take up the matter with you"—the bishop spread his hands—"so here I am."

"I see." The baron pursed his lips in a frown of vexation and ran a broad hand through his long, dark hair. "This is most disturbing. I made arrangements for the supplies the same day I returned from Elfael, and was glad to do it. Why, the wagoners reported a successful delivery with no difficulties along the way."

"I do believe you, baron," the bishop assured him. "It can only be that de Braose has taken the food and kept it for himself."

"So it would seem," Baron Neufmarché concurred. Rising from his chair, he crossed to the door in quick strides, opened it, and summoned the servant waiting outside. "Bring Remey here at once." The man hurried away, and the baron returned to his guest. "This will soon be put right."

"What do you intend—if I may be so bold?"

"I intend to send another consignment immediately," declared the baron. "What is more, I intend to make certain that it reaches you this time. I will give orders that the food is to be delivered to you and no one else."

"Baron Neufmarché," sighed Asaph, feeling the weight of care lift from his shoulders, "you have no idea how much this means to me. It is a blessing of the highest order."

"It is nothing of the kind," protested Neufmarché. "If I had been more diligent, this would not have happened, and you would not have had to undertake such an onerous errand. I am sorry." He paused. Then, his voice becoming grave, he said, "I can see now that we have no ally in Count de Braose. He is duplicitous and deceitful, and his word can no longer be trusted."

"Alas, it is true," confirmed Asaph readily.

"We must watch him closely, you and I," the baron continued. "I have received word of, shall we say, certain undertakings involving the count and his uncle." He offered a brief confidential smile. "But never fear, my friend; trust that I will do whatever I can to intercede for you."

Before the bishop could think what to say, the door opened and a thin man in a soft red hat entered the room. "Ah, there you are!" called the baron. "Remey, you will recall the supplies we sent to Count Falkes in Elfael, yes?"

"I do, my lord. Of course. I saw to it personally at your request."

"How many wagons did we send?"

The old servant placed a finger to his lips for a moment and then said, "Five, I believe. Three of grain, and two more loaded with meat and various other necessaries."

"That is correct, Remey," confirmed the baron. "I want you to ready another consignment of the same." He paused, glancing at the bishop, then added, "And double it this time."

"Ten wagons!" gasped Bishop Asaph. This went far beyond his most fervent hopes. "My lord baron, this is most generous—indeed, *more* than generous! Your largesse is as noble as it is needful."

"Think nothing of it," the baron replied grandly. "I am only too glad to be of some small service. Now then, perhaps I can persuade you to share a little sustenance with me before you return to Elfael. In fact, if you would consent to stay a day or so, you may depart with the first wagons."

"Nothing would please us more," replied the bishop, almost giddy with relief. "And tonight, Brother Clyro and I will hold vigil for you and extol your name before the Throne of Grace."

"You are too kind, bishop. I am certain I do not deserve such praise."

"On the contrary, I will spread word of your munificence

from one end of Elfael to the other so that all our people will know who to thank for their provision." Tears started to his eyes, and he dabbed them with his hands, saying, "May God bless you richly, baron, for troubling yourself on our behalf. May God bless you well and richly."

Bran spent the day getting to know the people of *Cél Craidd*, the hidden heart of the greenwood. A few were folk of Elfael, but many were from other cantrefs—chiefly Morgannwg and Gwent, which had also fallen under Norman sway. All, for one reason or another, had been forced to abandon their homes and seek the refuge of the wood. He talked to them and listened to their stories of loss and woe, and his heart went out to them.

That night he sat beside the hearth in Iwan's hut, and they talked of the Ffreinc and what could be done to reclaim their homeland. "We must raise a warband," Iwan declared, brash in his enthusiasm. "That is the first thing. Drive the devils out. Drive them so far and so hard they dare not come back again."

The three men faced one another across the small fire burning in the centre of the hut's single room. "We could get swords and armour," Siarles suggested. "And horses, to be sure. Good ones—trained to battle." The young man had been chief huntsman to the king of Gwent, but when the Ffreinc deposed his lord and took all hunting rights to themselves, Siarles had fled to the forest rather than serve a Ffreinc lord. He had assumed the position of Iwan's second. "De Braose has hundreds of horses. We'll raise a thousand," he said, exuberance getting the better of him. He considered this for a moment and then amended it, saying, "Not every warrior will need a horse, mind. To be sure, we must have footmen as well."

The mere thought of trying to find so many men and horses was laughable to Bran. Even if men in such numbers could somehow be found, arming and equipping a warband of that size could well take a year or more—and they must be housed and fed in the meantime. It was absurd, and Bran pitied his friends for their hopeless, pathetic dream; it might make the British heart beat faster, but it was doomed to failure. The Ffreinc were bred for battle; they were better armed, better trained, better horsed. Engaging them in open battle was certain disaster; every British death strengthened their hold on the land that much more and increased misery and oppression for everyone. To think otherwise was folly.

Listening to Iwan and Siarles, Bran grew more certain than ever that his future lay in the north amongst his mother's kinsmen. Elfael was lost—it had been so from the moment his father was cut down in the road—and there was nothing he could do to change that. Better to accept the grim reality and live than to die chasing a glorious delusion.

He looked sadly at the two men across from him, their faces eager in the firelight. They burned with zeal to drive the enemy from the valley and redeem their homeland. *Why stop there?* Bran thought. *They might as well hope to reclaim Cymru, England, and Scotland, too—for all the good it would do them.* Unable to endure the futile hope of those keen expressions, Bran rose suddenly and left the hut.

He stepped out into the moonlight and stood for a moment, feeling the cool night air wash over him. Gradually, he became aware that he was not alone. Angharad was sitting on a stump beside the door. "They have no one else," she said. "And nowhere else to go."

"What they want—," Bran began, then halted. Did anyone have even the slightest notion of the effort in time and money that it would take to raise a sufficiently large army to do what Iwan suggested? "It is impossible," he declared after a moment. "They are deluded."

"Then you must tell them. Tell them now. Explain why they are wrong to want what they want. Then you can leave knowing that, as their king, you did all you could."

Her words rankled. "What do you expect of me, Angharad?" He spoke softly so those inside would not overhear. "What they propose is madness—as you and I know."

"Perhaps," she conceded. "But they have nothing else. They have no kinsmen in the north waiting to take them in. Elfael is all they have. It is all they know. If their hope is mistaken, you must tell them."

"I will," said Bran, drawing himself up, "and let that be the end." He went back into the hut, taking his place at the fire once more.

"We could go to Lord Rhys in the south," Iwan was saying. "He has returned from Ireland with a large warband. If we convinced him to help us, he might loan us the troops we need."

"No," Bran said quietly. "There is no plunder to be had, and we have nothing to offer them. King Rhys ap Tewdwr will not get dragged into a war for nothing, and he has enough worries of his own."

"What do you suggest?" asked Iwan. "Is there someone else?"

Bran looked at his friend, the light still burning in his eyes;

he could not bring himself to snuff out that fragile flame. Angharad was right: the people had no one to lead them and nowhere else to go. For Iwan, and for them all, it was Elfael or nothing.

Bran hesitated, wrestling with the decision. *God have mercy*, he thought, *I cannot abandon them.* In that instant, a new path opened before him, and Bran saw the way ahead. "We don't have to fight the Ffreinc," he declared abruptly.

"No?" wondered Iwan. "I think they won't surrender for asking—a pleasant thought even so."

"Have you forgotten, Iwan? We went to Lundein and spoke to the king's justiciar," Bran said. "Do you remember what he said?"

"Aye," conceded the big man, "I remember. What help is that to us now?"

"It is our very salvation!" Iwan and Siarles exchanged puzzled glances across the fire. Clearly, they did not see, so Bran explained, "The cardinal said he would annul Baron de Braose's grant for six hundred marks. So we will simply *buy* Elfael from the king."

"Six hundred marks!" muttered Siarles in dull amazement. "Have you ever seen that much?"

"Never," allowed Bran. "In truth, I don't know if there is that much silver to be had beyond the March. But the terms were laid down by William's own man. The cardinal said we could have Elfael for six hundred marks."

"Aye," mused Iwan, rubbing his chin doubtfully, "that is what he said—and it is just as impossible now as it was then."

"A high price, yes, but not impossible. Anyway, it is far less than what would be needed to raise and feed an army of a thousand men—not to mention weapons and armour. For that, we'd need ten times more than the cardinal is asking."

The two others fell silent gazing at him, calculating the enormity of the sums involved. Bran let his words work for a moment and then added, "That aside, I agree about the horses."

"You do?" wondered Siarles, much impressed.

"Yes, but not a thousand. Three or four will suffice."

"What can we do with three horses?" scoffed the young forester.

"We can begin raising the six hundred marks to redeem our homeland."

PART FOUR

THE HAUNTING

Ten wagons laden with sacks of barley and rye, bags of dried beans and peas, and whole sides of beef and smoked pork trundled along the rising trackway through the forest. The supply van of Baron Neufmarché had spent all morning toiling up the winding incline of the ridge, and the crest was now in sight. Along with the wagons, the baron had sent an armed escort: five men-at-arms under the command of a knight, all of them in mail hauberks and armed with swords and lances, their shields and steel helmets slung behind their saddles. Their presence dared Count Falkes, or anyone else, to divert the consignment of supplies intended for the starving folk of Elfael.

The day had turned hazy and hot in the open places, the skies clear for the most part with but a smudgy suggestion of cloud to the west. The road, though deeply rutted and lumpy, was as dry as parchment. A drowsy hush lay over the rising woodland, as if the trees themselves dozed in the heat. The drivers did not press their teams too hard; the day was hot, the wagons were heavy, and they were loath to hurry. The food would arrive when it arrived, and that would be soon enough.

The six advance guards paused on the spine of the ridge and waited for the ox train to reach the top. From their high vantage point, the soldiers could see the Vale of Elfael spreading green and inviting to the north. "This is tedious work," muttered the knight leading the escort. Turning to one of his men, he said, "Richard, go down and tell them that we will ride on. There is a ford ahead—just there." He pointed down the descending slope to a place where a stream cut through the road as it pursued its switchback descent into the valley. "We will water the horses and wait for them there."

The man-at-arms gave a nod, put spurs to his horse, and trotted back down the slope. "This way," said the knight, and they rode down to the fording place, where they dismounted and stretched. After the animals had drunk their fill, the men drank, too, removing their round leather caps to lave cool water over their sweating heads. Kneeling in a sunny patch on the bank of the stream, the knight saw a shadow pass over him.

He watched the shade slowly engulf him, and thinking nothing more than that an errant cloud had passed over the sun, he ducked his head and continued cupping water to his mouth. Behind him, and a little way above, he heard the rustling of feathers and, still on his knees, craned his neck around to see a huge, dark, winglike shape disappear into the undergrowth—nothing more than a dull glimmering of black feathers, and then it was gone.

The sunlight returned, and the kneeling soldier was left with the strong sensation that something strange and unnatural had been watching him and, for all he knew, watched him still. The skin of his belly tightened beneath his chain mail tunic. Fear stretched both ways along his spine. The knight rose to his feet, replaced his leather cap, drew his sword, and prepared to fight. "To arms, men!" he cried. "To arms!"

Instantly, the soldiers unsheathed swords and levelled lances. They drew together to form a protective line and waited for the anticipated onslaught. The moment stretched and passed. The attack did not come.

The knight advanced cautiously to the place in the brush where the dark shape had disappeared. Gesturing for his men to maintain silence, he summoned them to him, indicating that the enemy was hiding in the underbrush. They paused at the ready, and then, hearing nothing, seeing nothing, they started into the brushwood, where they discovered a narrow trail used by animals when passing to and from the stream. Stopping every few steps to listen, the five soldiers advanced cautiously along the trackway.

A hundred paces farther along, the trail divided. One way led into a deep-shaded game run; arched over by intertwining limbs, it was straight and narrow and dark as any underground tunnel. The other was more open and meandered amongst the trees, below which stunted saplings formed a scrubby underbrush where an enemy might hide.

It could have been his overwrought imagination, but the knight felt dank and chill air seeping along the darker path. It came spilling out from the entrance of the game run like a vapour, invisible to the eye; nevertheless, he could feel it curling and coiling around his feet and ankles, climbing his legs. He stopped in his tracks and motioned the others behind him to halt as well.

Loath to take the darker path, the knight was considering their position when he heard a far-off whinny. It seemed to come from behind them in the direction of the stream. "The horses!"

Turning as one, the warriors ran back the way they had come, stumbling in their haste as they emerged once again on the low banks of the stream to find that their horses had vanished.

"God in heaven!" cried the knight. "We have been tricked! Get up there," he shouted, pushing two men along the upstream bank. "Find them!"

He sent his other two men-at-arms to search downstream and then ran to the road and hurried back to the ridgetop to see the ox-drawn wagons still some way off, creeping slowly up the last rise.

He returned to the fording place and sat down on a rock with his sword across his knees. Eventually, the two who had gone upstream returned to say they had found not so much as a hoofprint on the muddy bank. One of the guards who had been searching downstream returned with the same report—neither hide nor hair of any horse did he see.

"Where is Laurent?" asked the knight. "He was with you; what happened to him?"

"I thought he came back here," replied the soldier, glancing around quickly. "Did he not?"

"He did not," retorted the knight angrily. "As you can well see, he did not!"

"But he was just behind me," insisted the man-at-arms. Looking back along the bank, he said, "He must have turned aside to relieve himself."

Assuming this to be the case, they waited for a time to see if their missing comrade would reappear. When he failed to show up, the knight and his men walked back along the downstream bank. They shouted and called his name and listened for sounds of the absent soldier thrashing through the brush. The surrounding wood remained deathly still and quiet.

The five guardsmen were still shouting when the rider sent with the message for the wagons appeared. The knight turned on him. "Have you seen him?"

"Who, my lord?"

"Laurent—he's disappeared. Did you see anything amiss on the road?"

Catching the wild cast of the knight's eyes and frantic tone, he replied with studied caution. "Nothing amiss, my lord. All is well. The wagons will be here soon."

"All is *not* well, by heaven!" roared the knight. "Our horses have vanished, too."

"Vanished?"

"Spirited away!"

The rider's bald brow furrowed, and tiny creases formed at the corners of his eyes. "But I—are you certain, sire?"

"We watered the horses and knelt down to get a mouthful ourselves," explained one of the men-at-arms, pushing forward. "When we looked up"—he glanced around to gather the assent of his companions—"the horses had disappeared."

"One moment there, and the next gone?" wondered the rider. "And you saw nothing?"

"If we had, would we waste breath talking to you?" the knight charged angrily. Still gripping the hilt of his sword, he scanned the forest round about, a great, green, all-embracing wall. "Mark me, there is some witchery hereabouts. I can feel it."

They waited at the ford, armed and ready for whatever

might happen next, however uncanny, but nothing more sinister than clouds of flies gathering about their heads had befallen them by the time the first of the ox-drawn wagons reached them. The driver stopped to allow his team to rest before continuing the descent into the Vale of Elfael. While they waited, the knight questioned the lead wagoner closely, and then all the rest in turn as they drew up to water their animals, but none of the drivers had seen or heard anything strange or disturbing on the road.

When the oxen had rested, the wagon van of supplies resumed its journey to the monastery at Llanelli. While they were still some little way off, the wagons were seen by the guards at the count's fortress. Hoping for a way to ingratiate himself with the baron—and to distance himself from any whiff of thievery or misuse of this second shipment—Count Falkes sent his own contingent of soldiers down to help convey the much-needed food supplies the short remaining distance to the monastery.

The baron's guards grudgingly tolerated the count's men-at-arms, and the party continued on to Llanelli to supervise the unloading of the wagons at what remained of the monastery. While they watched the cargo being carried into the chapel, the soldiers began to talk and were soon relating the unchancy events that had just befallen them in the forest. Thus, word of the visiting soldiers' strange experience quickly reached Count de Braose, who summoned the baron's knight to his fortress.

"What do you mean the horses vanished?" inquired the count when he had heard what the knight had to say.

"Count de Braose," conceded the knight reluctantly, "we also lost a man."

"Men and horses do not simply dissolve into the air."

"As you say, sire," replied the knight, growing petulant. "Even so, I know what I saw."

"But you said you saw *nothing*," insisted Count Falkes.

"And I stand by it," the knight maintained stolidly. "I am no liar."

"Nor do I so accuse you," replied the count, his voice rising. "I am merely attempting to learn what it was that you saw—if anything."

"I saw," began the knight cautiously, "a shadow. As I knelt to drink, a shadow fell over me, and when I looked up, I saw . . ." He hesitated.

"Yes? Yes?" urged the count, impatience making him sharp.

Drawing a bracing breath, the knight replied, "I saw a great dark shape—very like that of a bird."

"A dark shape, you say. Like a bird," repeated Falkes.

"But larger—far larger than any bird ever seen before. Black as the devil himself, and a wingspread wide as your arms."

"Are you suggesting to me that this *bird* carried off your man and all the horses?" scoffed the count. "By heaven, it must have been a very Colossus amongst birds!"

The knight shut his mouth and stared at the count, his face growing hot with humiliation.

"Well? Go on; I would hear the rest of this fantastic yarn."

"We gave chase, sire," the knight said in a low, disgruntled voice. "We pursued the thing into the brushwood and found a deer track which we followed, but we neither saw nor heard anything again. When we returned to the stream, our horses were gone." He nodded for emphasis. "Vanished."

"You looked for them, I presume?" inquired the count.

"We searched both ways along the stream, and that is when Laurent disappeared."

"And again, I suppose no one saw or heard anything?"

"Nothing at all. The forest was uncannily quiet. If there had been so much as a mayfly to see or hear, that we would have. One moment Laurent was there, and the next he was gone."

Growing tired of the murky vagueness of the report, the count cut the interview short. "If there is nothing else, you may go. But do not for a single moment think to lay any of this at *my* feet. By the Holy Name, I swear I had nothing to do with it."

"I accuse no one," muttered the knight.

"Then you are dismissed. Take some refreshment for yourself and your men, and then you may return to the baron. God knows what he will make of the tale." When the knight made no move to leave, Count Falkes added, "I said, your service is completed. The supplies have been delivered, I believe? You may go."

"We have no horses, sire."

"And what do you imagine I should do about that?"

"I am certain Baron Neufmarché would deem it a boon of honour if you lent us some worthy mounts," the knight suggested.

The count glared at the man before him. "You want me to lend you horses?" He made it sound as if it was the most outlandish thing he had heard so far. "And what? Watch you make *my* animals disappear along with the others? I'll have none of it. You can ride back in the empty wagons. It would serve you right."

The knight stiffened under the count's sarcasm but held his ground. "The baron would be indebted to you, I daresay."

"Yes, I *daresay* he would," agreed the count. He regarded the knight; there was something in what he suggested. To have the baron beholden to him might prove a useful thing in future dealings. "Oh, very well, take some refreshment, and I will arrange it. You can leave tomorrow morning."

"Thank you, sire," said the knight. "We are most grateful."

When the knight had gone, Count Falkes put the matter out of his mind. Soldiers were a superstitious lot, all told, forever seeing signs and wonders where there were none. Even the most solid-seeming needed little prompting—a shadow in the woods, was that it?—to embark on a flight of delirious fancy and set tongues wagging everywhere. Probably the slack-witted guards, having ranged far ahead of the wagons, had emptied a skinful of wine between them and, in their drunken stupor, allowed their untethered horses to wander off.

Later that evening, however, as twilight deepened across the valley, the count was given opportunity to reappraise his hasty opinion when the missing soldier, Laurent, stumbled out of the forest and appeared at the gate of his stronghold. Half out of his head with fear, the fellow was gibbering about demons and ghosts and a weird phantom bird, and insisting that the ancient wood was haunted.

Before the count could interview the man in person, word had flashed throughout the caer that some sort of unworldly creature—a giant bird with a beak as long as a man's arm, wings a double span wide, and glowing red eyes—had arisen in the forest, called forth by means both mysterious and infernal to instil terror in the hearts of the Ffreinc intruders. This last appeared only too likely, the count considered, watching his men fall over themselves in their haste to hear the lunatic. This time tomorrow, the tale would spread from one end of the valley to the other.

Whatever it was that had frightened the stricken soldier, it would take more than some cockeyed tale involving an over-sized bird and the dubious misplacement of a few horses to make Count Falkes tremble in his boots. Nothing short of a midnight shower of fire and brimstone and the appearance of Lucifer himself could drive a de Braose from his throne once he had got his rump on it. And that was that.

CHAPTER 31

For Mérian, the invitation to attend the baron's festivities came as a command to undertake an onerous obligation. "Must we go?" she demanded when her mother informed her. "Must I?"

She had heard how the Ffreinc lived: how the men worshipped their ladies and showered them with expensive baubles; how the noble houses were steeped in lavish displays of wealth—fine clothes, sumptuous food, imported wine, furniture made by artisans across the sea; how the Ffreinc prized beauty and held a high respect for ritual, indulging many extraordinary and extravagant courtesies.

All this and more she had heard from one gossip or another over the years, and it had never swayed her from her opinion that the Ffreinc were little more than belligerent swine, scrubbed up and dressed in satin and lace, perhaps, but born to the stockyard nonetheless. The mere thought of attending one of their festive celebrations produced in her a dread akin to the sweating queasiness some people feel aboard ship in uneasy seas.

"It is an honour to be asked," Queen Anora told her.

"Then that is honour enough for me," she replied crisply. "Your father has already accepted the invitation."

"He accepted without my permission," Mérian pointed out. "Let him go without me."

This was not the last word on the subject—far from it. In the end, however, she knew she must accept her father's decision; she would pretend the dutiful daughter and go, like a martyr, to her fate.

Galled as she was to think of attending the event, she worried that she would not be properly dressed, that she would not know how to comport herself correctly, that her speech would betray her for a brutish Briton, that her family would embarrass her with their backward ways, and on and on. Just as there were a thousand objections to consorting with the Ffreinc, there was, she discovered, no end of hazards to fear.

As the baron's castle at Hereford loomed into sight, rising in the deepening blue of a twilight summer sky above the thatched rooftops of the busy town, Mérian was overcome by an apprehension so powerful she almost swooned. Her brother, Garran, saw her sway and grasped her elbow to keep her from toppling from her saddle. "Steady there, sister," he said, grinning at her discomfort. "You don't want to greet all those highborn Ffreinc ladies covered with muck from the road. They'll think you a stable hand."

"Let them think what they will," she replied, trying to sound imperious and aloof. "I care not."

"You do," he asserted. "Twitching like a sparrow with salt on its tail at the mention of the baron's name. Do you think I haven't seen?"

"Oh? And would it do you any harm to stand a little

closer to the washbasin, brother mine? I doubt highborn Ffreinc ladies look kindly on men who smell of the sty."

"Listen to that!" Garran hooted. "Your concern is as touching as it is sincere," he chortled, "but your counsel is misdirected, dear sister. It is yourself you should worry about."

And worry she did. Mérian had enough anxiety for the whole travelling party, and it twisted her stomach like a wet rag. By the time they reached the foot of the drawbridge spanning the outer ditch of the Neufmarché stronghold, she could scarcely breathe. And then they were riding through the enormous timber gates and reining up in the spacious yard, where they were greeted by none other than the baron himself.

Accompanied by two servants in crimson tunics, each bearing a large silver tray, the baron—his smooth-shaven face gleaming with goodwill—strode to meet them. "Greetings, *mes amis!*" bellowed the baron with bluff bonhomie. "I am glad you are here. I trust your journey was uneventful."

"Pax vobiscum," replied King Cadwgan, climbing down from his saddle and passing the reins to one of the grooms who came running to meet them. "Yes, we have travelled well, praise God."

"Good!" The baron summoned his servants with a wave of his hand. They stepped forward with their trays, which contained cups filled to the brim with wine. "Here, some refreshment," he said, handing the cups around. "Drink, and may it well become you," he said, raising his cup. He sipped his wine and announced, "The celebration begins tomorrow."

Mérian, having dismounted with the others and accepted the welcome cup, raised the wine to her lips; it was watered and cool and went down with undignified haste. When all had finished their cups, the new arrivals were conducted into the castle. Mérian, marching with the wooden stoicism of the condemned, followed her mother to a set of chambers specially prepared for them. There were two rooms behind a single wooden door; inside each was a single large bed with a mattress of goose down; two chairs and a table with a silver candleholder graced the otherwise bare apartment.

Food was brought to them, the candles lit, and a fire set in the hearth, for though it was a warm summer night, the castle walls were thick and constructed entirely of stone, making the interior rooms autumnal. Having seen to the needs of the baron's guests, the servants departed, leaving the women to themselves. Mérian went to the window and pushed open the shutter to look out and down upon the massive outer wall. By leaning out from the casement, she could glimpse part of the town beyond the castle.

"Come to the table and eat something," her mother bade her.

"I'm not hungry."

"The feast is not until tomorrow," her mother told her wearily. "Eat something, for heaven's sake, before you faint."

But it was no use. Mérian refused to taste a morsel of the baron's food. She endured a mostly sleepless night and rose early, before her mother or anyone else, and drawn by morbid curiosity, she crept out to see what she could discover of the castle and the way its inhabitants lived. She moved silently along one darkened corridor after another, passing chamber after chamber until she lost count, and came unexpectedly to a large anteroom that contained nothing more than a large stone fireplace and a hanging tapestry depicting a great hunt: fierce dogs and men on horseback chasing stags, hares, wild boars, bears, and even lions, all of which ran leaping through a wood-land race. Drawn to the tapestry, she was marvelling at the prodigious size and the tremendous amount of needlework required for such a grand piece when she felt eyes on her back.

Turning quickly, she found that she herself was the object of scrutiny. "Your pardon, Lady Mérian," said her observer, emerging from the shadowed doorway across the room. Dressed entirely in black—tunic, breeches, boots, and belt—save for a short crimson cloak neatly folded across his shoulders and fixed with a large brooch of fine yellow gold almost the same colour as his long, flowing hair, he wore a short sword at his side, sheathed in a black leather scabbard.

"Baron Neufmarché," she said, suddenly abashed. "Forgive me. I did not mean to trespass."

"Nonsense," he said, smiling, "I fear it is *I* who am tres-passing—on your enjoyment. I do beg your pardon." He moved to join her at the tapestry. She gazed at the wall hang-ing, and he gazed at her. "It is fine, is it not?"

"It is very beautiful," she said politely. "I've never seen the like."

"A mere trifle compared to you, my lady."

Blushing at this unexpected compliment, Mérian lowered her head demurely. "Here now!" said the baron. Placing a fin-ger beneath her chin, he raised her face so that he could look into her eyes. "I see I have made you uncomfortable. Again, I must beg your pardon." He smiled and released her. "That is twice already today, and I have not yet broken fast. Indeed," he said, as if just thinking of it for the first time, "I was just on my way to the table. Will you join me?"

"Pray excuse me, my lord," said Mérian quickly, "but my mother will have risen and is no doubt looking for me."

"Then I must content myself to wait until the feast," said the baron. "However, before I let you go, you must promise me a dance."

"My lord, I know nothing of Ffreinc dancing," she blurted. "I only know the normal kind."

Neufmarché put back his head and laughed. "Then for you, I will instruct the musicians to play only the *musique normale.*"

Unwilling to embarrass herself further, Mérian gave a small curtsy. "My lord," she said, backing away, "I give you good day."

"And good day to you, my lady," said the baron, smiling as he watched her go.

Mérian ducked her head, turned, and fled back down the corridor the way she had come, pausing at her chamber door to draw a breath and compose herself. She touched the back of her hand to her cheek to see if she could still feel the heat there, but it had gone, so she silently opened the door and entered the room. Her mother was awake and dressed in her gown. "Peace and joy to you this day, Mother," she said, hurrying to give her mother a kiss on the cheek.

"And to you, my lovely," replied her mother. "But you are awake early. Where have you been?"

"Oh," she said absently, "just for a walk to see what I might learn of the castle."

"Was your father or brother about?"

"No, but I saw the baron. He was going to break his fast."

"Did you see his wife, the baroness?"

"She was not with him." Mérian walked to the table and sat down. "Are they really so different from us?"

Her mother paused and considered the question. "I do not know," she said at last. "Perhaps not. But you must be on your best behaviour, Mérian," her mother warned, "and on your guard."

"Mother?"

The queen made no reply but simply raised an eyebrow suggestively.

"Whatever do you mean?" persisted Mérian.

"I mean," said her mother with exaggerated patience, "these Ffreinc noblemen, Mérian. They are rapacious and grasping, ever seeking to advance themselves at the expense of the Britons by any means possible—and that includes marriage."

"Mother!"

"It is true, Daughter. And do not pretend the thought of such a thing has never crossed your mind." Lady Anora gave her daughter a glance of shrewd appraisal and added, "More than one young woman has had her heart turned by a handsome nobleman—Ffreinc, English, Irish, or whatever."

"I would kill myself first," Mérian stated firmly. "Of that you can be certain."

"Nevertheless," her mother said.

Nevertheless, indeed.

And yet here they were, attending a feast-day celebration in the castle of a wealthy and powerful Ffreinc lord. Her mother was right, she knew, but she still resented such an untoward intrusion into what she considered the affairs of her own secret heart. She might not have the remotest intention of encouraging a dalliance with a loathsome Ffreincman, but she did not like having anyone, much less her mother, insinuating that she lacked the wits to govern her private affairs. And anyway, Baron Neufmarché was married and almost twice her age at least! What on earth was her mother thinking?

"Just you keep yourself to yourself, Mérian," her mother was saying.

"Mother, please!" she complained in a pained voice.

"Some of these noblemen need little enough encouragement—that is all I will say."

"And here was I," fumed Mérian, "thinking you had said too much already!"

On the same day that Baron Neufmarché's supply wagons departed, the second dispatch of Baron William de Braose's wagons arrived. As the heavy-laden vehicles trundled out across the valley floor, the sun dimmed in the west, leaving behind a copper glow that faded to the colour of an angry bruise. Nine wagons piled high with sacks of lime, rope, rolls of lead, and other supplies brought from Normandie were met by Orval, the count's seneschal, who instructed them to make camp below the caer. "Food will be brought to you here," he told them. "Stay with your teams tonight, and tomorrow you will be escorted to the building works."

The drivers passed a peaceful night at the foot of the hill beneath the fortress, moving on the next day to the three castle mounds now emerging on Elfael's borders. The farthest, a place newly dubbed *Vallon Verte*, took all of a long day to reach, and it was already growing dark by the time the wagoners began unhitching the oxen and leading them to the ox pen. Only when their animals were fed, watered, and put to rest for the night did the drivers join the masons and labourers gathered around their evening fire.

The workers camped a little distance away from the ditch beyond which rose the bailey mound where they had been working that day. Cups of ale and loaves of bread were passed from hand to hand as whole chickens, splayed on green elm branches, were turned slowly in the flames.

Men talked easily and watched the stars gather in the sky overhead as they waited for their supper. When they had eaten, they spread their bedrolls in the emptied wagon beds and lay down to pass a peaceful night amongst the heaps of stone and stockpiled timbers of the building site. It was not until one of the drivers went to yoke his team the next morning in preparation for the return journey that he noticed half of the oxen had disappeared. Of the twelve beasts to have entered the pen the night before, only six remained. Three of his own animals were missing, half of a second team, and one of a third.

He quickly called the other drivers to him, but other than standing and staring at the half-empty pen, no one had any explanation for the disappearance. They called the master, but he could offer nothing better than, "The Welsh are a thieving kind, as God knows. It's their nature. I say, find the nearest farmer and you'll find your oxen, like as not."

When asked, however, the master refused to spare any of his men from the building work to search for the missing beasts. They were still arguing over who should go to the fortress to request a party to track down the purloined animals when the count himself appeared. He had come with a small force to make a circuit of the construction works. Now that the long-awaited supplies had arrived, he wanted to make certain that nothing prevented the workmen from making good and speedy progress.

"Thieves, you say?" wondered Falkes when the drivers had explained the predicament. "How many?"

"Difficult to say, my lord," replied the driver. "No one saw them."

"No one saw anything?"

"No, my lord. We only discovered the theft a short while ago. It must have happened during the night."

"And the ox pens are not guarded, I suppose?"

"No, my lord."

"Why not?"

"No one steals oxen, my lord."

"I think," retorted the count, "you will find that they *do*. The Welsh will steal anything they can lay hands to."

"So it would appear."

"Indeed," replied the count sharply. "You will find them, or go back without them."

"We dare not go back without them," the driver said.

"Why not? The wagons are empty," Falkes pointed out. "You can get more oxen in Lundein."

"My lord," replied the driver gravely, "matched teams are scarce as bird hair just now. You won't find any for sale between here and Paris."

"Be that as it may," rejoined the count, "what do you expect *me* to do about it?"

"We thought—begging your pardon, sire—that his lordship might lend us some soldiers to find the thieves, my lord."

Unwillingness tugged the edges of the count's lips into a frown. First the missing horses, and now this. Was it really so difficult to keep animals from wandering off? "You want my men to search for oxen?"

"Five or six men-at-arms should be enough." Seeing the count's hesitation, the wagoner added, "The sooner we find the missing team, the sooner we can be on our way to fetch more supplies for the masons." When the count still failed to reply, he continued, "Now that the season is full on, the baron will not take kindly to any delays." As a last resort, he added, "Also, the workers will be wanting their pay."

Count Falkes regarded the empty wagons and the drivers standing idle. "Yes, yes, you have made your point," he said at last. "Ready your wagons and prepare to leave. We will find the stolen beasts. Oxen are slow; they cannot have gone far."

"Right you are, my lord," said the driver, hurrying away before the count changed his mind.

Turning to the soldiers who had accompanied him to the site, de Braose called the foremost knight to him. "Guiscard! Come here; a problem has arisen."

The knight attended his lord and listened to his instructions carefully. "Consider it done," he replied. "And the thieves, sire? What shall we do with them?"

"This land is now governed by the Custom of the March. You know what we do with thieves, do you not?"

A slow smile spread across the knight's smooth face. "Yes, I believe I recall."

"Then do it," ordered the count. "Show no mercy."

The knight bent his head in acknowledgement of his orders, then turned and started away. He had taken only a few paces when the count called after him, "On second thought, Guiscard, keep one or two alive, and bring them to me. We will draw and quarter them in the new town square and let their well-deserved deaths serve as a warning to anyone else who makes bold to steal from Baron de Braose."

"It will be done, sire." The knight mounted the saddle and called three men-at-arms to attend him.

"See you make some haste," the count shouted as they rode off. "The wagons must be on their way without further delay."

CHAPTER 32 ⚷

The day could not pass quickly enough for Mérian. In her impatience, she forgot her displeasure at her mother's meddling and her abhorrence of all things Ffreinc, and instead fell to fretting about clothes. She stood gazing with mounting chagrin at the gown spread out on her bed. Why, oh why, had she chosen that one? What had possessed her?

As much as she loathed the idea of consorting with Norman nobility, she did not want to give any of them the satisfaction of dismissing her as an ignorant British churl. When the time came to dress for the feast, she had worked herself into such a nervous state that she felt as if someone had opened a cage of sparrows inside her, and the poor birds were all aflutter to get out.

Trying her best to maintain her fragile composure, she forced herself to wash slowly and carefully in the small basin of cool water. She put on a fresh chemise of costly bleached linen and allowed her mother to brush her hair until it shone. Her long, dark tresses were gathered and braided into a thick and intricate plait, the end of which was adorned with a clasp of gold. Mérian then drew on her best gown of pale blue and, over it, a short, silk-embroidered mantle of fine cream-coloured linen. The gown and mantle were gathered at the waist by a wide kirtle of yellow satin, the beaded tassels of which almost brushed her toes. When she was ready, Queen Anora approved her daughter's choices and said, "But there is something missing . . ."

Suddenly stricken, Mérian gasped, "What? What have I forgotten?"

"Calm yourself, child," cooed her mother, bending to a small wooden casket that had travelled with them from Eiwas. Raising the lid, she produced a gossamer-thin veil of white samite hemmed with gold thread. She arranged the long rectangle of rare cloth with the point of one corner between Mérian's dark brows and the rest trailing down her back to cover, yet reveal, the young woman's braided hair.

"Mother, your best veil," breathed Mérian.

"You shall wear it tonight, my lovely," replied her mother. Bending to the casket once more, she brought out a thin silver circlet, which she placed on her daughter's head to secure the veil, then stepped back to observe her handiwork. "Exquisite," her mother pronounced. "A jewel to brighten any celebration. Let the Norman ladies gnaw their hearts with envy."

Mérian thanked her mother with a kiss. "I will be happy if I can survive the evening without falling over."

"Off with you now," said Anora, sending her away with a pat on the cheek. "Put on your shoes. The chamberlain will be here any moment."

Stepping into new soft leather slippers, never worn, Mérian tied the slender laces above her ankles, and as the knock sounded on the chamber door, she straightened, drew a deep, calming breath, and prepared to take her place amongst the highborn guests assembling in the baron's hall.

Though it was daylight still, the banqueting room was lit by rows of torches aflame in sconces on the walls. The immense oak doors were opened wide to allow the baron's guests to come and go as they pleased; iron candletrees in each corner and a bright fire in the hearth at the far end of the room banished the shadows and gloom like uninvited guests.

Boards had been set on trestles to form rows of tables down the length of the hall, at one end of which another table had been established on a riser so that it overlooked all the others. The room was aswarm with people—both guests in their courtly finery and servants in crimson tunics and mantles, bearing trays of sweetmeats and dainties to sharpen the appetite. Up in a small balcony in one corner of the hall, five musicians played music that sounded to Mérian like birds twittering in the trailing branches of a willow while water splashed in a crystal pool. It was so beautiful, she could not understand how it was that no one seemed to be listening to them at all. She had time enough to spare them only a fleeting glance before being drawn to observe the arrival of the baron and his lady wife.

"All hail the Lord of the Feast!" cried Remey, the baron's seneschal, as the couple appeared in the doorway. "Presenting my lord and lady, the Baron and Baroness Neufmarché. All hail!"

"Hail!" replied the guests with fervour. "Hail the Lord of the Feast!"

Baron Neufmarché, tall and regal in his black tunic and short red cloak, with his long, fair hair brushed back, the gold at his throat and on his tunic gleaming, stood on the threshold and passed a beneficent gaze over the glittering assembly. He

carried a small jewelled knife on his wide black belt and wore
a cross of gold on a gold chain around his neck. Beside him,
slender as a willow wand, stood the baroness, Lady Agnes. She
wore a pale gown of silvery samite that glistened like water in
the torchlight; on her head was a small, square-cornered caplet
beaded with tiny pearls. A double circlet of tiny pearls adorned
each slender wrist. Oh, but she was thin. The outlines of her
hip bones could be seen through the fine material of her dress,
and the bones at the base of her throat stood out like twin
arrow points. Her cheeks were hollow. Only when she smiled,
stretching her tight lips across her teeth, did a scrap of vitality
steal into her features.

Neufmarché and his wife were attended by a dark-haired
young woman—their daughter, Lady Sybil—whom Mérian
judged to be a few years younger than herself. The girl wore
a bored and aloof expression that declared to the world a
lively disdain for the gathering and, no doubt, her forced
attendance. Behind the imperious young lady marched a bevy
of courtiers and servants carrying trays heaped with tiny
loaves of bread made with pure white flour. Other servants
in crimson livery followed pulling a tun of wine on a small
wagon; still others brought casks of ale. Two kitchen servants followed bearing an enormous wooden trencher on
poles; in the centre of the trencher was a great wheel of soft
white cheese surrounded by brined onions and olives from
the south of France.

The servants proceeded to make a slow circuit of the
room so that the guests might help themselves to the cheese
and olives, and Mérian turned her attention to the other
guests. There were several young ladies near her own age, all
Ffreinc. As far as she could tell, there were no other Britons.

The young women were gathered in tight little gaggles and cast snide glances over their shoulders; none deigned to notice her. Mérian had resigned herself to having her mother's company for the evening when two young women approached.

"Peace and joy to you this day," one of the young women offered. Slightly the elder of the two, she had an oval face and a slender, swanlike neck; her hair was long, so pale as to be almost white, and straight and fine as silken thread. She wore a simple gown of glistening green material Mérian had never seen before.

"Blessings on you both," replied Mérian nicely.

"Pray, allow me to make your acquaintance," said the young woman in heavily accented Latin. "I am Cécile, and"——half-turning, she indicated the dark-haired girl beside her—"this is my sister, Thérese."

"I am Mérian," she responded in turn. "I give you good greeting. Have you been long in England?"

"Non," answered the young woman. "We have just arrived from Beauvais with our family. My father has been brought to lead the baron's warhost."

"How do you find it here?" asked Mérian.

"It is pleasant," said the elder girl. "Very pleasant indeed."

"And not as wet as we feared," added Thérese. She was as dark as her sister was fair, with large hazel eyes and a small pink mouth; she was shorter than her sister and had a pleasant, apple-cheeked face. "They told us it never stopped raining in England, but that is not true. It has rained only once since we arrived." Her gown was of the same shiny cloth, but a watery aquamarine colour, and like her sister's, her veil was yellow lace.

"Do you live in Hereford?" asked Cécile.

"No, my father is Lord Cadwgan of Eiwas."

The two young strangers looked at each other. Neither knew where that might be.

"It is just beyond the Marches," Mérian explained. "A small cantref north and west of here—near the place the English call Ercing, and the Ffreinc call Archenfield."

"You are Welsh!" exclaimed the elder girl. The two sisters exchanged an excited glance. "We have never met a Welsh."

Mérian bristled at the word but ignored the slight. "British," she corrected lightly.

"*Les Marchés,*" said Thérese; she had a lilting, almost wispy voice that Mérian found inexplicably appealing. "These Marches are beyond the great forest, *oui?*"

"That is so," affirmed Mérian. "Caer Rhodl—my father's stronghold—is five days' journey from here, and a part of the way passes through the forest."

"But then you have heard of the—" She broke off, searching for the proper word.

"*L'hanter?*" inquired the elder of the two.

"*Oui, l'hanter.*"

"The haunting," confirmed Cécile. "Everyone is talking about it."

"It is all *anyone* speaks of," affirmed Thérese with a solemn nod.

"What do they say?" asked Mérian.

"You do not know?" wondered Cécile, almost quivering with delight at having someone new to tell. "You have not heard?"

"I assure you I know nothing of it," Mérian replied. "What is this haunting?"

Before the young woman could reply, the baron's seneschal

called the celebrants to find places at the board. "Let us sit together," suggested Cécile nicely.

"Oh, do please sit with us," cooed her sister. "We will tell you all about the haunting."

Mérian was about to accept the invitation when her mother turned to her and said, "Come along, Daughter. We have been invited to join the baron at the high table."

"Must I?" asked Mérian.

"*Certainement,*" gushed Cécile. "You must. It is a very great *honneur.*"

"Precisely," her mother replied.

"But these ladies have kindly asked me to sit with them," Mérian countered.

"How thoughtful." Lady Anora regarded the young women with a prim smile. "Perhaps, in the circumstance, they will understand. You may join them later, if you wish."

Mérian muttered a hasty apology to her new friends and followed her mother to the high table where her father and brother were already taking their places at the board. There were other noblemen—all of them Ffreinc, with their resplendently jewelled ladies—but her father was given the place at the baron's right hand. Her mother sat beside her father, and Mérian was given the place beside the baroness, at her husband's left hand. To Mérian's relief, Lady Sybil was far down at the end of the table with young Ffreinc nobles on either side, both of whom appeared more than eager to engage the aloof young lady.

As soon as all the remaining guests had found places at the lower tables, the baron raised his silver goblet and, in a loud voice, declared, "Lords and ladies all! Peace and joy to you this day of celebration in honour of my lady wife's safe return from her sojourn in Normandie. Welcome, everyone! Let the feast begin!"

The feast commenced in earnest with the appearance of the first of scores of platters piled high with roast meat and others with bread and bowls of stewed vegetables. Servants appeared with jars and began filling goblets and chalices with wine.

"I do not believe we have met," said the baroness, raising a goblet to be filled. In her gown of glistening silver samite, she seemed a creature carved of ice; her smile was just as cold. "I am Baroness Agnes."

"Peace and joy to you, my lady. I am called Mérian."

The woman's gaze sharpened to unnerving severity. "King Cadwgan's daughter, yes, of course. I am glad you and your family could join us today. Are you enjoying your stay?"

"Oh, yes, baroness, very much."

"This cannot be your first visit to England, I think?"

"But it is," answered Mérian. "I have never been to Hereford before. I have never been south of the March."

"I hope you find it agreeable?" The baroness awaited her answer, regarding her with keen, almost malicious intensity.

"Wonderfully so," replied Mérian, growing increasingly uncomfortable under the woman's unrelenting scrutiny.

"Bon," answered the baroness. She seemed suddenly to lose interest in the young woman. "That is splendid."

Two kitchen servants arrived with a trencher of roast meat just then and placed it on the table before the baron. Another servant appeared with shallow wooden bowls which he set before each guest. The men at the table drew the knives from their belts and began stabbing into the meat. The women waited patiently until a servant brought knives to those who did not already have them.

More trenchers were brought to the table, and still more, as well as platters of bread and tureens of steaming buttered greens and dishes that Mérian had never seen before. "What is this?" she wondered aloud, regarding what appeared to be a compote of dried apples, honey, almonds, eggs, and milk, baked and served bubbling in a pottery crock. "It is called a *muse*," Lady Agnes informed her without turning her head. "Equally good with apricots, peaches, or pears."

Whatever apricots or peaches might be, Mérian did not know, but guessed they were more or less like apples. Also arriving on the board were plates of steamed fish and something called *frose*, which turned out to be pounded pork and beef cooked with eggs . . . and several more dishes the contents of which Mérian could only guess. Delighted at the extraordinary variety before her, she determined to try them all before the night was over.

As for the baroness, sitting straight as a lance shaft beside her, she took a bite of meat, chewed it thoughtfully, and swallowed. She tore a bit of bread from a loaf and sopped it in the meat sauce, ate it, and then, dabbing her mouth politely with the back of her hand, rose from her place. "I hope we can speak together again before you leave," she said to Mérian. "Now I must beg your pardon, for I am still very tired from my travels. I will wish you *bonsoir*."

The baroness offered her husband a brisk smile and whispered something into his ear as she stepped from the table. Her sudden absence left a void at Mérian's right hand, and the baron was deep in conversation with her father, so she turned to the guest on her left, a young man a year or two older than her brother. "You are a stranger, I think," he said, watching her from the corner of his eye.

"Verily," she replied.

"So are we both," he said, and Mérian noticed his eyes were the colour of the sea in deep winter. His features were fine—almost feminine, except for his jaw, which was wide and angular. His lips curled up at the corners when he spoke. "I have come from Rainault. Do you know where that is?"

"I confess I do not," answered Mérian, remembering her mother's caution and trying to discourage him with an indifferent tone.

"It is across the narrows in Normandie," he said, "but my family is not Norman."

"No?"

He shook his head. "We are Angevin." A flicker of pride touched this simple affirmation. "An ancient and noble family."

"Still Ffreinc, though," Mérian observed, unimpressed.

"Where is your home?" he asked.

"My father is King Cadwgan ap Gruffydd—of an ancient and noble family. Our lands are in Eiwas."

"In Wallia?" scoffed the young man. "You are a Welsh!"

"British," said Mérian stiffly.

He shrugged. "What's the difference?"

"*Welsh*," she said with elaborate disdain, "is what ignorant Saxons call anyone who lives beyond the March. Everyone else knows better."

"I have heard of this March," he said, unperturbed. "I have heard about your haunted forest."

Mérian stared at the young man, agitation knitting her brows as curiosity battled her reluctance to encourage any Ffreinc affinity. Curiosity won. "This is the second time this evening someone has mentioned the haunting." Searching the lower tables, she found the two girls she had spoken to earlier. "Those two—there." She indicated the sisters sitting together. "They spoke of it also."

"They would," muttered the young man, obviously irritated that his important news had been spoiled.

"Do you know them?"

"My sisters," he said, as if the word pained his mouth. "What did they say?"

"Nothing at all. The baron was seated, and we had to come to table, so I learned nothing more about it."

"Well then, I will tell you," said the young man, recovering something of his former good humour as he went on to explain how the forest was haunted by a rare phantom in the form of an enormous preying bird.

"How strange," said Mérian, wondering why she had heard nothing of this.

"This bird is bigger than a man—two men! It can appear and disappear at will and swoop out of the sky to snatch horses and cattle from the field."

"Truly?"

He nodded with dread assurance. Apparently, the thing was black from head to tail and twice the height of the tallest man, possessing glowing red eyes and a beak as sharp as a sword. He smiled grimly, enjoying the effect his words were having on the young woman beside him. "It can devour a human being whole with one snatch of its beak, and also outrun the fastest horse."

"I thought you said it swooped from the sky," Mérian pointed out, dashing cold water on his fevered assertions. "Is it a bird or a beast?"

"A bird," the young man insisted. "That is, it has the

wings and head of a bird, but the body of a man, only bigger. Much bigger. And it does not only fly, but hides in the forest and waits to attack its prey."

"How do you know this?" asked Mérian. "How does anyone know?"

Bending near, he put his head next to hers and said, "It was seen by soldiers—not so many days ago."

"Where?"

"In the forest of the March!" he replied confidently. "Some of the baron's own knights and men-at-arms were attacked. They fought the creature off, of course, but they lost their horses anyway."

The tale was so strange that Mérian could not decide what to make of it. "They lost their horses," she repeated, a sceptical note edging into her tone. "All of them?"

The young man nodded solemnly. "*And* one of the knights."

"What?" It was a cry of disbelief.

"It is true," he insisted hurriedly. "The knight was missing for three days but was at last able to fight free of the thing and escaped unharmed—except that he cannot remember what happened to him or where he was. Some are saying that the phantom is from the Otherworld, and everyone knows that any mortal who goes there cannot remember the way back—unless, of course, he eats of the food of the dead, and then he is doomed to stay there and can never return."

Speechless, Mérian could but shake her head in wonder.

"All the baron's court have been talking about nothing else," said the young man. "I have seen the man that was taken, but he will speak of it no more."

"Why not?"

"For fear that the creature has left its mark on him and will return to claim his soul."

"Can such a thing happen?"

"*Bien sûr!*" The young man nodded again. "It has been known. The priests at the cathedral have forbidden anyone to make sacrifice to the phantom. They say the creature is from the pit and has been sent by the devil to sift us."

An exquisite thrill rippled through Mérian's frame—half fear, half morbid fascination.

"You live beyond *les Marchés*," her companion said, "and yet you have no knowledge of the phantom bird?"

"None," replied Mérian. "I once heard of a great serpent that haunted one of the lakes up in the hills—Llyntalin, it was. The creature possessed the head of a snake and the slimy skin of an eel, but legs like those of a lizard, with long claws on its toes. It came out at night to steal cattle and drag them down into the bottom of the lake to drown."

"A wyrm," the young man informed her knowingly. "I, too, have heard of such things."

"But that was a long time ago—before my father was born. My grandfather told me. They killed it when he was a boy. He said it stank so bad that three men fell sick and one man died when they tried to bury it. In the end they burnt it where it lay."

"I would like to have seen that," the young man said appreciatively. Smiling suddenly, he said, "My name is Roubert. What is yours?"

"I am Mérian," she replied.

"Peace and joy to you, Lady Mérian," he said, "this night and all nights."

"And to you, Roubert," she smiled, liking this young man more and more. "Have you ever seen a wyrm?"

"No," he conceded. "But in a village not far from our castle in Normandie, there was a child born with the head of a dog. By this, the father knew his wife was a witch, for she had had unnatural relations with a black hound that had been seen outside the village."

"What happened?"

"The villagers hunted down the dog and killed it. When they returned home, they found the woman and the baby were also dead with the same wounds as those inflicted on the dog."

"Here now!" interrupted a voice next to Mérian. She turned to see Baron Neufmarché leaning across the empty place toward her. Glancing down the table, she saw that her father was deep in conversation with the Ffreinc nobleman next to him. "What is this nonsense you are telling our guest?"

"Nothing of importance, sire," answered the young man, retreating rapidly.

"We were speaking of the phantom in the Marches forest," volunteered Mérian. "Have you heard of this, sire?"

"Hmph!" puffed the baron. "Phantom or no, it cost me five horses."

"The creature ate your horses?" wondered Mérian in amazement.

"I did not say that," replied the baron. Smiling, he slid closer to her on the bench. "I lost the horses, it is true. But I am more inclined to the view that, one way or another, the soldiers were careless."

"What about the missing footman?" asked the young man.

"As to that," replied the baron, "I expect drink or too much sun will account for his tale." He paused to reconsider. "Still, I grant that he was a solid enough fellow. Whatever the explanation, the incident has much altered his mind."

Mérian shivered at the thought of something wild and freakish arising in the forest—the very forest she and her family had passed through on the way to Hereford.

"But come, my lady," said the baron with a smile, "I see I have upset you. We will not speak of such abhorrent things anymore. Here!" He reached for a bowl containing a pale purple substance. "Have you ever tasted *frumenty?*"

"No, never."

"Then you must. I insist," said the baron, handing her his own silver spoon. He pushed the bowl toward her. "I think you will like it."

Mérian dipped the tip of the spoon into the mushy substance and touched it to her tongue. The taste was cool and sweet and creamy. "It is very good," she said, handing back the spoon.

"Keep it," said the baron, closing his hand over hers. "A little gift," he said, "for gracing this celebration with your, ah, *présence lumineuse*—your radiant presence."

Mérian, feeling the heat of his touch on her skin, thanked him and tried to withdraw her hand. But he held it more tightly. Leaning closer, he put his mouth to her ear and whispered, "There is so much more I would give you, my lady."

CHAPTER 33

The knight called Guiscard, in command of eight doughty men-at-arms, ordered his troops to follow the tracks made by the missing oxen. Most of the hoofprints, as expected, led back toward the valley in the direction the wagons had come. A few, however, led out from the pen and down the hill to the nearby stream. "Here, men! To me!" shouted Guiscard as soon as he was alerted to this discovery. "We have them!"

When the searchers had assembled once more, they mounted their horses and set off together on the trail of the missing oxen, pursuing the track as it followed the stream, passing down around the foot of the castle work and behind the shoulder of the next hill. Once out of sight of the builders' camp, the trail turned inland, heading straight up over the hill and toward the forest a short distance to the northeast.

The searchers mounted the brow of the hill and started out across the wide grassy hilltop toward the leaf-dark woodland, blue in the distance and shimmering in the heat haze of summer. The tracks were easy to follow, and the soldiers loped easily through the long grass, slowing only as they

approached the beeches, elms, and finger-thin fir trees that
formed a protective bulwark at the edge of the forest.

Passing between the trunks of two large elms, the trail of
the missing oxen entered the wood as through a timber gate.
The light was somewhat poorer inside, but the beasts left
good, well-shaped prints in the soft earth—and, occasionally,
soft splats of droppings—which allowed the knight and his
men to proceed without difficulty. A few hundred paces inside
the wood, the ox trail joined a deer run, and the hoofprints of
the four heavy-footed beasts mingled with those of their
swift-running cousins.

The path traced the undulating hillside, rising and
falling with the rock escarpment beneath it, until it
descended into a deep-riven glen with a brook at the bottom. Here the trail turned to follow the trickle of water as
it flowed out from the forest interior, eventually joining the
stream that passed by the foot of the castle. They pushed
on, and after a time, the banks became steeper and rock
lined as the brook sank lower into the folded earth, dwindling to little more than a blue-black rivulet at the bottom
of a ravine of shattered grey shale.

The searchers moved deeper into the forest, where the trees
were older and bigger and the undergrowth denser. Sunlight
came in dappled fits and starts, striking green glints from
every leafy surface. When the search party came to the top of
a ridge, Guiscard halted his men and paused a moment to survey the path ahead. The air was still and humid, the trail dark
and close grown. The knight ordered his companions to dismount and proceed on foot. "The thieves cannot have gone
much farther," Guiscard told his men. "The only grazing is
behind us now. They will not want to stray too far from it."

"Who says the thieves intend to graze them?" wondered one of the men-at-arms.

"Valuable beasts like those?" scoffed the knight. "What else would they do with them?"

The man shrugged, then spat. "Eat them."

Guiscard glowered at the soldier and said, "Move on."

The trail pursued its way down the slope of the ridge beneath trees of ever-increasing size and age. The upper branches grew higher from the ground, lifting the roof of foliage and dimming the sunlight with a heavy canopy of glowing green leaves. On and on they went, and when the knight stopped again, the wood had become dark and silent as an empty church. The only sound to be heard was the rustling and chirping of small birds, unseen in the upper branches high above.

Thorny shrubs—blackberry and bilberry—grew man high on each hand; a few hundred paces farther along, the trail pinched down to a constricted corridor before disappearing into a tangled and impenetrable bank of brambles. As they neared the wall of thorns, they saw that the narrow trail turned sharply to the left. The oxen had passed between two overlapping hedges; the animals had been led single file in order to squeeze through, and there were tufts of tawny hair caught on some of the lower thorns. The silence of the forest had given way to the noisy chafe and chatter of crows emanating from the other side of the bramble bank. Easing cautiously through the thorny hedge, the searchers entered a clearing. The racket of the birds had risen to a piercing cacophony.

Gripping their lances, the soldiers crept out from the thorn hedge and into a small, sunlit meadow ringed about with birch and rowan trees. In the centre of the clearing was

a roiling, boiling black mound of birds: hundreds of them.
Crows, ravens, choughs, jays, and others were fighting over
something on the ground, and still more were circling and
diving in the air above this squirming, living heap of feathers,
wings, and beaks.

The air was loud with their shrieks and heavy with a
sweet, turgid stink.

"Drive them off," Guiscard ordered, and four of the men-
at-arms rushed the mound of birds, swinging their lances
before them and yelling as they ran.

The birds took flight at the sudden appearance of the
men and fled squawking and screeching into the sky; most
settled again in the branches of the surrounding trees, where
they continued to shriek their outrage at being driven from
their repast.

The birds gone for the moment, the knight and the rest of
the men approached the mound where their four comrades
were now standing still as stones, enthralled by the heap
before them.

"Out of the way," ordered Guiscard, striding up. The
footman stepped aside, and the knight took one look at the
mound before him and almost vomited.

Before him were what appeared to be the entrails and
viscera of the missing oxen—artfully heaped into a single,
glistening purple mound of rotting slime. Rising from the
centre of this putrefying mass was a long wooden stake,
and on the stake was the severed head of an ox. The skin
and most of the flesh had been ripped from the skull to
reveal the bloody bone beneath. Two of the hapless animal's hooves were stuffed in its hanging mouth, and its tail
protruded absurdly from one of its ears, and jutting from

the naked eyeballs of the freshly flensed skull were four long, black raven feathers.

The weird sight caused these battle-hardened men to blanch and brought the gorge rising to their throats. One of the soldiers cursed, and two others crossed themselves, glancing around the clearing nervously. "*Sacre bleu!*" grunted a soldier, prodding a lopped-off hoof with the blade of his lance. "This is the work of witches."

"What?" said the knight, recovering some of his nerve. "Have you never seen a slaughtered beast?"

"Slaughtered," muttered one of the men scornfully. "If they were slaughtered, where are the carcasses?" Another said, "Aye, and where's the blood and hide and bones?"

"Carried away by them that slaughtered the beasts," replied another of the soldiers, growing angry. "It's just a pile of guts." With that, he shoved his spear into the curdling bulk, striking an unseen bladder, which erupted with a long, low hiss and released a noxious stench into the already fetid air.

"Stop that!" shouted the man beside him, shoving the offender, who pushed back.

"Enough!" shouted the knight. Quickly scanning the sur-rounding trees for any sign that they were being watched, he said, "The thieves may still be close by. Make a circuit of the clearing, and give a shout when you find their trail."

Only too glad to turn away from the grisly mound in the centre of the glade, the soldiers walked to different parts of the perimeter and, bending low, began to look for the foot-prints of the thieves. One complete circuit failed to turn up anything resembling a human footprint, so the knight ordered them to do it again, more slowly this time and with better care and attention.

They were all working their way around the circle when a strange sound halted them in midstep. It started as an agonised cry—as if someone, or something, was in mortal anguish—and then rose steadily in pitch and volume to a wild ululation that raised the short hairs on the napes of the warriors' necks.

The crows in the treetops stopped their chatter, and a dread hush descended over the clearing. The unnatural calm seemed to spread into the surrounding forest like tendrils of a stealthy vine, like a fog when it searches along the ground, coiling, moving, flowing amongst the hidden pathways until all is shrouded with its vapours.

The searchers waited, hardly daring to breathe. After a moment, the eerie sound rose again, closer this time, growing in force, rising and rising—and then suddenly trailing away as if stifled by its own strength.

The carrion birds in the high branches took flight all at once.

The soldiers, holding tight to their weapons, gazed fearfully at the sky and at the wood around them. The trees seemed to have moved closer, squeezing the ring tighter, forming a sinister circle around them.

"Christ have mercy!" cried a footman. He flung out a hand and pointed across the clearing.

The soldiers turned as one to see an indistinct shape moving in the shadows beneath the trees at the edge of the glade. Straining into the darkness, they saw a form emerge from the forest gloom—as if the shadow itself was thickening, gathering darkness and congealing into the shape of a monstrous creature: big as a man, but with the head and wings of a bird, and a round skull-like face that ended in an extravagantly long, pointed black beak.

Like a fallen angel risen from the pit, this baleful presence stood watching them from across the clearing.

"Steady, men," said the knight, holding his sword before him. "Close ranks."

No one moved.

"Close ranks!" shouted Guiscard. "Now!"

The soldiers, shaken to action, moved to obey. They drew together, shoulder to shoulder, weapons ready. Even as they formed the battle line, the phantom melted away, disappearing before their eyes as the shadows reclaimed it.

The soldiers waited, bloodless hands gripping their weapons, staring fearfully at the place where they had last seen the creature. When a cloud passed over the sun, leeching warmth from the air, the terrified men bolted and ran.

"Stand!" cried the knight, to no avail. He watched his men deserting him, thrashing through the brush in their blind haste to escape the horror encircling them. With a last glance around the tainted meadow, brave Guiscard joined his men in flight.

Back at the builders' camp, the breathless searchers told what they had found in the forest and how they had been attacked by the forest phantom—a creature so hideous as to defy description—and only narrowly escaped with their lives. As for the missing oxen, they had been completely devoured by the creature.

"Except for the vitals," one of the men-at-arms explained to his astonished audience. "The devil thing devoured everything but the guts," he said. The soldier next to him took up the tale. "The bowels it vomited in the meadow. We must have startled it at its feeding," he surmised. Another soldier nodded, adding, "*C'est vrai.* No doubt that was why it attacked us."

But the soldiers were wrong. It was not the phantom that

fed on the stolen oxen. That very evening, in British huts and holdings all along the valley, a score of hungry families dined on unexpected gifts of good fresh meat that had been discovered lying on the stone threshold of the house. Each gift had been delivered the same way: wrapped in green oak leaves, one of which was pinned to the parcel by a long, black wing feather of a raven.

CHAPTER 34

Brother Aethelfrith paused on the road to drag a damp sleeve across his sweating face. The Norman merchants with whom he had been travelling had long since outpaced him; his short legs were no match for their mules and high-wheeled carts, and none of the four traders or their retainers had consented to allow him to ride in back of one of the wagons. To a man, all had made obscene gestures and pinched their nostrils at him.

"Stink? Stink, do I?" muttered the mendicant under his breath. He was a most fragrant friar, to be sure, but the day was sweltering, and sweat was honest reward for labours spent. "Normans," he grumbled, mopping his face, "God rot them all!"

What a peculiar people they were: big, lumpy lunks with faces like horses and feet like boats. Vain and arrogant, untroubled by any notions so basic as tolerance, fairness, equality. Always wanting everything their own way, never giving in, they reckoned any disagreement as disloyal, dishonest, or deceitful, while judging their own actions, however outrageously unfair, as lawful God-given rights. Did the

Ruler of heaven really intend for such a greedy, grasping, gluttonous race of knaves and rascals to supplant Good King Harold?

"Blesséd Jesus," he muttered, watching the last of the wagons recede into the distance, "give the whole filthy lot flaming carbuncles to remind them how fortunate they are."

Then, chuckling to himself over the image of the entire occupying population hopping around clutching painfully swollen backsides, he moved on. Upon cresting the next hill, he saw a stream and a fording place where the road met the valley. Several of the carts had paused to allow the animals to drink. "God be praised!" he cried and hurried to join them. Perhaps they would take pity on him yet.

Arriving at the ford, he called a polite greeting, but the merchants roundly ignored him, so he walked a little way upstream until he came to a shady place, where, drawing his long brown robe between his legs, he tucked the ends into his belt and waded out into the stream. "Ahh," he sighed, luxuriating in the cool water, "a very blessing on a hot summer day. Thank you, Jesus. Much obliged."

When the merchants moved off a short while later, he remained behind, content to dabble in the stream a little longer. By all accounts, Llanelli was a mere quarter day's walk from the ford. No one was expecting him, so he could take all the time he needed; and if he reached the monastery by nightfall, he would count himself fortunate.

The fat friar padded in the stream, watching the small, darting fish. He hummed to himself, enjoying the day as if it were a meal of meat and ale spread before him with lavish abundance. Upon reflection, he had no right to be so happy. His errand, God knew, was sin itself.

How he had come to the idea, he still could not say. An overheard conversation—a marketplace rumour, an errant word, perhaps, spoken by a stranger in passing—had worked away in him, sending its black roots deep, growing unseen until it burst forth like a noxious flower in full bloom. One moment, he had been standing before the butcher's stall, haggling over the price of a rind of bacon, and the next his bandy legs were scuttling him back to his oratory to pray forgiveness for the thoroughly immoral idea that had so forcefully awakened in his ever-scheming brain.

"Oh my soul," he sighed, shaking his head at the mystery of it. "The heart of man is deceitful above all things, and desperately wicked. Who can know it?"

Although he had spent the night on his knees, begging both forgiveness and direction, as dawn came up bright in the east, that heavenly guidance was no more in evidence than the pope's pardon. "If you have qualms, Lord," he sighed, "stop me now. Otherwise, I go."

Since nothing materialised to prevent him, he rose, washed his face and hands, strapped on his sandals, and hastened to consummate his scheme. It was *not*—and he was fiercely adamant about this part—for his own enrichment, nor did he desire any gain but justice. This was the heart of the matter. Justice. For, as his old abbot had often said, "When iniquity sits in the judgement seat, good men must take their appeals to a higher court."

Aethelfrith did not know how that appeal to justice might come about, but trusted that his information would give Bran all the inspiration he required to at least set the wheels in motion.

The shadows lengthened over the valley, and the road was

not shrinking; with grudging reluctance, Aethelfrith stepped from the water, dried his feet on the hem of his robe, and continued on his way. The merchants' van was well ahead of him now, but he dismissed the rude company from his thoughts. His destination was almost within sight. The Vale of Elfael stretched before him, its green fields spotted with slow-shifting cloud shadows. He doubted a more peaceful and serene dale could be found anywhere.

Buoyed by the beauty of the place, Brother Aethelfrith opened his mouth wide and began to sing aloud, letting his voice resound and echo out across the valley as he made his way down the long slope that would eventually bring him to Llanelli.

He was sweating again, long before reaching the valley floor. In the near distance he saw the old fortress, Caer Cadarn, rising on its hump of rock overlooking the road. "May your walls keep you safe as Jericho," Aethelfrith muttered, then crossed himself and hurried by.

The sun was touching the far western hills when he reached Llanelli—or what was left of it. The low wall of the enclosure had been taken down and most of the interior buildings either destroyed or converted to other uses. The yard had been enlarged to make a market square, and new structures—unfinished, their bare timbers rising from the builders' rubble—stood at each corner. All that remained of the original monastery was a single row of monks' cells and the chapel, which was only slightly larger than his own oratory. There seemed to be no one around, so he strode to the door of the chapel and walked in.

Two priests knelt before the altar, on which burned a single thick tallow candle that sent a black, oily thread of smoke into the close air. He stood in the doorway for a moment, then cleared his throat to announce his presence and said, "Forgive me, friends. I see I am interrupting your prayers."

The nearer of the two priests looked around and then nudged the other, who quickly finished his prayer, crossed himself, and rose to greet the newcomer. "God be good to you, brother," said the priest, taking in his visitor's robe and tonsure. "I am Bishop Asaph. How can I be of service?"

"Greetings in Christ and all his glorious saints!" declared the mendicant. "Brother Aethelfrith, I am, come on an errand of some . . . ah"——he hesitated, not wishing to say too much about his illicit chore——"delicacy and importance."

"Peace and welcome, brother," the bishop said. "As you can see, we have little left to call our own, but we will help you in any way we can."

"It is easily done and will cost you nothing," the friar assured him. "I am looking for Bran ap Brychan—I have a message for him. I was hoping someone here could tell me where to find him."

At this, a shadow passed over the bishop's face. His smile of welcome wilted, and his eyes grew sad. "Ah," he sighed. "I would that you had asked anything but that. Alas, you will not find the man you seek amongst the living." He shook his head with weary regret. "Our young Prince Bran is dead."

"Dead! Oh, dear God, how?" Aethelfrith gasped. "When did this happen?"

"Last autumn, it was," replied the bishop. "As to how it happened—there was a fight, and he was cruelly cut down when trying to escape Count de Braose's knights." The English monk staggered backward and collapsed on a bench against the wall. "Here; rest a moment," said Asaph. "Brother Clyro, fetch our guest some water."

Clyro hobbled away, and the bishop sat down beside his guest. "I am sorry, my friend," he said. "Your question caught me off guard, or I might have softened the blow for you."

"Where is he buried? I will go and offer a prayer for his soul."

"You knew our Bran?"

"Met him once. He stayed the night with me—he and that tall tree of a fellow—what was his name? John! They had a priest with them. Good man, I think. One of yours?"

"Iwan, yes. And Ffreol, perhaps?"

"The very fellows!" Aethelfrith nodded. "They were on their way to Lundein to see the king. I went with them in the end. Sorely disappointed they were. But I could have told them. The Ffreinc are bastards."

"From what we have been able to learn," Asaph said, "our Bran was captured on his way home. He was killed a few days later trying to escape." He regarded his visitor with soft-eyed sadness. "It pains me the more," he continued, "but Iwan and Brother Ffreol also fell afoul of Count de Braose."

"Dead, too? All of them?" asked Aethelfrith.

Bishop Asaph bent his head in sorrowful assent.

"Filthy Norman scum," growled the friar. "Kill first and repent later. That is all they know. Worse than Danes!"

"There was nothing to be done," Asaph said. "We said a Mass for him, of course. But"—he lifted his hands helplessly—"there it is."

"So now you have no king," observed Aethelfrith.

"Bran was the last of his line," affirmed the bishop. "We must be content now to simply survive and endure this unjust reign as best we can. And now"——his voice quivered slightly——"another blow has been dealt us. The monastery has been taken over for a market town."

"Scabby thieves, the lot of 'em!" muttered Aethelfrith. "Nay, worse than that. Even the lowest thief wouldn't rob God of his home."

"Baron de Braose has determined to install his own churchmen in this place. They are to arrive any day——indeed, when you came to the door, we thought it might be the new abbot come to drive us from our chapel."

"Where will you go?"

"We are not without friends. The monastery of Saint Dyfrig in the north is sister to Llanelli, or once was. We will go to them . . . and from there?" The bishop offered a forlorn smile. "It is in God's hands."

"Then I am doubly sorry," said Aethelfrith. "This world is full of trouble, God knows, and he spares not his own servants." Brother Clyro returned with a bowl of water, which he offered to their guest. Aethelfrith accepted the bowl and drank deeply.

"Why did you want to see our Bran?" asked the bishop when he had finished.

"I had a notion to help him," replied the friar. "But now that I see how events have fallen out, I warrant it a poor idea. In any event, it is of no consequence now."

"I see," replied the bishop. He did not press the matter. "Have you travelled far?"

"From Hereford. I keep an oratory there——Saint Ennion's. Have you heard of it?"

"Of course, yes," replied the bishop. "One of our own dear saints from long ago."

"To be sure," conceded Aethelfrith. "But it is home to me now."

"Then it is too far to come and return all at once. You must stay with us a few days"—the bishop lifted a hand in a gesture of helplessness—"or until the Ffreinc come to drive us all away."

Friar Aethelfrith spent the next day helping Asaph and Clyro pack their belongings. They wrapped the bound parchment copies of the Psalms and the book of Saint Matthew, as well as the small golden bowl used for the Eucharist on high holy days. These things had to be disguised and secreted amongst the other bundles of clerical implements and utensils, for fear that the Ffreinc would confiscate them if their value was known.

They finished their work and enjoyed a simple supper of stewed beans with a little sliced leek and burdock. The next morning, Brother Aethelfrith bade his friends farewell and started back to his oratory. The merchants he had followed to Elfael had also concluded their business, and as he passed Castle Truan—what the Normans were now calling Caer Cadarn—he saw five mule-drawn carts turn out onto the road and thought, now that the wagons were empty of goods, he might beg bold and ask for a ride.

So he quickened his pace and by midmorning had caught up with the wagon van when it paused to water the animals at the valley stream before starting up the long slope of the forested ridge. He came within hailing distance and gave a shout, which was not returned. "I see they still have some manners to learn," he muttered. "But no matter. They will have to be hard-hearted indeed to refuse my request."

As he neared the fording place, he saw that the traders were standing together in a clump, motionless, with their backs to him; they seemed to be staring at something on the far side of the stream.

He hurried to join them, calling, "Pax vobiscum!"

One of the traders turned on him. "Keep your voice down!" he whispered savagely.

Mystified, the friar shut his mouth with a click of his teeth. Taking his place beside the men, he stared across the fording place and into the wood. The mules, impassive creatures ordinarily, seemed restless and uneasy; they jigged in their traces and tossed their heads. And yet the wood beyond the stream seemed quiet enough. Brother Aethelfrith could see no one on the road; all seemed calm and tranquil.

"Forgive my curiosity, friend," he whispered to the man next to him, "but what is everyone looking at?"

"Gerald thought he saw the *thing*—the creature," the merchant whispered back, his voice tense in the unnatural silence. The only sound to be heard was the lazy, liquid gurgle of the water as it slipped around and over the stones.

"What creature?" wondered the priest. Nothing moved amongst the lush green foliage of the trees and lower brushwood.

"The phantom," the man explained. He turned his face to the bowlegged friar. "Do you not know?"

"I know nothing of any phantom," replied Aethelfrith. "What sort of phantom is it presumed to be?"

"Why," replied the merchant, "it takes the form of a great giant of a bird. Men hereabouts call it King Raven."

"Do they indeed?" wondered the friar, much intrigued. "What does it look like—this giant bird?"

The merchant stared at him in disbelief. "By the rood, man! Are you dim? It looks like a thumping great *raven*."

"Shut up!" hissed one of the others just then. "You will have the demon down on us!"

Before anyone could reply to this, one of the other traders threw out his hand and shouted, "There it is!"

Friar Aethelfrith glimpsed a flash of blue-black feathers glinting in the sun and the suggestion of a massive black wing as the creature emerged from the brushwood on the opposite bank a few score paces downstream. Two of the merchants gave out shouts of terrified surprise, and two others fell to their knees, clasping their hands and crying aloud to God and Saint Michael to save them. The rest fled back down the road to the safety of Castle Truan, leaving their carts behind.

"Christ have mercy!" gasped one of the remaining merchants as the creature's head came into view. Its face was an oval of smooth black bone, devoid of feathers, with two round pits where its eyes should have been. Save for the wickedly long pointed beak, its head most resembled a charred human skull.

Lifting its swordlike beak, the thing uttered a piercing shriek that resounded in the deathly silence of the wood. Even as the cry hung in the air, the phantom turned and simply melted back into the shadow of the wood.

The terror-stricken merchants leapt to their feet and ran for their wagons, lashed their mules to motion, and fled back into the valley. Of all those at the stream, only Aethelfrith was left to give chase—which he promptly did.

CHAPTER 35

Gathering up his robe, Aethelfrith strode boldly across the stream and started after the phantom. Upon reaching the far side of the stream, he paused and, finding nothing, proceeded into the brushwood, where the thing had vanished. There was no sign of the creature, and after a few paces he stopped to reconsider. He could hear the traders clattering away into the distance as their wagons bumped over the rutted road. Then, even as he was wondering whether to continue the chase or resume his journey, he saw the faint glimmer of glistening black feathers—just a quick flash before it disappeared into a hedge bank a few hundred paces down the trail. He hurried on.

The ground rose toward the ridge, and he eventually reached the top. Sweating and out of breath, he stumbled upon a game trail that led along the ridgetop. It was old and well established, overarched by the huge limbs of plane trees, elms, and oaks that formed a vault overhead and allowed only intermittent shafts of sunlight to strike down through the leaf canopy and illuminate the path. It was dark as a cellar, but since it was easier than pushing his way through the heavy underbrush, he decided to follow the run and soon realised just how quickly it allowed a man on foot to move about the forest.

The heat had been mounting steadily as the sun arced toward midday, and Aethelfrith was glad for the shade beneath the hanging boughs. He walked along, listening to the thrushes singing in the upper branches and, lower down, the click and chirrup of insects working the dead leaf matter that rotted along the trail. At any moment, he told himself, he would turn back—but the path was soft underfoot, so he continued.

After a time, the trail branched off; the left-hand side continued along the ridgetop, and the right-hand side descended the slope to a rocky hollow. Here the priest stopped to consider which path, if either, to take. The day was speeding from him, and he decided to resume his homeward journey. He turned around and started back, but he had not gone far when he heard voices: murmured only, light as thistledown on the dead-still air, there and gone again, and so faint as to be easily dismissed as the invention of his own imagining.

But years of living alone in his oratory with no company save his own inner musings had made his hearing keen. He held his breath and listened for the sound to come again. His vigilance was rewarded with another feather-soft murmur, followed by the unmistakable sound of laughter.

Frail as a wisp of cobweb adrift on the breeze, it nonetheless gave him a direction to follow. He took the right-hand trail leading down the back of the ridge. The path fell away steeply as it entered the hollow below, and Aethelfrith, his short legs unable to keep up with his bulk, plunged down the hill.

He entered the hollow in a rush, tripped over a root, and fell, landing with a mighty grunt at the feet of the great black phantom raven. He slowly raised his fearful gaze to see the ominous black head regarding him with malevolent curiosity. The fantastic wings spread wide, and the thing swooped.

The priest rolled on his belly and tried to avoid the assault, but he was too slow, and he felt his arm seized in a steely grip as he squirmed on the ground. "God save me!" he cried.

"Shout louder," hissed the creature. "God may hear you yet."

"Let be!" he cried in English, wriggling like an eel to get free. "Let me go!"

"Do you want to kill him, or should I?"

Aethelfrith twisted his head around and saw a tall, brawny man step forward. He wore a long, hooded cloak into which were woven a multitude of small tatters of green cloth; twigs and branches and leaves of all kinds had also been attached to the curious garment. Regarding the priest with a frown, he drew a knife from his belt. "I'll do it."

"Wait a little," spoke the raven with a human voice. "We'll not kill him yet. Time enough for that later." To the friar, he said, "You were at the ford. Did anyone else follow?"

Struggling in the creature's unforgiving clutch, it took the priest a moment to realise that the thing had spoken to him. Turning his eyes to his captor once more, he saw not the bone-thin shanks of a bird, but the well-booted feet and legs of a man: a man wearing a long cloak covered entirely with black feathers. The face staring down at him was an expressionless death's head, but deep in the empty eye sockets, Aethelfrith caught the glimmer of a living eye.

"I ask for the last time," the black-cloaked man said. "Did anyone follow you?"

"No, sire," replied the priest. "I came alone. God have mercy, can we not talk this out? I am a priest, am I not?"

"That you are, Aethelfrith!" said the creature, releasing him at once.

"Pax vobiscum!" cried the priest, scrambling to his feet. "I mean no harm. I only thought to—"

"Tuck!" exclaimed the man in the leafy cloak.

Reaching up a black-gloved hand, the creature took hold of the sharp raven beak and lifted it to reveal a man's face beneath.

"Blesséd Jesus," gasped the astonished friar. "Is it Bran?"

"Greetings, Tuck," laughed Bran. "What brings you to our wood?"

"You are dead!"

"Not as dead as some might wish," he said, removing the high-crested hood from his head. "Tell us quickly now—how did you come to be here?"

"A hood!" cried the friar, relief bubbling over into exultation. "It is just a hood!"

"A hood, nothing more," admitted Bran. "Why are you here?"

"I came to find *you*, did I not?" The friar stared at the strangely costumed man in amazement. "And here you are. Sweet Peter's beard, but you do not half frighten a body!"

"Friar Tuck!" called Iwan, stepping close. He gave the priest a thump on the back. "You held your life in your hands just then. What of the others—the men at the ford—did they see you?"

"Nay, John. They all ran away clutching their bowels." He smiled at the memory. "You put the fear of the devil in them, no mistake."

Bran smiled. "Good." To Iwan he said, "Bring the horses. We will meet Siarles as planned."

"Tuck, too?" wondered Iwan.

"Of course." Bran turned and started away.

"Wait," called the cleric. "I came to Elfael to find you. I have something important to say."

"Later," Bran told him. "We must be miles from here before midday. Our day's work has only begun. Come along," he said, beckoning the priest to follow. "Watch and learn."

The game run was narrow, and the horses were fast, pounding along the ridgetop track as the outreaching hazel branches whipped past. Bran, following Iwan's lead, slashed his mount across the withers with his reins, careering through the forest. The trail continued to climb as the ridge rose, bending around to the north; upon reaching the summit, they abandoned the run and struck off along another trail, moving west toward the edge of the forest. The riders might have travelled more quickly but for the extra weight behind Bran, clinging on for dear life.

The trail dropped sharply into a rocky defile. The pathway became rough under hoof, and the riders slowed. Stones the size of houses rose abruptly on each hand, forming a winding and shadowed corridor through which they had to pick their way carefully. When the path grew too narrow, they abandoned their mounts, tying them to a small pine tree growing in a crevice, and then proceeded on foot.

Silently, they stalked along a stone gallery so close they could have touched both sides with arms outstretched. This trail ended, and they stepped out into a small clearing, where they were met by another man—also dressed in a long, hooded cloak of green tatters. "Where have you been?" he whispered sharply. He saw the bandy-legged priest toiling along in Bran's wake and asked, "Where did you find that?"

Ignoring the question, Bran asked, "Are they here?"

"Aye," answered the man, "but they will soon be moving on—if they are not already gone." He darted away. "Hurry!"

Bran turned to his visitor and said, "You must swear a sacred oath to hold your tongue and keep silent."

"Why? What is going to happen?" asked Aethelfrith.

"Swear it!" insisted Bran. "Whatever happens, you must swear."

"On my naked soul, I swear silence," the friar replied. "May all the saints bear witness."

"Now stay out of sight." To Iwan, looking on, he said, "Take up your position. You know what to do."

All three moved off at a fast trot. Brother Aethelfrith stood for a moment, catching his breath, and then hurried after them. Soon the surrounding wood began to thin somewhat, and they came to a dell with huge boulders strewn amongst the standing trees like miniature mountains. At the far end of the dell, the forest ended, and the Vale of Elfael opened before them.

Beneath a great spreading beech tree at the forest's edge, three swineherds were taking their midday meal—two men and a boy, eating from a tuck bag they passed between them. All around them their scattered herd—thirty or more large grey-and-black-spotted swine—grubbed and rooted for last year's acorns and beech mast beneath the trees.

Without a word, Bran and his two companions left the trail, quickly melting into the shadowed greenwood. Aethelfrith knelt down on the path to catch his breath and wait to see what would happen.

Nothing happened.

His attention had begun to drift when he heard a shout from the swineherds. Turning his eyes back to the trio of herdsmen, the friar saw that all three were on their feet and staring into the wood. He could not see what had drawn their attention, but he could guess.

The three remained stock-still, unable or unwilling to move, rigid with fear. Then Aethelfrith saw what they had seen: the elusive black shape moving slowly in and out of the shadows amongst the trees. At the same time, two figures in green emerged from the wood behind the watching herdsmen. Keeping the low-hanging beech between the swineherds and the black shape that held their attention, the two green-cloaked men, using nothing more than short staves, quickly culled eight pigs from the herd and led them away into the wood.

Wonder of wonders, the swine followed the strange herdsmen willingly and without a sound. In less time than it would have taken Aethelfrith to tell, the livestock had been removed from the dell. Just as the animals disappeared into the forest, there arose a ghastly unnatural shriek from the surrounding wood. It was the same screech the priest had heard at the ford, only now he knew what it signified.

The swineherds, terrified by the inhuman cry, threw themselves to the ground and covered their heads with their mantles. They were still cowering there, not daring to move, when Iwan appeared and, with a gesture only, summoned Tuck to follow him. They returned to the horses then and waited for Bran, who soon joined them. "You can have Siarles's horse," Bran told the priest. "He is bringing the pigs."

The three retreated back down the narrow defile, retracing their steps until they reached a wider way, and then rode north into the heart of the forest. Unaccustomed to riding, it was all

Aethelfrith could do to remain in the saddle, let alone guide his mount. He soon lost all sense of distance and direction and contented himself with merely keeping up as he pressed deeper and ever deeper into the dark heart of the ancient wood.

Eventually, they slowed their horses and, after splashing across a brook and gaining a long, low rise, arrived at the great black trunk of a lightning-blasted oak. Here Bran stopped and dismounted. Aethelfrith, grateful for the chance to quit the saddle, climbed down and stood looking around. The trees were giants of the forest, their limbs huge and majestic, their crowns lofty. Their great girth meant that their trunks were far apart from one another and little grew in the shadows beneath them. Younger trees struggled up, straight and thin as arrows, to reach the sun; most failed. Unable to sustain their own weight, they fell back to earth—but slowly, slanting down at unnatural angles.

"This way," said Bran, motioning his guest to follow. He stepped through the split in the trunk of the blighted oak as through an open door. The friar followed, emerging on the other side into a wide, sunlit hollow large enough to contain a most curious settlement, a veritable village of hovels and huts made from branches and bark and—could it be?—the horns, bones, and skins of deer, oxen, and other beasts. On the far side of the glade were small fields, where a number of settlement dwellers were at work amongst the furrowed rows of beans, peas, and leeks.

"Passing strange," murmured Aethelfrith, oddly delighted with the place.

"This is Cél Craidd," Bran told him. "My stronghold. You are welcome here, Tuck, my friend. The freedom of my home is yours."

The cleric made a polite bow. "I accept your hospitality."

"Come along, then," said Bran, leading the way into the peculiar settlement, "there is someone else I would have you meet before we sit down to hear your news."

Bran, his cloak of black feathers gleaming blue and silver in the bright daylight, led the way to one of the hovels in the centre of the settlement. As they approached, an old woman emerged, pushing aside the deer hide that served as her door. She regarded the newcomer with a keen dark eye and then touched the back of her hand to her forehead.

"This is Angharad," said Bran. "She is our banfáith." Seeing that the priest did not understand the word, he added, "It is like a bard. Angharad is Chief Bard of Elfael."

To the old woman, he said, "And this is Brother Aethelfrith—he helped us in Lundein." Clapping a hand to the friar's shoulder, Bran continued, "He has come with news he deems so important that he has travelled all the way from Hereford."

"Then let us hear it," said Angharad. Stepping back, she pulled aside the deerskin and indicated that her guests should enter. The single large room had a bare earth floor; packed hard and swept clean, it was covered by an array of animal skins and handwoven coverings. More skins encircled a round firepit in the centre of the room, where a small fire flickered amongst the embers. There was a sleeping pallet on one side and a row of woven grass baskets.

Bran untied the leather laces at the neck of his feathered cloak and hung it on the tine of a protruding antler above one of the baskets; above the cloak, he hung the high-crested hood with its weird mask, then removed the black leather gauntlets and put them in the basket. He knelt over a basin on the floor to splash water on his face and drew his hands through his black hair. Shaking off the excess moisture, he arched his back and then suddenly slumped and sighed, and his body quivered as if with cold. The tremor passed, and Bran straightened. When he turned, he had changed slightly; he was more the Bran whom Aethelfrith remembered.

Angharad invited her guests to sit and stepped out to a barrel beside the door; she dipped out a bowl, which she brought to the priest. "Peace, friend, and welcome," she said, offering him the cup. "May God be good to thee all thy days, and strengthen thee to every virtue."

The priest bowed his head. "May his peace and joy forever increase," he replied, "and may you reap the rich harvest of his blessing."

"It is water only," Bran explained. "We don't have enough grain to make ale just now."

"Water is the elixir of life," declared the priest, raising the bowl to his lips. "I never tire of drinking it." He sucked down a healthy draught and passed the bowl to Bran, who also drank and passed it to Iwan. When the big man finished, he returned the bowl to Angharad, who set it aside and took her place at the fire ring with the men.

"I trust all is well in Hereford," said Bran, easing into the reason for the friar's journey to Elfael.

"Better than here," replied Aethelfrith. "But that could change." Leaning forward in anticipation of the effect his words would have, he said, "What if I told you a flood of silver was coming your way?"

"If you told me that," replied Bran, "I would say we will all need very big buckets."

"Aye," agreed the priest, "and tubs and vats and casks and

tuns and barrels and cisterns large and small. And I say you had best find them quickly, because the flood is on the rise."

Bran eyed the stout priest, whose plump cheeks were bunched in a self-satisfied grin. "Tell us," he said. "I would hear more of this silver flood."

CHAPTER 36

The rider appeared unannounced in the yard at Caer Rhodl. The horse was exhausted: hide wet with lather, spume pink with blood, hooves cracked. Lord Cadwgan took one look at the suffering animal and its dead-eyed rider and commanded his grooms to take the poor beast to the stables and tend it. To the rider, he said, "Friend, your news must be grievous indeed to drive a good horse this way. Speak it out, and quickly—there will be ale and warm meat waiting for you."

"Lord Cadwgan," said the rider, swaying on his feet, "the words I have are bitter ashes in my mouth."

"Then spit them out and be done, man! They will grow no sweeter for sucking on them."

Drawing himself up, the messenger nodded once and announced, "King Rhys ap Tewdwr is dead—killed in battle this time yesterday."

Lord Cadwgan felt the ground shift beneath his feet. Only months ago, Rhys, King of Deheubarth—and the man most Britons considered the last best hope of the Cymry to turn back the tide of the Ffreinc invaders—had returned from exile in Ireland, where he had spent the last few years ingratiating himself with Irish kings, slowly eliciting support for the British cause against the Ffreinc. Word had gone out that Rhys had returned with a massive warhost and was preparing to make a bid for the English throne while William the Red was preoccupied in Normandie. Such was the strength of King Rhys ap Tewdwr's name that even men like Cadwgan—who had long ago bent the knee to the Ffreinc king—allowed themselves to hope that the yoke of the hated overlords might yet be thrown off.

"How can this be?" Cadwgan wondered aloud. "By whose hand? Was it an accident?" Before the messenger could answer, the lord collected himself and said, "Wait. Say nothing." He raised his hand to prevent the reply. "We will not stand in the yard like market gossips. Come to my chambers and tell me how this tragedy has come about."

On his way through the hall, King Cadwgan ordered drink to be brought to his room at once, then summoned his steward. With Queen Anora and Prince Garran in attendance, he sat the messenger down in a chair and commanded him to tell all he knew of the affair.

"Word came to our king that Ffreinc marchogi had crossed our borders and set fire to some of our settlements," the messenger began after taking a long pull on the ale cup. "Thinking it was only a few raiders, Lord Rhys sent a warband to put a stop to it. When none of the warriors returned, the alarm was raised and the warhost assembled. We found the Ffreinc encamped in a valley inside our lands, where they were building one of those stone caers they glory in so greatly."

"And this inside the Marches, you say?" asked Cadwgan.

The messenger nodded. "Inside the very borders of Deheubarth itself."

"What did Lord Rhys say to that?"

"Our king sent word to the commander of the foreigners, demanding their departure and payment for the burned settlements on pain of death."

"Good," said Cadwgan, nodding his approval.

"The Ffreinc refused," continued the messenger. "They cut off the noses of the messengers and sent the bloodied men back to tell the king that the Ffreinc would leave only with the head of Rhys ap Tewdwr as their prize." The messenger lifted his cup and drank again. "By this we knew that they had come to do battle with our lord and kill him if they could."

"They left him no choice," observed Garran, quick to refill the cup. "They wanted a fight."

"They did," agreed the rider sadly, raising the cup to his lips once more. "Though the Ffreinc force was smaller than our own—fewer than fifty knights, and maybe two hundred footmen—we were wary of some treachery. God knows, we were right to be so. The moment we assembled the battle line, more marchogi appeared from the south and west—six hundred at least, two hundred mounted, and twice that on foot. They had taken ship and come in behind us." The messenger paused. "They had marched through Morgannwg and Ceredigion, and no one lifted a hand to stop them, nor to warn us."

"What of Brycheiniog?" demanded Cadwgan. "Did they not send the battle host?"

"They did not, my lord," replied the man curtly. "Neither blade nor shield of Brycheiniog was seen on the field."

Speechless with shock, King Cadwgan stared at the man before him. Prince Garran muttered an oath beneath his breath and was silenced by his mother, who said, "Pray continue, sir. What of the battle?"

"We fought for our lives," said the messenger, "and sold them dear. At the end of the first day, Rhys raised the battle call and sent to the cantrefs close about, but none answered. We were alone." He passed a hand before his eyes as if to wipe the memory from his sight. "Even so," he continued, "the fighting continued until the evening of the second day. When Lord Rhys saw that we could not win, he gathered the remnant of the warhost to him, and we drew lots—six men to ride with word to our kinsmen, and the rest to remain and seek glory with their comrades." The messenger paused, gazing emptily down. "I was one of the six," he said in a low voice, "and here I am to tell you—Deheubarth is no more."

King Cadwgan let out a long breath. "This is bad," he said solemnly. "There is no getting around it." *First Brychan at Elfael,* he thought, *and now Rhys at Deheubarth.* The Ffreinc, it seemed, would not be content with England. They meant to have all of Wales, too.

"If Deheubarth is fallen," said Prince Garran, looking to his father, "then Brycheiniog cannot be far behind."

"Who has done this?" asked Queen Anora. "The Ffreinc—whose warriors were they?"

"Baron Neufmarché," answered the messenger.

"You know this?" demanded Cadwgan quickly. "You know this for a truth?"

The messenger gave a sharp jerk of his chin sideways. "Not for a truth, no. The leaders amongst them wore a strange livery—one we have not seen before. But some of the wounded we captured spoke that name before they died."

"Did you see the end?" asked Anora, clasping her hands beneath her chin in anticipation of the answer.

"Aye, my lady. Myself and the other riders—we watched it from the top of the hill. When the standard fell, we scattered with the news."

"Where will you go now?" she enquired.

"I ride to Gwynedd, to inform the northern kingdoms," replied the messenger. "God willing, and my horse survives."

"That horse has run as far as it will go today and for many days, I fear," replied the king. "I will give you another, and you will rest and refresh yourself here while it is readied."

"You should stay here tonight," Anora told the messenger. "Continue on your way tomorrow."

"My thanks to you, my lady, but I cannot. The northern kings were raising warriors to join us. They must hear that they can no longer look to the south for help."

The king commanded his steward to bring food and make ready provisions the messenger could take with him. "I will see to the horse," said Garran.

"My lord king, I am much obliged." Having discharged his duty, the messenger slumped, grey faced, into the chair.

"We will leave you to your rest now," said the queen, leading her husband out.

Once out of hearing of the chamber, the king turned to his wife. "There it is," he concluded gloomily. "The end has begun. So long as the south remained free, it was possible to think that one day the Cymry might yet shake off the Ffreinc. There will be nothing to stop the greedy dogs now."

Queen Anora said, "You are client to Neufmarché. He will not move against us."

"Client I may be," spat the king bitterly. "But I am Cymry first, last, and always. If I pay tribute and rents to the baron, it is only to keep him far away from here. Now it seems he will not be satisfied with anything less than taking all of Cymru and driving us into the sea."

He shook his head as the implications of the catastrophe rolled over him. "Neufmarché will keep us only so long as it pleases him to do so. Just now he needs someone to hold the land and work it, but when the time comes to repay a favour, or provide some relative with an estate, or reward some service rendered—*then*," intoned Cadwgan ominously, "then all we have will be taken from us, and we will be driven out."

"What can we do?" asked Anora, bunching her mantle in her fists. "Who is left that can stand against them?"

"God knows," replied Cadwgan. "Only God knows."

Baron Neufmarché received the news of his resounding victory with a restrained, almost solemn demeanour. After accepting a report on the casualties suffered by his forces, he thanked his commanders for carrying out his orders so well and so completely, awarding two of them lands in the newly conquered territory, and another an advancement in rank to a lordship and the command of the unfinished castle that had so readily lured King Rhys ap Tewdwr to his doom. "We will speak more of this tonight at table. Go now; rest yourselves. You have done me good service, and I am pleased."

When the knights had gone, he went to his chapel to pray.

The simple room built within the stone walls of the castle was cool in the warmth of the day. The baron liked the air of calm quiet of the place. Approaching the simple wooden altar with its gilt cross and candle, he went down on one knee and bowed his head.

"Great God," he began after a moment, "I thank you for delivering the victory into my hand. May your glory increase. I beg you, almighty Lord, have mercy on those whose lives were given in this campaign. Forgive their sins, account their valour to their merit, and welcome them to your eternal rest. Heal the wounded, Lord Christ, and send them a swift recovery. In all ways comfort those who have suffered the pains of battle."

He remained in the chapel and was still enjoying the serenity when Father Gervais appeared. Aging now, though still vigorous, the cleric had been a member of the baron's court since coming to Beauvais as a newly shorn priest to serve Bernard's father.

"Ah, it is you, my lord," said the priest when the baron turned. "I thought I might find you here." The grey-robed priest came to stand beside his lord and master. "You are not celebrating the victory with your men?"

"God grant you peace, father," said Bernard. "Celebrating? No, not yet. Later this evening, perhaps."

The priest regarded him for a moment. "Is anything the matter, my son?"

Crossing himself, Neufmarché rose and, taking the priest by the arm, turned him and led him from the chapel, saying, "Walk with me, father. There is something I would ask you."

They climbed to the rampart and began making a slow circuit of the castle wall. "Earl Harold swore a sacred oath to Duke William, did he not?" said the baron after walking awhile. The sun was lowering, touching everything with gold. The summer air was warm and heavy and alive with the click and buzz of insects amongst the reeds and bulrushes of the nearby marshland below the east wall.

"An oath sworn on holy relics in the presence of the

Bishop of Caen," replied Father Gervais. "It was written and signed. There is no doubt about it whatsoever." Glancing at the baron, he said, "But you know this. Why do you ask?"

"The oath," said Bernard, "confirmed the promise made to William that he was to follow Edward as rightful King of England."

"D'une certitude."

"And the matter received the blessing of the pope," said Bernard, "who is God's vicar on earth."

"Again, that is so," agreed the priest. He glanced at the baron, who continued walking, his eyes on the stone paving at his feet. "My lord, are you fretting over the divine right again?"

The baron's head turned quickly. "Fretting? No, father." He turned away again. "Perhaps. A little." He sighed. "It just seems too easy . . ." Unable to find the words, he sighed again. "All this."

"And what do you expect? God is on our side. It is so ordained. William has been chosen of God to be king, and thus any enterprise that supports and increases his kingdom will rightly be blessed of God."

Bernard nodded, his eyes still downcast.

The priest was silent for a moment, then declared, "Ah! I have it. You worry that your support of Duke Robert will be held against you. That you will be called to reckoning, and the price will be too heavy to bear. That is what is troubling you, *n'est-ce pas?"*

"It has occurred to me," the baron confessed. "I sided with Robert against Rufus. The king has not forgotten, and neither will God, I think. There is an accounting to be rendered. Payment is due; I can feel it."

"But you were upholding the law," protested the priest.

"You will remember that at the time, Robert *was* the rightful heir. He had to be supported, even against the claims of his own brother. You were right to do so."

"And yet," replied the baron, "Robert did not become king."

"In his heavenly wisdom, God saw fit to bestow the kingship on his brother William," said Father Gervais. "How were you to know?"

"How *was* I to know?" repeated Bernard, wondering aloud.

"Précisément!" declared the priest. "You could not know, for God had not yet revealed his choice. And I believe that is why Rufus did not punish those who went against him. He understood that you were only acting in good faith according to holy law, and so he forgave you. He returned you to his grace and favour, as was only just and fair." The priest spread his hands as if presenting an object so obvious that it needed no further description. "Our king forgave you. *Voilà!* God has forgiven you."

In the clear light of the elderly priest's unfaltering certainty, Bernard felt his melancholy dissipating. "There is yet one more matter," he said.

"Let me hear it," said the priest. "Unburden your soul and obtain absolution."

"I promised to send food to Elfael," the baron confessed. "But I did not."

"But you did," countered the priest. "I saw the men readying the supplies. I saw the wagons leave. Where did they go, if not to the relief of the Welsh?"

"Before, I mean. I let the Welsh priest think that Count de Braose had stolen the first delivery, because it suited my purposes."

"I see." Father Gervais tapped his chin with an ink-stained finger. "But you made good your original vow."

"Oh yes—doubled it, in fact."

"Well then," replied the priest, "you have overturned the wrong and provided your own penance. You are absolved."

"And you are certain that my attainment of lands in Wallia is ordained by heaven?"

"Deus vult!" the priest confirmed. "God wills it." He raised his hand to the baron's arm and gave it a fatherly squeeze. "You can believe that. Your endeavours prosper because God has so decreed. You are his instrument. Rejoice and be grateful."

Bernard de Neufmarché smiled, doubts routed and faith restored. "Thank you, father," he said, his countenance lightening. "As always, your counsel has done me good service."

The priest returned his smile. "I am glad. But if you wish to continue in favour with the Almighty, then build him a church in your new territories."

"One church only?" said the baron, his spirits rising once more. "I will build ten!"

CHAPTER 37

Y̶ou cannot save Elfael one pig at a time,"
Brother Aethelfrith was saying.

"Have you *seen* our pigs?" Bran quipped. "They are mighty
pigs."

Iwan chuckled, and Siarles smirked.

"Laugh if you must," said the friar, growing peevish. "But
you will wish soon enough you had listened to me."

"The people are hungry," Siarles put in. "They welcome
whatever we can give them."

"Then give them back their land!" cried Aethelfrith. "God
love you, man; do you not see it yet?"

"And is this not the very thing we are doing?" Bran said.
"Calm yourself, Tuck. We are already making plans to do
exactly what you suggest."

The friar shook his tonsured head. "Are you deaf as well
as blind?"

"Why do you think we watch the road?" asked Iwan.

"Watch it all you like," snipped the priest. "It will avail
you nothing if you are not prepared for the flood I'm talking about."

The others frowned as one. "Tell us, then," said Bran. "What is it that we lack?"

"Sufficient greed," replied the cleric. "By the rood and Jehoshaphat's nose, you think too small!"

"Enlighten us, O Head of Wisdom," remarked Iwan dryly.

"See here." Tuck licked his lips and leaned forward. "Baron de Braose is building three castles on the northern and western borders of Elfael, is he not? He has a hundred—maybe two hundred—masons, not to mention all those workers toiling away. Workmen must be paid. Sooner or later, they *will* be paid—every last man—hundreds of them." Aethelfrith smiled as he watched the light come up in his listeners' eyes. "Ah! You see it now, do you not?"

"Hundreds of workers paid in silver," said Bran, hardly daring to voice the thought. "A river of silver."

"A *flood* of silver," corrected Aethelfrith. "Is this not what I am saying? Even now the baron is preparing to send his wagons with strongboxes full of good English pennies to pay all those workers. All the money you need will soon be flooding into the valley, and it is ripe for the taking."

"Well done, Tuck!" cried Bran, and he jumped to his feet and began pacing around the fire ring. "Did you hear, banfáith?" he asked, turning suddenly to Angharad sitting hunched on her three-legged stool beside the door. "Here is the very chance we need to drive the foreigners from our land."

"Aye, could be." She nodded in cautious agreement. "Mind, the Ffreinc will not send their silver through the land unprotected. There will be marchogi, and in plenty."

Bran thanked her for her word of warning, then turned to his champion. "Iwan?"

He frowned, sucking his teeth thoughtfully before

answering. "We have— what?—maybe six men amongst us who have ever held more than a spade. We cannot go against a body of battle-trained knights on horseback."

"Yet the silver will not leap into our hands of its own accord, I think," offered Siarles.

Angharad, frowning on her stool, spoke again. "If thou wouldst obtain justice, thou must thyself be just."

The others turned questioning glances toward Bran, who explained, "I think she means we cannot attack them without provocation."

The group fell silent in the face of such a challenge. "Truly," Bran said at last. Raising his head, he gazed across the fire ring, dark eyes glinting with merry mischief. "We cannot take on knights on horseback, but King Raven can."

Brother Tuck remained unmoved. "It will take more than a big black bird to frighten battle-hardened knights, will it not?"

"Well then," Bran concluded. His smile was slow, dark, and fiendish. "We will give them something more to fear."

Abbot Hugo de Rainault was used to better things. He had served in the courts of Angevin kings; princes had pranced to his whim; dukes and barons had run to his beck and bidding. Hugo had been to Rome—twice!—and had met the pope both times: Gregory and Urban had each granted him audience in their turn, and both had sent him away with gifts of jewel-encased relics and precious manuscripts. He had been extolled for an archbishopric and, in due time, perhaps even a papal legacy. He had governed his own abbey, controlled immense estates, held dominion over the lives of countless men and women, and enjoyed a splendour even the kings of England and France could sincerely envy.

Alas, all that was before the rot set in.

He had done what he could to prevent the debacle once the tide of fortune began to turn against him—benefactions and indulgences; costly gifts of horses, falcons, and hunting hounds to courtiers in high places; favourable endorsements for those in a position to speak a good word on his behalf. The reach of kings is long, however, and their memories for insults even longer. When William the Red cut up rough over the throne of England, Hugo had done what any right-thinking churchman would have done—the *only* thing he could have done. What choice did he have? Robert Curthose, the Conqueror's eldest, was the legitimate heir to his father's throne. Everyone knew it; most of the barons agreed and supported Robert's claim. Who could have known the deceitful William would move so swiftly and with such devastating accuracy? He cut the legs out from under his poor deluded brother with such uncanny ease, one had to wonder whether the hand of God was not in it after all.

Be that as it may, the whole sorry affair was the beginning of a long decline for Hugo, who had seen his own fortunes steadily wane since the day William the Red snatched away the crown. Now, at long last, the abbot was reduced to this: exile in a dreary backwater province full of hostile natives, to be bootlicker to a half-baked nobody of a count.

Hugo supposed he should be grateful, even for this little, but gratitude was not a quality he had cultivated. Instead, he cursed the rapacious Rufus; he cursed the blighted wilderness of a country he had come to; and he cursed the monstrous fate that had brought him so very low.

Low, he may be. Shattered, perhaps. Even devastated. But not destroyed. And never, ever finished.

He would, like Lazarus, rise again from this dismal hinterland tomb. He would use this opportunity, weak and slender though it was, to haul himself up out of the muck of his disgrace and reclaim his former stature. The de Braoses' new church might be an unlikely place to start, but stranger things had happened. That Baron William de Braose was a favourite of Red William was the single bright light in the whole cavalcade of misery he now endured. The road to the successful restoration of the abbot's wealth and power ran through the baron, and if Hugo had to wet-nurse his lordship's snotty-nosed nephew to ingratiate himself, so be it.

Time was against him, he knew. He was no longer a young man. The years had not mellowed him, however; if anything, they had made him leaner, harder, and subtler. Outwardly serene and benevolent, with a charitable smile—when it suited his interests—his scheming, devious soul never slept. Though his hair had gone white, he had lost none of it, nor any teeth. His body was still resilient and sturdy, with a peasant's enduring strength. What is more, he retained all the ruthless cunning and insatiable ambition of his younger years. Allied to that was the sagacity of age and the sly wisdom that had kept him alive through travails that would have consumed lesser men.

He paused in the saddle and gazed out over the Vale of Elfael: his new and, he fervently hoped, temporary home. It was not much to look at, although it was not without, he grudgingly admitted, a certain bucolic charm. The air was good and the ground fertile. Obviously, there was water enough for any purpose. There were worse places, he considered, to begin the reconquest.

Attending the abbot were two of Baron de Braose's knights. They rode with him for protection. The rest of his entourage and belongings would come in a week or so—three wagons filled with the few books and treasures left to him, and a smattering of more practical ecclesiastical accoutrements, such as robes, stoles, his mitre, crook, staff, standard, and other oddments. There would be five attendants: two priests, one to say Mass and another to carry out the details of administration, and three lay brothers—cook, chamberer, and porter. With these, chosen for their loyalty and unfaltering obedience, Abbot Hugo would begin afresh.

Once officially installed in his new church, Hugo would commence building his new empire. De Braose wanted a church; Hugo would give him an abbey entire. First would come a stone-built minster worthy of the name, and with it, a hospital—both inn for passing dignitaries and healing centre for those wealthy enough to pay for their care. There would be a great tithe barn and stable, and a kennel to raise hunting hounds to sell to the nobility. Then, when these were firmly established, a monastery school—the better to draw in the sons of the region's noblemen and worthies and reap fat grants of land and favours from appreciative parents.

With these thoughts, he lifted the reins and urged his brown palfrey on once more, following his escort to the count's fortress, where he would spend the night, continuing on to the church the next morning.

Within sight of their destination now, the riders picked up the pace. At the foot of the hill, they turned off the track and rode up to the fortress, passing over the narrow bridge and through the newly erected gate tower, where they were met by the snivelling nephew himself.

"Greetings, Abbot Hugo," called Count Falkes, hurrying to meet him. "I hope you have had a pleasant journey."

"Pax vobiscum," replied the cleric. "God be praised, yes. The journey was blissfully tranquil." He extended his hand for the young count to kiss his ring.

Count Falkes, unused to this courtesy, was taken aback. After a brief but awkward hesitation, he remembered his manners and pressed his lips to the abbot's ruby ring. Hugo, having made his point, now raised the hand over the young count in blessing. *"Benedictus, omni patri,"* he intoned, then smiled. "I imagine it must be easy to forget when one is unaccustomed to such decorum."

"Your Grace," replied the count dutifully. "I assure you, I meant no disrespect."

"It is already forgotten," the abbot replied. "I suppose there is little place for such ceremony here in the Marches." He turned to take in the hall, stables, and yard with a sweep of his keen eyes. "You have done well in a short time."

"Most of what you see was here already," the count conceded. "Aside from a few necessary improvements, I have not had time to construct anything better."

"Now that you say it," intoned the abbot, "I thought it possessed a certain quaint charm not altogether fitting the tastes of your uncle, the baron."

"We have plans to enlarge this fortress in due course," the count assured him. "The town and church are of more immediate concern, however. I have ordered those to be finished first."

"A wise course, to be sure. Make no mistake, I am most eager to see it all—especially the church. That is the solid cornerstone of any earthly dominion. There can be no true prosperity or governance without it." Abbot Hugo raised his hands and waved off any reply the count might make. "But, no, here I am, preaching to my host when the welcome cup awaits. Forgive me."

"Please, Your Grace, come this way," said Falkes, leading the way to his hall. "I have prepared a special meal in your honour—and tonight we have wine from Anjou, selected especially for this occasion by the baron himself."

"Do you indeed? Good!" replied Hugo with genuine appreciation. "It has been a long time since I held a cup of that quality. It is a delicacy I will enjoy."

Count Falkes, relieved to have pleased his demanding guest, turned to greet the churchman's escort; he charged Orval, the seneschal, with the care of the knights and then led the abbot into the hall, where they could speak in private before supper.

The hall had been renovated. A fresh layer of clay and gypsum had been applied to the rough timber walls, and after being pain-stakingly smoothed and dried, the whole was whitewashed. The small window in the upper east wall was now closed with a square of oiled sheepskin. A new table sat a short distance from the hearth, with a tall iron candletree at each end. A fire cracked smartly on the big hearth, more for light than heat, and two chairs were drawn up on each side, with a jar and two silver goblets on the table between them.

The count filled the cups and passed one to his guest, and they settled themselves in their chairs to enjoy the wine and gain the measure of each other. "Health to you, Lord Abbot," said Falkes. "May you prosper in your new home."

Hugo thanked him courteously and said, "Truth told, a

churchman has but one home, and it is not of this world. We sojourn here or there awhile, until it pleases God to move us along."

"In any event," replied the count, "I pray your sojourn amongst us is long and prosperous. There is great need here-abouts for a strong hand at the church plough—if you know what I mean."

"The former abbot incompetent, eh?" Raising his cup to his nose, he sniffed the wine, then sipped.

"Not altogether, no," said Falkes. "Bishop Asaph is capable enough in his way—but Welsh. And you know how contrary they can be."

"Little better than pagans," offered Hugo with a sniff, "by all accounts."

"Oh, it is true," confirmed the count. "They are an ill-mannered race—coarse, unlettered, easily inflamed, and contentious as the day is long."

"And are they really as backward as they appear?"

"Difficult to say," answered Falkes. "Hardheaded and stiff-necked, yes. They resist all refinement and delight in ostentation of every kind."

"Like children, then," remarked the abbot. "I also have heard this."

"You would not believe the fuss they make over a good tale, which they will stretch and twist until any truth is bent out of all recognition to the plain facts of the matter. For example," said the count, pouring more wine, "the locals will have it that a phantom has arisen in the forest round about."

"A phantom?"

"Truly," insisted the count, leaning forward in his eager-ness to have something of interest with which to regale his eminent guest. "Apparently, this unnatural thing takes the form of a great bird—a giant raven or eagle or some such— and they have it that this queer creature feeds on cattle and livestock, even human flesh come to that, and the tale is frightening the more timorous."

"Do you believe this story?"

"I do not," replied the count firmly. "But such is their insistence that it has begun disturbing my workmen. Wagoners swear they lost oxen to it, and lately some pigs have gone missing."

"Simple theft would account for it, surely," observed the abbot. "Or carelessness."

"I agree," insisted the count, "and would agree more heartily if not for the fact that the swineherds contend that they actually saw the creature swoop down and snatch the hogs from under their noses."

"They saw this?" marvelled the abbot.

"In full light of day," confirmed the count. "Even so, I would not put much store by it save they are not the only ones to make such a claim. Some of my own knights have seen it— or seen *something*, at least—and these are sturdy, trustworthy men. Indeed, one of my men-at-arms was taken by the creature and narrowly escaped with his life."

"*Mon Dieu, non!*"

"Oh yes, it is true," affirmed the count, taking another sip from his cup. "The men I sent to track down the missing oxen found the animals—or the little left of them. The thing had eaten the wretched beasts, leaving nothing behind but a pile of entrails, some hooves, and a single skull."

"What do you think it can be?" wondered the abbot, savouring the extraordinary peculiarity of the tale.

"These hills are known to be home to many odd happenings," suggested Falkes. "Who is to say?"

"Who indeed?" echoed Abbot Hugo. He drank from his cup for a moment, then mused, "Pigs snatched away in midair, whole oxen gorged, men captured . . . It passes belief."

"To be sure," conceded the count. He drained his cup in a long swallow, then admitted, "Yet—and I do not say this lightly—the affair has reached such a state that I almost hazard to think something supernatural does indeed haunt the forest."

All through the night, Bran sat hunched beside the hearth, arms around his knees, staring into the shimmering flames. Iwan, Aethelfrith, and Siarles had long ago crawled off to sleep, but Angharad sat with him still. Every now and then she would pose a question to sharpen his thinking; otherwise, the hudolion's hut remained steeped in a seething silence—the hush of intense and turbulent thought—as Bran forged the perfect weapon in the glowing fires of his mind.

He was not tired and could not have slept anyway, with his thoughts burning bright. As dawn began to invade the darkness in the east, the fires began to cool, and the shape of his cunning craftwork was revealed.

"That is everything, I think," he said, raising his head to regard the old woman across the smouldering fire ring. "Have I forgotten anything?"

He was rewarded with one of her wrinkled smiles. "You have done well, Master Bran." Raising her hand, palm outward, above her head, she said, "This night you have become a shield to your people. But now, in the time-between-times, you are also a sword."

Bran took that as high approval. He stood, easing out the kinks in his cramped muscles. "Well then," he said, "let us wake the others and get started. There is much to do, and no time to lose."

Angharad lifted her hand to the men slumped across the room. "Patience. Let them sleep. There will be little enough time for that in the days to come." Indicating his own empty sleeping place, she said, "It would be no bad thing if you closed your eyes while you have the chance."

"I could not sleep now for all of the baron's riches," he told her.

"Nor could I," she said, rising slowly. "Since that is the way of it, let us greet the dawn and ask the King of Hosts to bless our battle plan and the hands that must work to make it succeed." She stepped to the door and pushed aside the ox hide, beckoning him to follow.

They stood for a moment in the early light and listened to the forest awaken around them as the dawn chorus of birds filled the treetops. Bran looked out at the pitiful clutch of humble dwellings, but felt himself a king of a vast domain. "The day begins," he said after a moment. "I want to get started."

"In a little while," she suggested. "Let us enjoy the peace of the moment."

"No, now," he countered. "Bring me my hood and cloak; then wake everyone and assemble them. They should remember this day."

"Why this day above any other?"

"Because," explained Bran, "from this day on, they are no longer fugitives and outcasts. Today they become King Raven's faithful flock."

"The *Grellon*," suggested Angharad—an old word, it meant both "flock" and "following."

"Grellon," repeated Bran as the banfáith moved off to strike the iron and rouse Cél Craidd. He turned his face to the warm red glow of the rising sun. "This day," he declared, speaking softly to himself, "the deliverance of Elfael begins."

It is a very great honour," said Queen Anora. "I would have thought you would be pleased."

"How should I be pleased?"

"Relations are strained just now, it is true," her mother granted. "But your father thought that perhaps—"

"My father, the king, has made his views quite clear," Mérian insisted. "Don't tell me he has changed his opinion just because an invitation has come."

"This may be the baron's way of making amends," her mother countered. It was a weak argument, and Mérian regarded her mother with a frown of haughty disdain. "The baron knows he has done wrong and wishes to restore the peace."

"Oh, so now the baron repents, and the king dances dizzy with gratitude?" said Mérian.

"Mérian!" reprimanded her mother sharply. "That will do, girl. You will respect your father and abide by his decision."

"What?" demanded Mérian. "And is there nothing to be said?"

"You have said quite enough." Her mother, stiff backed, turned in her chair to face her. "You will obey."

"But I do not understand," insisted the young woman. "It makes no sense."

"Your father has his reasons," replied the queen simply. "And we must respect them."

"Even if he is wrong?" countered Mérian. "That is most unfair, Mother."

Queen Anora observed her daughter's distraught expression—brows knit, mouth pressed hard, eyes narrowed—and remembered her as an infant demanding to be let down to walk in the grass on the riverbank and being told that she could not because it was too dangerous so close to the water. "It is only an invitation to join the court for a summer," her mother said, trying to lighten the mood. "The time will pass quickly."

"Pass as it may," Mérian declared loftily, "it will pass without me!" She rose and fled her mother's chamber, stalking down the narrow corridor to her own room, where she went to the window and shoved open the shutters with a crash. The early evening air was soft and warm, the fading light like honey on the yard outside her window, but she was not in a mood to take in such things, much less enjoy them. Her father's decision seemed to her arbitrary and unfair. She should, she felt, have a say in it since it was she who must comply.

The baron's courier had arrived earlier in the day with a message asking if Mérian might come to Hereford to spend the remainder of the summer with his lordship's daughter, Sybil. He was hoping Mérian would help teach the young lady something of British customs and speech. Sybil would, of course, gladly reciprocate. Baron Neufmarché was certain the two ladies would become fast friends.

Lord Cadwgan had listened to the message, thanked the courier, and dismissed him in the same breath, saying, "I am much obliged to the baron. Please tell my lord that Mérian would be delighted to accept his invitation."

So that, apparently, was that: a decision that trod heavily on some of her most deeply held convictions, and Mérian was to have nothing to say about it. Since the downfall of Deheubarth, her father had been writhing like a frog in cinders, desperate to distance himself from the reach of Neufmarché. And now, all of a sudden, he seemed just as eager to court the baron's good favour. Why? It made no sense.

The very thought of spending the summer in a castle full of foreigners sent waves of disgust coursing through her slender frame. Her aversion, natural and genuine, was also an evasion.

For what Mérian refused to admit, even to herself, was that she had enjoyed the baron's feast immensely. Truth be told, she had glimpsed an attractive alternative to life in a crumbling caer on the Marches border. She did not allow herself to so much as imagine that she might acquire this life for herself— God forbid! But somewhere in her deepest heart lurked the hunger for the charm and grandeur she had experienced that glittering night, and, heaven help her, it all danced around the person of Baron Neufmarché himself.

For his part, he had made it abundantly clear that he found her beautiful and even desirable. The mere notion awakened feelings Mérian considered so unholy that she tried to suffocate the fledgling thought by depriving it of all rational consideration. On her return to Caer Rhodl after the feast in Hereford, she had considered herself safely out of harm's way and beyond the reach of the temptation the baron's court represented. And now, without so much as an "If you please, Mérian," she was to be sent away to the baron's castle like so much baggage.

She pushed away from the window and flopped back on

her bed. The thought that her father was simply using her to appease Neufmarché and further himself with the baron was too depressing to contemplate. All the same, that was the only explanation that made sense of the situation. If anyone else had suggested such a thing, she would have been the first to shout him down—all the while knowing it was her lot precisely.

In any event, the matter was closed to all appeal. Lord Cadwgan had made his decision and, regardless of anything Mérian or anyone else might say, would not reverse it. For the next few days, Mérian sulked and let everyone know exactly how she felt, delivering herself of long, soulful sighs and dark, moody glances until even Garran, her oblivious brother, complained about the damp chill in the air every time she passed by. But the evil day would not be held off. Her father commanded her to pack her belongings for her stay and had begun to make arrangements to take her to Hereford when Mérian received what she considered a reprieve. It came in the form of a summons for all the baron's nobles to attend him in council. The gathering was to be held at Talgarth in the baron's newly conquered territory, and all client kings and landed lords, along with their families and principal retainers, must attend. It was not an invitation that could be refused. Under feudal law, the unfortunate who failed to attend a formal council faced heavy fines and loss of lands, title, or in extreme cases, even limbs.

Baron Neufmarché did not hold councils often; the last had been five years ago when he had moved his chief residence to Hereford Castle. Then he had served notice that he meant to remain in England and expected his nobles to be ready and forthcoming with their support—chiefly in rents and services, but also in advice.

Lord Cadwgan took a cloudy view of the summons to Deheubarth—the scene of the late King Rhys ap Tewdwr's recent downfall and demise—considering it an insult to the Cymry and a none-too-subtle reminder of Ffreinc supremacy and ascendancy. The rest of the family felt likewise. Perversely, only Mérian welcomed the council, looking upon it as a pardon from the onerous duty that had been forced upon her. Now, instead of Mérian going alone into the enemy camp, the whole family would have to go with her.

"You need not look so pleased," her mother told her. "A little less gloating would better become you."

"I do not gloat," Mérian replied smugly. "But milk for the kit is milk for the cat—is that not what you always say, Mother?"

Three days of preparation followed, and the ordinarily sedate fortress shook life into itself in order to make ready the lord's departure. On the fourth day after receiving the summons, the entourage set out. All rode, save the steward, cook, and groom, who travelled in a horse-drawn wagon piled high with food supplies and equipment. The servants had dusted off and repaired the old leather tents Lord Cadwgan used for campaigns and extended hunting trips—of which there had been few in the last seven or eight years—in anticipation of making camp along the way and at the appointed meeting place.

"How long will the council last?" asked Mérian as she and her father rode along. It was early on the second day of travel, the sun was high and bright, and Mérian was in good spirits—all the more since her father's mood also showed signs of improving.

"How long?" repeated Cadwgan. "Why, as long as

Neufmarché fancies." He thought about it for a moment and said, "There is no way to tell. It depends on the business to be decided. Once, I remember, Old William—the Conqueror, mind, not the red-bearded brat—held a council that lasted four months. Think of that, Mérian. Four whole months!"

Mérian considered that if the baron's council lasted four months, then summer would be over and she would not have to go to Hereford. She asked, "Why so long?"

"I was not there," her father explained. "We were not yet under the thumb of the foreigners and had our own affairs to keep us occupied. As I recall, it was said the king wanted everyone to agree on the levy of taxes for land and chattels."

"Agree with him, you mean."

"Yes," said her father, "but there was more to it than that. The Conqueror wanted as much as he could get, to be sure, but he also knew that most people refuse to pay an unjust tax. He wanted all his earls, barons, and princes to agree—and to *see* one another agree—so that there could be no complaint later."

"Clever."

"Aye, he was a fox, that one," her father continued, and Mérian, after their stormy relations of late, was happy to hear him speak and to listen. "The real reason the council lasted so long came down to the Forest Law."

Mérian had heard of this and knew all right-thinking Britons, as well as Saxons and Danes, resented it bitterly. The reason was simple: the decree transformed all forested lands in England into one vast royal hunting preserve owned by the king. Even to enter a forest without permission of the warrant holder became a punishable offence. This edict, hated as it was from the beginning, made outlaws of all those who, for generations, had made their living out of the woodlands in one way or another—which was nearly everyone.

"So that was when it began?" mused Mérian.

"That it was," Cadwgan confirmed, "and the council twisted and turned like cats on a roasting spit. They refused three times to honour the king's wishes, and each time he sent them back to think about the cost of their refusal."

"What happened?"

"When it became clear that no one would be allowed to return home until the matter was settled, and that the king was unbending, the council had no choice but to assent to the Conqueror's wishes."

"What a spineless bunch of lickspits," observed Mérian.

"Do not judge them too harshly," her father said. "It was either agree or risk being hung as traitors if they openly rebelled. Meanwhile, they watched their estates and holdings slowly descending into ruin through neglect. So with harvest hard upon them, they granted the king the right to his precious hunting runs and went home to explain the new law to their people." Cadwgan paused. "Thank God, the Conqueror did not include the lands beyond the Marches. When I think what the Cymry would have done had *that* been forced on us . . ." He shook his head. "Well, it does not bear thinking about."

PART FIVE

THE
GRELLON

Despite Count Falkes's repeated offer to accompany him, Abbot Hugo insisted on visiting his new church alone. "But the work is barely begun," the count pointed out. "Allow me to bring the architect's drawings so you can see what it will look like when it is finished."

"You are too kind," Hugo had told him. "However, I know your duties weigh heavily enough, and I would not add to them. I am perfectly capable of looking around for myself, and happy to do so. I would not presume to burden you with my whims."

He rode out from the caer on his brown palfrey and arrived at Llanelli just as the labourers were starting their work for the day. The old church, with its stone cross beside the door, still stood on one side of the new town square. It was a rude wood-and-wattle structure, little more than a cow byre in Hugo's opinion; the sooner demolished, the better.

The abbot turned from the sight and cast his critical gaze across the square at a jumbled heap of timber atop a foundation of rammed earth. What? By the rod of Moses!—was *that* the new church?

He strode closer for a better look. A carpenter appeared with a coiled plumb line and a chunk of chalk. "You there!" the abbot shouted. "Come here."

The man glanced around, saw the priestly robes, and hurried over, offering a bow of deference. "You wish to speak to me, Your Grace?"

"What is this?" He flipped a hand at the partially built structure.

"It is to be a church, father," replied the carpenter.

"No," the abbot told him. "No, I do not think that likely."

"Yes," replied the workman. "I do believe it is."

"I am the abbot here," Hugo informed him, "and I say that"——he flapped a dismissive hand at the roughly framed building——"*that* is a tithe barn."

The carpenter cocked his head to one side and regarded the priest with a quizzical expression. "A tithe barn, Your Grace?"

"*My* church will be made of stone," Abbot Hugo told the carpenter, "and it will be of my design and raised on a site of my choosing. I will not have my church fronting the town square like a butcher's stall."

"But, father, see here—"

"Do you doubt me?"

"Not at all. But the count—"

"This is to be *my* church, not the count's. I am in authority here, *compris?*"

"Indeed, Your Grace," answered the confused carpenter. "What am I to tell the master?"

"Tell him I will have the plans ready for him in three days," declared the abbot, starting away. "Tell him to come to me for his new instructions."

With that, the abbot marched to the old chapel, paused

outside, and then pushed open the door. He was greeted by two priests; from the look of it, they had slept in the sanctuary amidst their bundled belongings.

"Who is in authority here?" demanded the abbot.

"Greetings in Christ, brother abbot," said the bishop, stepping forward. "I am Asaph, Bishop of Llanelli. We would have made a better welcome, but as you can see, this is all that is left of the monastery, and the monks have all been pressed to labour for the count."

"Be that as it may . . . ," sniffed Hugo, glancing around the darkened chapel. It smelled old and musty and made him sneeze. "I see you are ready to depart. I shall not keep you."

"We were waiting to pass the reins to you, as it were," replied Asaph.

"That will not be necessary."

"No? We thought you might like to know something about your new flock."

"Your presumption has led you astray, bishop. It is the flock that must get to know and heed the shepherd." Hugo sneezed again and turned to leave. "God speed you on your way."

"Abbot, see here," said the bishop, starting after him. "There is much we would tell you about Elfael and its people."

"You presume to *teach* me?" Abbot Hugo turned on him. "All I need to know, I learned from the saddle of my horse on the way here." He glanced balefully at the rude structure and the two lorn priests. "Your tenure here is over, bishop. God in his wisdom has decreed a new day for this valley. The old must make way for the new. Again, I wish you God's speed. I do not expect we will meet again."

The abbot returned to his horse across the square, passing the carpenter, who was now sitting on a stack of lumber with a saw across his lap. "What about this?" called the carpenter, indicating the unfinished jumble of timber behind him. "What am I to do with this?"

"It is a tithe barn," replied the abbot. "It will need a wider door."

You, Tuck, have the most important duty," Bran had told him as he boosted the priest into the saddle. "The success of our plan rests on you."

"Aye," he had replied, "you can count on me!" Borne on waves of hope and optimism, he had departed Cél Craidd with cheers and glad farewells still ringing in his ears.

Oh, but the fiery blush of enthusiasm for his part in Bran's grand scheme had faded to dull, muddy pessimism by the time Aethelfrith reached his little oratory on the Hereford road. *How, by the beards of the apostles, am I to discover the movements of the de Braose treasure train?*

As if that were not difficult enough, he must acquire the knowledge far enough in advance to give Bran and his Grellon enough time to prepare. To that end, he had been given the best of the horses so that he might return with the news at utmost speed.

"Impossible," Aethelfrith muttered to himself. With or without a horse. Impossible. "Never should have agreed to such a lack-brain scheme."

Then again, the idea had originated with himself, after all. "Tuck, old son," he murmured, "you've gone and put both feet in the brown pie this time."

As he approached the oratory, he was relieved to see that

no one was waiting for him. People had visited in his absence; small gifts of eggs, lumps of cheese, and beeswax candles had been placed neatly beside his door. After tethering his mount in the long grass around back, he filled a bucket from the well and left it for the animal. He gathered up the offerings from his doorstep and went in to light the fire, eat a bite of supper, and contemplate his precarious future. He fell asleep praying for divine inspiration to attend his dreams.

As the morning sun rose to dispel the mist along the Wye, so it brought a partial solution to Tuck's problem. Rising in his undershirt, he went out to the well to wash. Drawing his arms through the sleeves, he pushed the shirt down around his waist and splashed water over himself. The cold stung his senses and made him splutter. He dried himself on a scrap of linen cloth and stood for a moment, savouring the sweet air and calm of the little glade surrounding his cell. He watched the mist curling along the river, and it came to him that whatever else they did, the wagons would have to use the bridge at Hereford. It only remained to find out when. He could simply wait until the wagons passed his oratory on their way to Elfael; then he could saddle the horse and race to Bran with the warning and hope it gave him time enough. Bran had said they would need three days at least. "Four would be better," Bran had told him. "Give us but four days, Tuck, and we have a fighting chance."

He hurried back inside to pull on his robe and lace up his shoes. Taking his staff, he walked down to the bridge and into town. It was market day in Hereford, but there seemed to be fewer people around than usual—especially for a clear, fine day in summer. He wondered about this as he watched the farmers and merchants setting out their goods and opening their stalls.

As he loitered amongst the vendors, idly wandering here and there, he heard a cloth merchant complaining to another about the lack of custom. "Poor dealings today, Michael, m'lad," he was saying. "Might have stayed home and saved shoe leather."

"'Twill be no better next market week," replied the merchant named Michael, a dealer in knives, pruning hooks, and other bladed utensils.

"Aye," agreed the other with a sigh, "too right you are. Too right."

"Won't get better till the baron returns."

"Good fellows," said Aethelfrith, speaking up, "forgive me—I heard you speaking just now and would ask a question."

"Brother Aethelfrith! Mornin' to you," said the one named Michael. "God be good to you."

"And to you, my son," replied the friar. "Can you tell me why there are so few people at market today? Where has everyone gone?"

"Well," replied the cloth dealer, "sure as Sunday, it's the council, ent it?"

"The council?" wondered Aethelfrith. "I have been away on a little business and only just returned. The king has called a Great Council?"

"Nay, brother," replied the clothier, "not a king's council—only a local one. Neufmarché has convoked an assembly of all his nobles—"

"*And* their families," said Michael the cutler. "Off beyond the Marches somewhere. We'd ha' done better to follow the lot of them there."

"Indeed?" mused the priest. "I have heard nothing about this."

The two merchants, with no customers and time on their hands, were only too glad to oblige Aethelfrith of the news he had missed: the fierce battle and resounding defeat of the Welsh King Rhys ap Tewdwr, and the swift conquest of Deheubarth by the baron's troops. The cutler finished, saying, "Neufmarché called council to square things away, y'see?"

The squat friar nodded, thanked them, and asked, "When did they leave? Do you know? When did the council begin?"

The clothier shrugged. "I couldn't say, brother."

"Why, if I be not mistaken," said Michael, "it ent rightly begun as yet."

"No?"

"Don't see how it could." Michael picked up a small kitchen knife and tried its blade with his thumb. "The baron and his people rode out but yesterday—morning, it was, very early. I reckon 'twill take them two days at least to reach the moot—them and the other lords. The council would seem to begin a day or two after that. So make that three days—four, to be safe. Five, maybe six, at most."

"Too right," agreed the clothier. "And all that means we lose custom next week—and maybe the week after as well."

"Blessings upon you, friends!" called Aethelfrith, already darting away. He fled back across the bridge, his soft shoes slapping the worn timbers, and steamed up the hill to his oratory. He wasted not a moment, but threw a few provisions into a bag, saddled the horse, and rode out again.

He knew exactly when Baron de Braose's money train would roll.

CHAPTER 40

As Baron Bernard de Neufmarché gazed out upon the upturned faces of his subject lords gathered at Talgarth in the south of Wales, the treasure train of his rival Baron de Braose was approaching the bridge below his castle back in Hereford: three wagons with an escort of seven knights and fifteen men-at-arms under the command of a marshal and a sergeant. All the soldiers were mounted, and their weapons gleamed hard in the bright summer sun.

Hidden beneath food supplies and furnishings for Abbot Hugo's new church were three sealed strongboxes, iron-banded and bolted to the wagon beds. With ranks of soldiers leading the way and more riders guarding the rear, the train passed unhindered through Hereford. If any of Neufmarché's soldiers saw the train passing beneath the castle walls, they made no move to prevent it.

Thus, in accordance with Baron de Braose's plan, the wagon train rumbled across the bridge, through the town, and out into the bright, sunlit meadows of the wide Wye valley. It would take the slow ox train four days to pass through Neufmarché lands and the great forest of the March. But once past

Hereford, there would be no stopping the wagons, and the knights could breathe a little easier knowing that nothing stood between them and the completion of their duty.

The leader of this party was a marshal named Guy, one of Baron de Braose's youngest commanders, a man whose father stood on the battlefield with the Conqueror and had been rewarded with the lands of a deposed earl in the North Ridings: a sizeable estate that included the old Saxon market town of Ghigesburgh—or Gysburne, as the Normans preferred it.

Young Guy had grown up in the bleak moorlands of the north, and there he might have stayed, but thinking that life held more for him than overseeing the collection of rents on his father's estate, he had come south to take service in the court of an ambitious baron who could provide him with the opportunities a young knight needed to secure wealth and fame. Inflamed with dreams of grandeur, he yearned for glory far beyond any that might be acquired grappling with dour English farmwives over rents paid in geese and sheep.

Guy's energy and skill at arms had won him a place amongst the teeming swarm of knights employed by William de Braose; his solid, dependable, levelheaded northern practicality raised him above the ranks of the brash and impulsive fortune seekers who thronged the southern courts. Two years in the baron's service, Guy had waited for a chance to prove himself, and it had finally come. Certainly, marshalling the guard for some money chests was not the same as leading a flying wing of cavalry into pitched battle, but it was a start. This was the first significant task the baron had entrusted to him, and though it fell far short of taxing his considerable skills as a warrior, he was determined to acquit himself well.

Mounted on a fine grey destrier, he remained vigilant and pursued a steady, unhurried pace. To better safeguard the silver, no advance warning had been given; not even Count de Braose knew when the money would arrive.

Day's end found them camped beside the road on a bend in the river. High wooded bluffs sheltered them to the east, and the bow of the river formed an effective perimeter barrier on the other three sides. Any would-be thieves thinking to liberate the treasure would have to come at them on the road, and Guy positioned sentries in each direction, changed through the night, to prevent intruders from disturbing their peace.

They passed an uneventful night and the next morning moved on. Around midday they stopped to eat and to feed and rest the animals before beginning the long, winding ascent up out of the Vale of Wye. The first wagon gained the heights a little before sunset, and Guy ordered camp to be made in a grove of beech trees near an English farming settlement. Other than a herdsman leading a few muddy brown cows home to be milked, no one else was seen on the road, and the second night passed beneath a fair, star-seeded sky with serenity undisturbed.

The third day passed much the same as the previous day. Before climbing into their saddles on the fourth day, Guy assembled the men and addressed them, saying, "Today we enter the forest of the March. We will be wary. If thieves try to attack us, they will do so here, *compris*? Everyone is to remain alert for any sign of an ambush." He gazed at the ring of faces gathered around him: as solemn, earnest, and determined as he was himself. "If there are no questions, then—"

"What of the phantom?"

"Ah," replied Guy, "yes." He had anticipated such a question and was ready with an answer. "Many of you will have heard some gossip of this phantom, *non?*" He paused, trying to appear severe and dauntless for his men. "It is but a tale to frighten infants, nothing more. We are men, not children, so we will give this rumour the contempt it deserves." He offered a grimace of ridicule to show his scorn, adding, "It would take a whole forest full of phantoms to daunt Baron de Braose's soldiers, *n'est-ce pas?*"

He commanded the treasure train to move out. The soldiers took their mounts and fell into line: a rank of knights, three abreast to lead the train, followed by men-at-arms alongside and between each of the wagons, with four knights serving as outriders patrolling the road ahead and behind on each side. At the head of this impressive procession rode Guy himself on his fine grey stallion; directly behind him rode his sergeant to relay any commands to those behind.

By morning's end the money train had reached the forest edge. The road was wide, though rutted, and the wagon drivers were forced to slow their pace to keep from jolting the wheels to pieces. The soldiers clopped along, passing through patches of sunlight and shadow, alert to the smallest movement around them. It was cool in the shade of the trees, and the air was thick with birdsong and the sounds of insects. All remained peaceful and serene, and they met no one else on the road.

A little past midday, however, they came to a place where the road dipped low into a dell, at the bottom of which trickled a sluggish rill. Despite the fine dry weather, the shallow fording place was a churned mass of mud and muck. Apparently, herders using the road had allowed their animals to use it for a watering hole, and the beasts had transformed the road into a wallow.

Stuck in the middle of the ford was a wagon full of manure

sunk up to its axles. A ragged farmer was snapping the reins of his two-ox team, and the creatures were bawling as they strained against the yoke, but to no avail. The farmer's wife stood off to one side, hands on hips, shouting at the man, who appeared to be taking no heed of her. Both the man and his wife were filthy to their knees.

The road narrowed at the ford, and the surrounding ground was so soft and chewed up that Guy could see there would be no going around. Wary, senses prickling to danger, Guy halted the train. He rode ahead alone to see what had happened. "Pax vobiscum," he said, reining up behind the wagon. "What goes here?"

The farmer ceased swatting his team and turned to address the knight. "Good day, sire," the man said in rough Latin, removing his shapeless straw hat. "You see how it is." He gestured vaguely at the wagon. "I am stuck."

"I told him to put down planks," the farmwife called in shrill defiance. "But he wouldn't listen."

"Shut up, woman!" shouted the farmer to his wife. Turning back to the knight, he said, "We'll soon have it out, never fear." Eyeing the waiting train behind them, he said, "Maybe if some of your fellows could help—"

"No," Guy told him. "Just you get on with it."

"At once, m'lord." He turned back to the task of coaxing, threatening, and bullying the struggling team once more.

Guy rode back to the waiting train. "We will rest here and move on when they have cleared the ford. Water the horses."

The horses were watered and rested and the sun was beginning its long, slow descent when the farmer finally ceased shouting and slapping his team. Guy, thinking the wagon was finally free, hurried back down into the dell only to find the farmer lying on the grassy slope above the ford, his wagon as firmly stuck as ever.

"You! What in God's name are you doing?" demanded Guy.

"Sire?" replied the farmer, sitting up quickly.

"The wagon remains stuck."

"Aye, sire, it is that," agreed the farmer ruefully. "I have tried everything, but it won't budge for gold nor goose fat."

Glancing around quickly, the knight said, "Where's the woman?"

"I sent her ahead to see if there might be anyone coming the other way that could maybe lend a hand, sire," replied the farmer. "Seeing as how you and your men are busylike . . ." He left the rest of the thought unspoken.

"Get up!" shouted Guy. "Get back to your team. You have delayed us long enough."

"As you say, sire," replied the farmer. He rose and shambled back to the wagon.

Guy returned to the waiting train and ordered five men-at-arms to dismount and help pull the wagon free. These first five were soon as muddy as the farmer, and with just as little to show for it. So, with increasing impatience, Guy ordered five more men-at-arms and three knights on horseback to help, too. Soon, the muddy wallow was heaving with men and horses. The knights attached ropes to the wagon, and with three or four men at each wheel and horses pulling, they succeeded in hauling the overloaded vehicle up out of the hole into which it had sunk.

With a creak and a groan, the cart started up the greasy bank. The soldiers cheered. And then just as the wheels came free, there came a loud crack as the rear axle snapped. The hind wheels buckled and the cart subsided once more; men and horses, still attached to the ropes, were dragged down with it. The oxen could not keep their feet and fell, sprawling over each other. Caught in their yoke, they thrashed in the mud, kicking and bellowing.

Guy saw his hopes of a swift resolution to his problem sinking into the mire and loosed a spate of Ffreinc abuse on the head of the luckless farmer. "Loose those animals!" he ordered his men. "Then drag that cart out of the way."

Seven men-at-arms leapt to obey. Working quickly, they unyoked the oxen and led them from the wallow. Once free, the farmer led them aside and stood with them while the soldiers emptied his wagon, pitching the manure over the sides and then, slowly and with great effort, dragging the broken vehicle up the slippery bank and off the road.

"Thank you, sire!" called the farmer, regarding the wreck of his wagon with the dubious air of a man who knows he should be grateful but realises he is ruined.

"Idiot!" muttered Guy. Satisfied that his wagon train could now pass through, Guy rode back up the slope and signalled the drivers to come ahead.

When the first of the three teams had descended into the dell—which now resembled a well-stirred bog—Guy, taking no chances, ordered branches to be cut and laid down and ropes to be attached so riders could help pull the fully laden vehicle through the morass. Like a boat dragged across a tide-abandoned bay, the first wagon slid recklessly across. The laborious process was repeated for each of the two remaining wagons in turn.

Guy waited impatiently while the soldiers paused to clean the mud and ordure off themselves as best they could. His sergeant, a veteran named Jeremias, approached and said, "The sun is soon down, sire. Do you want to make camp now and journey on at daybreak tomorrow?"

"No," Guy growled, glancing at the miserable swamp now reeking with manure. "We've wasted enough time here today. I want to put this place behind us. We push on." Raising himself in the stirrups, he shouted, "Be mounted!"

A few moments later, all had regained the saddle. Guy waited until they had fallen into line and reformed the ranks, then called, *"Marcher sur!"* and the money train resumed its journey.

Once over the rim of the dell, the forest closed around them once more. The setting sun thickened the shadows beneath the overarching limbs, giving the riders the sensation of entering a dim green tunnel. Darkness crept in, closing silently around them. Guy was soon wishing he had not been so hasty in rebutting the sergeant's suggestion and decided that they would make camp at the next glade or meadow; but the underbrush crowded close on each side of the road, the tree trunks so close that the wagon wheels bumped over exposed roots, forcing the drivers to slow the pace even more. All the while, the last of the daylight steadily faded to a murky twilight, and the evening hush descended on the forest.

It was only then, in the quiet of the wood, that Marshal Guy de Gysburne began to wonder why it was that two bedraggled English farmers should speak such ready Latin. The thought had little time to take root in his awareness when the soldiers saw the first of the hanging corpses.

$\mathbf{M}$arshal Guy heard the low, tight-mouthed cursing of the soldiers behind him and knew that something was amiss. Without stopping, he turned in the saddle and looked back along the trailing ranks. He saw his sergeant and motioned him forward. "Jeremias," he said as the sergeant reined in beside him, "the men are muttering."

"They are, sire," confirmed the sergeant.

"Why is this?"

"Methinks it is the mice, sire."

"The mice, sergeant," repeated Guy, casting a sideways glance at the man beside him. He appeared to be earnest. "Pray explain."

With a tilt of his head, the sergeant indicated a branch at the side of the road a few paces away. Guy squinted at the overhanging branch, which looked no different from a thousand others seen that day—entirely unremarkable, except . . . except: hanging from the branch was a dead mouse.

The tiny corpse was suspended by a long hair from the tail of a horse, its sun-shrivelled body turning slowly in the light evening breeze. The marshal leaned from the saddle for a closer look and poked it with his finger as he passed. The little dead thing swung on its slender thread. Guy turned his face away and made a show of ignoring what he took to be a harmless, if somewhat sinister, prank.

The attitude was admirable but became increasingly hard to maintain. Try as he might to keep his eyes on the road before him, he could not prevent himself from glimpsing more of the things, and once he began to see them, he saw them everywhere. Swinging on their horsehair nooses from bushes and twigs, dangling from overhanging limbs and branches, high and low, on each side of the road, dead mice hung like grotesque fruit in an orchard of death.

The wagon train continued on into the gloaming, and the farther they went, the more of the weird little corpses they saw—and not mice only. Now, here and there amongst the hanging dead, were the bodies of larger creatures. He saw a vole first, and then another; then moles, shrews, and rats. Like the mice, the moles and rats were strung up with horsetail hair and left to twist gently in the breeze.

Soon, the soldiers were seeing dead rats everywhere— some shrivelled and desiccated as if dried in their skins, others that appeared freshly killed. But all, whether mummified or fresh, were hung by their necks, legs flat to their sides, tails stiff and straight.

Guy, glancing right and left, took them in with a shiver of disgust and, refusing to be cowed by the unnatural spectacle, rode on.

Then came the birds. Small ones first—sparrows, for the most part, but also wrens and nuthatches—scattered in amongst the rodents. The birds were dry husks of the creatures that had been—as if the avian essence had been sucked from them, along with all their vital juices—all of them suspended by their necks, wings folded tight against their bodies, beaks pointing skyward.

A few hundred paces down this weird gallery of death, the soldiers began seeing faces leering from the leaf-bordered shadows. They were not human faces, but effigies of twigs and bark and straw tied together with bits of leather and bone: heads, large and small, their eyes of stone and shell gazing sightlessly from the wood at the passing riders.

The muttering of the men became a low rumble. Everywhere a knight or soldier looked, another disembodied face met his increasingly unsteady gaze—as if the wood were populated with Greene Men, come to menace the intruders. Some of the larger ones had straw mouths lined with animal teeth, bared as if in the frozen rictus of death. These effigies mocked the riders. They seemed to laugh at the living, their mute voices shrill with the unspoken words: *As we are, soon you shall be.*

The soldiers proceeded along this eerie corridor in silence, eyes wide, shoulders hunched with apprehension. The farther they went, the more uncanny it became. The feeling of dread deepened moment by moment, as if each step brought them closer to a doom unknown and deeply to be feared.

Guy, resolute but anxious, was no less affected than his men; the weird sights around them seemed both purposeful and malevolent; yet the meaning of the macabre display—if meaning there was—escaped him.

Then, all at once . . .

"Yeux de Dieu!" swore Guy, jerking back the reins involuntarily. The big grey halted in the road.

Affixed to a tree beside the road was what appeared to be the figure of a man with huge hands and an enormous misshapen head, drenched in blood, his arms stretched as if to welcome passersby with a grisly embrace.

A second glance revealed that it was not a man at all, but a statue of cloth and straw affixed to a scaffold of tree limbs and topped with the head of a boar. The hideous thing had been drenched in blood and was covered with flies. *"Merde,"* Guy spat, urging his mount forward once more. "Pagans."

The heavy wagons rolled slowly past this grisly herald. Knights and men loosed curses even as they signed themselves with the cross.

The road descended gently into a shallow trough between the crests of two low hills. The forest pressed close, ominously silent. Guy, riding ahead, reached the bottom of the dell and, in the last light of day fading to the shadowy gloom of twilight, saw something lying across the road. Closer inspection revealed that a tree had fallen, its trunk spanning the road from side to side. There was no going around it.

Guy, now fully alert to danger, wheeled his mount. "Halt!" he shouted, his voice cracking loud in the deep forest hush. "Jeremias!" he said, indicating the tree behind him. "Remove it. Form a troop. Get it cleared away."

"At once, sire," replied the sergeant. Turning in the saddle, he called to the knights and men behind him. "First four ranks dismount!" he shouted. "The rest remain on guard."

Before the knights and men-at-arms could climb down from their saddles, there came a crashing from the surrounding wood—something huge and clumsy crashing through the tangled undergrowth toward the road. The soldiers drew their weapons as the unknown entity lumbered closer.

The bushes beside the road began quaking and thrashing from side to side. Guy's hand found his sword hilt and drew it. The sword was halfway out of the scabbard when, with the mewling, inarticulate squeal of a host of lost and tortured souls, the branches parted, and out from the vine-covered thicket to his left burst a herd of wild pigs.

Half-mad with fear, the animals tumbled through the opening and into the road. Whatever was driving the pigs terrified them more than the men on horseback, for the squealing, squalling animals, seeing their only path of escape blocked by the fallen tree, swirled around once, then lowered their heads and charged into the halted ranks of soldiers.

The hapless creatures—four sows with perhaps twenty or more piglets—darted in amongst the legs of the horses, instantly throwing the ordered ranks into rearing, kicking chaos. Some of the soldiers tried to ward off the pigs by stabbing at them with their swords, which only increased the confusion.

"Hold!" cried Guy, trying to make himself heard above the frantic neighing of the horses. "Hold the ranks! Let them pass!"

Catching a movement out of the corner of his eye, he turned and saw something alight on the trunk of the fallen tree. It seemed to simply materialise out of the darkness—a shadow taking substance, darkness contracting to itself and coalescing into the shape of a gigantic birdlike creature with the wings and high-domed head of a raven and the torso and legs of a man. The face of the phantom was a smooth, black skull with an absurdly long, pointed beak.

Guy gaped at the unearthly creature. His shouted orders clotted on his tongue. He swallowed and found his mouth had gone dry.

The phantom perched on the massive trunk of the fallen

tree, spread its great wings wide, and in a voice that seemed torn from the very forest round about, shrieked out a cry of raw animal rage that resounded through the forest, echoing amongst the treetops. Soldiers threw their hands over their ears to keep out the sound.

At once, the scent of smoke filled the air, and before Guy could draw breath to shout a warning to his men, twin curtains of flame leapt up on each side of the road along the length of the wagon train, which was now a confused mass of frightened men, pigs, and thrashing horses.

The phantom shrieked again. Lord Guy's grey destrier reared, its eyes rolling in terror. When Guy turned to look, the enormous raven had vanished. "Fall back!" cried the knight marshal. "Retreat!" His command was lost in the cacophony of pigs squealing, men shouting, and oxen bawling. "Turn around! Go back!"

As if in reply, the forest answered with a low groan and the shuddering creak of tree trunks cracking. The soldiers shouted—some pointing left, some right—as two huge oaks gave way on each side of the road, crashing to earth in a juddering mass of limbs and leaves. Knights on horseback scattered as the heavy pillars toppled, one atop the other, directly behind the last wagon in the train. The startled ox team surged forward, smashing into the stationary ranks directly ahead, overturning two horses and unseating their riders.

Trapped now in a corridor of flame and oily, pungent smoke, the wagons could neither turn around nor move off the road. The soldiers, still contending with the remaining pigs, strove to regain control of their mounts.

In the tumult and confusion, no one saw two furtive figures in deerskin cloaks rise from the bracken with pots of flaming pitch suspended from leather cords. Standing just beyond the shimmering sheet of fire, the skin-clad figures swung the pots in tight, looping arcs and let fly. The clay pots smashed into flaming shards, splattering hot, burning pitch over the sideboards of the nearest wagon.

The frightened oxen bolted, driving into the men and horses who could not get out of the way swiftly enough.

"Hold!" cried Guy. "Drivers, hold your teams!"

But there was no holding the terrified animals. They surged forward, heads down, driving into anything in their path. Knights and men-at-arms scattered, desperate to get out of the way of the wildly scything horns.

Some of the soldiers braved the wall of flames. Turning their mounts, they jumped the burning logs and struggled into the bramble-bound undergrowth. Those in the rearward ranks, seeing the flames and chaos ahead, abandoned their uncontrollable mounts and scrambled through the branches and over the fallen tree trunks blocking their retreat.

In the chaos of the moment, no one gave a thought to their trapped comrades; thoughts ran only to survival, and each man looked after himself. Once free, the men-at-arms took to their feet, running back down the road the way they had come.

The wagons were burning fiercely now, driving the horses and oxen wild with terror. There was no holding them. Everywhere, men were abandoning their saddles to flee the panic-stricken horses and flaming wagons.

Marshal Guy, his voice raw from shouting, tried to order his scattered retinue. With sword held high, he repeatedly called his men to rally to him. But the preternatural attack had overwhelmed them to a man, and Guy could not make himself heard above the clamour of beasts and men lost in the frenzy of escape.

In the end, he had no choice but to desert his own mount and follow his retreating men as they fled into the night. Working his way back along the riotous commotion of his flailing, devastated soldiers, Guy reached the rear of the treasure train and climbed onto the bole of one of the toppled oaks. There he took up the call to retreat. "Fall back! To me! Fall back!"

Those nearest swarmed over the fallen trunks, tumbling into the road and pulling the stragglers after them. When finally the last man had cleared the fiery corridor, Guy allowed himself to be pulled away from the wreckage by his sergeant. "Come, sire," said Jeremias, tugging him by the arm. "Let it go."

Still, Guy hesitated. He cast a last look over his shoulder at the inferno the road had become. Terrified horses still reared and plunged, hurling themselves headlong into the flames; the oxen lay dead—most had been killed by the knights in order to keep from being gored or trampled; discarded weapons and armour were strewn the length of the corridor. The rout was complete.

"It is over," said Jeremias. "You must rally the men and regain command. Come away."

Marshal Guy de Gysburne nodded once and turned away. A moment later, he was running into the flame-shattered darkness of a strange and hostile night.

CHAPTER 42

The sound of frightened, mail-clad soldiers in headlong retreat dwindled away, and soon all that could be heard was the hiss and crackle of the burning brush and wagons. For a moment, the forest seemed to watch and wait with breath abated, and then the scouring of the king's road began.

Seven men carrying spears leapt over the burning logs and into the fiery corridor. Clad in green cloaks, the hooded men made quick work dispatching any wounded animals. They then signalled the rest of their band, and within the space of six heartbeats, twenty more men and women crept out from hiding in the surrounding wood. Likewise dressed in long green cloaks with leaves and twigs and bits of rag sewn onto them, they were the Grellon: King Raven's faithful flock.

Quickly removing their cloaks and hoods, the Grellon set about quenching the flames of the burning wagons and surrounding vegetation—using hides that had been soaked in the stream. As soon as the fires were out, torches were lit and sentries posted, and the flock fell to their appointed tasks with silent and urgent efficiency. While some of the band butchered the horses and oxen where they lay, others led the living animals away into the forest. Once the animals had been cared for, the workers unloaded the still-smouldering wagons, carefully examining the cargo. Much had been damaged by the flames, of course, but much remained unharmed; everything was carried off to be hidden in the wood for later use.

Once the vehicles had been unburdened of their baggage, the iron-bound strongboxes were prised from the planks before the wagons themselves were broken apart and hauled into the forest. The useable parts—wheels, harness, yokes, and iron fittings—would find their way back into service, and the rest would be scattered, hidden, and left to rot.

While the wagons were being dismantled, the discarded bits of armour and weapons, saddles and tack—as well as anything else of value—were heaped together in a single pile that was then sorted into bundles and carried off. Meanwhile, the leavings of the butchered animals were placed in a ready-dug pit near the road, which was then filled in and covered with bracken and moss, freshly dug elsewhere and transplanted. When everything of value had been salvaged, the tree trunks blocking the road were removed—an arduous task made more difficult by the necessity of having to work in darkness—and the pitch-bearing logs were rolled back into the underbrush; any scorched branches were carefully trimmed back to green growth.

Their work finished, the forest dwellers gathered up the meat of the slaughtered beasts and crept away, melting back into the darkness from which they had sprung.

When the sun rose upon the forest the next day, there was little to mark the odd, one-sided battle that had been fought in that place—saving only some singed tree limbs that could not be reached, broken earth, and a few damp, dark patches where the blood of an ox or a horse stained the road.

Loss of all goods and chattels under your care, loss of horses and livestock, loss of church property and sacred relics—not to mention loss of the treasure you were sworn to protect," Abbot Hugo de Rainault intoned solemnly as he stared out the window of the former chapter house he had commandeered for his own use. "Your failure is as ignominious as it is complete."

"I lost no men," Marshal Gysburne pointed out.

"Mon Dieu!" growled Hugo. "Do you think Baron de Braose will care about that?" He levelled a virulent stare at the knight. "Do you *think* at all?"

Guy de Gysburne held his tongue and waited for the storm to pass. Of the two men before him, the abbot was the more outraged and possessed far greater ability to make his anger felt. Next to the fiery Hugo's scathing excoriations, the irate Count Falkes seemed placid and reasonable, if perturbed.

"At the very least, Gysburne, you will be imprisoned," said Count Falkes, breaking in.

"At worst, you face execution for malfeasance and gross neglect of duty," said the abbot, concluding the thought in his own way.

"We were ambushed. I did my duty."

"Did you? Did you?" demanded Hugo. "No doubt that will be of great comfort when your head is on the block."

"Execute a knight in service?" scoffed Guy; the bravado was thin and unconvincing.

"Do not imagine such a fate unlikely. The baron may think it worthwhile to make an example of you."

Guy, standing at attention with his hands clasped behind him as he bore the brunt of their anger, now turned in appeal to the count. "Lord Falkes," he said, "you saw the place of ambush; you saw how——"

"I saw very little indeed," Falkes replied with cool disdain. "A few bloodstains and some withered foliage. What is that?"

"It is my point exactly," insisted Guy, his voice rising with frustration. "Someone removed the wagons and oxen— removed *everything!*"

"Yes, yes, no doubt it was this creature—this phantom."

"I did not say that," muttered Guy.

"Phantom?" asked Abbot Hugo, raising one eyebrow with interest.

Falkes gave the priest a superior smile and explained about the birdlike creature haunting the forest of the March. "The folk of Elfael call it the Hud," he said. Waving his hand dismissively, he added, "I am sick of hearing about it."

"Hood?" questioned the abbot. "Is that what you said?"

"Hud," corrected Falkes. "It means sorcerer, enchanter, or some such. It is a tale to frighten children."

"*Something* attacked us in the forest," the marshal said. "It commanded wild pigs, killed oxen, and burned our wagons."

"Yes, yes," replied Falkes impatiently, "and then carried everything away, leaving nothing behind."

"What do you want of me?" demanded Guy, tiring of the interrogation.

"I want the baron's money back!" roared Falkes. Guy lowered his head, and Falkes let out a sigh of exasperation. "*Mon Dieu!* This is hopeless." Looking to the abbot, he said, "Do

what you will with him. I am finished here." With a last con-
demning glance at the miserable Guy de Gysburne, he paid
the abbot a chilly farewell and strode from the room.

In a moment, they heard the clump of hooves in the yard as
the count rode away. "A man in your precarious position,
Gysburne," said the abbot quietly, "might rather ask what *I* can
do for you." Clasping his hands before him, he regarded the
dishevelled knight with a pitying expression. "I do not know
what happened out there," Hugo continued in a more sympathetic tone, "but I see that it has shaken you and your men."

Gysburne clenched his jaw and looked away.

"There will be hell to pay, of course," resumed the abbot.
"Yet I can ensure that the brunt of this catastrophe does not
fall solely on your shoulders."

"Why should you help me?" asked the knight without
looking up.

"Is not clemency an attribute of the Holy Church?"
Abbot Hugo smiled. Guy's gaze remained firmly fixed on the
floor at his feet. "If further explanation is needed, let us just
say that I have particular reasons of my own."

The abbot crossed to the table on which cups and a jar
were waiting. He placed his hands flat on the table. "You will,
of course, return to face the wrath of Baron de Braose," he
said. "However, I propose to send you with a letter informing the baron of certain mitigating facts which should be
taken into consideration, facts which will ultimately exculpate
you. Furthermore, I am prepared to argue, not for imprison-
ment or dismissal, but for your reassignment. In short, I
might be persuaded to ask the baron to assign you to me here.
I would then be willing to take full responsibility for you and
your actions."

At this, the knight raised his eyes.

The abbot, pacing slowly around the small room of the former chapter house, continued, "After the debacle in the forest last night, de Braose will not refuse me. Far from it. He will think it a most salubrious suggestion—all the more when I offer to make up the pay for the workers out of my own treasury."

"You would do this?" wondered Guy.

"This and more," the cleric assured him. "I will request troops to be placed under my command. You, my friend, shall lead them."

Abbot Hugo paused again to regard the unlucky knight. He might have chosen someone older and more experienced for what he had in mind, but Gysburne had dropped into his lap, so to speak, and another opportunity might be a long time coming. All things considered, Sir Guy was not such a bad choice. "I trust this meets with your approval?"

"What about the count?"

"Count Falkes will have nothing to say about it one way or the other," the abbot assured him. "Well?"

"Your Grace, I hardly know what to say."

"Swear fealty to me as God's agent by authority of the Holy Church, and it is done."

"I swear it! On my life, I do so swear."

"Splendid." Hugo returned to the table and poured a cup of wine for his guest. "Please," he said, offering the goblet to the knight. Guy accepted the cup, almost expecting it to burn his hand. Even if it had been offered by the devil himself, he would still be bound to receive it. The calamity in the forest had left him with no better choice.

The abbot smiled again. Distressing as the loss of his

property was, the strange turn of events had nevertheless provided him a welcome means of increasing his authority. With his own private army, he would be the most powerful prelate in all Wallia. "As you will appreciate, I lost a very great deal last night. The *church* lost treasure of significant value. That cannot be allowed to happen again." He poured wine into the second cup. "That *will not* happen again."

"No, Your Grace," agreed Guy. He raised his cup and wet his lips. Although greatly relieved not to have to return to Baron de Braose empty-handed, the knight had yet to obtain the measure of the abbot: less a saint, he thought, than a merchant prince in priestly robes. Job's bones, he had met more holy-minded pickpockets!

Guy took another sip of wine, and his thoughts returned to the events of that morning.

As soon as he had regrouped his men—who were still exhausted and shaken by the unnatural events in the haunted wood—he had started out by dawn's first light to bring the count and abbot the bad news. "It was most uncanny beginning to end," he had reported. "On my life, it seems the very stuff of nightmares." He then went on to explain, to an increasingly outraged and disbelieving audience, all that had transpired in the forest.

"Fool!" the abbot had roared when he finished. "Am I to believe that you think there is more to this affair than the rapacious larceny of the reprobate and faithless rabble that inhabit this godforsaken country?"

At those words, the unearthly spell surrounding the entire incident had relinquished some of its power over him. Guy de Gysburne stood blinking in the sunlight of the abbot's reception room. It was the first time he had stopped to consider that the attack had been perpetrated by mere mortals only—cunning mortals, perhaps, but flesh-and-blood humans nonetheless. "No, my lord," he had answered, feeling instantly very embarrassed and overwhelmingly absurd.

Obviously, it had all been an elaborate trap—from the dead creatures strung up along the roadside, to the flames and falling trees that had cut off any chance of escape . . .

But no.

Now that he thought about it, the ambush had begun well before that—probably with the broken wagon axle earlier in the day: the hapless farmer and his shrewish wife, loud and overbearing, impossible to ignore as they stood arguing over the spilled load, standing in mud where no mud should have been . . .

Yes, he was certain of it. The deception had begun far in advance of the actual attack. Moreover, the individual elements of the weird assault had taken a considerable amount of time to prepare—perhaps many days—which meant that someone had known when the treasure train would pass through the forest of the March. Someone had known. Was there a spy in the baron's ranks? Was it one of the soldiers or someone else who had passed along the information?

As Guy sat clutching his cup, his heart burned for revenge. The offer of a new position with the abbot notwithstanding, he vowed to find whoever had ruined his position with the baron and make them pay dearly.

"Mark me, lord marshal, these pagan filth will learn respect for the holy offices. They will learn reverence for the mother church. Their heinous and high-handed deeds will not go unpunished." Though the abbot spoke softly, there was no mistaking the steel-hard edge to his words. "You, Marshal

Gysburne, will be the instrument of God's judgement. You will be the weapon in my hand."

Sir Guy could not agree more.

The abbot poured another cup and lifted it in salute. "Let us drink to the prompt recovery of the stolen treasure and to your own swift advancement."

The marshal raised his cup to the abbot's, and both men drank. They then put their heads together to compose the letter to be delivered to the baron. Before the wax was dry on the parchment, Guy was already scheming how to find the stolen treasure, expose the traitor in their midst, and exact revenge on those who had disgraced him and robbed the abbot.

CHAPTER 43

Under the keen watch of sentries hidden in the brush along the road, the Grellon walked hidden pathways. Moving with the stealth of forest creatures, men, women, and children ferried the plunder back to their greenwood glen on litters made of woven leather straps stretched between pine poles. It took most of the day to retrieve the spoils of their wild night's work and store it safely away. Thus, the sun was low in the sky when Bran, Iwan, Tuck, Siarles, and Angharad finally gathered to open the iron-banded caskets.

Iwan and Siarles set to work, hacking at the charred wood and metal bands of the first two strongboxes. The others looked on, speculating on what they would find. Under the onslaught of an axe and pick, Iwan's box gave way first; three quick blows splintered the sides, and three more released a gleaming cascade of silver onto the hearthside floor. Tuck scooped up the coins with a bowl and poured them into his robe, as Siarles, meanwhile, chopped at the top of the chest before him and presently succeeded in breaking open the ruined lock.

He threw open the lid. The interior was filled with cloth bags—each one tied by a cord that was sealed in wax with the baron's crest. At a nod from Bran, he lifted one out and untied the string, breaking the seal, and poured the contents into Brother Tuck's bowl: forty-eight English pennies, newly minted, bright as tiny moons.

"There must be over two hundred pounds here," Siarles estimated. "More, even."

Iwan turned his attention to the third box. Smaller than the other two, it had suffered less damage and proved more difficult to break open. With battering blows, Iwan smashed at the lock and wooden sides of the chest. The iron-banded box resisted his efforts until Siarles fetched a hammer and chisel and began working at the rivets, loosening a few of the bands to allow Iwan's pick to gain purchase. Eventually, the two succeeded in worrying the lid from its hinges; tossing it aside, they upended the box, and out rolled plump leather bags—smaller than the baron's black bags, but heavier. When hefted, they gave a dull chink.

"Open them," Bran commanded. He sat on his haunches, watching the proceedings with dazzled amazement.

Plucking a bag from the chest, Iwan untied the string and shook the contents into Bran's open hand. The gleam of gold flashed in the firelight as a score of thick coins plopped into his palm.

"Upon my vow," gasped Aethelfrith in awe, "they're filled with flaming *byzants*!"

Raising one of the coins, Bran turned it between his fingers, watching the lustrous shimmer dance in the light. He felt the exquisite weight and warmth of the fine metal. He had never seen genuine Byzantine gold *solidi* before. "What are they worth?"

"Well now," the priest answered, snatching up a coin from

the floor. "Let me see. There are twelve pennies in a shilling, and twenty shillings in a pound—so a pound is worth two hundred and forty pennies." Tapping his finger on his palm as if counting invisible coins, the mendicant priest continued, amazing his onlookers with his thorough understanding of worldly wealth. "Now then, a mark, as we all know, is worth thirteen shillings and four pence, or one hundred sixty pennies—which means that there are one and a half marks in one pound sterling."

"So how much for a byzant?" asked Siarles.

"Give me time," said Tuck. "I'm getting to that."

"This will take all night," complained Siarles.

"It *will* if you keep interrupting, boyo," replied the priest testily. "These are delicate calculations." He gave Siarles a sour look and resumed, "Where was I? Right—so that's . . ." He paused to reckon the total. "That's over five pounds." He frowned. "No, make that six—more."

"A bag?" asked Bran.

"Each," replied the priest, handing the byzant back to him.

"You mean to say *this*," said Bran, holding the gold coin to the light, "is worth ten marks?"

"They are as valuable as they are scarce."

"Sire," said Iwan, dazzled by the extent of their haul, "this is far better than we hoped." Reaching into another of the leather bags, he drew out more of the fat gold coins. "This is a . . . a miracle."

"The Good Lord helps them who help themselves," Friar Tuck said, pouring coins from the fold of his gathered robe into the bowl on the floor before him. "Blesséd be the name of the Lord!"

"How much is there altogether?" wondered Bran, gazing at the treasure hoard.

"Several hundred marks at least," suggested Siarles.

"It is more than enough to pay the workers," observed Angharad from her stool. "Much more." She rose and gathered a deerskin from her sleeping place. Spreading it on the floor beside the kneeling priest, she instructed, "Count it onto this."

"And count it out loud so we can all hear," added Siarles.

"Help me," said the priest. "Put them into piles of twelve."

The two fell to arranging the silver coins into little heaps to represent a shilling, and then Brother Tuck began telling out the number, shilling by shilling. Siarles, using a bit of charred wood, kept a running tally on a hearthstone, announcing the reckoning every fourth or fifth stack, and calling out the total at each mark: one hundred . . . one hundred seventy-five . . . two hundred . . .

The women of Cél Craidd brought food—a haunch of roast meat from one of the slaughtered oxen and some fresh barley cakes made from the supplies intended for Abbot Hugo. Bran and the others ate while the counting continued.

After a while, they heard voices outside the hut. "Your flock grows curious," Angharad said. "They have been patient long enough. You should speak to them, Bran."

Rising, Bran stepped to the door and pushed aside the ox-hide covering. Stepping out into the soft night air, he saw the entire population of the settlement—forty-three souls in all—ranged on the ground around the door of the hut. Wrapped in their cloaks, they were talking quietly amongst themselves. A fire had been lit and some of the children were running barefoot around it.

"We are still counting the money," he told them simply. "I will bring word when we have finished."

"It is taking a fair sweet time," suggested one of the men.

"There is a lot to count."

"God be praised," said another. "How much?"

"More than we hoped," replied Bran. "Your patience will be rewarded, never fear."

He returned to Angharad's hearth and the counting. "Three hundred fifty . . . ," droned Siarles, making another mark on the stone, ". . . four hundred . . ."

"Four hundred marks!" gasped Iwan. "Why were they carrying so much money?"

"Something is happening that we have neither heard nor foreseen," Angharad replied, "and this is the proof."

Tuck, still counting, gave a cough to silence them. And the total continued to grow.

When the last silver penny had been accounted, the total stood at four hundred and fifty marks. Then, turning his attention to the leather bags in the last casket, the friar began to count out the gold coins to the value of ten marks each. The others looked on breathlessly as the friar arranged the golden byzants in neat little towers of ten.

When he finished, Tuck raised his head and, in a voice filled with quiet wonder, announced, "Seven hundred and fifty marks. That makes five hundred pounds sterling."

"Do I believe what I am hearing?" breathed Iwan, overwhelmed by the enormity of the plunder. "Five hundred *pounds* . . ." He turned his eyes to Bran and then to Angharad. "What have we done?"

"We have ransomed Elfael from the stinking Ffreinc," declared Bran. "Using their own money, too. Rough justice, that."

Turning on his heel, he moved to the door and stepped out to deliver the news to those waiting outside. Angharad went with him and, raising her hands, said, "Silence. Rhi Bran would speak."

When the murmuring died down, Bran said, "Through our efforts we have won five hundred pounds—more than enough to pay the redemption price Red William has set. We have redeemed our land!"

The sudden outcry of acclamation took Bran by surprise. Hearing the cheers and seeing the glad faces in the moonlight took him back to another place and time. For a moment, Bran was a child in the yard at Caer Cadarn, listening to the revelry of the warriors returning from a hunt. His mother was still alive, and as Queen of the Hunt, she led the women of the valley, singing and dancing in celebration of the hunters' success, her long, dark hair streaming loose as she spun and turned in the rising glow of a full moon.

Nothing could ever bring her back or replace the warmth he had known in the presence of that loving soul. But this he could do: he could reclaim the caer and, under his rule, return the court of Elfael to something approaching its former glory.

Angharad had once asked him what it was he desired. He had suspected even then that there was more to the question than he knew. Now, suddenly, he beheld the shape of his deepest desire. More than anything in the world, he wanted the joy he had known as a child to reign in Elfael once more.

Angharad, standing at his side, felt the surge of emotion through him as a torrent through a dry streambed, and knew he had made up his mind at last. "Yes," she whispered. "This night, whatever you desire will bend to your will. Choose well, my king."

Raising his eyes, he saw the radiant disc of the moon as it cleared the sheltering trees, filling the forest hollow with a soft, spectral light. "My people, my Grellon," Bran said, his voice breaking with emotion, "tonight we celebrate our victory over the Ffreinc. Tomorrow we reclaim our homeland."

Mérian had determined to endure the baron's council with grace and forbearance. Spared the greater evil of having to spend the summer in the baron's castle in Hereford, she could afford to be charitable toward her enemies. Therefore, she vowed to utter no complaint and to maintain a respectful courtesy to one and all in what she had imagined would be a condition little better than captivity.

As the days went by, however, her energetic dislike for the Ffreinc began to flag; it was simply too difficult to maintain against the onslaught of courtesy and charm with which she was treated. Thus, to her own great amazement—and no little annoyance—she found herself actually enjoying the proceedings despite the fact that the one hope she had entertained for the council—that she might renew her acquaintance with Cécile and Thérese—was denied her: they were not in attendance.

Their brother, Roubert, cheerfully informed her that his sisters had been sent back to Normandie for the summer and would not return until autumn, or perhaps not even until next spring. "It is good for them to acquire some of the finer graces," he confided, adopting a superior tone.

What these graces might be, he did not say, and Mérian did not ask, lest she prove herself a backward hill-country churl in need of those same finer graces. She welcomed Roubert's company but felt awkward in his presence. Although he always appeared eager to see her, she sensed a natural haughtiness in him and a veiled disdain for all things foreign—which was nearly everything in fair Britain's island realm, including herself.

Aside from Roubert, the only other person near her own age was the baron's dour daughter, Sybil. Mérian and the young lady had been introduced on the first day by Neufmarché himself, with the implied directive that they should become friends. For her part, Mérian was willing enough—there was little to do anyway with the council in session most of the day—but so far had received scant encouragement from the young noblewoman.

Lady Sybil appeared worn down by the heat of the summer sun and the innate discomforts of camp. Her fine dark hair hung in limp hanks, and dark shadows gathered beneath her large brown eyes. She appeared so listless and unhappy that Mérian, at first annoyed by the young woman's affected swanning, eventually came to pity her. The young Ffreinc noblewoman languished in the shade of a canopy erected outside the baron's massive tent, cooling herself with a fan made of kidskin stretched over a willow frame.

"*Mère de Dieu*," sighed the young woman wistfully when Mérian came to visit her one day, "I am not . . . um"—she paused, searching for a word she could not find—"*accoutumé* so much this heated air."

Mérian smiled at her broken English. "Yes," she agreed sympathetically, "it is very hot."

"It is always so, *non?*"

"Oh no," Mérian quickly assured her. "It is not. Usually, the weather is fine. But this summer is different." A cloud of bafflement passed over Lady Sybil's face. "Hotter," Mérian finished lamely.

The two gazed at each other across the ditch of language gaping between them.

"There you are!" They turned to see Baron Neufmarché striding toward them, flanked by two severe-looking knights dressed in the long, drab tunics and trousers of Saxon nobility. "My lords," declared the baron in English, "have you ever seen two more beautiful ladies in all of England?"

"Never, sire," replied the two noblemen in unison.

"It is pleasant to see you again, Lady Mérian," said the baron. Smiling into her eyes, he grasped her hand and lifted it to his lips. Turning quickly, he kissed his daughter on the forehead and rested his hand on her shoulder. "I see you are finding pleasure in one another's company at last."

"We are trying," Mérian said. She offered Sybil a hopeful smile. Clearly, the young woman had no idea what her father was saying.

"I hope that when the council is over, you still plan to attend us in Hereford," the baron said.

"Well, I . . . ," Mérian faltered, unable to untangle her mixed emotions so quickly. After all, when originally mooted, the proposition had been greeted with such hostility on her part that now she hardly knew *what* she felt about the idea.

Neufmarché smiled and waved aside any excuse she might make. "We would make you most welcome, to be sure." He stroked his daughter's hair. "In fact, now that you know each other better, perhaps you might accompany Sybil to our estates in Normandie when she returns this autumn. It could be easily arranged."

Uncertain what to say, Mérian bit her lip.

"Come, my lady," coaxed the baron. He saw her hesitancy and offered her a subtle reminder of her place, "We have already made arrangements, and your father has consented."

"I would be honoured, sire," she said, "seeing my father has consented."

"Good!" He smiled again and offered Mérian a little bow of courtesy. "You have made my daughter very happy."

A third soldier came rushing up just then, and the baron excused himself and turned to greet the newcomer. "Ah, de Lacy! You have word?"

"*Oui, mon baron de seigneur,*" blurted the man, red-faced from rushing in the heat. The baron raised his hand and commanded him to speak English for the benefit of the two knights with him. The messenger gulped air and dragged a sleeve across his sweating face. Beginning again, he said, "It is true, my lord. Baron de Braose did dispatch wagons and men through your lands. They passed through Hereford on the day the council convened and returned but yesterday." The man faltered, licking his lips.

"Yes? Speak it out, man!" Calling toward the tent, the baron shouted, "Remey! Bring water at once." In a moment, the seneschal appeared with a jar and cup. He poured and offered the cup to the baron, who passed it to the soldier. "Drink," Bernard ordered, "and let us hear this from the beginning— and slowly, if you please."

The messenger downed the water in three greedy draughts. Taking back the cup, the baron held it out to be refilled, then drank a little himself. "See here," he said, passing the vessel to the nobles with him, "de Braose's men passed through my lands without permission—did you mark?" The nobles nodded grimly. "This is not the first time they have trespassed with impunity. How many this time?"

"Seven knights and fifteen men-at-arms, not counting

ox herds and attendants for three wagons. As I say, they returned but yesterday, only—most were afoot, and there were no wagons."

"Indeed?"

"There is rumour of an attack in the forest. Given that some of the men were seen to be wounded, it seems likely."

"Do they say who perpetrated the attack?"

"Sire, there is talk . . . rumours only." The soldier glanced at the two noblemen standing nearby and hesitated.

"Well?" demanded the baron. "If you know, say it."

"They say the train was attacked by the phantom of the forest."

"Mon Dieu!" exclaimed Remey, unable to stifle his surprise.

The baron glanced hastily over his shoulder to see the two young women following the conversation. "Pray excuse us, ladies. This was not for your ears." To the men, he said, "Come; we will discuss the matter in private." He led his party into the tent, leaving Mérian and Lady Sybil to themselves once more.

"Le fantôme!" whispered Sybil, eyes wide at what she heard. "I have heard of this. It is a creature *gigantesque*? *Oui*?"

"Yes, a very great, enormous creature," said Mérian, drawing Sybil closer to share this delicious secret. "The people call him King Raven, and he haunts the forest of the March."

"Incroyable!" gasped Sybil. "The priests say this is very impossibility, *n'est-ce pas*?"

"Oh no. It is true." Mérian gave her a nod of solemn assurance. "The Cymry believe King Raven has arisen to defend the land beyond the Marches. He protects Cymru, and nothing can defeat him—not soldiers, not armies, not even King William the Red himself."

CHAPTER 44

Dressed as humble wool merchants, Bran, Iwan, Aethelfrith, and Siarles swiftly crossed the Marches and entered England. Strange merchants these: avoiding towns entirely, travelling only by night, they progressed through the countryside—four men mounted on sturdy Welsh horses, each leading a packhorse laden with provisions and their wares, which consisted of three overstuffed wool sacks. Laying up in sheltered groves and glades and hidden glens along the way, they slept through the day with one of their number on watch at all times.

They arrived in Lundein well before the city gates were open and waited impatiently until sleepy-eyed guards, yawning and muttering, drew the crossbeams and gave them leave to enter. They went first to the Abbey of Saint Mary the Virgin, where, after a cold-water bath, the travellers changed into clean clothes and broke fast with the monks. Then, groomed and refreshed, they led their packhorses through the narrow streets of the city to the tower fortress. At the outer wall of the tower, they inquired of the porter and begged audience with Cardinal Ranulf of Bayeux, Chief Justiciar of England.

"He is not here," the porter informed them. "He is away on king's business."

"If you please, friend," said Aethelfrith, "could you tell us where we might find him? It is of utmost importance."

"Winchester," replied the porter. "Seek him there."

Bran and Iwan exchanged a puzzled glance. "Where?"

"Caer Wintan—the king's hunting lodge," the friar explained for the benefit of the Welsh speakers. "It is not far—maybe two days' ride."

The four resumed their journey, pausing long enough to provision themselves from the farmers' stalls along the river before crossing the King's Bridge. Once out of the city, they turned onto the West Road and headed for the royal residence at Winchester. Riding until long after dark, rising early, and resting little along the way, the travellers reached the ancient Roman garrison town two days later. Upon asking at the city gate, they were directed to King William's hunting lodge: a sprawling half-timbered edifice built by a long-forgotten local worthy, and carelessly enlarged over generations to serve the needs of various royal inhabitants. The great house was the one place in all England the Red King called home.

Unlike the White Tower of Lundein, the Royal Lodge boasted no keep or protective stone walls; two wings of the lodge enclosed a bare yard in front of the central hall. A low wooden palisade formed the fourth side of the open square, in the centre of which was a gate and a small wooden hut for the porter. As before, the travellers presented themselves to the porter and were promptly relieved of their weapons before being allowed into the beaten-earth yard, where knights, bare to the waist, practised with wooden swords and padded lances.

They tied their horses to the ringed post at the far end of the yard and proceeded to the hall. They were made to wait in an antechamber, where they watched Norman courtiers and clerks enter and leave the hall, some clutching bundles of parchment, others bearing small wooden chests or bags of coins. Bran, unable to sit still for long, rose often and returned to the yard to see that all was well with Iwan and Siarles, who waited with the horses, keeping an eye on their precious cargo. Brother Aethelfrith, meanwhile, occupied himself with prayers and psalms that he mumbled in a low continuous murmur as he passed the knots of his rope cincture through his pudgy hands.

The morning stretched and dwindled away. Midday came and went, and the sun began its long, slow descent. Bran had gone to see if Iwan had watered the horses when Aethelfrith called him back inside. "Bran! Hurry! The cardinal has summoned us!"

Bran rejoined Tuck, who was waiting for him at the door. "Mind your manners now," the friar warned, taking him by the arm. "We need not make this more difficult than it is already. Agreed?"

Bran nodded, and the two were conducted into Ranulf of Bayeux's chamber. A whole year and more had passed, and yet the same two brown-robed clerics sat at much the same table piled high with rolled and folded parchments, still scratching away with their quill pens. Between them in a high-backed chair sat the cardinal, wearing a red satin skullcap and heavy gold chain. His red hair was cut short; it had been curled with hot irons and dressed with oil so that it glimmered in the light from the high window. Three rings adorned the fingers of his pale hands, which were folded on the table before him. Eyes closed,

Cardinal Ranulf rested his head against the back of his chair, apparently asleep.

"My lord cardinal," announced the porter, "I bring before you the Welsh lord and his priest."

"And his *English* priest," added Aethelfrith with a smile. "Don't you be forgetting."

"Cardinal," said Bran, not waiting to be addressed, "we have come about the de Braose grant."

The chief justiciar slowly opened his eyes. "Have I seen you before?" he asked, passing a lazy glance over the two men standing before him at the table.

"Yes, sire," replied the friar respectfully. "Last year it was. Allow me to present Lord Bran of Elfael. We discussed the king's grant of Elfael to Baron William de Braose."

Recognition seemed to come drifting back to the cardinal then. Presently he nodded, regarding the slim young man before him. "Just so." The Welsh lord appeared different somehow— leaner, harder, with an air of conviction about him. "Do you speak French?" inquired the cardinal.

"No, my lord," answered Aethelfrith. "He does not."

"Pity," sniffed Bayeux. Changing to Latin, he asked, "What is your business?"

"I have come to reclaim my lands," replied Bran. "You will recall that you said the grant made to Baron de Braose could be rescinded for a fee—"

"Yes, yes," replied the cardinal as if the memory somehow pained him, "I remember."

"I have brought the money, my lord cardinal," answered Bran. He raised a hand to Tuck, who hurried to the door and gave a whistle to the two waiting outside. A moment later, Iwan appeared, lugging a large leather provision bag. Approaching the cardinal, the champion hoisted the bundle onto the table, opened it, and allowed some of the smaller bags of silver to spill out.

"Six hundred marks," said Bran. "As agreed." He put his hand to the sack. "Here is two hundred. The rest is ready to hand."

Ranulf reached for one of the bags and weighed it in his palm as he raised his eyes to study Bran once more. "That is as it may be," he allowed slowly. "I regret to inform you, however, six hundred marks was last year's price."

"My lord?"

"If you had redeemed the grant when offered," continued the cardinal, "you could have had it for six hundred marks. You waited too long. The price has gone up."

"Gone up?" Bran felt the heat of anger rising to his face.

"Events move on apace. Time and tide, as they say," intoned the cardinal with lofty sufferance. "It is the same with the affairs of court."

"Pray spare me the lesson, my lord," muttered Bran through clenched teeth. "How much is required now?"

"Two thousand marks."

"You stinking bandit!" Bran spat. "We agreed on six hundred, and I have brought it."

The cardinal's eyes narrowed dangerously. "Careful, my hotheaded prince. If it were not for the king's need to raise money for his troops in Normandie, your petition would not be considered at all." He reached a hand toward one of the money sacks. "As it is, we will accept this six hundred in partial payment of the two thousand—"

"You want money?" cried Bran. He saw the cardinal, officious and smug in his sumptuous robes as he reached for the coins; his vision dimmed as the blood rage came upon him. "Here is your money!"

Reaching across the table, he seized the cardinal by the front of the robe, pulled him up out of his chair, and thrust him down on the table, crushing his face against the coins spilled there. Ranulf let out a strangled cry, and his two scribes jumped up. As the nearest one bent to his master's aid, Bran took up an ink pot and dashed the contents into his face. Instantly blinded, the clerk fell back, bawling, shaking black ink everywhere. The other started for the door. "Stay!" shouted Bran, his knife in his hand.

Iwan, uncertain what was happening, glanced nervously at his lord. Tightening his grip on the money sack, he backed toward the door. Cardinal Ranulf, squirming under his grasp, pulled free, falling back in his chair. Bran leapt onto the table and kicked the pile of parchments, scattering letters, deeds, and royal writs across the room. He kicked another pile and then jumped down, seizing the cardinal once more. "Does the king know what you do in his name?" asked Bran.

The cardinal spat at him, and Bran slammed his head down on the table. "Answer me, pig!"

"Bran!" Iwan put a hand to his lord's shoulder to pull him away. "Bran, enough!"

Shaking off Iwan's hand, Bran pulled the cardinal up, wielding the knife in his face and shouting, "Does the king know what you do in his name?"

"What do you think?" sneered the cardinal. "I act with William's authority and blessing. Release me at once, or I will see you dance on the gibbet before the day is out."

"Pray forgive him, Your Eminence," said Tuck, pushing in beside Bran. "He is overwrought and emotional." Taking Bran's hand in both of his own, it took all his considerable strength to wrest the knife from his grasp and pull him away. "If you please, sire, accept this six hundred marks in part payment for the whole. We will bring you the rest when we have it."

He looked to Bran, indicating that an answer was required. "Not so?"

Bran took a step back from the table. "They get nothing from me—not a penny."

"Bran, think of your people," pleaded Aethelfrith.

But Bran was already walking away. He signalled Iwan and Siarles, still holding the leather bags. "Bring the money," he told them. The two scooped the loose coins and money bags back into the sacks and then hurried to follow their lord.

"I will have you in chains!" shouted the cardinal. "You cannot treat the royal justiciar this way!"

"Again I beg your indulgence, Your Eminence," said Friar Tuck, "but my lord has decided to take his appeal to a higher court."

"Fool, this is the king's court!" the cardinal roared. "There is none higher."

"I think," replied Tuck, hurrying away, "you will find that there is one."

Tuck rejoined the others in the yard. Bran was already mounted and ready to ride. Iwan and Siarles were securing the money sacks when from the hall entrance burst Cardinal Ranulf, shouting, *"Saivez-les! Aux armes!"*

Some of the knights still lingering in the yard heard the summons and turned to see the cardinal. Red-faced and angry, his robes splotched with black ink, hands outthrust, he was pointing wildly at the departing Britons.

"Aux armes! Gardes!" bawled the cardinal. "To arms! Seize them!"

"Iwan! Siarles!" shouted Bran. Slapping the reins across his mount's withers, he started for the gate. "To me!"

The porter, hearing this commotion, stepped from his hut just in time to see Bran bearing down on him. He flung himself out of the way as Bran slid from his still-galloping horse and dove into the hut, appearing three heartbeats later with the weapons that had been given over on his arrival. Raising his longbow and nocking an arrow to the string, he loosed one shaft at a bare-chested knight who was readying a lance for Iwan's unprotected back. The arrow sang across the yard with blazing speed, striking the knight high in the chest. He dropped to the ground, clutching his shoulder, writhing and screaming.

Iwan finished tying the money sack and swung into the saddle. Siarles followed an instant behind, and both rode for the open gate. Tuck's horse, skittish with the sudden commotion, reared and shied, unwilling to be mounted. The friar held tight to the reins and tried to calm the frightened animal.

Meanwhile, the porter, having regained his feet and his wits, threw himself at Bran and received a jab in the stomach with the end of the bow. He crumpled to his knees, and Bran, returning to the business at hand, raised the bow, drew, and buried a second shaft in the doorpost a bare handsbreadth from the cardinal's head. Ranulf yelped and stumbled back into the hall. The porter struggled to his knees again—just in time to receive a sidelong kick to the jaw, which took him from the fight. "If you want to live," said Bran, "stay down."

Iwan reached the porter's hut, and Bran, darting inside again, retrieved the champion's bow and sword. "Ride on ahead!" shouted Bran, handing the champion his weapons; he galloped away, leading the packhorse. "Wait for me at the bridge!"

Siarles followed, holding tight to the reins of the second

packhorse. He paused at the porter's hut long enough to snatch his bow and a sheaf of arrows from Bran's grasp. "Go with Iwan."

"My lord, I won't leave you behind."

"Keep the money safe," Bran shouted. "I'll bring Tuck. Wait for us at the bridge."

"But, my lord——," objected Siarles.

"Just go!" Bran waved him away as he darted back into the yard.

The friar had his hands full now; he was surrounded on three sides by Ffreinc knights—two holding the padded lances they had been using when the fight began, and one wielding a wooden practise sword. One of the knights made a lunge with his lance, striking the priest on the back of the neck. Tuck fell, still clinging to the reins of his rearing mount, and was dragged backward.

Bran, running to the middle of the yard, loosed a shaft as the knight drove in to crush Tuck's skull with the butt of the lance. The arrow struck just above the hip, throwing the knight sideways; his lance spun from his hand. "Pick it up!" shouted Bran. Out of the corner of his eye, he saw the dull glint of metal as two helmeted heads appeared in the doorway of the hall. He sent another arrow into the doorway to keep them back and shouted for Tuck to release the horse. "The spear, Tuck!" he cried, pointing to the weapon on the ground. "Use it!"

Understanding came to him at last. The friar let go of the reins and snatched up the practise weapon just as the knight with the wooden sword closed on him. Spinning the shaft like a quarterstaff, Tuck dealt the man a solid blow on the forearm as the wooden blade swung down. The sword slipped from his grasp. As the soldier grabbed his broken arm, Tuck swung hard at the man's knee; the soldier's leg buckled, and he went down. Meanwhile, Tuck, spinning on his toes, whirled around to face his last assailant. He neatly parried one swipe of the padded lance and dodged another before landing a doublehanded blow on top of the knight's unprotected head. The lance pole bounced and split with a resounding *crack!* as the knight dropped senseless to the ground.

"Away, Tuck!" cried Bran. Seizing the reins of the friar's skittish horse, he held the animal until the priest gained the saddle and, with a slap on the beast's rump, sent him off. "Fly!"

Bran turned around to face the next assault, only to find himself alone in the yard. There were other soldiers in hiding close by, he guessed, but none brave enough to face his bow until they could better protect themselves. He walked to the soldier squirming in the dirt with an arrow in his hip. "If you're finished with this, I'll be having it back," Bran told him. Placing a foot on the wounded man's side, he gave a hefty yank and pulled the arrow free; the knight screamed in agony and promptly passed out. Bran set the bloody arrow on the string and, watching for anyone bold enough to challenge him, backed toward the gate and his own waiting mount.

Upon reaching his horse, he cast a last look at the hall, where a knight's red-painted shield was just then edging cautiously into view from the open doorway. He drew and loosed. The arrow blazed across the distance and struck the shield just above the centre boss. The oak shaft of the arrow shattered, and the shield split. Bran heard a yowl of pain as the splintered shield disappeared. Smiling to himself, he climbed into the saddle, wheeled his horse, and rode to join his swiftly fleeing band.

CHAPTER 45

The fields and groves of Winchester fell away behind the steady hoofbeats of the horses. Bran pushed a relentless pace, and the others followed, keeping up as best they could. When Bran finally paused to rest his mount, the sun was a golden glow behind the western hills. The first stars could be seen in patches of clear sky to the east, and the king's town was but a dull, smoke-coloured smudge on the southern horizon.

"Do you know what this means?" demanded Tuck. Out of breath and sweating from the exertion, he reined in beside Bran and gave vent to his anger.

"I suppose it means we won't be asked to join the king's Christmas hunt," replied Bran.

"It means," cried Tuck, "that a worse fate has befallen Elfael than any since Good King Harold quit the battle with an arrow in his eye. Christ and all his saints! Attacking the cardinal like that—you could have got us all killed—or worse! What were you thinking?"

"Me? You blame me?" shouted Bran. "You cannot trust these people, Tuck. The Ffreinc are two-faced liars and cheats, every last one—beginning with that red-haired mag-got king of theirs!"

"Well, boyo, you showed *them*," the friar growled. "This time tomorrow there will be a price on your head—on *all* our heads, thanks to you."

"Good! Let Red William count the cost of cheating Bran ap Brychan."

"For the love of God, Bran," Tuck pleaded, "all you had to do was swallow a fair-sized chunk of that blasted Welsh pride and you could have had Elfael for two thousand marks."

"Yesterday it was six hundred marks, and today two thousand," Bran spat. "It'll be ten thousand tomorrow, and twenty the day after! It is always more, Tuck, and still more. There is not enough silver in all England to satisfy them. They'll never let us have Elfael."

"Not now," Tuck snapped. "You made fair certain of that, did you not?"

Bran, glaring at the fat priest, turned his face away.

Iwan and Siarles, leading the packhorses, reined up then. "Sire," said Iwan, "what about the money? What are we going to do now?"

"Why ask me?" Bran replied, not taking his eyes from the far horizon. "I had one idea and risked everything to make it work—we all did—but it failed. I failed. I have nothing else."

"But you will think of something," said Siarles. "You can always come up with something."

"Aye, and it had better be quick," Friar Tuck pointed out. "After what happened back there, the Ffreinc will be fast on our trail. We cannot stand here in the middle of the road. What are we going to do?"

Can't you see? thought Bran. *We tried and failed. It is over.*

Finished. The Ffreinc rule now, and they are too powerful. The best we can do is take the money and divide it out amongst the people. They can use it to start new lives somewhere else. For myself, I will go to Gwynedd and forget all about Elfael.

"Bran?" said Iwan quietly. "You know we will follow you anywhere. Just tell us what you want to do."

Bran turned to his friends. He saw the need in their eyes. It was as Angharad had said: they had no one else and nowhere else to go. For better or worse, beleaguered Elfael was their home, and he was all the king they had.

Well, he was a sorry excuse for a king—and no better than his father. King Brychan had cared little enough for his people, pursuing his own way all his life. *"You are not your father,"* Angharad had told him. *"You could be twice the king he was—and ten times the man—if you so desired."*

Yet here he was, set to follow in his father's footsteps and go his own way. Was this his fate? Or was there another way? Competing thoughts roiled in his mind until one finally won out: he was *not* his father; it was not too late; he could still choose a better way.

God in heaven, thought Bran, *I cannot leave them. What am I to do?*

"What are you thinking, Bran?" asked Aethelfrith.

"I was just thinking that the enemy of my enemy is my friend," said Bran as the words came to him.

"Indeed?" Tuck wondered, regarding him askance. "And who is this dubious friend of yours?"

"Neufmarché," said Bran. "You said the baron had called a council of his vassals and liege men—"

"Yes, but—"

"The place where they are meeting, could you find it?"

"It would not be difficult, but—"

"Then lead me to him."

"See here, Bran," Tuck remonstrated, "let us talk this over."

"You said the Ffreinc will be searching for us," he countered. "They will not think to look for us in the baron's camp."

"But, Bran, what have we to do with the baron?"

"There is no justice to be had of England's king," Bran answered, his voice cutting. "Therefore, we must make our appeal wherever we find a ready ear."

Turning in the saddle, the priest appealed to Iwan. "Talk to him, John. I've grown fond of this splendid neck of mine, and before I risk it riding into the enemy's camp, I would know the reason."

"He has a fair point, Bran," said the champion. "What have we to do with Neufmarché?"

Bran turned his horse around to address them. "The king weighs heavily on de Braose's side," he said, his face aglow in the golden light of the setting sun. "With the two of them joined against us, we need a powerful ally to even the balance." Regarding Tuck, he said, "You have said yourself that Neufmarché and de Braose are rivals—"

"Rivals, yes," agreed Tuck, "who would carve up Cymru between them—and then squabble over which one had the most." He shook his head solemnly. "Neufmarché may hate de Braose every mite and morsel as much as we do, but he is no friend to us."

"If we make alliance with him," said Bran, "he will be obliged to help us. He has the power and means to rid us of de Braose."

"Tuck is right," said Iwan. "Besides, how can we persuade him to ally with us? We have nothing to offer him that he wants."

"Even so," said Siarles, "would Neufmarché make such a bargain?"

"Aye, and if he did," added Tuck, "would he keep it?"

Bran paused in silent reflection. Could Neufmarché be trusted? There was no way to tell. "Lord Cadwgan in Eiwas holds him trustworthy and just. He and his people have been treated fairly. But whether the baron honours his word or not," Bran said, the words like stones in his mouth, "we will be no worse off than we are now."

"This is a remedy of last resort," Tuck argued. "Let us exhaust all other possibilities first."

"We have done that, my friend. We have. All that is left us now is to watch the Ffreinc grow from strength to strength at our expense. Baron de Braose and the Red King mean us nothing but harm. As for Neufmarché? We have nothing to lose." Bran offered a bitter smile. "If we must sleep with the devil, let us do it and be done. This is nothing more than what my father should have done long ago. If Brychan had sworn allegiance to the Ffreinc when he had the chance, we would not be in this predicament now."

The others, unable to gainsay this argument, reluctantly agreed.

Bran, brightening at last, said, "Lead the way, Tuck, and pray with every breath that we find the friend we seek."

Baron Bernard de Neufmarché had dismissed the last of the day's petitioners and returned to his tent, where, after summoning Remey to bring him refreshment, he removed his short cloak and eased himself into his chair. It had been a

long day but, in balance, a good one and a fitting conclusion
to a council that had, in the end, satisfied his every demand.
Convening at Talgarth—the scene of vaunted Lord Rhys ap
Tewdwr's recent demise—had been the masterstroke, provid-
ing a strong and present reminder to all under his rule that he
was not afraid to deal harshly with those who failed to serve
him faithfully. The point had been made and accepted.
Tomorrow the council would formally end, and he would
send his vassals home—some to better fates than they had
hoped, others to worse—and he would return to Hereford to
oversee the harvest and begin readying the castle for the influx
of fresh troops in the spring.

"Your wine, sire," Remey placed a pewter goblet on the
table beside the baron's chair. "I have ordered sausages to be
prepared, and there is fresh bread soon. Would you like
anything else while you wait?"

"The wine will suffice for now," the baron replied, easing
off his boots and stretching his legs. "Bring the rest when it
is ready—and some of those *fraises*, if there are any left."

"Of course, sire," replied the seneschal. "The sessions
went well today, I assume?"

"They went very well indeed, Remey. I am content." Baron
Neufmarché raised his cup and allowed himself a long, satisfying sip, savouring the fine, tart edge of the wine. Councils
always brought demands, and this one more than most—owing
to the prolonged absence of the king. Royal dispatch fresh
from Normandie indicated that the conflict between Red
William and his brother, Duke Robert, had bogged down; with
summer dwindling away, there would be no further advances at
least until after harvest, if then. Meanwhile, the king would
repair to Rouen to lick his wounds and restock his castles.

Thus, the king's throne in England appeared likely to remain vacant into the foreseeable future. An absent king forced the lesser lords to look for other sources of protection and redress. This, Neufmarché reflected, created problems and opportunities for the greater lords like himself, whose influence and interests rivalled the king's. A baron who remained wary and alert could make the most of the opportunities that came his way.

He was just congratulating himself on the several exceptional opportunities that he had already seized this day when one of the squires who served as sentry for the camp appeared outside the tent. Bernard saw him hovering at the door flap and called, "Yes? What is it?"

"Someone requests audience, sire."

"Affairs are concluded for the day," Neufmarché replied. "Tell them they are too late."

There was a short silence, and then a small cough at the door flap.

"What? Did you not hear what I said? The council is over."

"I have told them, sire," the squire replied. "But they insist."

"Do they!" shouted the baron. Rising from his chair, he stumped to the doorway in his stocking feet and threw back the hanging flap. "I am at rest, *idiot!*"

The squire jumped back, almost colliding with the two strangers behind him—Welshmen from the look of them: a young one, dark and slender, with a puckered scar along his cheek, and an older one, broad and bandy-legged, who, despite his outgrown tonsure, appeared to be a priest of some kind. Both men were dusty from the road and stank of the saddle.

"Well?" demanded the baron, glaring at the strangers who had disturbed his peace. "What is it? Be quick!"

"Pax vobiscum," said the fat priest. "We have come on a matter we think will be of special interest to you."

"The only thing that interests me right now," snarled the baron, "is a cup of wine and the comfort of my chair—which I possessed until your unseemly interruption."

"William de Braose," said the young man quietly.

Neufmarché turned a withering gaze upon the lithe stranger. "What about him?"

"His star ascends in the king's court while yours declines." The young man smiled, the scar twisting his expression into a fierce grimace. "I would have thought the humiliation of that would be a constant embarrassment to a man like you. Am I wrong?"

"Impudent knave!" spat Neufmarché, thrusting forward. "Who are you to speak to me like this?"

The stranger did not flinch but replied with quiet assurance. "I am the man who offers you a way to reverse your sorry fate."

Baron Neufmarché succumbed to his own curiosity. "Come inside," he decided. "I will listen to what you have to say." Holding the flap aside, he invited the strangers to enter and dismissed the squire. "I would ask you to sit," the baron said, returning to his camp chair, "but I doubt you will be here that long. For I warn you, the moment I lose interest in your speech, I will have you thrashed and thrown out of this camp."

"As you say," replied the young man.

Taking up his cup once more, the baron said, "You have until this cup is drained." He drank deeply and said, "Less now. I would speak quickly if I were you."

"De Braose is a tyrant," the young man said, "with little understanding of the land he has taken, and none at all of the people under his rule. Most of them have fled, and those that remain are made to perform slave labour at the cost of their own fields and holdings. If they were allowed to return to their homes, to work the land and tend their herds, Elfael would enjoy prosperity unequalled by any other cantref. All that is required is someone who can guide the will of the people— someone the Cymry will follow, who can deliver them to you."

The baron sipped again, more slowly this time, and considered what he had heard. "You can do this?"

"I can." There was no hint of hesitation or doubt in the young man.

"Your offer is tempting, to be sure," allowed the baron cautiously. Putting the cup aside, he said, "But who are you to make such an offer?"

At this, the bowlegged friar spoke up. "Before you stands Bran ap Brychan, the rightful heir to Elfael. And I am Aethelfrith, at your service."

Neufmarché gazed at the young man before him. It never ceased to amaze him how very often events beyond his reckoning conspired to bring his plans to bountiful fruition. Here, he had not lifted a hand, and the prize plum had simply dropped into his lap. "The rightful heir is dead," he said, feigning indifference. "At least, that is what I heard."

"To my great relief," replied Bran, "it remains a rumour only. Still, it serves a useful purpose."

"When the time is right," put Aethelfrith, "we will make his presence known, and his people will rally to him and overthrow the de Braose usurpers."

"In exchange for your promise to restore me to the throne," Bran said, "I would pledge fealty to you. Elfael would then abide in peace."

Now the baron smiled. "What you have said has roused my interest—and more than you know." He rose and walked to the rear of the tent. "Will you take some wine?"

"It would be an honour," replied Tuck. "There is much to discuss."

"A moment, please," said the baron. "I will order cups to be brought." With that, he disappeared through the rear flap into the room used by his servants for preparing food for the baron and his guests. "Remey!" Neufmarché called aloud. "Wine for my visitors." The servant, just returning from the kitchen tent with a trencher of sausages, appeared at his summons. Stepping quickly to meet him, the baron raised a finger to his lips for silence, leaned close, and whispered, "Fetch me four knights—armed and ready to fight. Bring them here at once."

Remey's brow wrinkled in confusion. "Sire? Is something amiss?"

"No time to explain—but the two Welshmen are to be taken captive. Indeed, they will not leave this place alive. Understand?" The aging seneschal inclined his head in a compliant nod. "Go," said Neufmarché, taking the trencher from his hands. "I will keep them occupied until you return."

Remey turned on his heel and padded away. The baron returned to his audience room with the sausages, which he placed on the table, inviting his guests to help themselves. "Sit you down, please. Enjoy!" he said with expansive warmth. "The wine will come in a moment. In the meantime, I would hear more about how you plan to bring about de Braose's defeat."

CHAPTER 46

The last day of the baron's council found Mérian in a pensive mood. Having resigned herself to the fact that she would leave the council and return, not to Caer Rhodl, but to Castle Neufmarché in Hereford, she was nevertheless apprehensive. A sojourn amongst the Ffreinc in the baron's household? Secretly she was fascinated by the thought—even regarding the prospect of a winter spent in Normandie in a kindly light. Even so, she could not deny the feeling that she was behaving as something of a traitor. A traitor to what? Her family? Her country? Her own ideas about who and what the Ffreinc were?

She could not decide.

Her father had as much as commanded her to go. Her own mother had told her, "It is important that you do well in the baron's court, Mérian. He likes you, and we need his friendship just now." Although she did not say it outright, her mother had given her to know that by currying favour with the baron, she was helping her family survive. In short, she was little more than a hostage to the baron's good pleasure.

She told herself that Cymru would be the same whether

she was attached to the baron's court or not. She told herself that in all likelihood, her poor opinion of the Ffreinc was based on hearsay and ignorance and that this was a chance to discover the truth. Of course, she still considered the Ffreinc enemies, but was not a Christian required to love her enemy? From the time she was old enough to stand beside her mother in church, she had been instructed to love her enemies and do good to those who persecuted her. So if not the Ffreinc, then who? She told herself that any young woman in her position would welcome the chance to advance herself in this way, and that she should be grateful.

She told herself all these things and more. Yet the feeling of betrayal would not go away.

It was with these thoughts turning over in her mind that she made her way amongst the untidy sprawl of tents to the baroness's pavilion in the centre of the camp. Mérian had been sent to find Sybil and inform her friend that she had said her good-byes to her parents and that her things were packed and awaiting collection by the baron's servants. As she passed the baron's tent, however, a shout brought her up short. She stopped.

It sounded like an argument had broken out. There was a crash, as if a table had been overturned, and suddenly, out of the tent burst four marchogi dragging two men between them. At the sight of the young noblewoman standing directly in their path, the soldiers halted. The foremost prisoner raised his head. Even with the blood streaming from a cut above his eye, even though she never thought to see him again amongst the living, she knew him.

"Bran!" She blurted the name in startled amazement. "Is it you?"

"Mérian," gasped Bran, no less astonished to see her.

"Step aside, lady," said one of the knights, jerking Bran to his feet.

Without thinking, Mérian held up her hand. "Stop!" she said, and the soldiers paused. She stepped nearer. "I thought you died—everyone said so."

"Wishful thinking."

"You know this man?" The voice was Neufmarché's. He stepped from the tent and came to stand beside Mérian.

"I did once," Mérian replied, turning to the baron. "I—until this moment, I thought him dead! Why are you treating him so? What has he done?"

"He claims to be the heir of Elfael," the baron replied. "Is this true?"

"It is," Mérian granted.

"That is all I need to know." The baron, sword in hand, waved the soldiers on. "Take them away."

"I am sorry you had to see that, my dear—," the baron began. He did not finish the thought, for as the knights, still distracted by Mérian, stepped past her, Bran twisted in their grasp and shook himself free. Snatching a dagger from the belt of his nearest captor, he spun on his heel, grabbed Mérian, and pulled her roughly to him. Neufmarché made a clumsy attempt to snatch her from Bran's grasp, and almost lost his hand.

"Stay back!" Bran shouted, raising the naked blade to Mérian's slender neck.

"Bran, no—," Mérian gasped.

One of the knights made a sudden lunge toward him. Bran evaded the move, pressing the knife to Mérian's throat and drawing a frightened scream from the young woman. "If you have any care for her at all," he snarled, "you will stand aside."

"Stand easy, men," the baron told his soldiers. To Bran he said, "Do you imagine this will aid you in any way?"

"That we will soon discover," he said. Turning to the soldiers holding Tuck, he commanded, "Release the priest."

The knights looked to the baron. He saw the sharp blade pressed against the soft white flesh—flesh he coveted—and could not bear to see it harmed. Neufmarché surrendered with a nod. "Do it," he said dully. "Let him go."

"Tuck," called Bran, "bring the horses!"

The English friar shook free of his captors, giving one a pointed kick, saying, "That is for laying unclean hands on one of God's humble servants." He hurried to where the horses had been left on the nearby picket line.

"Bran, let me go," pleaded Mérian, her fear quickly melting into anger. "This is not meet."

"I asked you to come with me once," he said, his mouth close to her ear. "You refused. Now it seems you are to join me whether you will or no."

Tuck hurried back, leading the horses. He passed one pair of reins to Bran and scrambled into the saddle. Bran, stepping gingerly backward to the horse, pulled Mérian with him. "Climb up and be quick," he told her, maintaining his grip on the knife. Gathering her skirts, she put her foot to the stirrup, and Bran, with a sudden movement, boosted her onto the horse and, quick as a cat, vaulted up behind her.

"Farewell, baron," said Bran, shaking out the reins. "Had you been true, you would have enjoyed the spectacle of your rival's downfall. Now you will have to content yourself with the knowledge that this day you sealed your own."

"I will track you down like an animal," said Neufmarché.

"When I find you, I will gut you and hang your carcass for the birds."

"You must catch me first, Neufmarché," said Bran. "And if we are followed from this place, Mérian's lovely corpse will be all you find on the trail."

"Don't waste your breath on them," said Tuck. "Let us hie from this vipers' den."

"Away, Tuck!" With that, Bran slapped the reins across the shoulders of his mount, and the horse leapt ahead. The fat priest followed, and the two riders disappeared with their hostage, passing between the close-set tents and out of sight. The soldiers watched in flat-footed amazement.

"After them!" shouted the baron. "Mérian is not to be harmed."

"What about the other two?" asked one of the knights.

"Once the lady is safe—and only then," the baron cautioned, "kill them. If anything happens to her, your lives are forfeit."

The four knights ran for their horses and clattered off in pursuit of the fugitives. Baron Neufmarché watched until they were out of camp and then returned to his tent, his spirits soaring with jubilation. By the time his knights returned with Mérian, the last heir to the throne of Elfael really would be dead, his unwanted presence a fast-fading memory. The troops promised by his father, the duke, would arrive with the first ships in the spring, and in the council just concluded, he had—through bargaining, wheedling, threatening, and cajoling over many days—finally obtained the support of his vassal lords for his threefold plan.

The unexpected appearance of Elfael's prince might have swiftly undone all his hard work over the last many days, but fortunately, that problem would be swiftly resolved when the knights returned with his head in a sack. Thus, no sooner than it had arisen, the unforeseen impediment had been cleared. The conquest of Wales could begin.

Friar Tuck was first to reach the little dell where the four had made camp—not far from the fields where the council was meeting, but hidden in a fold between two hills. "Iwan! Siarles!" he shouted, thundering down the hillside to the stand of beech trees where they had camped. "To arms! The Ffreinc are coming!"

The two men appeared, drawing their swords as they ran. Iwan took in the situation at a glance, thrust his sword into the turf, and raced back for his longbow. Tuck reached the shelter of the trees and threw himself from the saddle as Iwan appeared, clutching two bow staves in one hand and a sheaf of arrows in the other. "There are four of them!" cried Tuck. "Bran has a woman with him and cannot outpace them much longer. We had but a few yards' start on them."

"Four only?" said Iwan, tossing a bow to Siarles. "The way you were shouting, I thought all the Normans in England were on your tail—and their hounds as well."

"What woman?" wondered Siarles, bracing the bow against his leg to string it.

"Our escape required a hostage," Tuck explained. "For God's sake, hurry!"

A cry arose from the rim of the dell. They turned to see Bran pounding down the gentle slope, encumbered by a squirming, screaming female. His mount was tired and clearly labouring. Even as they watched, he was overtaken by the two Ffreinc knights sweeping up behind him with swords raised.

"For the love of God!" cried Tuck. "Hurry!"

"All in good time, brother," said Iwan, passing a handful of arrows to Siarles. "It does not do to hurry an archer. It makes him miss."

With quick downward jabs, the two stuck the arrows point first in the turf and, plucking one each, nocked it to the string.

"Left!" said Iwan.

"Right!" answered Siarles, and with almost languid motion, the two pressed the longbows forward as if trying to step through them. There was a single dull thrum and fizzing hiss as the arrows flew. The knight on the left, standing in his stirrups, his arm raised high, ready to begin the fatal downward slash with his blade, was struck in the centre of the chest. Already unbalanced, the impact slammed him backward over the rump of his horse, dead when he hit the ground. The rider on the right had time but to glance once at the suddenly empty saddle of his companion before Siarles's arrow buried itself in his chest. The sword spun from his hand, and he clutched the arrow, fighting to turn his galloping mount—a fight he lost when Siarles's second arrow struck just below the first and knocked him from the saddle.

Bran galloped on. The two remaining knights appeared on the rim of the dell and started down. "Left!" said Iwan again and loosed. The arrow, a blurred streak in the air, seemed to lift the soldier up ever so slightly as the horse ran out from under him.

The sole remaining knight must have seen the two riderless horses breaking off to the side, for he tried to halt his headlong pursuit. With a cry of dismay, he jerked the reins back hard. The horse's churning hooves slipped in the long grass, and the animal slid. The knight, occupied with his stumbling mount, did not see the arrow that flung him from the saddle. He landed heavily on his side, rolled over, and did not move again.

"Get their horses!" shouted Bran to Siarles as he reined his lathered mount to a halt. "Tuck! Iwan! Break camp. It will not be long before Neufmarché realises his knights are not coming back—and then he will come in force." The two hurried off to gather the water and provisions and saddle the horses.

"Let me go!" shouted Mérian, scratching at Bran's hands. He released his hold and let her fall. She landed in an awkward sprawl, her mantle sliding up over bare legs. Her shoes had come loose and been lost in the mad dash from the baron's camp. "You did that on purpose!" she raged, pulling down her mantle and scrambling to her feet. Bran slid down from the saddle. Livid with rage, dark eyes ablaze, Mérian flew at him with her fists. "How dare you! I am not a sack of grain to be picked up and thrown over your shoulder. I demand—"

"Enough!" Bran snapped, grabbing both of her wrists in one strong hand.

"Take me back at once."

"So your friend the baron can carve my head from my shoulders?" he said. "No, I think I would rather live a little longer."

"My father will do the same unless you let me go. Whatever trouble you're in will not be helped by taking me. I am certain that it can be cleared up if we all just—"

"Mérian!" Bran's hand flicked out and connected with her

cheek in a resounding slap. "Do you understand what just happened here?" He pointed to the dead knights on the hillside. "Look out there, Mérian. This is no misunderstanding. The baron means to kill me, and I do not intend to give him another chance."

"You hit me!" she said darkly. "Never do that again."

"Then do not give me cause."

Siarles returned, leading three horses. "One got away," he said.

"Go help Iwan and Tuck," Bran told him, taking the reins. "Three is enough."

"What are you going to do?" asked Mérian, her voice shaking with anger.

"Get as far away from here as possible," he replied, examining the horses. There was blood on one of the saddles, and the horse that had stumbled had a ragged gash in a foreleg. Bran released the animal and, selecting one for Mérian, pulled her around to the side and held out the stirrup for her. "Mount up."

"No."

"You are acting like a child."

"And you are acting like a brigand," she said. Raising both hands, she pushed him over backward, turned, and started running—gaining only a few paces before she felt his arms around her waist, lifting her from her feet.

"I *am* a brigand," he said. Lugging her back to the horse, he heaved her clumsily into the saddle and proceeded to tie her feet to the stirrups with the straps used to secure a lance. "Do not try me again, Mérian, or I might forget I ever loved you."

"You flatter yourself," she snarled. "But you were ever a flatterer and a liar."

Iwan, Tuck, and Siarles emerged from the beech grove just then, leading two horses. "Ready!" called Iwan.

"Ride out," Bran said. Holding tight to the reins of Mérian's mount, he swung up into the saddle. "Come, my lady," he said, his voice cold and cutting. "Let us hope that, along with your loyalty and good sense, you have not also forgotten how to ride."

"Where are you taking me?"

"To Cél Craidd," he replied. "Our fortress may not be as fine and rich as Castle Neufmarché, but it is blessedly free of Ffreinc, and you will receive a better welcome there than I received at the baron's hands."

"They will find me, you know," she said, trying to sound brave and unconcerned. "And you will pay dearly for what you've done."

"They will find you when I choose to let them find you, and *they* are the ones who will count the cost."

Turning his eyes to the line of advancing twilight away to the east, Bran gazed at the gathering darkness and embraced it like a friend. He lifted his head, squared his shoulders, and drew the evening air deep into his lungs. When he glanced again to Mérian, his eyes were veiled with the night, and she realised Bran was no longer the boy she had once known. "But now," he said, his words falling like a shadow between them, "it is time for this raven to fly."

≒ EPILOGUE ≒

Nine days after the searchers returned to Castle Neufmarché in Hereford with the sorry news that they had failed to turn up any sign of the Welsh outlaws' trail, a solitary rider appeared at the door of the Abbey of Saint Dyfrig—the principal monastery of Elfael in the north of the cantref near Glascwm. "I am looking for a certain priest," the rider announced to the brother who met him at the gate. Wearing a dark green hooded cloak and a wide-brimmed leather hat pulled low over his face, he spoke the Cymry of a trueborn Briton. "I was told I might find him here."

"Who is it you seek?" asked the monk. "I will help you if I can."

"One called Asaph, a bishop of the church."

"Then God has rewarded your journey, friend," the monk told him. "He is here."

"Fetch him, please. My time is short."

"This way, sir, if you please."

The brother led the visitor to the guest lodge, where he was given a cup of wine, a bowl of soup, and some bread to refresh himself while he waited. Lifting the bowl to his lips, he drank down the broth and used the bread to sop up the last drops. He then turned his attention to the wine. Sipping from his cup, he leaned on the doorpost and gazed out into the yard at the monks hurrying to and fro on their business. Presently, the doorkeeper appeared, leading a white-robed priest across the yard.

"Bishop Asaph," said the monk, delivering his charge, "this man has come asking for you."

The priest smiled, his pale eyes crinkling at the corners. "I am Asaph," he said. "How may I serve you?"

"I have a message for you," said the stranger. Reaching into a pouch at his belt, he brought out a piece of folded parchment, which he passed to the bishop.

"How very formal," remarked the bishop. He received the parcel, untied the leather binding, and unfolded it. "Excuse me; my eyes are not what they were," he said, stepping back into the light of the yard so that he could see what was written there.

He scanned the letter quickly and then looked up sharply. "Do you know what this letter contains?" The rider nodded his assent, and the bishop read the message again, saying, ". . . and a sum of money to be used for the building of a new monastery on lands which have been purchased for this purpose the better to serve the people of Elfael should you accept this condition." Raising his face to the stranger, he asked, "Do you have the money with you?"

"I do," replied the rider.

"And the condition—what is it?"

"It is this," the messenger informed him. "That you are to preside over a daily Mass and pray for the souls of the people of Elfael in their struggle and for their rightful king and his court, each day without fail, and twice on high holy days."

The rider regarded the bishop impassively. "Do you accept the condition?"

"Gladly and with all my heart," answered the bishop. "God knows, nothing would please me more than to undertake this mission."

"So be it." Reaching into his pouch, the messenger brought out a leather bag and passed it to the senior churchman. "This is for you."

With trembling hands the bishop opened the curiously heavy bag and peered in. The yellow gleam of gold byzants met his wondering gaze.

"Two hundred marks," the rider informed him.

"Two *hundred*, did you say?" gasped the bishop, stunned by the amount.

"Begin with that. There is more if you need it."

"But how?" asked Asaph, shaking his head in amazement. "Who has sent this?"

"It has not been given for me to say," answered the rider. He stepped to the bench and retrieved his hat. "It may please my lord to reveal himself to you in due time." He moved past the bishop into the yard. "For now, it is his pleasure that you use the money in the service of God's kingdom for the relief of the folk of Elfael."

The bishop, holding the bag of money in one hand and the sealed parchment in the other, watched the mysterious messenger depart. "What is your name?" asked Asaph as the rider took up the reins and climbed into the saddle.

"Call me Silidons, for such I am," replied the rider. "I give you good day, bishop."

"God with you, my son!" he called after him. "And God with your master, whoever he may be!"

Later, as the monks of Saint Dyfrig's gathered at vespers for evening prayers, Bishop Asaph recalled the condition the messenger had made: that he perform a Mass each day for the people of Elfael and the king. Lord Brychan of Elfael was dead, sadly enough. If any soul ever needed prayer, his surely did—but who amongst the living cared enough to build an entire monastery where prayers could be offered for the relief of that suffering soul?

But no . . . no, the messenger did not name Brychan. He had said, *"The people in their struggle and for their rightful king and his court . . ."* Sadly, the king and heir were dead—so who *was* the rightful ruler of Elfael?

Bishop Asaph could not say.

Later that night, the faithful priest led the remnant of Elfael's monks, the handful of loyal brothers who had entered exile with him, in the first of many prayers for the cantref, its people, and his mysterious benefactor. "And if it please you, heavenly Father," he whispered privately as the prayers of the monks swirled around him on clouds of incense, "may I live to see the day a true king takes the throne in Elfael once more."

⊰ ROBIN HOOD IN WALES? ⊱

It will seem strange to many readers, and perhaps even perverse, to take Robin Hood out of Sherwood Forest and
relocate him in Wales; worse still to remove all trace of
Englishness, set his story in the eleventh century, and recast
the honourable outlaw as an early British freedom fighter.
My contention is that although in Nottingham, the Robin
Hood legends found good soil in which to grow, they must
surely have originated elsewhere.

The first written references to the character we now know
as Robin Hood can be traced as far back as the early 1260s.
By 1350, the Robin Hood legends were well-known, if some-
what various, consisting of a loose aggregation of poems and
songs plied by the troubadours and minstrels of the day.
These poems and songs bore little relation to one another and
carried titles such as "Robin Hood and the Potter," "Robin
Hood's Chase," "Robin Hood and the Bishop of Hereford,"
"The Jolly Pinder of Wakefield," "The Noble Fisherman,"
"Robin Whood Turned Hermit," "Robin Hood Rescuing
Three Squires," and "Little John a'Begging."

As the minstrels wandered around Britain with their lutes

and lyres, crooning to high and low alike, they spread the fame
of the beloved rogue far and wide, often supplying local place-
names to foster a closer identification with their subject and
give their stories more immediacy. Thus, the songs do not
agree on a single setting, nor do they agree on the protago-
nist's name. Some will have it Robert Hood, or Whoode, and
others Robin Hod, Robyn Hode, Robinet, or even Roger.
Other contenders include Robynhod, Rabunhod, Robehod,
and, interestingly, Hobbehod. And although these popular
tales were committed to paper, or parchment, by about 1400,
still no attempt was made to stitch the stories together to form
a whole cloth.

In the earliest stories, Robin was no honourable Errol
Flynn-esque hero. He was a coarse and vulgar oaf much given
to crudeness and violence. He was a thief from the beginning, to be sure, but the now-famous creed of "robbing from
the rich to give to the poor" was a few hundred years removed
from his rough highwayman origins. The early Robin robbed
from the rich, to be sure—and kept every silver English penny
for himself.

As time went on, the threadbare tales acquired new and
better clothes—until they possessed a whole wardrobe full of
rich, colourful, sumptuous medieval regalia in the form of
characters, places, incidents, and adventures. Characters such
as Little John, Friar Tuck, Will Scarlet, and Sir Guy of
Gisbourne joined the ranks one by one in various times and
places as different composers and writers spun out the old
tales and made up new ones. The Sheriff of Nottingham was
an early addition and, contrary to popular opinion, was not
always the villain of the piece. The beautiful, plucky Maid
Marian was actually one of the last characters to arrive on the

scene, making her debut sometime around the beginning of the sixteenth century.

Others are notable by their absence. In the early tales there is no evil King John and no good King Richard—no king at all. And the only monarch who receives so much as a mention is "Edward, our comely king," though which of the many Edwards this might be is never made clear.

So we have an amorphous body of popular songs and poems about a lovable rascal whose name was uncertain and who lived someplace on the island of Britain at some unknown time in the past. Of all the possibilities to choose from in locating the legend in place and time, why choose Wales?

Several small but telling clues serve to locate the original source of the legend in the area of Britain now called Wales in the generation following the Norman invasion and conquest of 1066. First and foremost is the general character of the people themselves, the Welsh (from the Saxon *wealas*, or "foreigners"), or as they would have thought of themselves, the Britons.

In AD 1100, Gerald of Wales, a highborn nobleman whose mother was a Welsh princess, wrote of his people: "The Welsh are extreme in all they do, so that if you never meet anyone worse than a bad Welshman, you will never meet anyone better than a good one." He went on to describe them as extremely hardy, extremely generous, and extremely witty. They were also, he cautioned, extremely treacherous, extremely vengeful, and extremely greedy for land. "Above all," he writes, "they are passionately devoted to liberty, and almost excessively warlike."

Gerald painted a picture of the Cymry as a whole nation of warriors in arms. Unlike the Normans, who were sharply divided between the military aristocracy and a mass of peasants, every single Welshman was ready for battle at a moment's notice; women, too, bore arms and knew how to use them.

Within two months of the Battle of Hastings (1066), William the Conqueror and his barons, the new Norman overlords, had subdued 80 percent of England. Within two years, they had it all under their rule. However—and I think this is significant—it took them over two *hundred* years of almost continual conflict to make any lasting impression on Wales, and by that late date it becomes a question of whether Wales was really ever conquered at all.

In fact, William the Conqueror, recognising an implacable foe and unwilling to spend the rest of his life bogged down in a war he could never win, wisely left the Welsh alone. He established a baronial buffer zone between England and the warlike Britons. This was the territory known as the March. Later, this sensible no-go area and its policy of tolerance would be violated by the Conqueror's brutish son, William II, who sought to fill his tax coffers to pay for his spendthrift ways and expensive wars in France. Wales and its great swathes of undeveloped territory seemed a plum ripe for the plucking, and it is in this historical context (in the year AD 1093) that I have chosen to set *Hood*.

A Welsh location is also suggested by the nature and landscape of the region. Wales of the March borderland was primeval forest. While the forests of England had long since become well-managed business property where each woodland was a veritable factory, Wales still had enormous stretches of virgin wood, untouched except for hunting and hiding. The forest of the March was a fearsome wilderness when the woods of England resembled well-kept garden preserves. It would have been exceedingly difficult for Robin and his outlaw band to actually hide in England's ever-dwindling Sherwood, but he could have lived for years in the forests of the March and never been seen or heard.

This entry from the Welsh chronicle of the times known as *Brenhinedd Y Saesson*, or *The Kings of the Saxons*, makes the situation very clear:

> Anno Domini MLXXXXV (1095). In that year King William Rufus mustered a host past number against the Cymry. But the Cymry trusted in God with their prayers and fastings and alms and penances and placed their hope in God. *And they harassed their foes so that the Ffreinc dared not go into the woods or the wild places, but they traversed the open lands sorely fatigued, and thence returned home empty-handed. And thus the Cymry boldly defended their land with joy.* (emphasis mine)

That, I think, is the Robin Hood legend in seed form. The plucky Britons, disadvantaged in the open field, took to the forest and from there conducted a guerrilla war, striking the Normans at will from the relative safety of the woods—an ongoing tactic that would endure with considerable success for whole generations. That is the kernel from which the great durable oak of legend eventually grew.

Finally, we have the Briton expertise with the warbow, or longbow as it is most often called. While one can read reams of accounts about the English talent for archery, it is seldom recognized—but well documented—that the Angles and Saxons actually learned the weapon and its use from the Welsh. No doubt, the invaders learned fear and respect for the longbow the hard way before acquiring its remarkable potential for themselves.

As military historian Robert Hardy has observed, "The Welsh were the first people on the British Isles to have and use longbows. The Welsh became experts in the use of the longbow, and used the longbow very effectively in battles against the invading English." The Welsh repelled Ralph, Earl of Hereford, in 1055 using the longbow. There is a story about Welsh longbowmen penetrating a four-inch-thick, solid oak door with their arrows at the siege of Abergavenny Castle. Hardy goes on to say,

> Like the Welsh, the English learned an important lesson by fighting against the longbow. That lesson being that the longbow is a formidable weapon when used correctly. With the eventual defeat of the Welsh, and "alliance" of the English and Welsh, the English employed Welsh longbowmen in its own army. During this time, the English began a campaign to train their own longbowmen as well.

In his book *Famous Welsh Battles*, British historian Philip Warner writes:

> There were no easy victories over the Welsh. They were greatly esteemed and widely feared, whether fighting as mercenaries in the Middle Ages or engaging in guerrilla combat. From south Wales came a new weapon, the longbow, as terrifying as modern weapons of mass murder. Some 6 feet long and discharging an arrow 3 feet in length, averaging

12 arrows a minute, they blanketed a target like a dark, vengeful cloud. In the next moment all would be groans, screams and confusion.

Taken altogether, then, these clues of time, place, and weaponry indicate the germinal soil out of which Robin Hood sprang. As for the English Robin Hood with whom we are all so familiar . . . just as Arthur, a Briton, was later Anglicised—made into the quintessential English king and hero by the same enemy Saxons he fought against—a similar makeover must have happened to Robin. The British resistance leader, outlawed to the primeval forests of the March, eventually emerged in the popular imagination as an aristocratic Englishman, fighting to right the wrongs of England and curb the powers of an overbearing monarchy. It is a tale that has worn well throughout the years. However, the real story, I think, must be far more interesting.

And so, in an attempt to centre the tales of this British hero in the time and place where I think they originated—*not* where they eventually ended up—I have put a British Rhi Bran, and all his merry band of friends and enemies, in Wales.

—Stephen Lawhead

ACKNOWLEDGMENTS

The author gratefully acknowledges the assistance of Mieczys aw Piotrowski and the cooperation of Józef Popiel, Director of Biaowieski National Park, Poland, who kindly allowed me to roam freely in the last primeval forest in Europe.

PRONUNCIATION GUIDE

Many of the old Celtic words and names are strange to modern eyes, but they are not as difficult to pronounce as they might seem at first glance. A little effort—and the following rough guide—will help you enjoy the sound of these ancient words.

Consonants – As in English, but with the following exceptions:

c:	hard, as in *c*at (never soft, as in *cent*)
ch:	hard, as in Ba*ch* (never soft, as in *church*)
dd:	a hard *th* sound, as in *th*en
f:	a hard *v* sound, as in o*f*
ff:	a soft *f* sound, as in o*ff*
g:	hard, as in *g*irl (never soft, as in *George*)
ll:	a Gaelic distinctive, sounded as *tl* or *hl* on the sides of the tongue
r:	rolled or slightly trilled, especially at the beginning of a word
rh:	breathed out as if *h-r* and heavy on the *h* sound
s:	soft, as in *s*in (never hard, as in *his*); when followed by a vowel it takes on the *sh* sound
th:	soft, as in *th*istle (never hard, as in *then*)

Vowels – As in English, but generally with the lightness of short vowel sounds

a:	short, as in c*a*n
á:	slightly softer than above, as in *a*we
e:	usually short, as in m*e*t
é:	long *a* sound, as in h*ey*
i:	usually short, as in p*i*n
í:	long *e* sound, as in s*ee*
o:	usually short, as in h*o*t
ó:	long *o* sound, as in w*o*e
ô:	long *o* sound, as in g*o*
u:	usually sounded as a short *i*, as in p*i*n
ú:	long *u* sound, as in s*ue*
ù:	short *u* sound, as in m*u*ck
w:	sounded as a long *u*, as in h*ue*; before vowels often becomes a soft consonant as in the name Gwen
y:	usually short, as in p*i*n; sometimes *u* as in p*u*n; when long, sounded *e* as in s*ee*; rarely, *y* as in wh*y*

The careful reader will have noted that there is very little difference between *i*, *u*, and *y*—they are almost identical to non-Celts and modern readers.

Most Celtic words are stressed on the next to the last syllable. For example, the personal name Gofannon is stressed go-FAN-non, and the place name Penderwydd is stressed pen-DER-width, and so on.

AVAILABLE EVERYWHERE
Book Two in the King Raven Trilogy

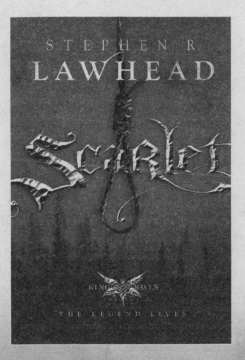

As the story of King Raven continues, the stakes grow ever higher and the lives of Bran's band hang ever more in the balance. Will Scarlet is about to be hung. Bran discovers a secret that leads them on a desperate sea voyage to France in a daring attempt to reveal the plot against King William by his brother, Duke Robert, and the greedy Baron de Braose.

Will Bran's loyalty regain him the throne of Elfael? Or will his efforts only increase the sheriff's determination to destroy King Raven?

THE DRAGON KING TRILOGY

AVAILABLE IN THE YOUNG ADULT SECTION
of bookstores everywhere

Stephen Lawhead's best-selling
trilogy is now available for
a new generation of readers.

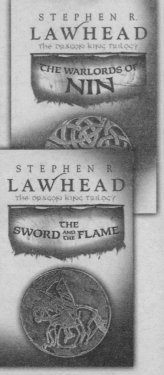

STEPHEN R.
LAWHEAD
THE DRAGON KING TRILOGY
THE WARLORDS OF
NIN

STEPHEN R.
LAWHEAD
THE DRAGON KING TRILOGY
IN THE HALL OF
THE DRAGON KING

STEPHEN R.
LAWHEAD
THE DRAGON KING TRILOGY
THE
SWORD AND THE FLAME

THOMAS NELSON
Since 1798

An excerpt from *The Paradise War*,
Book One in the Song of Albion trilogy

Chapter I
AN AUROCHS IN THE WORKS

It all began with the aurochs.

We were having breakfast in our rooms at college. Simon
was presiding over the table with his accustomed critique on
the world as evidenced by the morning's paper.

"Oh, splendid," he sniffed. "It looks as if we have been
invaded by a pack of free-loading foreign photographers keen
on exposing their film—and who knows what else—to the
exotic delights of Dear Old Blighty. Lock up your daughters,
Bognor Regis! European paparazzi are loose in the land!"

He rambled on awhile, and then announced: "Hold on!
Have a gawk at this!" He snapped the paper sharp and sat up
straight—an uncommon posture for Simon.

"Gawk at what?" I asked idly. This thing of his—reading
the paper aloud to a running commentary of facile contempt,
scorn, and sarcasm, well mixed and peppered with his own
unique blend of cynicism—had long since ceased to amuse
me. I had learned to grunt agreeably while eating my egg and
toast. This saved having to pay attention to his tirades, elo-
quent though they often were.

"Some bewildered Scotsman has found an aurochs in his
patch."

"You don't say." I dipped a corner of toast triangle into
the molten center of a soft-boiled egg and read an item about

a disgruntled driver on the London Underground refusing to stop to let off passengers, thereby compelling a train full of frantic commuters to ride the Circle Line for over five hours. "That's interesting."

"Apparently the beast wandered out of a nearby wood and collapsed in the middle of a hay field twenty miles or so east of Inverness." Simon lowered the paper and gazed at me over the top. "Did you hear what I just said?"

"Every word. Wandered out of the forest and fell down next to Inverness—probably from boredom," I replied. "I know just how he felt."

Simon stared at me. "Don't you realize what this means?"

"It means that the local branch of the RSPCA gets a phone call. Big deal." I took a sip of coffee and returned to the sports page before me. "I wouldn't call it news exactly."

"You don't know what an aurochs *is*, do you?" he accused. "You haven't a clue."

"A beast of some sort—you said so yourself just now," I protested.

"Really, Simon, the papers you read—" I flicked his upraised tabloid with a disdainful finger. "Look at these so-called head-lines: 'Princess Linked to Alien Sex Scheme!' and 'Shock Horror Weekend for Bishop with Massage Parlor Turk!' Honestly, you only read those rags to fuel your pessimism."

He was not moved. "You haven't the slightest notion what an aurochs is. Go on, Lewis, admit it."

I took a wild stab. "It's a breed of pig."

"Nice try!" Simon tossed his head back and laughed. He had a nasty little fox-bark that he used when he wanted to deride someone's ignorance. Simon was extremely adept at deri-sion—a master of disdain, mockery, and ridicule in general.

I refused to be drawn. I returned to my paper and stuffed the toast into my mouth.

"A pig? Is that what you said?" He laughed again.

"Okay, okay! What, pray tell, is an aurochs, Professor Rawnson?"

Simon folded the paper in half and then in quarters. He creased it and held it before me. "An aurochs is a sort of ox."

"Why, think of that," I gasped in feigned astonishment. "An ox, you say? It fell down? Oh my, what *won't* they think of next?" I yawned. "Give me a break."

"Put like that it doesn't sound like much," Simon allowed. Then he added, "Only it just so happens that this particular ox is an ice-age creature which has been extinct for the last two thousand years."

"Extinct." I shook my head slowly. "Where do they get this malarkey? If you ask me, the only thing that's extinct around here is your native skepticism."

"It seems the last aurochs died out in Britain sometime before the Romans landed—although a few may have survived on the continent into the sixth century or so."

"Fascinating," I replied.

Simon shoved the folded paper under my nose. I saw a grainy, badly printed photo of a huge black mound that might or might not have been mammalian in nature. Standing next to this ill-defined mass was a grimlooking middle-aged man holding a very long, curved object in his hands, roughly the size and shape of an old-fashioned scythe. The object appeared to be attached in some way to the black bulk beside him.

"How bucolic! A man standing next to a manure heap with a farm implement in his hands. How utterly homespun," I scoffed in a fair imitation of Simon himself.

"That manure heap, as you call it, is the aurochs, and the implement in the farmer's hands is one of the animal's horns."

I looked at the photo again and could almost make out the animal's head below the great slope of its shoulders. Judging by the size of the horn, the animal would have been enormous—easily three or four times the size of a normal cow. "Trick photography," I declared.

Simon clucked his tongue. "I am disappointed in you, Lewis. So cynical for one so young."

"You don't actually believe this"—I jabbed the paper with my finger—"this trumped-up tripe, do you? They make it up by the yard— manufacture it by the carload!"

"Well," Simon admitted, picking up his teacup and gazing into it, "you're probably right."

"You bet I'm right," I crowed. Prematurely, as it turned out. I should have known better.

"Still, it wouldn't hurt to check it out." He lifted the cup, swirled the tea, and drained it. Then, as if his mind were made up, he placed both hands flat on the tabletop and stood.

I saw the sly set of his eyes. It was a look I knew well and dreaded. "You can't be serious."

"But I am perfectly serious."

"Forget it."

"Come on. It will be an adventure."

"I've got a meeting with my adviser this afternoon. That's more than enough adventure for me."

"I want you with me," Simon insisted.

"What about Susannah?" I countered. "I thought you were supposed to meet her for lunch."

"Susannah will understand." He turned abruptly. "We'll take my car."

"No. Really. Listen, Simon, we can't go chasing after this ox thing. It's ridiculous. It's nothing. It's like those fairy rings in the cornfields that had everybody all worked up last year. It's a hoax. Besides, I can't go—I've got work to do, and so have you."

"A drive in the country will do you a world of good. Fresh air. Clear the cobwebs. Nourish the inner man." He walked briskly into the next room. I could hear him dialing the phone, and a moment later he said, "Listen, Susannah, about today . . . terribly sorry, dear heart, something's come up . . . Yes, just as soon as I get back . . . Later . . . Yes, Sunday, I won't forget . . . cross my heart and hope to die. Cheers!" He replaced the receiver and dialed again.

"Rawnson here. I'll be needing the car this morning . . . Fifteen minutes. Right. Thanks, awfully."

"Simon!" I shouted. "I refuse!"

This is how I came to be standing in St. Aldate's on a rainy Friday morning in the third week of Michaelmas term, drizzle dripping off my nose, waiting for Simon's car to be brought around, wondering how he did it.

We were both graduate students, Simon and I. We shared rooms, in fact. But where Simon had only to whisper into the phone and his car arrived when and where he wanted it, I couldn't even get the porter to let me lean my poor, battered bicycle against the gate for half a minute while I checked my mail. Rank hath its privileges, I guess. Nor did the gulf between us end there. While I was little above medium height, with a build that, before the mirror, could only be described as weedy, Simon was tall and regally slim, well muscled, yet trim—the build of an Olympic fencer. The face I displayed to the world boasted plain, somewhat lumpen features, crowned with a lackluster mat the color of old walnut shells. Simon's features were sharp, well cut, and clean; he had the kind of thick, dark, curly hair women admire and openly covet. My eyes were mouse gray; his were hazel. My chin drooped; his jutted.

The effect when we appeared in public together was, I imagine, much in the order of a live before-and-after advertisement for *Nature's Own Wonder Vitamins & Handsome Tonic*. He had good looks to burn and the sort of rugged and ruthless masculinity both sexes find appealing. I had the kind of looks that often improve with age, although it was doubtful that I should live so long.

A lesser man would have been jealous of Simon's bounteous good fortune. However, I accepted my lot and was content. All right, I was jealous too—but it was a very contented jealousy.

Anyway, there we were, the two of us, standing in the rain, traffic whizzing by, buses disgorging soggy passengers on the busy pavement around us, and me muttering in lame protest. "This is dumb. It's stupid. It's childish and irresponsible, that's what it is. It's nuts."

"You're right, of course," he agreed affably. Rain pearled on his driving cap and trickled down his waxed-cotton shooting jacket.

"We can't just drop everything and go racing around the country on a whim." I crossed my arms inside my plastic poncho. "I don't know how I let you talk me into these things."

"It's my utterly irresistible charm, old son." He grinned disarmingly. "We Rawnsons have bags of it."

"Yeah, sure."

"Where's your spirit of adventure?" My lack of adventurous spirit was something he always threw at me whenever he wanted me to go along with one of his lunatic exploits. I preferred to see myself as stable, steady-handed, a both-feet-on-the-ground, practical-as-pie realist through and through.

"It's not that," I quibbled. "I just don't need to lose four days of work for nothing."

"It's Friday," he reminded me. "It's the weekend. We'll be back on Monday in plenty of time for your precious work."

"We haven't even packed toothbrushes or a change of underwear," I pointed out.

"Very well," he sighed, as if I had beaten him down at last, "you've made your point. If you don't wish to go, I won't force you."

"Good."

"I'll go alone." He stepped into the street just as a gray Jaguar Sovereign purred to a halt in front of him. A man in a black bowler hat scrambled from the driver's seat and held the door for him.

"Thank you, Mr. Bates," Simon said. The man touched the brim of his hat and hurried away to the porters' lodge. Simon glanced at me across the rain-beaded roof of the sleek automobile and smiled. "Well, chum? Going to let me have all the fun alone?"

"Curse you, Simon!" I shouted, yanked the door open, and ducked in. "I don't need this!"

Laughing, Simon slid in and slammed the door. He shifted into gear, then punched the accelerator to the floor. The tires squealed on the wet pavement as the car leapt forward. Simon yanked the wheel and executed a highly illegal U-turn in the middle of the street, to the blaring of bus horns and the curses of cyclists.

Heaven help us, we were off.

The story continues in Chapter Two . . .